ALL
THESE
ASHES

ALL
THESE
ASHES

JAMES
QUEALLY

Copyright © 2021 by James Queally
Cover and jacket design by 2Faced Design

ISBN 978-1-951709-50-1
eISBN: 1-978-1-951709-66-2
Library of Congress Control Number: available upon request

First hardcover edition September 2021 by Polis Books, LLC
44 Brookview Lane
Aberdeen, NJ 07747
www.PolisBooks.com

POLIS BOOKS

Dedication:

For The Clinton Avenue Five, whose story should not be lost to history

CHAPTER ONE

S HAYNA BELL REFUSED to die on her sixteenth birthday.

She brought her fist down against the old wooden door. Once, twice. Ten times. Until the heat on her skin forced her to retreat. Until the smoke creeping into her nose and over her tongue crawled into her throat, prompting a guttural, violent cough that nearly sent her to the floor.

Backpedaling down the wooden stairs and into the basement, she nearly tripped over her younger sister's prone form. Adriana had been curled up there, crying, little yelps escaping her lips ever since the door slammed shut. But now she wasn't moving. For just one second, Shayna was appreciative of the smoke obscuring her vision. Thick, gray, charcoal smoke. The kind that billows from a burning building. The kind that kills you on your sixteenth birthday.

Shayna clawed at her dress, grateful she'd gotten done up for the rendezvous that had gone horribly wrong, feeling lucky that the royal blue garment came with a shoulder wrap she was able to stretch over

1

her mouth and nose.

The smoke would kill you before the flames, or at least that's what the man in the Newark Fire Department uniform had said during that one safety drill they held in the Weequahic High School gym every year.

Shayna wished he was here now, destroying the door with an axe, freeing her and her sister and her cousins, getting them out before the smoke choked them to death. Or before the building collapsed on top of them.

She looked to the door again, remembering her last failed attempt to break free, wondering if escape would even do her any good.

They were still out there. They had to be.

Either way, Shayna was going to need help to bring the door down and Adriana wasn't getting up. Just thirteen, with bones thin like a bird's, she wasn't qualified for the task anyway.

Shayna turned to Lavell and Kurtis, her cousins, the two brothers who probably agreed on little aside from the fact that they didn't want to be in this basement as it turned into a little hell.

Lavell, the skinny one of the two, had been staring at her the whole time, arms wrapped around his knees, tears running down his face then disappearing so fast they might as well have turned into steam. Kurtis, with his wide shoulders and workhorse frame and body perfect for barreling through the door, was lying face down.

His hands were tucked toward his stomach, trying to pin shut the hole that matched the one through his back.

Kurtis had been shot with the same gun used to march them past the now locked door. The gun held by the same person who'd shoved Shayna down the stairs before she'd woken up in an inferno. Probably the same person who'd set the blaze swallowing everything around them. Probably the same person who'd tried to sentence four people to death.

The smell of rot filled Shayna's nose, a reminder of her decrepit surroundings. The abandoned buildings, the row of leftover homes they pretended were their own private neighborhood. The little world they were going to start together. The place where their secret wasn't a scandal but a preview of the promise of when they could just exist side by side.

Right up until that promise was betrayed with a bullet.

Shayna ran for the door again, the need to know why pushing her, even as the smoke starved her lungs, making every move ten times more difficult than it needed to be. Shayna pounded, punched, screamed, prayed.

Not caring that the heat was making her flesh one shade darker. Not caring that she was too small to break through. Barely noticing the nails driven into the door at odd angles, ensuring the basement would be her tomb.

Shayna's legs started to sink away from her body, the rest of her frame folding over with them. She collapsed into a ball on the stairs. Her vision strained, blurred, faded. Her brain flickered on and off, a fluorescent in its final moments.

Shayna Bell was going to die on her sixteenth birthday.

All she could do now was pray for one grim gift: that the fireman was right. That the smoke would put her to sleep before the fire made her suffer.

CHAPTER
TWO

THERE WERE TIMES I missed being a reporter.

Fighting my way through a tangle of limbs outside a Hoboken apartment complex, sweating through a jacket I had to wear because it was somehow pouring in eighty-five-degree heat, was not one of them.

"Jesus, kid, drop your shoulder. This ain't a fucking prayer circle," shouted Mickey Teague, the photographer I'd worked with at least three times in the past two months and thought about killing no less than six.

He wanted me to move forward, with no regard of what that might mean for the rib cages and ankles of the other reporters around us. Reporters who themselves had no regard for what shoving toward the apartment complex might mean for the young woman who was probably looking down on us wondering what the fuck she did to deserve this.

Nothing, of course. She'd done nothing.

Teague lost what little patience he had and put a hand in the small of my back, using my frame to part the sea of interns and desperate freelancers between us and the Hoboken police car parked at the entrance to the Hudson Arms luxury apartment complex. I barely got my hands up in time to keep my face from colliding with the cruiser window. A waft of tobacco breath told me Teague was still moving, so I shimmied right, narrowly avoiding his drunk circus bear frame as it crashed into the spot where I'd been standing.

"See, Avery, that's how you get in position for a shot. It's called being a professional," Teague hissed. "Though, I guess it helps not being a pussy too."

Teague was no professional. None of us were.

Professionals didn't form a mosh pit of microphones and cameras hoping to get a quote or picture of the abject grief and confusion that would surely be etched across a woman's face less than twelve hours after she found out her fiancé had died. That he'd killed himself. That he'd done so after shooting eight people at a bar. That the life they'd planned together was over, replaced by one defined by his crime.

"Hey, professional," I whispered to Teague, getting my face closer to his cologne of sweat and more sweat than I wanted to. "You wanna stay here, or you wanna get the wood for tomorrow's paper?"

"We got the best perch for the assignment, Avery. There is no wood here," he replied, repeating the slang for a tabloid front page that I'd honestly never bothered to look up the origin of.

"There is if someone gets an exclusive shot of Miss Holly Hox's tear-drenched face," I said.

Teague pulled back from his camera to motion toward the cop car we were pressed against, and the cops adjacent to it.

"How do you figure that? You gonna charge past the boys in blue?" he asked. "I heard some crazy shit about you and the police in Newark, but you can't be that stupid."

"Stupid is standing here and trying to get a slightly better version of the same static shot every other paper and TV station will have tomorrow," I said. "Smart is being the one that gets her to talk. Or at least the picture of her when she refuses to."

Teague looked back down his lens, as if he was making sure he'd perfectly framed his absolutely useless shot. But I'd gotten to him. I saw him tapping his fingers against the side of the camera.

"You know…we can just split up. You stay here. I'll go inside," I said. "This way you don't miss anything, and if there's a way to get the shot, I can just snap it on my iPhone."

"You think they're gonna put a fucking iPhone photo on the front?" Teague asked.

Of course they would. The *Manhattan Bugle-Bulletin* would embed a screenshot of a tweet on the front page if it was something no one else had. But Teague was proud and he was mean and he seemed like the kind of photographer who feared getting scooped more than he feared actual physical harm.

"You get ten minutes," he replied. "But if we miss something out here, the desk will know why and it'll be the last time I let you work with me."

It was cute how he thought that was a threat.

I led him down Sinatra Drive. Having a reasonable amount of personal space after two hours in that musty pile of humanity felt amazing. I shook out each of my arms, watching rainwater spray from my jacket, feeling the swamp that had matted against my chest run down other body parts.

Teague stomped to catch up to me as I turned left on 14th Street, the apartment complex getting further and further out of view.

"Hey, fuck-O, I thought the plan was to get in the apartment," he said.

"It is. So, it would help if we had a reason to be in the apartment," I replied.

We came to a stop outside Napoli's, a by-the-slice place about three blocks from the building. I looked at Teague, assuming he'd make the connection, but he just kept glaring at me like I was something he'd stepped in.

Without even looking at the menu I ordered five pies—two plain, two pepperoni, one white—some wings and calamari.

"We're gonna distract the cops with a free meal?" Teague asked as I sat at a table near the cashier.

"Luxury apartments like this almost always have a delivery entrance. This one certainly does, we passed it walking here," I replied. "I ordered enough that the guard will believe it'll take two of us to carry it. We get in, we go straight for the apartment number we have for Miss Hox, and knock. She answers, tears up the minute I mention her dearly departed. You point and click."

Teague scratched his nose, then nodded. A smile crept over his face.

"Alright, alright, Avery," he growled. "Maybe you still got what it takes."

What did it take? A lack of empathy? An inability to realize the people we covered had pain beyond what we printed? Or maybe it just took a bank account bordering on overdrawn and safety in the knowledge that front page offerings paid double.

Teague started talking again, sharing some war story from an assignment fifteen years ago, claiming he'd won a fight that he'd surely never been in. I tuned him out, wondering if the part of my brain whispering, "Russ, you need the money," could raise its decibel level and shout down the part screaming, "Russ, you're about to do something terrible."

Sure, Miss Hox had married a monster. But she was a victim here too. She had a right to her pain. A right the *Bugle-Bulletin's* readers didn't. Sure, maybe she'd actually want to talk. I'd spoken to widows who found the experience cathartic, felt like doing the interview helped chronicle their lost loved one's legacy. At least it gave them something to do. Gave them some sense of control in the wake of chaos.

But this ambush? She hadn't asked for this. This wasn't gonna help anybody but me.

I looked back at the cashier. Noticed a delivery guy had come back and moved toward the bathroom, depositing his Napoli's hat atop the display glass. The cashier turned around and shouted, "Hey, Bobby," to get his attention. The only other employee I could see was sliding his massive oar under a browning circle of dough.

With no one looking, I hopped up, snatched the hat and jammed it into my waistband.

Five minutes later we were back out in the rain, each carrying a stack of pies topped by containers of wings and squid. When we got a little bit away from the eatery, I placed the pies on the hood of a parked car and put on the store's hat. Teague caught on, put his boxes down the same way and unzipped his jacket, playing with the camera strap on his neck until the lens was tucked against his chest and out of sight.

We walked back in silence, turning down an alley when I saw the delivery entrance. It was a downward ramp that led to a non-descript metal door and one man dressed in an all-black suit. Security, but not police, which was as fortunate as it was logical. The cops would handle crowd control given the massive media presence, but they weren't going to lock down the entire building.

I kept my eyes straight as we approached the door, pausing briefly to seem like I was struggling with the pizzas, stepping too hard in a puddle like I might slip. I tilted the boxes just enough that one of the calamari orders slid off and blessed the concrete in red sauce.

"There goes my goddamn tip," I said, making sure to make eye contact with the doorman as I flashed him a receipt. "I'm going up to 324."

I had no idea whose apartment 324 was, but it wasn't Miss Hox's. The guard looked us over once, hand wandering toward a phone box that he'd probably have used to call and check in with the tenant if we weren't drenched and stepping around rain-soaked seafood on our way to the door.

"Tell them I knocked it off the box when I opened up," he said with a soft smile.

Nice guy. Hopefully, that would help him when his bosses started looking for someone to fire for letting reporters slip in.

We made it to the elevator without a problem. Once inside, we put down the food and situated ourselves. I pulled a notepad from my jacket pocket, seeing the ink from old notes melt away into incomprehensible nothing on each soaked page. Professionals remembered to bring pencils in case of inclement weather. I searched my pockets, finding only pens.

Teague got his camera out and fiddled with it for a few seconds, before flipping over one of the lids and pulling out a slice.

"Really?" I asked.

Teague didn't respond, just chewed. Of course, his stomach wasn't in knots. The people we were about to hurt didn't matter to him. They were just another photo.

The elevator dinged. Sixth floor. Miss Hox was in 607. Probably looking at pictures of her fiancé, maybe thinking about the night he proposed, trying to line that moment up with the one where she saw his picture on the news above the words "suspected gunman."

I stopped at the door. Teague took his stance, lens hovering over my shoulder. My finger stopped a millimeter from the bell. I didn't want to do this, but I needed the money, and someone else would if I didn't. The news wasn't meant to be polite. Just honest, unflinching.

I pressed the button. Voices rose up on the other side of the door, a mix of alarm and confusion. I heard Teague's breathing pick up slightly. Was he...excited?

"You think she'll smile?" he asked.

The door opened.

She did not smile.

Miss Hox met us with a face streaked with tears and eyes so red they bordered on swollen. Her hair was splayed about in frizzled clumps.

"Who are...?" she started.

I felt Teague lean in for the shot over my shoulder. I saw Miss Hox's eyes widen as she realized what was about to happen. I closed mine and listened. The whisper in my head finally raised its voice.

My right elbow shot up, catching the underside of Teague's camera, sending his lens and flash toward the ceiling where they couldn't capture anything useful.

"I'm sorry," I said.

"What the fuck is wrong with you?" Teague shouted as he tried to aim a second time.

I thrust my elbow back again, this time catching the lens. Something broke, but the sound of it was drowned out by the door slamming shut. Feeling the slightest sense of relief, I started walking back toward the elevator.

"You wanna explain what in the goddamn hell that was?" Teague asked as I headed for the exit.

I didn't. At least not to him.

He wasn't the type to understand that some stories just aren't worth telling.

The meter at the gas pump climbed higher and higher, lurching over fifty dollars as my Impala's hungry tank drank like it might never taste fuel again. The credit card I was about to swipe already had a four-digit balance, like most of its neighbors in my wallet.

The slight high I'd felt after breaking Teague's camera, and by extension not being a total piece of shit, evaporated as soon as I got into my car and started doing some simple math. The combination of pride, decency, or ego that sent my elbow into his lens would cost me at least $300 now that I had no story to file. The *Bugle-Bulletin* routinely ignored expense reports from freelancers if the expenditures didn't result in a story, so I'd pissed away the gas money and the tab I'd run up on my pizza-based ruse as well.

That was approximately $300 less to throw at my credit card debt as it experienced a growth spurt. Three hundred dollars less to put towards my way more than $300 per month rent. Three hundred dollars less to put towards groceries. And there would be more $300 holes in my meager budget to come.

The *Bulletin-Bugle* freelance gigs were my only real source of income now, and I imagined those were going to dry up after Teague went back to the newsroom and explained to the photo desk why he had a busted camera. I'd be lucky if they didn't try to bill me for his equipment too, another four-digit invoice to add to the pile of bills I already couldn't afford. I was making a habit of making enemies of middle-aged men who could fuck up my bank accounts.

Two years earlier, I'd been the police beat reporter at the *Signal-Intelligencer* in Newark, the Garden State's largest newspaper. A fight with a managing editor left me unemployed and with a sour reputation in the incestuous Tri-State area media scene, so I cashed in some favors with some cop sources I'd never be able to use again and got fast-tracked for a PI's license.

Cops quickly became the bulk of my client base, and I got a reputation as someone the men and women of the Newark Police Department could turn to when they needed information that could disrupt an administrative beef or internal affairs probe. Then people started coming to me with real, indictable problems and I'd started to wonder what the fuck I was doing with my life.

So, I took a case that raised some hell for the NPD. National headline hell. CNN realized Newark existed kind of hell. The department was now under federal investigation hell. A year had passed and the courts were still trying to figure out how many defendants needed retrials kind of hell.

People died kind of hell.

To the shock of no one, the whole situation left me persona non grata among most police officers in Newark and beyond, which made my PI's license little more than a piece of paper I'd need to put in a box when I got evicted from my apartment.

Sweat beads formed over my brow as I kept driving down the 1&9, south from Jersey City to Newark. A few minutes passed and I wiped at my face again as I dipped off the highway and into the city's East

Ward, the Ironbound neighborhood where I lived, worked, slept and generally tried to hide out from anything that cost money.

I waved my hand over the Impala's air conditioning vent and felt nothing but lukewarm wind coming out. I fiddled with the settings, hoping I'd just spun a dial the wrong way. But with my luck, the suddenly tropical climate of my car probably meant the A/C was busted. Another problem beyond my budget.

Fresh out of patience and disposable income, I wondered if I had any leftovers in the fridge as I parked outside of my apartment. There was probably some Chinese. There was always Chinese.

I stepped out of my car, the reunion with the humid rain making me feel all the sweat and grime of my day again, leaving me desperate for a shower. Trudging down the block with my head down, I didn't notice the broad-shouldered man in the overcoat heading for my staircase until we'd nearly bumped shoulders.

"Avery," growled a voice that for two years had almost always meant trouble in my life.

I looked up to see Bill Henniman, one of those middle-aged men who'd taken a pair of scissors to my purse strings the year before. The Newark police lieutenant had played a pivotal role in spreading the word that my business services were no longer required by anyone in blue.

The last time he'd been in my apartment, he'd threatened me.

The last time I'd seen him, we'd taken a stab at making peace.

But it was the time between those two run-ins that still kept me up at night. The time when he'd shot someone in front of me.

"No," I said.

"Huh?"

"I'm going to ask why you're here, then you're gonna tell me, which means we'll have to talk," I said. "I've been in the rain all day losing money and cultivating a migraine, so I'm pretty much done with human contact right now."

"I knew coming here was a terrible idea," he replied, letting out a sigh that sounded like air rushing from a balloon.

"Finally, we agree on something," I said.

I made it halfway up the rain-slick stairs, then realized I didn't hear his footsteps going the other way.

I turned around. There had to be a good reason he was standing in a downpour and seeking my attention. Normally, I was the type of guy tried to avoid, not seek out.

Reporter curiosity: lead suspect in the serial murder of thousands of cats.

"What are you doing here?" I asked.

"I want to hire you," Henniman replied.

Somewhere, nine more lives ended.

Henniman followed me into the de facto office of my two-bedroom apartment. Only one of the rooms was actually home to a bed, but putting a wall between the place where I slept and the place where the filing cabinets were seemed like a good way to prevent workaholism.

At least that had been the idea, back when I had enough work to worry about that.

I flipped a light switch and directed the lieutenant to an Ikea-adjacent chair I'd bought off Craig's List for twelve dollars. It creaked under his weight. That's what twelve-dollar chairs do. The thing had collapsed at least three times before, but the seat and backing seemed content to work through their divorce each time I forced the single screw holding them together back into place.

"When did you become such a neat freak?" Henniman asked, waving a hand across the room, toward the desk lined with short, compact piles of manila folders.

"It was messier when I had clients," I replied. "Remember when I had those?"

"You could have one any second now," he said, slipping the verbal jab, pointing a finger at himself.

Henniman wasn't one for reflection. Or he'd selectively forgotten that the last time he was in my apartment, he'd threatened to pull a favor and have my license revoked.

"Just like that?" I asked. "You want to forget about everything and be friends?"

"I never said anything about friends," he replied. "I have a case. You look desperate for some paying work. What does last year have to do with now?"

"Did you forget about the part where you blew up my life?"

Henniman laughed, but it came out more like a cough, rising up from his belly, making everything shudder between there and his neck.

"Blew up your life?" he asked. "Did you forget about the part where I saved it?"

I gave him a hard stare, but all I saw was the year before. The flop motel. The gunshot. The body of our mutual friend leaking out on me. The last few seconds that I'd been blissfully ignorant of how warm someone else's blood feels when it stains you.

It took me a minute to see the vacancy in his eyes. He'd left the room, gone back to the same scene with me. The gunshot had taken a piece of him too, even though he was the one who'd done the shooting.

"Are you familiar with the Twilight Four?" he asked, cutting off any avenue to discuss our painful past.

I blinked a few times, trying to reorient myself in the present. Twilight Four. It sounded familiar. I'd seen the words splashed across framed front pages in the *Signal-Intelligencer* newsroom back when I still worked there. It sounded like the title of a future Netflix documentary.

"Rings a bell, but I think it went down before I was at the paper," I replied.

"It went down before you were in Kindergarten," he shot back, smirking.

"Oh, good. You're gonna do the grizzled veteran thing. That's fine. You've been doing this job since I was in diapers, you solved your first case before I solved the mysteries of puberty. I get it," I said. "Yet, you're still here asking for my help, so why don't you go ahead and tell me about the thing I need to help you with?"

Henniman stood up, rolling his shoulders, unknotting them.

"It started out as a missing persons case in 1996," he said. "Four teenagers, all related, all disappeared on the same night. Shayna Bell. Her younger sister, Adriana. Their cousins from their mother's side, Kurtis and Lavell Dawkins. Youngest was thirteen. Oldest sixteen. Didn't gain much attention at first, and it really shouldn't have."

I opened my mouth to speak, but Henniman held his hand up, eyes wandering to the ceiling.

"This might take a while to explain, but it'll only take half that while if you don't hit me with the director's commentary every time a thought pops into your head," Henniman said. "They were teens, gone in the summer. No motive, no known enemies, no crime scene, no evidence of anything awful. They wouldn't be the first kids to just fuck off for a few days."

He eyed me. I behaved. He continued.

"But as the weeks turned into a month and that turned into two, the Bell girls' oldest sister started raising hell. She stirred up some attention from the newspapers. You know how the department reacts to pressure, so suddenly there's a task force dedicated to solving this missing persons case that is clearly no longer a missing persons case," Henniman said. "The detectives were fucked from the start. Months behind. None of the early leg work had been done. No timelines. No one entirely certain when each of the four were last seen or where. Four Black kids missing and a hint of the police screwing up. Do I need to tell you what happened next?"

I thought of how I'd spent the earlier part of my day. How the New York tabloids only seemed to cross the river when a tragedy and a narrative shook hands.

"A lot of people like me asking a lot of questions that a lot of people like you couldn't answer," I said.

Henniman nodded.

"We had nothing to give them. But the family kept talking, and suspicion started becoming fact. There were stories about it being a hate crime, an initiation rite for a biker gang or a Klan revival out of Gloucester County or somewhere else in the South Jersey confederacy. There was the inevitable speculation that the girls' parents killed them after someone got an interview with a distant cousin with an axe to grind," he said. "On and on. The department and the family were both so desperate everyone was swiping at any and every rumor. None of it even close to real. But we had nothing to disprove any of it either. We couldn't even be sure they were dead. We had no bodies. No crime scene. It was like they blinked out of existence."

I'd stood up at some point during Henniman's speech, more enthralled by his tale than I wanted to be.

"So why are you coming to me about a cold case that happened before I ever set foot in Newark?" I asked.

"'Cause it's not a cold case," he replied. "About eight years ago, I solved it. Or at least I thought I did."

Henniman leaned back against the far wall, crossed his arms and slumped his head. For someone who couldn't stand most journalists, the man wasn't half bad at pacing a story.

"I was only a few years into Major Crimes then. Still a detective. Ended up working a gun task force with the ATF, trying to disrupt a ring that was arming half the assholes in Newark and Jersey City, group making Iron Pipeline runs."

Most of the guns that killed people in New Jersey's largest city weren't actually from New Jersey. Someone pulled the trigger in Newark, sure, but you could usually trace the path of the bullets to an illegal parking lot sale in Pennsylvania or, in Henniman's case, a van that hauled stolen firearms up I-95 from the Carolinas.

"I wanted to show I belonged in this unit. Every time we had a takedown like this, especially with the chance to hold federal sentencing guidelines over someone, I went hunting for informants. Someone to make me look smart," I said. "On this one, as we were walking them out of the warehouse, I noticed this one guy wouldn't make eye contact with anyone. Not the cops, not his future co-defendants. I get up close to him, he's all sickly skin and eyes desperate not to cry. A really stupid neck tattoo to boot, one that's gonna work like a bullseye inside. Doesn't look like he could survive a varsity locker room, much less a stint in a federal pen. I decide that's my guy."

Henniman paused, like he was waiting for me to compliment his snitch Spider-Sense.

"We get him in a room. Tell him he's facing a minimum of seven years and the feds can pick and choose where he goes. Promise him a trip to Leavenworth. Kansas. No one is visiting him after he goes in. No one is gonna recognize what's left of him if he ever comes back. Of course, he asks if there's anything he can do to help himself. I figure maybe he's going to cough up a bunch of buyers, other gun runners..."

"Instead, he tells you he knows what happened to the Twilight Four," I reply. "And you believe him, even though you've got the guy so shit scared he's gonna tell you he shot Hoffa and the body's in his attic."

"I didn't believe a fucking word out of his mouth. But like I said, this case was Newark legend. I had to at least check it out, in case I'd hit the lottery. And parts of what he said fit. My new friend's name was Isiah Roust, and he had a Newark address in the '90s. Somewhere around Weequahic, same as the victims," Henniman said, referring to the neighborhood in the South Ward. "The guy he put in as the killer was also a local. Military background. And he just so happened to be in a serious relationship with the missing girls' eldest sister, Cynthia Bell, the one who the media kept putting at the front of the story."

Henniman paused and made eye contact, like he was checking that I'd followed along.

"Roust said our killer had been messing around with Shayna. So not only was he stepping out on his maybe future wife, but he was looking at a statutory rape charge," Bill said. "She'd threatened to tell the parents, according to Roust, and our killer couldn't have that. The others just got caught in the middle."

"This Roust guy have any proof of that beyond his say-so?" I asked.

"No. But he knew how they died, said the killer told him all about it," Henniman replied. "Fire at an abandoned house. NFD was beyond understaffed at the time, barely handling priority calls. Wasn't unheard of for them to just let empty buildings burn back then. But there are records of rowhouses going up around the same time the kids vanished. Never could match the particular fire Roust described to one with an exact date and time though. We do a little more digging and find out our supposed killer broke up with Shayna's older sister right after the disappearance. Moved out of the city."

That didn't mean anything to me, but it might have meant everything to a juror.

"We talk to this man. The one Roust pointed too," Henniman said. "He doesn't have an alibi for the night of the fire. It'd been more than twenty years, who can remember what they did on some random Thursday?"

"That's not proof beyond a reasonable doubt," I said.

"There are at least twelve people who will disagree with you," Bill replied. "Our case wasn't exactly strong, but his defense was basically non-existent. We had Roust swearing up and down the man confessed. Cynthia, the sister, turned on him on the stand, pointing out that she'd always suspected something was strange about him ending their relationship not long after the kids vanished. That he'd retreated from her, turned cold. And we found an eyeball witness who said he saw Shayna and our guy talking the day the kids vanished. Our guy, meanwhile, refuses to take the stand in his own defense. Jury decides that it walks like a killer, looks like a killer. Guilty on all counts. Locked away for the last eight years, set to stay that way for the rest of his life. Until last week."

"What happened last week?"

"His case was up on appeal," Henniman said. "Then the prosecutor's office dropped everything without prejudice."

I chewed my lip. Knowing Henniman, knowing he was one of

those true believer cops, I could guess what he wanted to hire me for.

"So, you want me to do what exactly? Hunt around and help discredit whatever got his case kicked, help you shove this man back in a box because your shitty police work couldn't get it done the first time?"

Henniman pressed two fingers against each of his temples and rubbed them in slow circles, closing his eyes. He grabbed a notepad off my desk, tore off half a page, and started writing something.

"No, I want you to help fix my shitty police work," he replied.

He handed me the scrap. The top line was a name: Abel Musa. Underneath it was a room number and an address I recognized as Newark University Hospital.

"And fix it while it still matters. Musa's dying. Pancreatic cancer," Henniman said. "I think he'd like to die an innocent man."

CHAPTER
THREE

I F I WAS gonna clear Abel Musa's name, I'd need to do it quick.

He didn't move his head as I hovered in the doorway to his hospital room. Slumped over and crumpled like laundry someone had thrown on the chair he was sitting in, I wasn't sure if he could.

Henniman had sworn he'd called ahead and added me to the list of approved visitors, but I was still nervous to enter Musa's room. I shouldn't have been—this was no different than any of a thousand door knock interviews I'd done as a reporter—but I wasn't a reporter anymore. The freelance gigs I'd been picking up for the New York City tabloids mostly consisted of stakeouts, ambush interviews and shouting questions in a media scrum I knew would never be answered. The conversations didn't require skill, and they rarely lasted more than fifteen seconds.

What I'd done in the past year wasn't journalism, it was stenography with a splash of breaking and entering, like the incident in Hoboken the day before. Even then, the only good work I'd done hadn't ended up in a newspaper.

Picking Musa's brain would be the first god's honest act of reporting I'd done in almost two years, and I wasn't exactly sure how to approach it. Sure, as a crime reporter, you get calls and letters from people claiming their years-ago convicted son or daughter is innocent on a weekly basis. I'd had this conversation before. But always as a politely disinterested listener, reading NBA think pieces from the safe end of a phone call and barely taking notes, because I usually had a dozen other stories to chase, most of them with a toe dipped in reality.

Musa was the only name on my list this time. Or at least the only one that wouldn't lead to me working with scum like Teague again.

I'd spent the night before my hospital visit reading articles on the Twilight Four case and Musa's murder trial. The photos showed a tall, thick, proud Black man. A tree that couldn't be chopped down. His jaw was locked in nearly every photo, never betraying any reaction. Not when you could see some of the victims' loved ones shouting in the gallery. Not when a prosecutor jabbed an accusatory finger in his face in a way that would have made most men flinch. Not when he was sentenced to life in prison to pay for the loss of four lives that he swore he hadn't taken.

Whatever panic or frustration or fear Abel Musa had been feeling was for him and him alone then. But now, propped up in a hospital chair that looked too large for his withering frame, that thousand-yard stare was the only quiet dignity Musa seemed to have left.

He was looking right at me, but with eyes so tired and blank I wasn't entirely sure he could see anything. I waved. No reaction. I looked out toward the nurse's station, but no one standing there seemed interested in acknowledging me.

I turned back to Musa, who was slunk so low in his seat I thought it might swallow him, and took a cautious step forward. A cartoon tip toe. He didn't do anything, so I took another step. Still nothing.

No longer worried I was invading or about to scare the frail man, I started walking like a normal person.

"No, don't stop," he said, his voice so low and smoky it was like someone strangled a whisper. "That shit was funny."

I snapped to attention, as the corners of his lips bent up in a mocking smile.

"Sorry, sorry. I just, there was no one here and you don't know me so I wasn't sure what to…" I stammered.

Musa looked like he wanted to follow his grin with a laugh, but instead his mouth curled and shot up a glob that splashed to the floor next to him as he keeled over at the waist. It was gray, thick. Slightly bloody.

I ran over to his side, looking back at the nurse's station for help, finding none. I dropped to one knee and put a hand on Musa's back, like I had any idea what I was doing, and followed the wire running near his hands, looking for a call button. When I found it, one of Musa's fishbone thin fingers stopped me.

"Don't waste their time," he hissed.

I watched his other quaking hand pull a cloth up and clear away the rest of the fluid from his mouth. Slowly, looking like his body might break with every inch it traveled, he shuffled back into a seated position.

He studied my face for a second, squinting, maybe straining for a memory.

"You don't know me," I said. "My name is…"

"I don't need you to tell me what I know," he replied. "I know I don't get visitors. I know I don't know you. Means you want something, or someone who wants something sent you."

"Bill…Bill Henniman," I said. "He sent me, about your case. About the—"

"The detective?" he asked, eyes widening just slightly.

I nodded. He nodded back.

Then he held up the wire in his hand. His thumb was pressed to the call button for the nurse.

"Is everything alright, Mr. Musa?" asked the first of two women in scrubs to appear.

"No. I don't know who this man is," he said, his voice suddenly jumping up a few octaves, that knowing hiss evolving into a worried whine. "I don't know why he's here."

"Woah, woah. I'm on his visitor list," I said, holding my hands up toward the nurses. "I'm here to ask him about—"

"The cops sent him!" Musa said, his voice still noticeably in a higher pitch than it had been before the nurses showed up. "Please, get him out! I'm done with cops! No more cops!"

I thought about correcting him. But between the two nurses a half-step away from calling security and the terminally ill patient having a panic attack, I wasn't likely to find any agreeable parties.

Henniman had clearly left out a few details. The lieutenant hadn't taken many follow-up questions in my office, knowing me well enough to be sure my curiosity would guide me to Musa's hospital bed. But why wouldn't he warn me not to mention his name?

Was he unaware it would set Musa off? Or did he want me to see the panic?

I started walking out, half turning to take one more look at Musa. He was still freaking out with both nurses preening over him. We made eye contact briefly, and for a second, something in his expression changed.

The sly smirk was back. He wasn't scared, he just didn't want to talk. And he was smart enough to know how to turn the nurses into his own private security.

Calling out a cancer patient as manipulative didn't seem like the best move, so I turned to leave. But as I stepped into the hallway, I saw a familiar face that likely meant I'd be staying longer.

"I think there's a little confusion here," said Keyonna Jackson, her voice filling the room and taking command of it, like it had at so many rallies across Newark in the past few years. "Russ isn't working for the cops. I doubt they'd even have him anymore, ain't that right, Russ?"

Key would know. If Henniman was the last nail in the coffin of my

PI business, Key was the one who'd started building the pine box in the first place.

I sat across a table from Keyonna Jackson like I had dozens of times before, wondering if she could help me, wondering if the assistance would be worth the accompanying headache.

This was how it always started. Each of us sizing up the other, trying to figure out what they wanted. Usually, we opted for a place with better food at least, but the dishwater flavored coffee of the hospital cafeteria would have to do.

Our roles had changed plenty of times over the years: source and reporter, client and investigator, friend and foe. But at its core, the dynamic was pretty simple: if one of us needed something, the other was usually willing to help procure it. I cared about her, but I wouldn't admit it out loud unless she took one of my relatives hostage. One I actually liked.

Key had risen to prominence in Newark as the force behind citywide anti-violence demonstrations in the early 2010s, speaking out against anyone who would do harm to Brick City residents, rarely seeing much difference between cops and criminals. Megaphone in hand, she'd blocked streets and snarled traffic every other Wednesday for years as the city's homicide count crept into the triple digits. She'd get in the face of a mayor just as quick as she'd snap at a sixteen-year-old wannabe banger talking the kind of shit that can lead to gunfire in the South Ward.

Sometimes, she got a little out there for my tastes—reforming police departments was one thing, abolishing the cops altogether was another—but Key had the right intentions at heart. She really believed Newark could rise above its reputation, and I admired that.

We didn't always agree on tactics, though.

It had been about a year since Key had directed me toward a grieving father and a cell phone video that would change the city as much as it changed me. She'd put me on a collision course with the police department, and in the ensuing fiasco, she'd leaked that footage to my old newspaper. There were protests. People got hurt, arrested. Worse.

As she twisted off the cap of a Diet Coke bottle and took a quick swig, I realized it was no coincidence that I'd run into her outside the hospital room of another ticking time bomb for the NPD.

"You know, after everything that happened last year, I assumed you might change up a little," Key said. "But here we are. Sitting across a table from one another. You running errands for cops, me about to warn you why maybe you shouldn't. Again."

"You're oversimplifying," I said.

"Am I?" she asked. "What were you doing in Abel's room?"

Of course, Key was on a first name basis with the man. She made it her business to know everything and anything she could about any misstep made by Newark's police. Whether that was because she was a tireless activist or a relentless opportunist depended on who you asked.

"Running down something for a potential client," I said.

"That client happen to be a cop?" she asked.

"Not at liberty to discuss."

"Yet for some reason, Abel was up there screaming, 'No more cops,' when I walked in, and you used to have a lot of cop friends, didn't you? Specifically, the one who put Abel away for something he says he didn't do," she said, dramatically scratching her chin before making a pensive face at me. "I think I'm deducing something."

"Don't I get to ask you what you're doing here?"

"You do," she replied. "But I asked you first."

There was no reason to hold out on Key, other than the fact that she was being slightly more smug than usual.

"Honestly? I didn't know that man's name, or any of the story that ended with him in that hospital bed, until yesterday. Henniman came to my door and told me a story. I'm not exactly swimming in clients right now, and you know why," I said. "Not all of us…"

I stopped myself, because doctors advise against picking at scabs.

But then I scratched anyway, like everyone does.

"Not all of us benefitted from what happened last year," I said, jabbing a finger in her direction.

While I'd ended up nearly out of work and mostly out of money after playing a part in exposing the scandal that had placed Newark's police department under a federal watchdog, virtually everyone else involved had come out unscathed or leveled up.

Dina, my ex-girlfriend, who'd written the story that forced the Department of Justice to send people from D.C. to the Bricks, had graduated from the *Signal-Intelligencer* to the *Washington Post*. Henniman, despite himself being wrist deep in the muck we'd raked, seemed to still have his badge.

As for Key, well, I'd known her approximately six years. Through five and a half of them, I could bet any amount of money that she'd be wearing some combination of an oversized t-shirt bearing the names of a few homicide victims, New Balance sneakers and Mom jeans. But recently, she'd been showing up places with a burgundy blazer and what occasionally looked like a pantsuit. She still kept the t-shirts on underneath the suit jackets, though.

"I told you what I was doing here," I said. "So why don't you tell me what Newark's next mayor wants with Mr. Musa?"

"You're really just gonna assume I'm here because of Councilwoman Pereira?" she asked.

"You hate that blazer," I said. "But I assume she makes you wear it on official business."

Key sat there, titled her head just slightly, and folded her right hand over her left fist as a little scowl appeared on her face. It was her way of telling me I was right without saying it, 'cause if she ever admitted I was right about anything, she'd burst into flames.

"Key, look at me. I barely know what I'm doing here, and I'm just smart enough to guess what you're doing here. I got a cop I kinda sorta don't trust but whose money I kinda sorta definitely need asking me to look into this. Now you're here on a mission from the woman who might be running the city in a few months," I said. "I feel like I'm about to step in shit. Again. And I've still got shit on my shoes from last year."

She shook her head and craned her neck upwards, like she was searching for an answer in the blinding hospital fluorescents.

"There's an innocent man dying upstairs and most of the world thinks he's a killer," she said. "And here you are making this about you?"

"It's a gift."

"I should slap you," she said.

"Info first," I replied. "Slaps after."

"What did Henniman tell you?" she asked.

Not much, but I needed to tell her even less than that. Key was generous with information, infamous for sending mass texts to the people who filled her marches when she had even the slightest bit of controversial intel. That was a problem before she had a city councilwoman in her contacts list.

"Henniman worked the Twilight Four killing. Not the original missing persons, obviously, but he picked it up as a cold case years later," I said. "He rang Musa up on the murders. Musa got convicted, then he got released. Supposedly, because of the cancer. But Henniman seems to think he's innocent. Didn't really offer much of a why."

"And were you even slightly curious why Henniman was trying to hire someone he hates to look into his screw up instead of fixing it himself?" she asked.

"Well, I assumed since the prosecutor's office released Musa on compassionate grounds, the police department's official position was that he's just dying, not innocent," I replied. "So, I'd guess Henniman's bosses don't want him investigating this."

"Henniman's bosses don't want him investigating anything," she replied, looking a little too self-satisfied with that knowledge.

"You got cop sources now?" I asked.

She tapped the laminate clipped to her blazer.

"I got a secure pass to city hall now. People talk," she replied. "Henniman was neck deep in the shit we dredged up last year. He got to keep his job, but that was about it. He's in a rubber room now, processing public records requests all day. The city is just hoping he becomes a pension check they mail every two weeks."

Great. Henniman had swam over to the shipwreck that was my life after barely escaping the pull of his own.

"You still haven't answered me, Key," I said. "You know why I'm here. Why does the councilwoman want you here?"

Sure, it'd been a while since I'd done the reporter thing, but some stuff just stays with you. Like how to work a source. Like how to ask questions you already know the answer to just to make sure the person you're talking to is playing fair.

The woman Key was working for, Mariana Pereira, wasn't stretching her limbs for the jump from city councilwoman to mayor because she was a policy genius. At least not solely for that reason. She'd gained from the fiasco Key and I had helped cause the year before too. Become the star of her own viral cell phone video, the kind that made her synonymous with confronting police misconduct.

"This may shock you, Russ, but I agree with your cop friend. I don't think Abel killed those kids either. I think him getting sick was just the last cruel coincidence for him in a long line of them, something that made it easy for the prosecutors to kick his case without too much attention," Key said. "I knew Cynthia Bell. The marches in the '90s, when she was calling out the NPD for failing to find her sisters? Those were some of my first protests. Abel got diagnosed more than a year ago. Before his newest appeal was filed. If this was really about him being sick—"

"Then why wait so long to petition for his release?" I replied, taking another sip of the crap coffee.

"Right. Something's off," she said. "Now, I'd be here any which way. But you're right, it wouldn't exactly hurt the councilwoman to learn this was yet another NPD fuck-up under the current administration's watch."

"I hear you," I replied. "If Henniman tells me anything that sounds like police incompetence ruining Abel Musa's life, I'll send you a text. Or a DM. Do you have Signal? I hear that keeps the government from listening."

Key looked like she was thinking about slapping me again.

"But seriously, I'll let you know what I hear," I said. "Right after you get Musa to talk to me."

"And why the hell would I do that?" she asked.

"'Cause he won't talk to Henniman. And if I can do something Henniman can't, that gives the lieutenant more reason to talk to me," I said. "Makes it more likely he'll tell me something you want to know."

"I don't remember you being the sharing type," she said.

I stood up, went to take a final sip of coffee and found the cup empty. My back pocket was light of the change necessary for a refill.

"It's like you said, I'm real good at making things about me. And right now, I've got bills to pay."

I went back to the hallway outside Musa's room, put my hand against the glass separating me from him, and thought about the best way to be selfish.

Sure, the main task at hand seemed like it might be altruistic: help clear the name of an innocent man.

But if Bill Henniman and Keyonna Jackson were circling the same case, I doubted they were working toward the same goal.

Henniman wasn't telling me everything. But I knew a lieutenant's pay topped out above six figures, and he'd been at that rank, with no kids, for a while. I could probably pull a rate out of my ass that covered a few months' rent and he wouldn't blink.

But Key's presence, and her new job, gave me pause. The woman she was working for, Mariana Pereira, was anything but token opposition in the pending mayor's race. Mariana was a rising star among Essex County Democrats. Young. Smart. Portuguese. The daughter of Tiago Pereira, the restaurant owner and unofficial "mayor" of the Ironbound neighborhood where I lived. The police scandal I'd helped expose the year earlier had made Newark's longtime mayor, Cleanthony Watkins, vulnerable, and Mariana's mix of heritage and left-of-left-wing politics had energized a base separate from that of the incumbent.

Some people claimed Pereria's politics leaned toward socialism, but that kind of alarmist rhetoric usually only impacted right-leaning voters, and you were more likely to find a velociraptor than a conservative in Newark.

She had a real chance to win. I'd already pissed off the police. I wasn't entirely sure I wanted to piss off their eventual boss too.

I didn't know how long it would take Key to convince Musa to talk to me, or if she'd even be able to deliver. Feeling my light wallet again, I thought about calling Henniman, asking him to sit down and let me look through his old case files, see what that jarred loose. At the very least he could expense my dinner.

As I turned to leave, wondering exactly what kind of takeout Bill would be willing to cover, something grabbed my shoulder hard enough to stop me from moving.

"Hold on just a second, sir," said the voice belonging to the suit-clad arm on my left. I traced the vice grip on my shoulder to a blank expression wearing an earpiece. He had a friend on the right in the same budget Secret Service getup.

I went to swat away the hand on my shoulder, not expecting to be successful, more testing the reaction. Sure enough, the guy took hold of my wrist with one hand, twisted it down and placed the palm of his other hand in my elbow, getting control of my left side as efficiently as possible.

They didn't work for the hospital.

"Sir, please calm down. We just need to check you out," said the one who'd been on my right and wasn't holding my arm hostage.

"Check me out for what?" I asked.

"Weapons. Contraband. Maybe a notepad," said a voice I really hoped I'd never hear again. "You used to be dangerous with one of those things."

At least now I knew this was all a show, a power trip.

When the goons let me go, I found myself face-to-face with the used car salesman bitten by a radioactive can of hairspray who handled press relations for Newark City Hall.

"Russell Avery," said Dameon Lynch, the mayoral spokesman who'd been the bane of most Brick City reporters' existences for at least two decades. "Sorry for the show of force, but we're in a very competitive election cycle right now. Can't be too careful with a regular Raymond Chandler like yourself walking around."

"Marlowe," I spat back.

"Huh?"

"Philip Marlowe's the PI, Chandler's the author," I said. "If you're gonna make a shitty joke, at least know what the fuck you're talking about, Lynch."

He dug his hands deeper into the pockets of his form-fitting slacks. Lynch was the kind of attractive that always pissed me off: pretty face, bleached teeth, always filling out business attire the way people on TV seem too. I'd look like wait staff at a golf course bar and grill if I rocked a polo and khakis. He looked like the guy whose name was on the country club.

"How are the *Signal-Intelligencer*'s readers surviving without your eloquence?" Lynch asked, playing with the ever-present Bluetooth in his ear.

"Poorly. But hey, cursing you out instead of pretending I like you is one of the few perks of unemployment," I said. "So are you wasting taxpayer money just to screw with me, or is there an actual reason you're here?"

Two more sets of muscles that happened to be attached to brain stems showed up down the hall, their appearance answering my question. Each flanked a tall, lithe black man wearing a smile practiced at countless press conferences and council hearings.

Newark Mayor Cleanthony Watkins nodded his head at Lynch and moved toward the bedside of the man his city had supposedly wronged, before pointing at me and flashing a thumbs-up. Whether he remembered me or was just the kind of asshole who wanted people to say he never forgot a face was up for debate.

Lynch went to say something again, but I tuned out his inevitable bland insult and thought about being selfish again.

A wrongful conviction.

A cold case that had haunted the city for decades.

A veteran cop looking for redemption.

Two mayoral candidates circling the case, adding a little political intrigue to boot.

It had been a while since my name had graced the front page of a newspaper, but I knew how to formulate a headline. This wasn't just a case. It was a story.

One I could write the hell out of.

One that, if told right, could help me get my life back in order.

CHAPTER
FOUR

'D SPENT YEARS trying to turn Bill Henniman into a source.

The Major Crimes lieutenant had been plugged into almost all of Newark's newsworthy homicides and drug investigations during my time as a reporter, perched atop a pile of information that would have fit nicely on the *Signal-Intelligencer*'s front page most days. Getting his cell phone number back then would have been like striking oil in your backyard.

I'd made overtures for drinks. I'd delivered my practiced speech about how going in depth on some of the department's toughest cases might give the public a different perspective on policing. When I found out he collected challenge coins—which are basically cop-themed bottle caps commemorating a certain department's units or historic moments on the job that some of the boys in blue treated like macho trading cards—I'd even made a point to snag a few off the beaten path ones while visiting friends out of state.

But Henniman had been a cop's cop, tribal and unflinching,

convinced he and his colleagues were living by some warrior code that the rest of us just couldn't understand. He saw the press as less than an enemy, but nothing even close to a friend. When I bugged him after a news conference and opened my palm to reveal challenge coins from the Durham P.D. Bomb Squad, Henniman just met me with his exhausted-by-everything glare and asked if I was trying to bribe him.

I didn't get that cell phone number.

But now, as I parked the Impala on one of Verona's endlessly impeccable suburban side streets, I had Henniman's digits, his home address and, maybe for the first time ever, something he wanted. If Key was right, and she usually was, the lieutenant had been excommunicated from his church. If he was really being boxed up and shipped out of the Newark Police Department, he couldn't risk getting caught digging into this against orders. Not if he wanted his pension.

He needed me involved, even just as a cutout, to keep his fingerprints off the investigation. Which meant giving me the kind of access he thoroughly enjoyed denying back when I carried a press credential.

Roughly twenty-four hours had gone by since Henniman had shown up on my doorstep and told me a story interesting enough to send me to Abel Musa's hospital room. He'd left a few things out of that tale, like the fact that Abel Musa either didn't know the detective was trying to clear his name or didn't believe him.

I was going to have to ask Henniman about those lies of omission, but that probably meant he was going to yell at me, so that would have to wait. The lieutenant had called me over to review the case file on the Twilight Four, and I needed to squeeze every piece of information I could out of him while I was on his good side. Information that would be invaluable to any investigation he wanted to hire me to launch.

Or any article I wanted to write.

The thought of using Henniman's cold case to reinvigorate my journalism career wasn't merely renting space in my head, it had leased the property with an option to buy. Writing something that set an innocent man free was one of those things every reporter puts on their bucket list. A story like that could make a career, or in my case, revive a dead one. I was a long, long way from proving, or even necessarily believing, that Abel Musa was innocent. But if things played out that way, I'd be the first to know, and I'd have access to files and interviews and voices no one else would.

I'd be able to own the story in a way I probably hadn't owned any other in my five years chronicling Newark's bloodiest and most brutal happenings. I'd have to reactivate my Twitter account. I'd probably end up on a few podcasts. But most importantly, I might be able to land a job that allowed me to tear up my godforsaken PI's license and stop working for people like Bill Henniman.

Which meant, at least for the next few days or weeks, I'd need to be exceedingly nice to Bill Henniman.

As he unlocked the varnished wood door to his home, I met him with a smile so wide I thought I'd strain something.

"How are we doing this morning, Lieutenant?" I asked, extending a hand holding a black coffee from the above-average Montclair deli I'd hit up on the ride over.

Henniman looked at me like I was offering him a grenade.

"I already brewed a pot," he said, then stepped aside to let me in.

Okay, maybe exceedingly nice was too much. Maybe we could work our way up to regular nice. Or just not enemies.

Henniman's door opened into a vestibule with a rack lined with interchangeable pairs of black and brown dress shoes on the left and a small desk scattered with a mix of mail, opened and unopened, on the right. The floor was a high dark blue carpet with stains probably older than I was.

The foyer led into a living room where an American flag hung across one wall behind a brown leather couch and a New Jersey Devils logo banner filled the space behind the TV on the other. Some shelves were hammered into the free space on the walls, homes for pictures that mostly looked like a timeline of Henniman's career: academy graduation, detective's shield, sergeant's stripes, etc.

No family, or at least none that I could recognize. I knew Henniman was divorced, possibly twice, but there wasn't even anything resembling a favored uncle or cousin among his framed and treasured memories. I looked down at his waist as he led me deeper into the home, noticed the holstered sidearm there, and assumed his badge was still on.

Off duty probably wasn't a concept Bill Henniman believed in, which made me worry about how he was going to handle it if Key's prophecy came true and he was put out to pasture. I'd read an article recently about how a cluster of NYPD officers had eaten their guns in the past six months. All recent retirees. All ill-equipped to ride off into civilian life.

I didn't particularly like Henniman, but I didn't want that end for him. After all, the guy had saved my life.

"Let me see your phone," he growled.

"Uh, what?"

"Your phone," he said. "I need to see it."

"Why?"

"Because I'm not going to hire you if you don't give it to me."

My sympathies toward Bill's potential empty home life suddenly made a left turn toward somewhere else. Journalist Me would have told him to fuck off. Bumbling But Still Profitable PI Me from a year earlier would have told him to fuck off. But Current Day Me needed the check he was going to cut, so Current Day Me gave his ego a holiday, unlocked the phone and handed it over.

Bill jabbed at the screen and then his own, making slow, deliberate pokes, looking like the relative hopelessly confused by the tablet someone thought was a great Christmas gift. When he handed it back to me, a little square with two stick figures arm in arm was on my home screen.

"The Find My Friends app?" I asked. "We're friends now, Bill? Besties?"

"I need your help, but we need to make one thing clear. This is still my case. I make the calls," he said. "I need to know where you are and what you're up to."

"You think I'm going to run off the leash and get into traffic?" I asked.

"That wouldn't bother me," he said. "But if you shit on the carpet, I have to clean it up."

Henniman turned and walked toward the dining room, like that was a natural place to end the discussion. Like he hadn't just demanded I submit to GPS monitoring.

The table at the center was dominated by open manila folders, each one revealing what appeared to be a polaroid degraded by time. The images were surrounded by a mixture of decades-old handwritten notes on curled paper and fresher typed pages that I assumed came from Henniman's cold-case investigation. There were six faces in the photos: one that looked like a much younger Abel Musa, one I didn't recognize and four teens striking varying poses, all blissfully unaware of how close their stories were to ending.

"Who's he?" I asked, finger aimed at the man I didn't know.

"We'll get to him," Henniman replied. "If you're going to learn the players, you're going to do this in the right order."

Rent was due in a week. Rent was due in a week.

"Fine by me. This case has been living with you for years," I said, managing to avoid gritting my teeth. "Lead the way."

Henniman moved around the table and plucked a polaroid of a Black teenage girl with wide eyes and shoulder-length frizzy hair that teased toward the edges of a tank top. She sported denim shorts that cut high on her thigh, and her expression was stuck between a high-beam smile and a confident smirk, like she wasn't sure if she wanted the photographer to see a woman or a girl.

"Shayna Bell," Henniman said. "Sixteen years-old when she disappeared. This was taken two months before that. Young woman was on her way. Probably had more book smarts then than I do now. Was burning through Advanced Placement classes and made time to letter for the Weequahic High School volleyball team on top of that. No one had any good reason to want her dead."

"Except Abel Musa," I replied. "According to your informant."

Henniman shook his head.

"What did I say about doing this in the right order?" he asked. "Don't poison the well. If we're going to give this thing a legitimate second look, we need to start in the same place as the original case detectives. With nothing."

I felt my body tense up to argue, but that was just instinct when interacting with Henniman. He was right. The lieutenant clearly didn't trust his informant anymore, even if he hadn't told me why. That same informant's claims about Musa had colored his entire investigation.

"So, who was Musa back then?" I asked.

"Boyfriend to the older sister, Cynthia, and by all accounts, a good one. They'd apparently been flirting with the idea of marriage before the Bells' lives went to hell," he said. "Otherwise, he was a local Mr. Fix-It. Earned his taxable income at a body shop on Clinton Avenue, but he was never far from his toolbox, did odd jobs at low cost for most anyone who asked. Apparently, that was how he met Cynthia and the rest of our eventual ghosts."

I bristled slightly at the language but let it go. Henniman snatched up another polaroid, this one next in line from Shayna's, a younger girl with a tight braid and big pools for eyes who had no qualms about baring her teeth for the camera.

"Adriana. Thirteen. Shayna's youngest. Followed big sister everywhere, considered her both protector and best friend by all accounts. With the age difference between her and the other kids, family always assumed she'd just been tagging along for whatever happened to her sister," Henniman said. "There was always the chance she ran away separately, maybe got picked off by some monster with a thing for young girls, but most of the family interviews from that time say her and Shayna were last seen leaving the family home together."

Henniman came around to my side of the table, waving a hand

to brush me back as he scooped up pictures of two boys with similar faces on different bodies. One was husky, wearing a serious expression as his broad shoulders filled out a Weequahic High School football sweatshirt. The other was made of stilts, his face half hidden by a Newark Bears baseball cap, body trying to escape the frame like he'd been retreating from the camera lens when the picture was snapped.

"Kurtis and Lavell Dawkins. Sixteen and fifteen, respectively," he said. "I'm sure you can guess which one played O-line. They were Shayna's cousins, but their parents were out of the picture. Stayed in a foster home in the North Ward. Kurtis, the big one, had a minor marijuana arrest a few months before vanishing. I imagine if this had been known to be a murder at the beginning, the department might have looked at the drug angle more forcefully."

"But you didn't know it was a murder then," I said, taking a step back from Henniman. "And if we're ruling out your CI for the purposes of this thought exercise, then you still don't know that now. We keep talking about this like it's a crime, but what if the original detectives were right. What if this was, and always has been, a missing persons case?"

"You actually think that or are you asking just to ask?"

"I could pull out a notepad if it makes you feel more comfortable," I said.

Henniman rolled his eyes.

"Doesn't make sense as a disappearing act," he said. "No one who knew these kids back then suggested they had anything to run from. Now there were issues between the Dawkinses and their foster parents. Lavell, the smaller brother, had made an abuse allegation. But nothing ever came of it. Even if something had, that doesn't explain the girls. And besides, if they had run, none of these four had the means or money to get far."

"What if they didn't run?" I asked. "Maybe someone took them?"

"Was never any evidence this was a kidnapping," he said. "No ransom note. And the Bells weren't poor, but they weren't rich either."

"Trafficking?" I asked.

"That might have made sense if it weren't for the two boys, but again, no evidence of that."

Both our eyes traveled to the sixth polaroid on the table. The man I didn't recognize. Henniman seemed hesitant to move for it.

"No evidence meaning you or the original detectives couldn't find any?" I asked, picking up the picture of who I assumed to be the CI. "Or no evidence meaning it was never looked for because you were so sure about what this guy was selling you?"

Henniman took the snapshot out of my hands. He looked like he wanted to fling it across the room, but instead locked onto the dead eyes staring back at him. The picture showed someone tall and, at best guess, Hispanic. Someone on the precipice between adolescence and adulthood, string bean thin. His hands were jammed in his pockets and messy brown hair drooped across his face, obscuring the unkempt stubble growing around his chin. He was trying to look hard, but he just looked nervous. This had to be Isiah Roust, the informant that Henniman had used to walk Abel Musa into a jail cell.

"I told you, parts of his story made sense," the lieutenant said.

"What made you so sure about him then and so convinced he's wrong now?" I asked. "What changed?"

Henniman kept the picture pinned between his middle and index fingers, slowly shaking the polaroid. He looked like he was getting angry. I didn't need that.

"Bill," I said. "If you fucked up, you fucked up. The important part is you want to make it right now. But if I'm going to work with you on this, I need to know everything. You sent me to Musa's hospital bed yesterday, not warning me he would freak out at the mention of your name. I know we're a long way from trusting each other. You literally just put a digital leash on me. But there's no point in hiring me if you're gonna hold out."

Henniman's grip tightened on the picture.

"Musa is never going to believe I've got his best interests in mind, and I don't blame him. I honestly just figured you'd be smart enough to keep me out of it when you went to see him," Henniman said. "As for Roust…"

He sighed and flicked the informant's picture face down on the table like a mucked poker hand.

"Last year, Roust got in a car accident down in Asbury Park, that's where he lives now," he said. "Had Xanax in his system, and the person he rear-ended was older, got hurt bad enough that the Monmouth prosecutor hung an ADW charge on him. While he's waiting for trial, he ends up housed next to someone the cops down there liked for a series of home invasions and rapes. Like magic, he confesses to Roust."

"Oh shit," I replied, sure where this was going.

"He'd read enough newspaper clippings to know Asbury Park PD was looking for a certain height, weight and complexion. Pieced together enough quotes from anonymous sources in those reports, the kind of info that the police hadn't officially given out, that it seemed legitimate," Henniman said. "The perp they wanted had been using protection, wiping down surfaces. With no forensics, this jailhouse confession was mana from heaven."

Henniman dropped the picture and picked up a thick binder.

"Preliminary hearing transcripts from Monmouth County. Roust got destroyed on cross. Mixed up details between three different crime scenes because, of course, his cellmate hadn't told him jack shit," Henniman said. "He cooked the goddamn story."

"When did this happen?" I asked.

"Maybe three months ago," he replied. "Musa had already appealed his conviction, claiming insufficient evidence, and he lost. But you know how it goes for lifers. He filed again, and this would have come up in discovery."

"Meaning it would have become public," I said.

Henniman nodded.

"So, Musa's compassionate release…" I started.

"Probably had very little to do with compassion," Henniman

replied. "County prosecutor is a Democrat too, backed by the same people as Mayor Watkins."

Essex County's political machinery was old, but it was well maintained. Those who'd once benefitted from it and moved to other parts of the state didn't forget where they came from. People looked out for each other, ran slates that tended to get re-elected over and over, barring disaster. Watkins had already endured one, courtesy of the scandal I'd helped uncover the year before. His faint re-election hopes would not have survived a second.

I looked down at the table. The pictures stared back up. With Henniman removing the informant's polaroid, it was a spread of five stolen lives.

I wasn't terribly surprised to find myself standing in the middle of it, but I was still struggling to understand my dance partner's presence.

"Why do you care?" I asked.

Henniman looked at me like he was choking on something.

"Why do I... Did you fall asleep somewhere during this fucking conversation?" he asked. "We got the wrong guy."

"Maybe," I said. "Probably. But this can't be the first time someone has challenged your work. This is definitely the first time you've gone outside the department, maybe even against the department. Now you're breaking bread with me, a guy most of your fellow badges would probably love to see face down in the Passaic River. It wasn't that long ago you were at my door, threatening me, when I tried to shed light on the Newark PD's sins. So, I need to know why. Why do you care this time? Why this case?"

Henniman closed his eyes and scratched at the bridge of his nose. Another sigh escaped his lips. This case had clearly lived with Henniman. Haunted him. He looked remorseful, and Henniman didn't do remorse. He'd more or less ruined my business and almost put me in handcuffs a year ago, and he hadn't even offered to buy me a beer in return.

"You want to know why I care, then there's someplace I need to take you," Bill replied. "Tonight, would have been Shayna Bell's fortieth birthday."

I'd spent a lot of time writing about death, but very little getting comfortable with confronting it.

Back when I was a reporter, interviewing those who'd recently lost their spouse or child or sibling, I'd often ask them about "what happened," "the incident" or some other neutered description of their personal tragedy.

Rarely, would I say "dead." Like my word choice would somehow convince reality to take a day off.

As we approached the Eastern shore of Weequahic Lake, entering a crowd of less than fifty people staring out at a quartet of candles lined up near the water, I felt that same anxiety crawling into my stomach. That I was invading and about to be found out.

There were four pictures near the candles, each from a childhood frozen in amber. Shayna Bell. Her sister, Adriana. Kurtis and Lavell Dawkins. All shown about the same age they were in the fading photos in Henniman's murder file.

The crowd we'd folded into was largely Black, almost entirely older than me. I guessed these were the Dawkinses and Bells who lived close enough to come back and remember, maybe some neighbors who'd never left Weequahic. A few older women appeared to be praying the rosary, but a handful of heads raised up and noticed Henniman and I lurking toward the back. The lieutenant didn't notice or care. I certainly did.

Most of these people had been mourning for more than twenty years. I'd only truly been invested in their pain for a little over twenty hours. This felt wrong.

My eyes wandered over to the right side of the candles, where three television cameras stood in a row, all trained on the pop-up memorial. The media presence wasn't terribly shocking, given Musa's recent release from custody. This would be a logical follow-up piece, even if they didn't know that the real story might be far more complicated.

A few TV reporters milled around the cameras, some I recognized from past crime scenes and miseries. One was locked in a conversation with a woman whose motions were too excited and exaggerated for the occasion, but that was because they were usually too excited and exaggerated for everything.

Keyonna Jackson half turned to the crowd, as if she was checking for something, then went back to the reporter.

Spotting Key was like solving the first clue on a crossword puzzle. The next answer fell into place when I found Dameon Lynch, the mayor's spokesman and known cause of many migraines, shaking the hands of a pastor and playing the same game as Key. Making friends and winning influence, treating this like a networking event, even if the guests of honor were all dead. It didn't take long for me to notice Mayor Watkins doing the same thing, just with a different group of people near a car in an adjacent parking lot who were too far away for me to make out.

If Key and Lynch and Watkins were all there, that meant Councilwoman Pereira was either just out of my sight or on her way. After all, the cameras weren't simply here for the past.

"Is this what you brought me here for?" I asked Henniman. "We already knew this case was turning political."

"Just wait," he said, hands folded, eyes toward the ground.

I looked back to Watkins. The mayor moved toward the front of the crowd, stopped and stood at parade rest. A trio of Newark police officers followed him at a short distance, presumably his dignitary detail. City cops acting as his private security. One of them might have been the one who grabbed me at Lynch's behest at the hospital, but I couldn't be sure.

The people he'd been speaking to were advancing from the parking lot toward the candles, six men and women who seemed to be orbiting around a seventh. The short woman at the center was dressed in all black, with shoulder-length hair framing a face in Sunday church makeup. She walked while mouthing words I couldn't hear. I focused on her face, the narrow eyes and high cheek bones and crease lines along her forehead, the round but not heavy frame, and saw what might have happened if Shayna Bell had a chance to grow old.

The crowd of onlookers grew quiet, and Key cut her chatter with the cameramen short and took up a place near the front as well, eyeing Lynch as she moved. The woman who'd been at the center of the procession from the parking lot came to a stop near the candles and turned toward all of us, raising her hands as if they were in prayer and touching them to her lips, nodding toward everyone with eyes that were slightly damp. The man who had been holding her hand let go. Another from her flock carried over a microphone, a cable and small wattage amplifier, the kind of setup I imagined Key used back when she was disrupting city hall instead of working inside it.

"Shayna was the kind to count heads for her birthday every year, so thank you all for coming. This size crowd would have made her smile, or at least kept her from crying," the woman said, sharing a sad smirk of her own as she gripped the microphone with both hands. "For the few of you who don't know, my name is Cynthia Bell. We're here tonight to make sure four names are never forgotten."

She let one hand fall from the microphone and extend toward the candles.

"Kurtis. Lavell. Our baby, Adriana. And, of course, Shayna," she said. "Twenty-four years since they were called away from us. Taken too fast by…well, we don't need to speak his name. He doesn't matter."

Cynthia slowly dropped to one knee, scooping up the picture of Shayna, struggling a little as she rose again.

"You're forty today, girl," she said. "And we all knew how you liked a party, so we're throwing you another one."

I looked toward Henniman, who was listening intently, eyes locked onto Cynthia. I could have done a backflip and he wouldn't have noticed.

"Some of you know this was one of Shayna's favorite spots," Cynthia said, gesturing toward the lake, which was glistening under a bright summer moon behind her. "She used to run the loop around the water in the summers, always starting and ending on this spot. Used to say there's almost no place quiet in Newark, but this came closest."

Cynthia went to bend down for another picture, but one of the men who'd helped her over from the parking lot hustled to the candles and handed up Adriana's image.

"Our littlest one followed her here often, though, in truth, she followed Shayna everywhere. She'd make a game of it, almost like hide and seek," Cynthia said, pecking a quick kiss on the forehead of the child in the frame. "Baby girl worshipped her older sister. I wish we'd gotten to spend more time together, but all those years between us, you know how it is. I was taking classes at Essex County Community when she still had braces. But even more, I just wish you had the chance to grow up outside Shayna's shadow, show us all the beautiful woman you would have become."

Cynthia waved her hand, and the man who'd handed her Adriana's picture did the same with photos of Kurtis and Lavell.

"And the boys. What's that thing they say about your cousins, they're your first best friends?" Cynthia asked. "Kurtis looked out for Shayna like the brother she never had, and Lavell was the sweetest little boy…if you could ever pull his nose out a book and get him talking."

The Twilight Four case had clearly never gone cold for Cynthia Bell. The tremble in her voice, the short breaths between words, betrayed pain that wasn't quite fresh, but nowhere near dulled by the years since she'd last seen her loved ones.

"You know, every now and again, I catch myself thinking about how long it's been since I've seen their faces. And it tears me up like it does right now," Cynthia said, her eyes now averted from the crowd, staring down at the pictures that had returned to their places near the candles. "And then I stop. I say, Cynthia, they're gone, but it hasn't been that long. 'Cause once a year, just for a little bit, you get to feel them again. Sense them again. I believe that. I really do. That when we all come together like this, it calls them back home for just a little bit. Shayna's running out by the lake. Adriana's hiding, watching. Lavell's reading on one of these benches. Kurtis is standing off to the side, trying to pretend like he don't care, when he's really looking out to make sure no one messes with his family."

Cynthia's voice trailed off and her shoulders pinched toward her neck. She ran her lips over one another and shook her head. I didn't know if Cynthia offered the same eulogy every year or scratched the depths of her sadness for new details to mark the grim occasion each time, but the task had exhausted her either way.

"Well, I think I need to sit down. But I understand we have a few guests here tonight who might want to say a few words about my family," Cynthia said.

I looked left, found Lynch whispering something to Watkins. The spokesman had probably written whatever the mayor was about to say, and Watkins had surely rehearsed it on the drive over. He strode toward Cynthia, hands out to his sides before he brought them up and under the woman's trembling palms, nodding his head and mouthing, "Thank you." He'd definitely planned that too. The shift from her genuine pain to his practiced brand almost made me dizzy.

"Good evening, good people," Watkins said, voice booming with the confidence of a preacher who could also sell you a luxury car. He wasn't using the microphone. He didn't need too.

"Now, I can't claim to be here as a mourner. I didn't know these beautiful babies, much as it saddens me to know they're gone. I can't ever understand what you're all feeling," he said, before his eyes wandered toward the cameras. "What I am here to do is assure you the man responsible for this will never, ever walk these streets again. I will respect Cynthia's wishes. I won't speak the animal's name. But I imagine most of you know what happened. That he's lying in a hospital bed right now instead of a cell where he belongs. I'll have you know I went by University yesterday to look him in the eye and tell him that I will make it my personal mission to see that he never leaves that room.

To let him know that if he happens to make a miraculous recovery, I will push the prosecutor's office to shove him back in the hole he was meant to rot in."

Watkins's face turned intense. His eyes narrowed and his nostrils flared. Just enough that you might think the anger was real.

"Our city will never forget these boys and girls," he said. "But we will damn sure forget that man ever walked this earth."

A few of the men in the crowd clapped and Cynthia let out a loud "yes." The rest of the mourners seemed to be nodding in acknowledgment. I looked to Henniman again. His expression was guarded, but his fists were clenched.

Before returning to the audience, Watkins clasped Cynthia Bell's hands once more, as if to say they were in this together. As if the city's most powerful man could stand next to a woman scarred by one of its worst crimes and even suggest he'd learned the same lessons about struggle. Cynthia reclaimed the microphone and looked over to where Key had been.

"Would anyone else like to speak?" she asked.

I followed her gaze and found Mariana Pereira had snuck in at some point, purposefully unnoticed. The North Ward councilwoman was wearing a black blouse and jeans with minimal makeup, like she'd just left a shift at her father's famous Ironbound restaurant. She hadn't come for the cameras.

"I'm just here out of respect for who we lost, Mrs. Bell," Mariana said, voice low enough that I wouldn't have heard her if I was standing any further away. "But thank you for offering."

Cynthia nodded, seemingly content with the show of respect. I studied Key for some kind of reaction, but her face was blank. I didn't know if she was here on a personal or political mission, but it seemed the councilwoman had chosen the former.

The crowd moved closer to the candles, and Cynthia began to lead them in a chorus of "Happy Birthday" for Shayna. Henniman tapped me on the shoulder and started moving back toward the car, so I followed.

We made it halfway before the pained voice that had led the ceremony cried out Bill's name.

Henniman and I both spun around and saw Cynthia Bell walking quickly through the grass, having left someone else to lead the birthday choir.

"You didn't say hello," she said.

"I didn't want to intrude," Henniman replied, politeness in his voice I didn't know he was capable of. "With the politicians and…well, everything with him…it just seemed wrong."

Cynthia shook her head and rubbed a hand on Henniman's cheek. I wasn't sure which one was older, but something felt maternal about it.

"Detective, you're the only reason we know what happened. You're the only reason I know enough to even hold these memorials, to know they're not just out there, lost," she said. "You always have a place here."

Henniman nodded. He looked at her, then at me, but said nothing.

"Who's this?" she said.

"A colleague," he replied.

"Another detective?" she asked.

"Sort of," I said, instantly earning a look from Henniman that said I wasn't supposed to speak.

"It's complicated," Bill said. "He's just helping me close a few doors."

Cynthia's face twisted.

"About…about my sisters?" she asked. "Is this about their case?"

Henniman looked deflated. He grasped Cynthia's hands. I wasn't sure who was holding up who.

"There's nothing to worry about for now, Cynthia. It's just procedure. With Musa getting released to the hospital, I just need to look at a few things, and I need fresh eyes," he said.

Cynthia met me with something closer to suspicion than contempt.

"What do you mean, for now?" she asked, a stammer in her voice. "Did something happen?"

"Cynthia," he said, composing himself, his own hands now

traveling to her shoulders. "Do you still trust me?"

She nodded.

"If or when there's something new to know, you will be the first to know," he said. "I promise you. I'll do what needs to be done."

Cynthia's eyes wandered from Bill's to mine. Maybe she trusted the detective, but I was a new part of the equation, something that might change the math to a result she didn't like.

"Okay...okay," she said, voice shaking like it had when she held the microphone, eyes looking a little more wary of Bill then they had at first.

With seemingly nothing left to say but goodbye, Cynthia did so and returned to the family she had left.

We resumed our march toward the car. Henniman didn't say anything. He didn't need to. His passion for the case made more sense than it had in the morning. That woman deserved answers, and Bill clearly wanted to find them, no matter how painful they were.

But that task might have been easier if there wasn't a Newark police cruiser blocking us from leaving.

I didn't used to be the kind of person who got nervous when police showed up unannounced.

For most of my life, the cops had simply been the guys who stopped the robbers. The guys you tipped your hat to and said, "Stay safe," if you bumped into them in uniform. The Finest. Like one of my uncles said: "Don't want trouble with the police? Don't do anything stupid."

That mantra made sense to me as a white kid hanging out above the poverty line in a North Jersey suburb. It still seemed logical in my early days as a reporter, when I spent most of my time chronicling homicides and framing the world through the worst things cops ever see.

But the past two years had taught me how outdated my uncle's mantra was, that the definition of stupid was subjective. That just because the uniform said hero, it didn't mean the person underneath was fit for a cape.

The Newark PD cruiser blocking our exit was perpendicular to the back bumper of Henniman's ride, the two cars forming a capital T. Three men in plain clothes were standing near it, one slouching with his ass on the hood and legs kicked out toward us, the others roaming either side of the car, hands near their belts.

"Friends of yours?" I asked, assuming we were still out of earshot.

"They used to be," Henniman grumbled back.

As we got closer, I started sizing up the trio. The one leaning on the hood was white, with black hair just long enough that a stalk swept his eyebrow. There was an odd shape to his nose, like it had been broken before. He stood over six feet and had a frame filling out a tight t-shirt and jeans that belied little, if any, body fat. The two cops hovering nearby were a mismatch if they were partners. One sported a goatee and wore a polo shirt and jeans that revealed a forearm sleeve tattoo with enough spider webs to fulfill the dreams of many a Hot Topic employee. The other was a skinnier Black guy with a suit that hung loose who seemed to be shifting from foot to foot. He straightened up when we got closer. Great, he wanted to be intimidating too.

"Nelson," Henniman said to the cop near the hood.

"Bill," the man replied.

"It's still lieutenant."

"Not anymore, Bill. At least not to us," Nelson said. "Not much longer to anyone, from what I hear."

"A good detective knows better than to believe every rumor they hear. Thought I taught you that," Henniman replied. "Either way, I'm still a lieutenant, Detective Nelson. Even if I'm not your lieutenant. But I hope I don't need to pull rank to get you to move that car."

Best I could guess, these were some of Henniman's former associates from the Major Crimes division, one of the NPD's elite assignments. Henniman had once run the unit, before his career got derailed by the scandal that I'd had no small part in exposing a year ago. Before he'd saved my life by killing one of Major Crimes' former legends.

"No worries, Bill. This isn't about you anyway," Nelson said. "New captain told us about your history with this case. That you come to this memorial every year. That you wouldn't be here for any reasons you're not supposed to be."

Nelson's eyes lingered on Henniman's for a second longer than they needed too, punctuating his point before turning to me.

"We'll be gone as soon as we have a word with…well, I hope he's not your friend, but the guy next to ya," Nelson said.

I made a big show of looking around the empty parking lot.

"Who? Me?" I asked. "'Cause you're not blocking my car. Hell, condition my car's in, I could just leave it here, no one's boosting that heap. So, I can just walk."

I started to step away, just to see what would happen. Nelson placed a hand on my chest as I crossed his path. The tattooed officer stepped in front of the cruiser's push bar to cut me off.

"Uh, Nelson?" I asked.

"Detective," he replied.

"Oh, like how he's a lieutenant?" I asked. "Unless you've got a valid reason to stop me, Nelson, I'm gonna need you to take your fucking hand off me."

Something between a laugh and a cough came out of Nelson's mouth. He pulled his hand back but waved over the other officer in the loose suit, effectively surrounding me.

"Heard you had a mouth," Nelson said. "But relax, no need to involve the ACLU. We just need to talk to you about a harassment complaint."

"They sent three guys from Major Crimes to investigate a harassment complaint? Bullshit," I said, turning toward Henniman. "Guess things really went to hell fast when you left the unit, huh?"

Bill didn't even look at me. He had his arms crossed, eyes jumping between Nelson and the others, an uneasy look on his face. I should have known better. Whatever avarice was brewing between Henniman and the department, he wasn't going to side with me over brother officers.

"The person making the complaint is involved in one of our cases," Nelson said, not bothering with my insult. "So maybe you talk a little less shit, answer a few more questions, and this is over in five minutes."

The only person they could have been referring to was Musa.

"So, you're here to tell me the guy in a hospital bed with pancreatic cancer, who thinks your department framed him for four murders, who thinks people wearing the letters NPD on their shirt ruined his life…he filed a police report?" I asked.

"I'm here to tell you not to bother the man," Nelson replied, stepping to me, the other cops closing rank in sync. "Or else you might risk arrest."

A cop was getting in my face about Abel Musa for the second day in a row. Yesterday, it had happened because Dameon Lynch spotted me in the hospital. Clearly, my presence had not gone unnoticed during the memorial either.

"Listen, I'm no attorney, but you're clearly a dipshit, so let me try and explain this to you," I said. "To get a prosecutor to do anything with a harassment charge, you'd need proof I bugged the guy more than once or caused him alarm knowing he didn't want to hear from me. None of that happened, and Abel Musa sure as shit didn't call your squad room anyway. Which means you're here to cause me a headache because the mayor's office told you to. Which means I'm leaving."

I tested the waters again and found Nelson's hand on my chest, this time with the requisite muscle behind it to push me back.

"I didn't say you could leave."

"Was he this stupid when he worked for you?" I asked, turning toward Henniman.

Nelson responded with a half shove, enough to make me rock back on my heels and think about falling. Bill hadn't moved, meaning I wasn't sure if I was outnumbered three-to-one or four-to-one.

"Detective," Henniman said, still not moving. "You made your point. Now do the smart thing and walk away before this becomes a problem."

Well, three-on-two was less terrible.

I wasn't exactly spoiling for a fight with the cops, especially not while trying to revive a career that mostly involved writing about them, but these guys didn't seem like they were here to do anything that would go in a police report either. Not if Lynch had sent them, which seemed like a pretty safe bet.

Nelson stood up straight, setting off an alarm in my head about the obvious height and weight disparity between me and the guy who liked putting his hands on me. The other officers closed ranks on each of his shoulders.

"And how's it gonna become a problem, Bill?" Nelson asked. "Or are you gonna side with him over us again?"

I turned toward Bill. The man's practiced stoicism was gone, his face wearing something resembling indignance.

"Careful, son," Henniman said, his voice both grave and concerned. He was closing the gap on the younger lion now. "Don't start talking about things you don't understand."

Nelson erased the rest of the space between them. I backpedaled a bit, and Nelson's friends kept their distance too. This wasn't our fight anymore.

"What's there to understand, Bill?" he asked. "You're a fucking cop killer."

The insult got caught in Nelson's throat, probably because Henniman's hand was wrapped around it. The old cop got low and drove his hips, forcing Nelson back by his neck until his body hit the cruiser. The other cops seemed as surprised as I was by the lieutenant's speed. The skinny Black officer stepped in my path, while the one with the Hot Topic ink raced to help Nelson, who was trying and failing to disconnect Henniman's death grip.

Officer nu-metal managed to get his hands around Henniman's waist and pull him back just enough for Nelson to breathe. Half-choked and fully incensed, Nelson threw an overhand right that brought Henniman to a knee. Hot Topic started driving forearms into the Lieutenant's back. Bill had fought well, if briefly, but he was on the wrong end of the numbers game. He kept trying to find his feet, but the younger officers had the stamina to keep raining blows.

The cop blocking my way turned around to watch the assault. If he seemed timid before, he seemed outright unnerved now. His hand was shaking. Maybe he was new to the unit. This clearly wasn't the job he signed up for.

If he hated the type of bully nonsense Nelson seemed to get off on, there was an alternate universe where I could have made him a friend. Or at least a source.

Unfortunately, he was in my way. And I owed Henniman.

I drove the point of my knee into the underside of the officer's balls, hoping my guess about Lynch was right and these guys weren't here in any official capacity.

With his reproductive organs relocated into his midsection, I had little trouble getting hold of the back of his neck and driving his body into the side of Henniman's car.

Nelson and his friend were too busy throttling Bill to notice I'd dropped their partner. Or that I'd pulled out my cell phone, turned it sideways and pressed record.

"Detective," I shouted, and they both turned their heads, clearly identifiable faces now in frame. "Mind stepping away from the lieutenant?"

"You little fuck," Nelson said, out of breath, starting toward me.

"Wouldn't do that," I said, continuing to backpedal. "There were already TV cameras here, people I knew. Promise I can hit send before you can get this thing out of my hands."

I was bluffing. Nelson must have played poker because he read it after a few seconds and kept advancing. Then he hit the ground.

Henniman was up, a collapsible baton extending from his hand. I didn't know where he pulled it from, but I was glad he had it. Nelson groaned and searched the asphalt with his hands, trying to stand up, but Henniman's foot found his jaw and put him down for good. The lieutenant turned to Hot Topic and held the baton high.

"You gonna move the fucking car now?" he asked.

Two minutes later, we were driving out of the parking lot. Henniman had some blood dribbling from his nose, a scowl on his face and a puffiness in his eyes that wasn't from Nelson's fists. He'd been injured before a punch was thrown.

Now I understood why Bill hired me. Sure, he wanted fresh eyes on the case. And he knew I could talk to people who wouldn't talk to him.

But mostly, he had no one else to turn to.

CHAPTER
FIVE

THE NEXT MORNING, I got to pretend I had a career again.

I popped out of bed around 8 a.m. without the aid of a cell phone alarm, took a shower and put up a pot of coffee. By 8:30, I had pants on and began scrounging my kitchen for breakfast. I needed something to fuel the headlong dive I needed to make into the copies of police reports, interview notes and court transcripts that Henniman had made for me before we'd left for the memorial.

But I wasn't adept at groceries, or general adulthood. Outside of a few bananas that seemed to have gone black overnight, my kitchen lacked breakfast materials beyond coffee. So, I got dressed like I was going to work—I even put on a short sleeve button-down to make sure I was all business—and started the four-block walk from my apartment to Ferry Street.

Ferry was the Ironbound's main thoroughfare, running north from Newark Penn Station to St. Stephan's Church, connecting with Market Street at each point to form two thirds of a misshapen triangle.

The always-busy block was dotted with bars, cafes, barbecue spots and tapas restaurants all serving a combination of Portuguese, Brazilian and Spanish influenced fare. Locally owned businesses occupied the spaces between spots to stuff your face, laundromats and family pharmacies and convenience stores whose owners sometimes lived in one of the apartments upstairs.

Occasionally, a chain store peeked its head out—a Boost Mobile here, a McDonald's there—but for the most part the Ironbound was a self-sustaining economy. Dollars stayed in this community, allowing the Ironbound to stay what it had been for nearly one hundred fifty years. Newark's Plymouth Rock.

The neighborhood had been a landing spot and forward base for generations of Irish, German Polish and Italian immigrants as far back as the late 1800s. But it was the Portuguese influx, which reached its peak in the 1970s, that had shaped the modern-day Ironbound.

The neighborhood was more of a melting pot now than it once was. While some of the older locals still referred to Ferry as Portugal Avenue, a wide range of Latinos also now called the Ironbound home. You might hear as much Spanish as Portuguese in the neighborhood, not that I could tell the difference, nor was I alone in failing to notice the distinction. I wasn't the only white guy who'd swooped in for the reasonable rent prices either.

Still, the best food on Ferry was Portuguese. Formosa at the corner of Madison and Ferry had a simple menu, an owner who had been in the neighborhood for decades and the best Pasteis de Nata on the block. I could already taste the cinnamon crusting on the delicious little egg tarts when I stepped through the door.

You got in line as soon as you entered Formosa, joining the row of bodies snaking toward the pastry display cases on the left, salivating over the various treats hiding behind glass until one of the five employees running around behind the counter deigned to notice you. The rest of the room was dominated by about fifteen small tables with two chairs on either side, nearly each one filled by an older member of the neighborhood's original Portuguese delegation, reading the *Luso-Americano* newspaper and nibbling at some of the items on the menu I'd never explored.

I shuffled from foot to foot as the line crawled. Formosa was always worth the wait, but I was busy and briefly considered grabbing a Sausage McMuffin instead. Then a hand reached over the counter, waving a brown bag in my direction containing something so fresh I could feel the warmth radiating from it.

"You look like you're in a rush, Mr. Tracy," said the man holding out the breakfast pastries.

I looked up to find Tiago Pereira, Formosa's owner and the so-called Ironbound mayor, smiling at me from over the counter. His face was framed by his bushy silver moustache and beard, hair so thick it was like a platinum wig for his face. He was wearing an apron over a white t-shirt and seemed just as eager to stem the growing line as the employees thirty years younger than him dashing around behind the counter.

It had been a long time since Tiago needed to rock an apron or bother with a customer. He'd owned Formosa since the mid-1980s, and his other property, Marisqueira Pereira, was a wildly popular seafood restaurant that drew people who'd never been to Newark into the neighborhood for dinner. Still, Tiago would sweep the sidewalk if he thought it was too messy for his customers, and he made a habit of knowing his regulars and their orders. Sometimes he even blessed them with so bad they're good Dad jokes or pet names. Once he learned what I did for a living, I'd been reborn as Dick Tracy in his eyes.

I handed Tiago a few bills and nudged my head toward the sidewalk, hoping he'd follow. Sometimes it was the only break the old man allowed himself. I peeked into the bag, tempted to take a deep inhale. Four custard cups. Just the sugar rush I needed to tear through legal documents.

"I promise you, the omelets are good too," Tiago said as he escaped from behind the counter.

"You could put one in the bag, you know," I replied.

"You'd eat the pastries first and the eggs would get cold."

"You know your customers well," I said, a little laugh escaping.

"No, I just raised a boy once," he replied, voice trailing off for just a second. "So what case are you trying to crack today? You're not usually in so early."

"Nothing you'd be interested in," I replied, trying to avoid discussing a quadruple murder before breakfast. "Though I did run across your daughter's new friend while working on something the other day. What did she bring her on as anyway, a campaign advisor?"

Tiago's face seemed to sour at the mention of Key.

"Miss Jackson?" he asked. "That woman…she is a friend of yours, right?"

"I think the term is frenemy," I replied.

"Huh?"

"Nothing," I said. "We've worked together before. She can be… abrasive, but she's a good person. She'll do right by Mariana."

Tiago turned his head toward the bakery, craning his neck, like he was trying to spot something at one of the tables. I sometimes forgot how tall Tiago was. A shade over six feet, maybe had an inch or two on me. His neck and arms were covered in lean, ropey muscle, the kind that developed from seven-day work weeks instead of a gym membership. He shook his head before turning back to me with an expression that was a little tired and a little concerned.

"Something wrong here, Tiago?" I asked.

"No, well, not with your friend. Sorry," he said. "I just thought I saw something."

"So that's a yes," I said, waving him over toward a bench. "Here. Sit. I'll eat, we'll consider it a business breakfast."

"I'm not hiring you, Dick Tracy," Tiago said, his smile threatening to reclaim its place.

"I'm hearing that a lot these days," I replied. "That's fine. You let me cut the line. I'm just paying you back for that."

Tiago nodded and we took a seat.

"You know I've always supported my daughter. Whatever she wanted to do. Going away to school, walking away from the family businesses, even going into politics," he said. "As a councilwoman, she helps the neighborhood. She helps our people. She does so much good. But all this. Mayor? It worries me."

"She has a good chance to win," I said.

"That's what worries me," he replied.

I cocked my head to the side, trying to track the contradiction in his commentary. I decided to bite into one of the custard cups instead of saying anything that might upset Tiago.

"Lately, I've noticed men coming around who aren't from the neighborhood. At the bakery. At the restaurant. Maybe reporters. Maybe they work for the mayor. I don't know," he said. "You were a journalist. Is this normal? If she wins, does it stop?"

With Dameon Lynch at Watkins's right hand, it wouldn't surprise me if he was sending people around the Pereira family businesses to snoop. It was a pretty standard tactic. Let them know you're looking, even if you're not sure there's anything to find. It had certainly rattled Tiago, which would slot in nicely on my list of two hundred reasons to hate Lynch.

Of course, Watkins's longevity in Newark politics wasn't based solely on his charm. The man had heavy support within the Newark Police Department and heftier financial backing from the city chapter of the Fraternal Order of Police, the result of him mostly turning a blind eye to years of excessive force complaints and questionable shootings. Even with the federal government knocking at the door, threatening a sea change in the way the city's cops operated, Watkins had expressed hesitance toward signing any kind of consent decree that would mandate reform. The mayor liked to say change was better handled at the local level, but anyone paying attention could see his political survival instincts kicking in.

Tiago's daughter had shown no such fear of alienating the badge-wearing voting bloc. She'd won a crowded race for the North Ward City Council slot roughly two years earlier, but the calls for her to seek the big chair hadn't started until the winter before. Mariana was the only elected official to take part in the protests over the murder of Kevin Mathis, whose death was the first in the series of dominos that changed my life and dragged some of the Newark Police Department's ugliest sins into daylight the year before.

During one otherwise peaceful demonstration on Ferry, the NPD called an unlawful assembly a lot quicker than they were probably legally allowed to. Mariana was one of a handful of people who stayed in the street, facing down a skirmish line of officers dressed for combat. They repeatedly warned her she could face arrest or the use of less lethal munitions. She repeatedly warned them that they were violating her constituents' constitutional rights.

One officer—who either didn't know Mariana was a city councilwoman or thought the NPD's use-of-force policy was more like a suggestion—decided to silence Mariana by skipping a foam round off the street and into her thigh. With Newark already drawing airtime from CNN during the Mathis protests, footage of the conflict went viral and endeared Mariana to Key and the activist crowd looking to unseat Watkins.

Tiago had more reasons to worry about his daughter than he probably realized.

"Scrutiny's standard in politics, Tiago. Is there something in particular you're worried about? Something you need me to check out? I know you said you're not hiring me, but I can work on commission for these," I said, waving the bag of pastries.

"No, no," he said, seemingly laughing more for my benefit than his own. "I just worry sometimes. This neighborhood, it's ours, you know. But the city? The people who run it? They've always looked like you or looked like the mayor. I think sometimes maybe Newark is okay with us having our neighborhood, but how would they handle it if we were in charge? Maybe they don't want that. Maybe they'll do something to stop her. My family has worked extremely hard to build what we have here, and I don't want to see someone try to tear it down just to keep their job."

I checked my phone. It was past nine now. I had a mountain of paperwork to sift through, and as much as I respected Tiago, I didn't really have time to wrestle with his unspecified fears.

"Listen, Tiago, if something weird happens, or if you even think there's something weird going on, you call me," I said, handing him a business card. "I've dealt with the mayor's people before, and they can be a handful. They can get a little dirty. But that's exactly why your daughter is running, right? To fix that?"

"That's good," he said. "Maybe you should work on her campaign."

I half laughed, half died inside. Tiago was too nice of a man to have to suffer one of my rants on politics and public relations.

"Only if she pays me in these," I said, taking another bite and flashing him the kind of smile I could only produce when eating something Tiago had cooked.

B ack home, filled with enough sugar and dough to qualify as a meal, I took my first few sips of coffee and sat down in my office, happy I had a reason to use it.

I woke up my laptop and opened the websites that housed the big, scary numbers associated with my student loan and credit card debt. It'd been a minute since I had a reason to look at them and do something besides scream "fuck" at varying decibel levels.

Henniman had plunked down $5,000 to retain my services after our brawl with his old colleagues at the park. That was a little more than what lived in my rapidly eroding savings account, which I'd been using to cover my rent while my credit cards covered the groceries.

I didn't negotiate when he suggested the number. I didn't even ask a question. It wasn't like I had rates, or a website or an actual business model anyway. Two years ago, I'd started fixing problems on referral and I was making enough to live without too much fiscal panic.

But that was then. Now, as I stared at the computer and my quadruple digit credit card balances, I pulled up the calculator on my phone and started trying to figure out how much of Henniman's money I could use to keep from drowning. And how much more I'd need to reach dry land.

About a third of Henniman's donation wiped out my Visa balances and halved what was left on my Macy's card. When the fuck did I get a Macy's card?

I looked back and forth between Henniman's files and my bank account. The cash infusion would be enough to hold off any debt collectors, but it wasn't going to fix any of my long-term fiscal headaches. There were more credit cards with more four-digit balances, and Henniman was my lone source of income for the near future. I needed to figure out a way to stretch that.

The thought of my byline hovering between a headline about the Twilight Four and a story that contained words and phrases like "exonerated," "exclusively obtained" and "first reported by" floated around my head again.

Helping Henniman could be the right thing to do for the universe and my bottom line. There would be a story to write here, I just needed to figure out what it was.

I grabbed the files and placed them gently on the floor. They could wait. They were static, unaffected by time. I could send some flares out into the world first, poke around about my freelance options during normal business hours, then start pulling apart witness statements and trial transcripts and police and arson reports from the '90s after the sun went down.

My brain conjured up a pre-emptive headache at the thought of all that reading. Most crime reporters would kill for the kind of access Henniman was granting me, but in truth, those files might as well have had teeth. I'd never been much of a document reporter, always concerned that I wasn't quite smart enough to isolate the crucial detail or pattern lurking in a 3,000-page response to a public records request.

I was a shoe leather and social engineering guy, a talker. Why pull apart pages when you can make sources tell you what's hiding in them?

A blank Word document stared at me until I got a second cup of coffee and typed "Interview List" in bold black letters atop the page. I tapped my fingers against the keyboard for a second, hearing an endless snare drum until the words "Original Detectives" flowed out of me.

I peeked inside the first folder, cautious not to alert Pandora to the crack in the seal of the box. Thankfully, Bill kept things in chronological order and the original missing persons files from 1996 were near the top. The initial investigators were easy to spot. Unfortunately, it was just as easy to find their obituaries once I punched their names into a search engine.

A conversation with Cynthia Bell would be critical at some point, but it probably wouldn't come easy. She'd seemed, understandably, panicked at the idea Henniman was looking at the case again. It was clear she was sure of Abel Musa's guilt, and getting her to cooperate with an investigation that might upend that truth was going to be a challenge.

I'd also need to find Isiah Roust, Henniman's old CI with a potential talent for fictionalizing confessions. If he'd lied about Musa, there had to be a why there. But that wasn't a conversation I could have without Henniman present.

My fingers walked the desk again until they found the cliff leading to Henniman's files. There'd be more names to put on the list in there. All I had to do was dig in.

Instead, I opened a web browser and screwed around on social media for a bit. Procrastination comes as naturally to a reporter as writing, and I didn't have a deadline. Technically, I didn't even have a story. But if this went the way I was hoping, and Musa was cleared, I'd need to have a place to publish fast. So, I avoided the files again and started scrolling through my phone for the names of old colleagues, most importantly ones who'd left the *Signal-Intelligencer* and wouldn't catch any flak from editors for helping me out.

I found an old boss who'd moved on to a New York City tabloid. A health reporter I'd once teamed up with for a project on opioid addiction who now had a national presence at Buzzfeed. A Trenton bureau escapee who covered federal law enforcement for a non-profit focused on criminal justice in the city.

I sent them all some variation of a "long time, no see" e-mail, weaving in an old after work drinking story that would pester the ghost of our friendship enough to at least compel a response, asking them how freelancing worked at their publications and hinting I might have something interesting about a Newark cold case.

For a brief second, I let myself glimpse a future where I walked into a newsroom again, intercepting a city editor as they headed for a meeting, insistent I knew something so important it couldn't wait. I let myself dream about helping people through stories again.

With all my flares shot and my interview list still close to blank, I looked back at Henniman's files and exhaled. It was almost noon. It was time to do some actual work.

Or it would have been if my phone hadn't buzzed. There was a message on Signal, the encrypted texting app most reporters used, hoping it provided protection from snooping. I had no idea how, or if, Signal actually worked. But it seemed to make people who wanted to leak things feel comfortable enough to take the risk.

The text was from a Bergen County area code. It was only four words long:

"Abel Musa is innocent."

A series of bubbles appeared, followed by one more message:

And I can help you prove it."

CHAPTER
SIX

S OURCES RARELY APPEAR out of thin air. Not unless they want
something.

There were few universal truths in reporting, and fewer I
actually believed in. But whenever someone came to me swearing they
knew "The Big Thing," I was usually more concerned with why they
were telling me than what they actually knew.

Playing whistleblower is risky, after all. People lose jobs. People get
hurt. Death is a non-zero possibility.

If Abel Musa was innocent, a lot of people in city government would
be humiliated. Some might wind up unemployed. Cleanthony Watkins
would likely have to print up business cards that said something other
than "Mayor" for the first time since dial-up connections were a thing.

That's a lot of power to go up against. That's a lot of reasons to keep
your mouth shut.

So, as I leaned against a fence behind a restaurant called Don Pepe,
staring at the half-full parking lot, I started to wonder why it had been

so easy to convince the anonymous phone number that we should meet face-to-face.

We'd texted back and forth throughout the day, but I'd failed to glean anything useful from the person. They wouldn't say how they got my number or hint at what they knew or how they knew it. All the texter would tell me was they worked for the city—meaning they could have been the police chief, a clerk at the Sewer & Water Department, or anything in between—and they lived close enough to meet me in Newark without too much notice.

In fifteen minutes, I was supposed to be inside, sitting at a table in the back left corner of the old Portuguese seafood spot, the one that charged twice as much as Tiago did to serve me food about half as good. I hadn't seen anyone I knew come or go, but I also didn't know who I was supposed to be looking for. Maybe that meant my texter was inside before I got there. Or they hadn't arrived yet. Or they weren't coming and just wanted to make sure I'd be in a certain place at a certain time, which they'd already achieved.

I'd built fruitful relationships in the past with sources who started out as dummy e-mail addresses or website commenters or hastily created Twitter accounts that still had that little egg as a profile picture. But that was when my contact information frequently appeared at the end of *Signal-Intelligencer* articles, and people frustrated with their bosses or workplaces had reason to think telling me one thing might accomplish another.

No one would have any reason to contact me about Abel Musa unless they already knew I was investigating something connected to Abel Musa. That list was pretty short. Henniman and Key had no reason to play games with me, and Cynthia Bell had met me for all of ten seconds.

That really only left two options: a disgruntled cop or prosecutor who'd been involved with Musa's appeal, or someone who wanted to fuck with me. Don Pepe was less than two miles from city hall, the FBI's local field office, the federal courthouse and a Newark police precinct. Not exactly the spot a cop would pick to play Deep Throat unless they wanted to lose their job.

Which probably meant someone was fucking with me. Which was fine. But I still wanted to know who before I walked through the door.

"Don Pepe," said the voice that picked up after I dialed the restaurant.

"Hi, how are you doing? Sorry to be a pest but I'm running late and wanted to see if I could push back my reservation tonight."

"We're pretty packed," the person replied as I looked at a row of open spaces in the parking lot. "That's gonna be tough. What was the last name?"

"Avery, should be for two at seven p.m.," I replied.

"Avery, Avery…" the maître d' muttered to himself, as I heard the sound of pages flipping in the background. "Not seeing it."

Swing and a miss. Though I guess it was a good thing my would-be source wasn't being that obvious. Still, Mystery Texter did have a specific table in mind. They likely called ahead. I didn't know who they were, and we only had one other name in common.

"Is it under, uh…Musa?" I asked. "Abel Musa."

He didn't respond. I wondered if he recognized the name from the news and was thinking about telling his manager that an accused quadruple murderer might be trying the *camarones provenzal* that night.

"Mr. Musa sat down ten minutes ago," the man replied. "Who is this?"

The doctors at University Hospital were pretty incredible, but they probably hadn't cured cancer in the past twenty-four hours. Abel Musa sure as shit was not inside the restaurant waiting for me. So, who was?

"This is Abel Musa," I said.

"Excuse me?"

"Did I stutter?" I asked. "Who the hell did you give my table too?"

"The man said—"

Well, Mystery Texter was a guy. That halved the haystack.

"What man?" I asked, raising my voice to the appropriate "Karen wants to see the manager" volume. "Did you check his ID? Did it say Abel Musa? Or did you just give away my table?"

"Sir, I'm sure we can accommodate you..."

"Can you? You just told me you were pretty packed."

I was almost screaming now. A pair of kids on a nearby street corner looked at me like I was crazy, which was fine, 'cause that's what I was going for. I'd waited plenty of tables and tended a few bars before I found a full-time journalism gig. You never want to be the person who puts the nutjob on the phone with your manager.

"What does he look like?" I asked.

He stammered more than spoke, so I just kept yelling over him.

"The-the-the-the man you gave my table to!" I shouted. "I didn't stutter, so why are you? Who is he?"

"Sir, I'm not going to—"

"Yes, yes, you are. Or do I have to tell the manager that you just give away reservations to anyone who happens to read a name off the guest book when they walk in?" I asked.

"One moment," he said, surrendering to my customer from hell routine. I'd been on the wrong end of it so many times it was easy to drum up.

"It's a man in a suit. Slicked black hair. Bluetooth in his ear," the maître d' said. "He's only ordered a white zinfandel so far. I can ask him to move."

Knowledge of his shitty wine choice was irrelevant. But the combination of too much hair product, an ever-present earpiece and someone manipulating me made the man's identity perfectly clear.

I hung up and gritted my teeth. Then I headed for the door, wondering what headache Dameon Lynch was gonna cause me this time.

Lynch was lost in his phone, swiping with one hand, fidgeting with his earpiece with the other. That made it really easy to grab his glass of Zinfandel and empty the contents onto his head before he had time to react.

The voice of Newark City Hall popped out of his chair and swatted at his hair and face like he was under attack by a swarm of bees. The sticky sweet wine was already mixing in with the military-grade grooming product he used to achieve his impossibly coiffed appearance, ensuring his next shower would be a project.

"What is wrong with you?" he asked.

"There's a list, but mostly financial insecurity and a short temper," I replied. "You're lucky I didn't flip the table."

"Because I used a little subterfuge to get you here?" he asked.

"No, because you sent cops to get physical with me twice in two days, and then you pulled this stupid bullshit," I replied.

He kept waving his hand near his hair, like that might air dry the mess I'd made, but all it did was speed up the pink droplets sliding down his too tanned face.

"Do you have any facts to support that allegation?" he asked.

"I'm not at the paper anymore, as you so often like to remind me, so that doesn't matter," I replied.

It was around then that I noticed most of the restaurant was watching us. I looked over my shoulder and saw the maître d' approaching. Now he had a face to match the crazy voice from the phone.

"Is everything alright, sir?" he asked Lynch.

Lynch looked like he wanted to complain and have whatever passed for a bouncer at Don Pepe throw me out. But that would have rendered his stupid little ruse pointless.

"Everything's fine, my friend just has a...difficult sense of humor," he said, sitting down.

Lynch reorganized his table setting, folded a napkin back over his lap and motioned for me to join him, like this was a normal business meeting and not one that started with a lie and misdemeanor battery.

"Was all this cloak and dagger shit really necessary?" I asked as I sat down.

A busboy came by and nervously poured water. Maybe he was worried I'd hurl liquids in his direction too.

"Would you have met up with me otherwise?" Lynch asked.

"Of course not."

"Then it was necessary," he said, rolling his eyes and straightening the creases on his suit jacket. "I do wish you'd get over this rivalry you think we have. There's no reason for you to hate me."

There were plenty of reasons. Press secretaries and reporters lived at cross purposes. Technically, Lynch's job was to provide information, but only the sanitized kind. His real job had always been to block me from learning anything worth knowing. He was also from Philly, making him an asshole on an almost biological level.

But in Lynch's case, things went beyond the usual flack-reporter feud.

"I can think of three reasons," I replied. "Stephanie. Krystal. And Deonna."

"Excuse me?"

"We're not on the record, Lynch. Hell, I don't even know what that would mean for me anymore," I said. "You don't have to pretend you don't know who they are."

He held his hands out, offering a half-hearted shrug, expression never changing.

Dameon Lynch would never admit those were the names of the three city hall employees who'd contacted me four years earlier, describing late-night text messages from burner phones, bumping bodies in hallways with hands landing in places that couldn't be coincidental. The way the longtime married mayor always announced he'd be staying at his second apartment downtown when they were around. The way he reacted when they kept telling him no.

It took me months to convince them to go on the record. Late-night calls that were more therapy sessions than interviews. Interviews that turned into confessions. Deonna had caved to his whims at one point, thinking Watkins's lust could be satiated with one visit to the apartment. Not knowing he'd want it to be a weekly occurrence. Not knowing the things he'd call her, the threats he'd make, when she stopped showing up.

Two weeks before the story was to publish, Lynch asked me to get drinks. Tried to coax names out of me. Told me he'd heard whispers I was working on a story about sexual harassment and that he wanted to make sure I didn't print something I couldn't take back. That I was a good reporter with good intentions and he didn't want to see my career collapse under a libel lawsuit. He kept slipping in names.

Each of theirs came up at one point. I didn't betray them. Not intentionally. But he must have read something in my face, because Deonna was the first to recant a week later. Her brother worked for the housing department, and he'd gotten suspended out of nowhere.

Stephanie backed off next, and while I could never be sure, the social media images of her moving into a new apartment in the Dumbo section of Brooklyn led me to assume Lynch and a duffel bag of money got to her before I could place a check-in call.

Krystal still wanted to fight it. She'd been born in Newark. Didn't want to see her city run by a lecherous piece of shit. But it was years before the words "Me" and "Too" had become conjoined twins. One woman's word, even with some corroborating texts and really specific details, wasn't going to be enough against a sitting mayor.

She was devastated when I told her the story was dead. She told me I was a failure. She wasn't wrong.

Lynch got off easy when I dumped the wine glass on his head. I should have ordered a bottle and broken it across his jaw.

He flagged the waiter down, but kept his eyes trained on me.

"Another glass, please, and an extra napkin if you can spare it," he said.

"Oban, eighteen year," I added, before the waiter could ask or Lynch could offer.

Lynch's eyes bugged. I didn't really care about the scotch, but the reaction suggested this was on his tab, not the city's. He was here on his own accord.

"Expensive pour," he said. "I took you for a shot and beer type. I'm impressed."

"Wow, you really commit to the role," I replied. "You're trying to glad hand? Work me? I dumped a glass of wine on your head, like, three minutes ago."

"There's no upside in revenge. Though you will be getting a receipt for my dry cleaning," he said. "I didn't want to be seen at your apartment or office, whatever you call it. You would not have taken my calls. I needed you in a place, and now you're here. All you've achieved is mussing my hair."

There was a lot for me to hate about Dameon Lynch, but if I had to zero in on one thing, it was his calm. Lynch seemed to have an internal reset button, an ability to shrug off slights in deference to achieving what he wanted. I'd seethe over an unjust parking ticket for weeks and plot revenge against the meter maid's entire family. You could set Lynch on fire, but he'd figure out a way to get you back at the table if he needed something from you while he was still smoldering.

The waiter dropped off our drinks, including Lynch's extra napkin. He dabbed at his forehead and the collar of his damp shirt again. I waited for a scowl, a complaint, something. But he just placed the cloth on his lap and leaned forward, elbows on the table, chin leaning on his folded hands. Waiting.

"Are you going to tell me what you want?" I asked.

Lynch reached down and produced the brown messenger bag I'd seen him carry everywhere since we first met at one of Watkins's press conferences years earlier.

"That what's going to clear Abel Musa's name?" I asked.

"Nothing short of an act of God can clear Abel Musa's name. I assumed you dispensed with that fantasy once you realized I was the one contacting you," he said. "But Mr. Musa is, nonetheless, the reason we're here. Your obsession with him is troubling."

"Obsession? I tried to talk to the man once."

"Then you showed up at a memorial for his victims. A memorial I've attended for the past eight years and never seen you at once," Lynch said. "And you appear to be running around with the disgraced detective who hasn't done any good for this city since arresting Musa all those years ago. Why you're trying to save your business, or your career, is beyond me. But you clearly seem to be in need of something to do. So, I'm here to provide a better use of your time."

"Ya know, doing this job as long as you have, I thought you'd have the basics down by now," I said. "When has telling me the story's not a story ever worked? Has it ever worked on any reporter?"

"Plenty. And unsurprisingly, they all remain gainfully employed," Lynch said. "But I'll bite. Officially, on the record. Abel Musa is a murderer. There is nothing conspicuous about his release, nothing noteworthy, except perhaps evidence of the existence of karma, seeing that he is now terminally ill after being spared the death sentence he so richly deserved. You can quote that. I'm not here to protect anyone from secret truths being unearthed, Mr. Avery. If anything, I'm here to help you expose some."

I wanted to laugh, but he was too confident. He pulled two white envelopes from the bag, both brimming at the lip. The corner of a photograph seemed to be peeking out of one, but not far enough that I could see who or what had been captured in the frame.

"Off the record, of course, I can't say I missed our verbal sparring matches from your time at the paper. But your sudden re-appearance in my life did make me curious. I obviously read about your involvement in last year's running catastrophes with the police department, but then you seemed to slink away again until I saw you at the hospital. So, I got to wondering where you had gone in between," Lynch said. "And what did I find? A depressingly small amount. The occasional byline in a disreputable tabloid, the domain name for your little PI business website lapsed. And all that credit card debt…you're underwater, Mr. Avery. I'm simply here to remind you how to swim."

"You looked into my fucking finances, Lynch?" I asked. "Now

who's obsessed?"

"Running a credit check on you took no more than ten minutes of my time," he replied. "You need money. You need viable work. You're not going to find either by chasing down an embarrassing non-story, so allow me to point you in a direction that might provide both."

Lynch opened the envelope on the left and shook some of its contents onto the table, cupping a hand around what was there in case an erstwhile waiter or busboy happened to peek.

I leaned in to see what hook Dameon Lynch had been baiting me with all day and instantly regretted it.

The pictures showed two young women poolside, both in their mid-to-late twenties or early thirties, starring at each other, , skin glistening in the sun. The one with the dark hair and ruby red lipstick on the left seemed to have walked her hand on the thigh of her friend on the right. The images laid out across the table like a comic strip and I watched them tell a story that went from low-level flirt to full-on lip lock. The last one showed them walking away, arm and arm, in the direction of what looked like a hotel.

Lynch opened the second envelope, and more pictures rained down. Explicit ones, showing what happened once the women got upstairs. But there were more images in that pile, taken in what seemed to be a variety of locations. The more photos Lynch displayed, the less clothing each woman wore. Things got NC-17 in a hurry. These photos probably hadn't been meant for anyone but the people in them.

The women's hair styles changed as I kept looking, a streak of red coming and going from the younger woman's appearance, depending on where the photo was taken. Whatever this relationship was, it hadn't been brief.

I couldn't tell exactly where the pictures were taken, but the youth in the face of the woman on the left at least gave me an idea of when. She'd looked older when I saw her the night before.

Mariana Pereira. Newark's North Ward councilwoman, and maybe, its next mayor.

"I'm sure you recognize one of the parties here," Lynch said. "The other, I'm told, was a canvasser in her initial council race. In other words, a subordinate. I imagine a campaign sexual misconduct piece might put your name back on a front page faster than your misguided cold case crusade."

"No," I replied.

"No, this isn't a story? No, you don't believe me?" he asked. "If it's the latter, I assure you I have some documentation confirming the younger woman's employment."

"No, I'm not getting involved in this," I said. "This isn't news, this is mudslinging. You're afraid that she can take you in November."

"Ms. Pereira doesn't inspire fear in the mayor, I can promise you that. He doesn't even know I'm here," Lynch said. "But I will admit to being personally concerned that the city's voters might have the wrong impression of the councilwoman based solely on that video and her unfortunate run-in with the police last year. They deserve a fuller portrait, including how she might deploy her influence to force her own desires—"

"Stop. Don't. Do not go there. You of all people do not get to fucking go there," I said. "The woman is saying this was non-consensual?"

Lynch didn't speak.

"The woman saying she felt pressured?" I asked.

Still nothing. He had a script. I'd knocked him off it.

"You haven't talked to her," I said.

"The provenance of this information is irrelevant. The reality of it is," Lynch said. "I'm not here to tell you what to do, Russell. But as much as you irritate me, I have always respected you as a journalist. Quite frankly, you entertain me. Your ability to navigate spin has always impressed. All I'm asking is that you use those same critical eyes now. You're chasing this Musa canard because you're seeing what you want to see, an opportunity and a chance to right a perceived wrong. I'm offering you the same. Don't run away from it just because you don't like where it's coming from."

Lynch stood up, sliding the envelopes my way, then scooping up his wine and draining the glass.

"I'll get the bill on my way out. Don't waste that scotch," he said. "Depending on what you do here, it might be a while before you can afford more."

CHAPTER
SEVEN

I DIDN'T WASTE THE scotch.

Then I went home, where I also made sure I didn't waste the two glasses worth of bourbon left in the Woodford Reserve bottle I'd bought before money got tight. The combination of a pending headache and the sudden awareness of my limited liquor budget redirected me to the fridge, where I snatched up one of the loose Presidente beers I'd grabbed at the corner store. Then another. Thankfully, sleep snuck up from behind twenty minutes into an old episode of *Burn Notice* before I could track down drink number six.

Dozing off probably spared me from a serious hangover, but I was still rubbing my temples and taking slow, labored sips from a purple Gatorade as I sat in the Impala the next morning. Lynch's comments had plotted my course, but they hadn't sent me straight to Mariana Pereira's door like he'd probably hoped.

I'd taken the pictures he left on the table. Of course, I'd taken the pictures. You don't leave live ammunition laying around like that.

Sifting through the two envelopes he'd put in front of me, I found the additional evidence Lynch promised. Somehow, he'd also gotten chat logs between Mariana Pereira and the other woman, explicit exchanges that functioned as captions to the photos.

Most of it was simply the embarrassing sex talk many of us have and all of us hope never sees the light of day. Kink specifics and a likely clue into what I'd find in Mariana's browser history. None of that would have mattered if the women hadn't seemed to enjoy leaning into the boss-employee dynamic of their fling. There were references to fooling around in a campaign office. The "Maybe I'll give you a promotion if…" kind of flirting that's only a problem in lawsuits and political campaigns. If Lynch wanted to paint a picture that Mariana Pereira was unethical, that she leveraged her position into dalliances with her staff, she'd basically handed him the brush.

But did Lynch really think I was desperate enough to write that kind of story? Maybe that was what he took away from looking into my finances, or maybe he was having trouble getting traction for the story elsewhere and getting a little desperate himself. I tried to tell myself he was wrong, that I'd never write that kind of garbage, even if it might force some editors to remember I existed. But if that was true, then why hadn't I thrown out the photos?

Not liking any of the answers to that question, I decided to focus on the Twilight Four instead. I reached down into my backpack, pulled out the documents from Henniman's file relating to Kurtis and Lavell Dawkins, and focused on a different puzzle for the time being.

Lynch had been right about one thing. In the brief time I'd been looking into the Twilight Four killings, I'd been doing it at someone else's direction. Henniman had sent me to Musa. Henniman had been over my shoulder the first time I saw the case files. Henniman had taken me to the Bell family memorial at Weequahic Lake. Hell, he'd even driven me there.

There was nothing wrong with what Bill was doing, but by his own estimation, he'd gotten the case wrong the first time. It needed fresh eyes.

It seemed the Bell family was the sun the Twilight Four killings orbited around. Cynthia had been the speaker for her dead relatives in the press. Sixteen-year-old Shayna, with her big smile and bright future, was the victim most of the articles focused on.

But there were two headstones somewhere with the last name Dawkins on them. When we first looked at the files in Henniman's home, Bill seemed to run past the Dawkins boys' struggles with their foster family as a possible motive.

A second look at those concerns led me to Highland Avenue, a side street off the Bloomfield Avenue corridor near Branch Brook Park, one of the few parts of Newark that seemed like it melted into suburbia. My eyes were trained on a two-story home with a wide porch and enough grass out front for kids to run around in, the kind of residence where a family might grow. A house that was a rare specimen in the Brick City's sprawl of co-ops, projects, duplexes and cramped apartments.

The house marked the last known address of Kurtis and Lavell Dawkins, a plot of land that had belonged to Anthony and Lorena D'Agostino for much longer than the boys had been dead. The D'Agostinos, at least according to the notes in Henniman's file, had been serving as foster parents for decades. Lorena had told the initial case detectives that she couldn't have children of her own, so she took up fostering as opposed to adoption in the hopes of turning her misfortune into civic engagement.

Part of me wondered if the minimum $700 monthly boarding stipend the state gives out per foster kid had anything to do with the D'Agostinos' goodwill.

Lavell didn't seem ready to see his foster parents canonized for sainthood either. According to Henniman's files, the boy was having trouble walking at school one day. A trip to the nurse's office revealed deep bruising on his thighs. Lavell accused Anthony of beating him, but none of the other foster kids in the D'Agostino residence would corroborate the claim, and there was no way to be sure the contusions on the boy were the result of an angry stepparent. An investigation by the state Department of Children & Family services went nowhere, because that's where they always go.

Lavell's allegation came about six months before the children disappeared. The D'Agostinos were fostering three other kids beyond the Dawkins kids at the time, meaning they were pulling in at least $3,500 from the state per month. Neither mentioned a job during their only substantive interview with the police, and the transcripts didn't exactly paint them as grief-stricken. They hadn't appeared in any of the news stories about the vanished kids either.

Still, if someone killed four kids, they had to have a reason. Silencing a child abuse allegation and preserving a monthly state check seemed more like a motive than anything else I'd come across yet.

If Lavell's claim was true, maybe his big brother stepped to his defense and the D'Agostinos decided they needed to get rid of both boys. Maybe they told their cousins about it, putting Shayna and Adriana in the crosshairs as well.

Nothing else made immediate sense. Kurtis had that drug arrest not long before the fire, but it was for marijuana possession. That sounded more "dumb high school kid mistake" than something that might have led to a drug-motivated homicide. Adriana was thirteen, and I was struggling to see who would need an eighth-grader dead so bad they would be willing to dig three additional graves.

I stepped out of the car and into the August heat, immediately regretting my decision to wear jeans and a button-down. But I needed to talk to the D'Agostinos, and the easiest way to spark a conversation was to approach them as a reporter, which meant dressing like an adult. My legs cried sweat, longing for the freedom of the basketball shorts I'd been wearing when I woke up.

As I started walking toward the D'Agostino residence, I noticed a bicycle racing up the sidewalk on their side of the block. A Black teen, no older than fifteen, was pedaling fast enough that the chain looked like it might snap. A younger boy, twelve if I had to guess, maybe a sibling, was riding on pegs on the back wheels, his hands digging into the shoulders of the driver.

The bike came to a stop on the lawn of the D'Agostino residence, and the older boy jumped off it so fast that it tipped over and took the smaller kid with it. Someone sitting on the porch in shorts and a wife-beater unfurled his arms and walked to the top step, glaring at the two kids on the lawn. He looked older than both, but he probably still couldn't buy beer without a fake ID.

"Miss Lore is gonna hear about this," the bike rider said as the boy who had been on the pegs chased him, a backpack slipping off his shoulder.

"It wasn't my fault," the child replied, his voice a fearful whine. "He was riding too fast and the bag just slipped."

The cyclist spun around and blasted the kid with a two-handed shove, the meat of his palms hitting both shoulders so hard the smaller one tripped over the bicycle and landed on his back. The backpack opened up and what looked like comic books flew out. I couldn't make out the titles from a distance, but the tiny body always carrying something to read reminded me of the way Cynthia had described Lavell.

"Don't. No crying," the fifteen-year-old said back. "You fuck up. You own it. Like the rest of us."

I kept moving up the street slowly. The little one was scrambling to shove the contents of his backpack into the bag when I noticed something else on the ground where he'd fallen. Small bundles. Round in shape. I couldn't be sure what they were, but they didn't look like anything a twelve-year-old should have been carrying.

"Both of you. Quiet. Now," the oldest one said from the porch.

"But, Ray, you don't understand," said the one who reminded me of Lavell. "He was rushing me. Now he's gonna tell Miss Lore it's my fault and—"

"Stop. Talking," said the porch guard, whose name appeared to be Ray. His eyes would have been burning holes through the petrified little kid if they weren't too busy clocking me closing in on the porch.

The teen went to shove the little one again, but Ray was already moving down the steps and grabbing the back of the bike rider's t-shirt like it was a dog's leash.

"Inside," he said. "Both of you."

Nearly getting hurled into the stairs was enough for bike kid to flee. The littlest one was still collecting himself, rubbing the back of his head from the fall and squeezing his arm. We made eye contact briefly, but as Ray got closer, the boy got smart and ran inside too.

"Help you?" Ray asked, meeting me on the sidewalk before I could get any closer to the door.

"Just wanted to talk to Mr. D'Agostino," I said.

"Not home," he replied, crossing his arms, digging his knuckles under his biceps to make them pop out more.

It was a standard bouncer move. Which would have been fine if we were standing outside of a nightclub instead of a foster home.

"Mrs. D'Agostino?" I asked.

"Her neither."

"Your brother seems to disagree," I said, nudging my head toward the door.

Ray shook his head, eyes not even bothering to meet mine anymore.

"Not my brother. And not what he said. Have a nice day."

He turned his back on me. I didn't have a ton of options other than trying to run by him for the doorbell, which would have probably ended with my head and the concrete having a disagreement.

A scream came from the doorway, a high-pitched one. Ray moved quickly toward the sound and I followed behind. We both looked up to see the little comic book fan rushing out of the house, tears streaming down his face.

"It wasn't my fault! I didn't mean it and it wasn't my—"

He froze when he found Ray at the top of the porch steps, his little body just barely halting its momentum before he ran face first into the larger boy's waist. A white woman came scrambling behind him in a run that was more of a propulsive stumble, strands of black hair that were ceding ground to gray running wild around her face.

The woman, who I presumed was Lorena D'Agostino, slowed and stood up straight as she noticed me behind Ray on the porch steps. She was in what might have been a band t-shirt, before one hundred laundry spins dissolved the logo into a splotch of color, and black leggings. Her face was all creases, except one that dead-ended at a black mole on her right cheek. A pink tongue flicked out from behind her teeth then went back in as she caught her breath.

"What? Who?" she asked, before turning to Ray while pointing at me. "Who's that?"

"I'm—" I started.

"I didn't ask you," Lorena said, stepping to Ray as if he couldn't sneeze and break her in half. "Who is that? And why is he here?"

"I'm—" I tried again.

"Still not asking you," she said.

"He, uh, just showed up, Miss Lore," Ray replied. "I told him to leave, but, like, then—"

"Then he didn't," she said. "So now I have to deal with it. Typical."

The woman was almost standing on her toes to get in Ray's face, close enough that spittle had to be glazing his cheek.

I looked back and forth from Ray to the little boy. Watching the way the big one shrunk from her, the way the little one was sweating.

"Mrs. D'Agostino. My name is Russell Avery," I said, extending a hand. "I was hoping to talk to you and your husband for a story I'm writing about—"

"My husband is dead, and you'll still have better odds getting an interview out of him than me," she said.

Lorena D'Agostino stepped back, cleared her hair from her face and took a stance in the center of the porch, like it was a stage.

"You. Leave," she said, pointing a finger at me before aiming a thumb over her shoulder. "You two. Inside. Now. We need to have a conversation."

Ray marched instantly. The youngest boy looked at me for a few seconds, eyes starting to water, before he dropped his head and followed. The sound of the door slamming punctuated the exchange.

As the little boy left, I made note of two things: the panic in his eyes and his decision to wear a long-sleeve shirt in August.

I was sweating through dress clothes for a reason. He might have been too. Hiding the same kind of damage Lavell Dawkins might have suffered more than twenty years ago.

It took all day, but Henniman's files finally won the battle for my attention.

The boxes of documents had to overcome a grueling slate of opponents, including my cell phone and the last two Presidente bottles in the fridge. But with Lorena D'Agostino and Abel Musa less than chatty, research seemed my only recourse. I made some coffee, separated out the folders documenting decades of misery and decided to act like an adult.

Assuming Isiah Roust hadn't completely concocted the murders out of thin air, someone had killed Shayna, Adriana, Kurtis and Lavell. Which meant someone had a reason to want them dead.

The way Lorena D'Agostino had acted was certainly a red flag. Her current crop of foster children seemed genuinely afraid of her. The image of that panicked child was not going to leave my head. Had Lavell Dawkins been that same boy trying to outrun a much younger Lorena three-plus decades earlier?

Lavell had accused his foster father of abuse, and Lorena said her husband was dead, but that didn't mean she hadn't picked up a few tricks for beating her young charges into obedience from the dearly departed.

I'd run a records check on the D'Agostino family after my visit to their home, and the results were relatively boring. The county assessor's website showed the upscale home near Branch Brook Park had been bequeathed to Anthony when his parents, who had owned a successful trucking company, died in the early 1980s. They hadn't left him the business, and it was easy to see why. Neither Anthony's nor Lorena's employment history screamed success story, at least from what was publicly available.

Lorena also lacked a criminal record. Anthony had been arrested for DUI twice in the '90s, but he hadn't hurt anyone or caused a crash. DUI somehow wasn't on the list of crimes that could disqualify a person from being a foster parent.

Next, I opened Henniman's file on Kurtis Dawkins and began flipping through pages. The football player had also been sixteen when he disappeared, and while he wasn't the model student-athlete his cousin Shayna was, he seemed to be relatively well liked around Weequahic High.

I couldn't find any evidence that Kurtis shared his younger brother's belief that their foster parents were abusive, though I did locate a 1994 police report detailing the former running back's marijuana arrest. According to a narrative provided by an Officer Russell Thomas, Kurtis had been picked up in a schoolyard in a group of five kids. Officer Thomas said he rolled up because he noticed teens inside the area after dusk. There was a small amount of marijuana in a backpack that Officer Thomas found between the kids, and Kurtis Dawkins's ID was inside. When no one claimed ownership of the drugs, Kurtis wound up in handcuffs.

Things never got to the point of charges though. Henniman had marked something down about Officer Thomas putting in a good word for the kid and the NPD never bothered following up with the prosecutor's office. Nice guy.

I let my conspiracy brain run for a minute, considered that Kurtis had maybe told the police something he wasn't supposed to in order to get out of trouble, but he only had enough pot in his possession to spark a schoolyard joint. That was barely trouble to begin with, even back in the '90s.

A fishing trip through Adriana's and Shayna's files came up just as empty. The thirteen-year-old girl was a thirteen-year-old girl, and the documents on Shayna mostly expanded upon the rosy portrait painted by her family at the memorial. I found one line highlighted by Henniman from Cynthia Bell's second interview with police back in '96. She thought Shayna had been dating someone but didn't know who. If the police back then knew who the boyfriend was, or had questioned him, it wasn't reflected in the file.

I switched gears and pulled out the thick folder of information on Abel Musa, which likely included trial transcripts and minute orders and all sorts of courthouse minutiae that would make my eyes bleed.

The evidence against Musa, outside of Isiah Roust's now-dubious insistence the man had confessed, seemed scant. Musa obviously knew the victims, at least the Bell sisters, since he had been in a romantic relationship with Cynthia. He'd lived in the same neighborhood as the Bells as well. He broke things off with Cynthia and relocated to Elizabeth less than a year after the teens disappeared, and while I could see how that might look suspect to a jury, it ultimately didn't mean anything. Maybe he cheated on her. Maybe the neighborhood handyman found a better garage to work for in Union County. There was nothing to corroborate Roust's claim that Musa had been doing something untoward with Cynthia's younger sister either. From there, the gaps in the prosecution's case only got larger. There was zero physical evidence. The victims' bodies had never been recovered. The police didn't even have a crime scene, only an approximation of one based on Roust's testimony.

Everything hinged on the CI, character witnesses, Musa's lack of an alibi, and a jury made of Newarkers likely hungry to be play a role in closing one of the city's oldest open wounds.

Cynthia had testified to her suspicions that Shayna had a secret boyfriend, something she hid from the rest of her family, but she couldn't provide a name, much less a face. Still, Musa didn't have an alibi for the night the kids went missing or much of an explanation for the timing of his breakup with Cynthia and his decision to leave the neighborhood.

Roust had offered up a compelling narrative, and the transcripts showed Cynthia taking the stand for an entire day that featured several departures into wails and tears. A day that Musa sat silently, which was enough for the newspaper clips at the time to describe him as "menacing."

Musa was a military veteran. But fighting in Vietnam didn't give you the hero pass with the public most other wars did. The crime that had put him in the cell where Roust allegedly obtained his confession wasn't helping his optics either. He'd been in a bar fight with three others outside Edison and claimed self-defense. But he'd hospitalized two of his opponents, maiming one with a beer bottle. It looked like a bartender had testified on Musa's behalf, claiming the men he'd fought with had hurled racial slurs and started the fight. But Musa still wound up pleading to assault and got a twelve-month stretch, one that had overlapped with Roust's stint in East Jersey State Prison in the mid-2000s.

I fished for the transcript of Roust's initial statement to Henniman. It was possible the informant was just a spectacular liar, but I was having trouble believing he'd stitched together a coherent confession out of nothing.

Roust's commentary was light on quantifiable fact: he talked about the purported relationship between Abel and Shayna, how the guilt had ripped at Musa and that's why he had to get out of the neighborhood. It was all vague, fueled by emotion. All of it, except the description of the fire.

According to Roust, Musa had gone looking for Shayna the night the kids disappeared. He was armed with a Saturday night special he'd allegedly bought in the neighborhood. His plan was to drive Shayna out somewhere remote, a place he knew in Sussex County, shoot her and leave the body hidden in an expanse of farmland that might take a couple of days to discover. But the night of, Shayna had been with her sister and cousins when Musa came to pick her up.

Kurtis, the big protector, thought Musa was acting suspicious. There was an argument and things turned violent fast, according to Roust. Kurtis was shot, and Musa panicked. He marched them all at gunpoint into an abandoned home, nailed the basement door shut and set the building ablaze with a mixture of bleach, cooking oil and kerosene. All items he'd apparently had in the bed of his pick-up truck.

I went back to the trial testimony, looking for the comments made by a retired Newark arson investigator named Mickey Lalor. While the prosecution couldn't definitively ID a crime scene, they had asked the fire department to put together a list of possible incidents that could have been the blaze Roust described.

The fire department and the city had been in a dispute over a new labor contract around the time the kids disappeared. Newark's Bravest had been engaging in sickouts, so the department's resources were spread extremely thin. Engine companies were only responding to priority calls, and abandoned buildings didn't meet that definition. But that didn't mean the NFD wasn't documenting the fires it couldn't race to immediately.

I paused for a second, looking back and forth between Roust's testimony and that of the fire department investigator. Making sure I wasn't simply seeing what I wanted to see.

The night that Shayna, Adriana, Kurtis and Lavell were last seen, there had been a four-alarm blaze at the Carmel Tower apartments, a high-rise with at least one hundred residents. The fire department had, understandably, devoted most of its available hands there.

The night the kids had gone missing, a trio of formerly abandoned rowhouses had also been swallowed up in the South Ward. A blaze that, upon later investigation, the fire department believed might have been caused by homeless people warming themselves. There were traces of kerosene and cooking oil at the scene. The building had collapsed in on itself, covering up the basement. With no reported injuries, the city's resources stretched thin and the tract of land set for redevelopment about a year or two later, no one had bothered excavating anything.

Isiah Roust might have lied about who set the fire.

But it sure seemed like he knew the truth about how it was set.

CHAPTER
EIGHT

FINDING ISIAH ROUST wasn't the hard part.

Winning the cooperation of the person who could make him talk, however, had proved to be something of a pain in the ass.

The twice-convicted felon and possibly twice-unreliable state witness was on probation, meaning his home address, work address and general habits and movements would be known to law enforcement. One phone call from Bill Henniman would produce all that information.

A quick search for the last criminal complaint with Roust's name on it had given me his Asbury Park address. But after my swing-and-miss at the D'Agostino residence, I didn't want to make the ninety-minute drive down the shore just to have another door slammed in my face.

With Henniman, I was at least guaranteed to get some questions in. Probation comes with a laundry list of requirements, including compliance with random visits from law enforcement. Legally speaking, Bill could make Roust talk.

Without him, I was risking a fifty-mile drive that might end with me picking up a slice at Porta and turning around. I'd heard good things, but the favored pizza of hungover hipsters didn't really seem worth all that effort.

"The whole reason I'm in this mess is because that man is a lying piece of shit," Bill had replied when I called him in the morning, excitedly rambling about what I thought was a mini-breakthrough in the investigation. "We can't trust a word he says."

"It's a thread worth pulling on, man," I shot back. "Besides, Roust screwed you. Don't you want to know why?"

That prompted about twenty minutes of negotiating. I promised to buy him a beer at Wonder Bar, but he shrugged me off. I jokingly suggested Roust might run and it would give Bill an excuse to take a swing at him, but he just let out a huff.

It wasn't until I posed a simple question that Henniman finally caved.

"What else are you doing today?"

He was silent. It was Saturday. I thought back to the house with the pictures mostly occupied by brother cops, and our encounter with cops a day later that illustrated how few boys in blue saw Bill as a brother anymore.

I'd struck a nerve I hadn't meant to. But by the early afternoon, a visibly annoyed but otherwise subdued Bill Henniman was in the passenger seat of my car, occasionally complaining about the music. I'd thrown on Drive-By Truckers, deciding old cop plus southern rock would equal palatable for the lieutenant. I was wrong.

We exited my car and headed toward the south side of the convention center. Henniman nodded at the "Greetings From Asbury Park" sign, a solemn little hat tip. Guess I should have gone with the Boss on the drive instead.

We made our way toward the Silverball Museum, a pinball enthusiast's version of heaven that sat off the boardwalk between two restaurants. According to Henniman's probation contacts, Roust had found work there as a mechanic, tinkering with the bumpers and flippers on the ancient machines when they went kaput.

Stepping into the Silverball from the beach was like falling through a hole in the space-time continuum. The "museum" was mostly an arcade, complete with coin-operated turnstiles at the entrance. A claw game filled with stuffed animals that hadn't been won since it was first turned on and a fortune teller machine built before Hollywood made Zoltar a household name flanked the door.

I walked over to a cashier who seemed more focused on the hot dogs rolling on the steamer next to him than customer service and bought one-hour wristbands for both of us. All the machines inside the Silverball were free, you just had to cough up a few bucks for an allotment of time.

"So, what's our play?" I asked Bill as we eyed several rows of blinking machines.

"What play? He's on probation. We see him. I tell him we have questions. He has to answer them or else he gets violated," Henniman replied, then raised a hand as I started to object. "I know it's not technically that simple, but before you try to teach me something about my job again, let me remind you he knows it's a borderline act of God that he's not in prison, and isn't likely to push back."

Henniman started walking away from me toward the back corner of the arcade.

"Where are you going?"

"I see a Skeeball machine back there. I said I'd come. I didn't say I'd help," he replied. "You let me know when you find him."

I wandered over to a pinball machine with Arnold Schwarzenegger's face emblazoned over the scoreboard and decided that would be my stakeout spot. I sucked at pinball, but I remembered the *Terminator: Judgment Day* machine from when I was a kid, and instinctively pulled the trigger on the gun that was supposed to launch the ball into play.

I absent-mindedly pressed flippers, losing two balls in less than two minutes as I kept scanning the room for Roust. Henniman's erstwhile snitch would standout eventually.

Most of the Silverball's employees seemed like they attended high school a short bike ride from the front door. The photo of Roust I'd plucked from the state department of corrections website showed a man in his mid-forties who looked a decade older than that. His eyes had sunken and the long sad boy hair from his younger days was now splayed and thinning. He'd filled out over the years, but with middle age flab rather than muscle. The new mugshot also showed an unfortunate neck tattoo that looked like a cellmate's first draft instead of legitimate ink.

My third ball disappeared down the hole. Arnold announced he'd be back. I wouldn't.

I moved down a different aisle, looking at some of the arcade cabinets, hoping to find a less frustrating way to kill time. The sight of the '90s Simpsons' beat 'em up brought a smile to my face, so I settled in to smashing Mr. Burns's goons over the head with Marge's vacuum. Everyone always made the mistake of playing as Bart, but the Simpson matriarch had the most reach to clear the screen.

Twenty minutes later, I noticed a small crowd forming around a *Back to the Future* pinball machine. It seemed like a kid was about to summon their inner Marty McFly and shatter the high score.

I was getting tired of waiting for Roust. Maybe the repair man needed a reason to be on the floor.

I strolled behind the four people crowding the machine, checking on Henniman as I slid by. He was still battering the Skeeball ramp, hurling each shot so hard the balls were rebounding off the netting above the machine before somehow plunking into the 100 ring.

The *Back to the Future* game was at the end of a row, powered by a black cable running a small distance to a wall outlet next to the archway leading to the restrooms. The twelve-year-old at the controls was only a few thousand off the high score, with just one ball left. He was sweating. His grandparents couldn't have been prouder.

I genuinely felt bad about kicking the plug out as I went past.

The boy howled in frustration and immediately started banging the sides of the machine with his palms. Henniman turned around as I leaned against a wall next to him.

"Oh no, the machine broke," I whispered.

"That kid's going to cry," he replied.

"Hey, I gave you a chance to come up with a plan. You chose Skeeball."

Henniman nudged his head to the red lights above the ramp, showing he'd tallied an absurd 400.

"At least I got to keep my high score," he said.

The boy's tantrum had drawn someone in a blue polo shirt from the back of the building. Someone who stood about five foot seven with an unfortunate neck tattoo. It looked like it was supposed to be an ace of spades, which would have been bad enough on its own. But someone had messed up the tip of the playing card suit, making it look like either a shrub or a butt plug, depending on the eye and kink level of the beholder.

The sight of Isiah Roust sucked out what little joy was in Henniman's heart. As Roust tried to stem the child's tantrum, the lieutenant marched across the room with murder in his eyes. It occurred to me that Bill probably hadn't seen Roust since the moment he learned the ex-CI ruined his career. It then occurred to me that Roust couldn't help us if Bill ripped his head off and punted it into the ocean.

Thankfully, a woman appeared halfway between Bill and his target.

"You need to move," he growled.

"And you need to stop stalking him," she whispered back.

Henniman stood straight up. I came to a halt right behind him. The woman tapped the badge on her belt.

"I got a call that someone was looking for Roust," said the woman, who I assumed was his probation officer. "And since you two aren't the only ones lately, I'd sure as hell like to know why."

Despite my best efforts, I still wound up sitting at the hipster pizza place without talking to Roust.

The slice in front of me was topped with vegan mozzarella, vegan parmesan, and, most likely, regret. I held it up at an angle, waiting to see if any of the cheese would slide or obey gravity or do any of the things an honest counter slice would do.

The woman who had intercepted us inside the Silverball Museum, dooming us to pizza that shouldn't legally be allowed to be referred to as pizza, eyed us as she chewed what was allegedly a gluten-free garlic knot.

Monmouth County Probation Officer Leanne Cooley had already cleared her plate and was now studying my abandoned slice. The brunette with the candy pink nails on the same hands as knuckles that had clearly punched something lately had her elbows on the table and a smile on her face, like she was sitting across from two old friends she'd bumped into in public, not two interlopers stalking her charge.

After stopping Henniman's death march—which I'd quietly appreciated, 'cause I wasn't sure I could've done it—Leanne had ushered us out of the arcade, whispering something about how we were going to spook "him." I'd presumed the "him" she was talking about was Roust, which made little to no sense, because I assumed probationers know what their probation officers look like.

But she'd rushed us a block or two away to Porta, promised to explain over a pie and then proceeded to order everything on the menu that I was pre-destined to hate.

"Wasting food doesn't sit with me," she said.

There was a little bit of a twang in her voice. I couldn't tell if it was South Jersey or the actual South.

"This doesn't qualify as food," I replied.

"Oh lord. Are you a New Yorker or something? Think your bagels are better too?"

"North Jersey and—"

"Here it comes. Tell me it's Taylor Ham. Get it over with."

"Stop," Henniman said. "Just, please, don't. He does the banter shit all day, every day. I am not taking two doses of it."

"You don't like my banter?" I asked.

Henniman took a sip of his water, sucked in an ice cube and bit down hard enough to shatter a tooth.

"Even your questions about banter are fucking banter," he growled, before turning toward Officer Cooley. "I don't know you, but you're on the job, so out of respect I let you walk us away from the man we drove here to see. That was the one shred of patience I had. I don't want to eat this dog shit pizza. I don't want to listen to the two of you fail at stand-up comedy. I want you to tell me why the fuck I'm not talking to Isiah Roust."

"He always this pleasant?" Leanne asked me.

I looked at Henniman, who looked less than pleasant.

"Any response I give is going to be considered banter, isn't it?" I asked.

He didn't speak. He didn't move. If he was breathing, he might have found a way to do it via sneer.

"Maybe just tell him why you dragged out us of there. Please?" I asked her.

Leanne rubbed her thumb and forefinger over the last bit of her garlic knot, then dropped it on the plate and turned to Henniman.

"Well, since your friend was so polite," she started. "I picked you two off in there because I prefer getting a heads-up when another cop wants to chat with one of my probationers, especially one as squirrely as Roust. And the people in my office down here respect that. That friend you called to ask about Roust happens to be my captain. He let me know what you were up to."

"He's someone we need to speak to for a murder investigation," Henniman said. "I'd imagine that trumps anything down here."

"An official murder investigation?" she asked, before pointing one of those Barbie nails at me. "Because, down here, we don't usually bring civilians along for interviews during murder investigations. Also, I was just being cute with the *down here* thing. This is Asbury Park, not bumblefuck."

Bill looked displeased. I let out a little chuckle. The woman's taste in pizza might have been shit, but her smack talk game made it easy to forget that.

"I've been more than a little curious about Roust's whole deal since he got assigned to me," she said. "My boss isn't usually a quota type, but he's been extremely interested in him. Asking me about the most ticky-tack possible violations. Did he miss a meeting with me because he missed a bus? Was he late for work? Normally, our chief is a rehabilitation type. Wants to see people succeed. So, with him acting all *Hang 'Em High* and Roust going from a model probationer to the way he's been lately…"

"What do you mean, the way he's been lately?" Henniman asked.

"The meetings started about two months ago," she replied.

The time stuck out to me. I'd need to check to be sure, but Musa's appeal had been scheduled to land on a judge's bench about two months ago. That was around the time Henniman said the Essex County Prosecutor's Office started spinning the wheels that led to Musa's compassionate release. I zoned in on what Leanne had said about her boss looking for any reason to violate Roust and started to wonder if someone in the Watkins administration or the NPD was trying to call in a favor. Whatever Roust knew, it would be harder for him to leak it if he was back inside a prison cell.

"What meetings, with who?" Henniman asked.

"Well, I don't know yet," Cooley replied. "I don't know what Roust did to make you look like you wanna kill him, but he's been pretty well-behaved on my watch. Goes to work. Goes to his AA meetings. Goes home. Not much variety to his routine. Until two months ago. Now he goes to the dog park up on the north end of the beach once weekly. I don't know who he's talking to. I haven't been getting that close. But it's looked pretty animated."

"Maybe he just likes dogs?" I asked.

"Roust doesn't have a dog. Neither does whoever he seems to be meeting with," she replied.

"What do they look like?" Henniman asked.

"A guy, best I can tell. Always has a hat on. Like I said, I've been keeping my distance. I like my probationers trusting me," she said. "My boss isn't the only one who believes in second chances, and nearest I can tell, Roust isn't doing anything sideways, just suspicious, which I'm supposed to be watching for. He doesn't know I've been keeping such close tabs, and he'd be likely to change up whatever he's doing if I interfered or spot-checked him...or let two out-of-towners rush him at his job."

"You say rush, I say interrogate," Henniman replied. "What is this hands-off bullshit? If you think he's up to something, that's exactly why you should've let me question him. Instead of us sitting here trying to understand the not that complex mind of a twice-convicted scumbag over a shitty pie."

The waitress had been approaching with a water pitcher, stopped cold and turned around.

"You really need to switch to decaf," she said to Henniman. "I don't have a problem with you questioning him. I just want you to question him when it might actually accomplish something. it's Saturday, and he gets off work soon."

"So?" Henniman asked.

"Saturday's dog park day," she said.

Thirty minutes later, the three of us were leaning against a rail overlooking the beach, watching late afternoon waves crash as we waited for Roust. Leanne said he normally walked up the boardwalk and through the convention center toward the dog beach, since he'd lost his driver's license on account of the DUI that put him on her to-do list in the first place.

Roust's shift was supposed to end at 4:30. I went back and forth between checking the doors to the Silverball and dicking around on my phone as the minutes ticked by. There was no Roust by 4:35.. At 4:40, someone in one of the arcade's blue polos went by, but they were thirty years old and three arrests shy of being Roust. , Five minutes after that, Henniman was asking if Leanne was sure about Roust's work schedule.

Five minutes after that, she was walking inside the arcade. Five minutes after that, she was bracing for a tirade as she explained to Henniman that Roust told his boss he wasn't feeling well and left work early.

"He looked fine," she said.

"Because he was fine," Henniman replied. "He probably caught sight of me when you got in our way and bailed."

"Well, this is why you should have contacted his probation officer directly instead of—"

I pushed myself away from the rail and started walking toward my car before they could start arguing again.

"Where are you going?" Bill asked.

"To see if he's still at the dog beach. You two can come if you take a break from yelling at one another."

Which they did. For the ten minutes it took me to drive up Kingsley Street and find parking again. The dog beach had a lovely mix of Corgis, Huskies and the friendliest German Shepherd I'd ever seen, but no Isiah Roust. We were getting dangerously close to having wasted an entire day, and I was not looking forward to hearing Bill shout about how I'd mishandled our approach and Leanne's interference on the drive home.

Departing beachgoers would worsen the weekend traffic, giving him an extra hour to tear into me between Asbury and Newark.

"Enough. Let's just bang on his door," Henniman said from the passenger seat of my car.

"Because he went home from work sick?" Leanne asked.

"No, because he changed up his routine on one of the days you said he'd already been acting suspicious, that just so happens to coincide with us coming down here to question him," Henniman replied. "We tried this your way, all it got us was a bad lunch and no answers. I'm not going to tell you how to do your job. But I am gonna go ahead and do mine."

"So, what's your plan when he doesn't answer the door?" she asked. "Probationers are subject to search at any time, but you can't just go into his apartment without a reason."

"Then we'll get him coming or going," Bill replied. "This isn't a discussion, and if it was, you're outvoted and he's driving."

I didn't necessarily disagree with Bill, even if he was being a dick about it. I turned to Leanne in the backseat.

"Sorry, but he's technically my client," I said. "You're welcome to come along though."

"Client?" she asked. "You know, despite the results, I've made some pretty honest attempts at helping you two without really knowing what you're into."

"We get to talk to Roust, I promise I'll tell you whatever you want to know," I replied.

Henniman gave me a look, apparently unaware of how empty promises worked. I was quickly developing a soft spot for Leanne and wanted to reward her curiosity, but Bill was paying the, well, bills.

We drove up 3rd Street, away from the beach and back into the belly of Asbury where people worked and slept and lived irrespective of the summer shore crowd. Roust laid his head in a rented apartment on the first floor of a two-family home, according to Leanne. The only entrance was a side-door halfway down a driveway. There were no cars parked there when I pulled to a stop across the street. But Roust didn't drive, and his windows weren't visible from the front of the property, so we couldn't tell if he was home without knocking.

Henniman was out of the car before I killed the engine. I hopped out to follow and Leanne was a breath behind that.

"We got a plan here?" I asked.

"Bang on door. Ask questions," Bill replied. "Like we should have a few hours ago."

Leanne was on our heels, offering up even keel suggestions like, "Maybe he'll open up if he hears a familiar voice," and, "You need reasonable suspicion," but Bill was locked on target.

The lieutenant's fist was raised overhead and smashing into the side door seconds later. Four loud hammer knocks.

"Isiah Roust! Newark Police! Open up!" he shouted.

A muffled series of sounds came back. Feet moved quickly across a floor. Maybe more than one pair. A panicky voice repeated the word "shit" multiple times. Glass broke.

"Sounds like someone's in trouble," Bill said, looking a little too happy about it. "That count as reasonable suspicion to you? Or would you be more comfortable with exigent circumstances? 'Cause he sounds distressed."

He was looking at Leanne. She nodded, but didn't look thrilled about it. Bill took a step back and ducked his shoulder. She grabbed him, reached down and picked up an out of place rock near the doormat. She slipped off the top half, revealing a hidden space in the plastic. "Told you I've been keeping a close eye on him."

Bill was through the door as soon as he was able, gun already drawn. Leanne followed suit. I knew they were probably relying on training so ingrained it was instinct, but I had my concerns about Bill running gun first toward a man he despised.

The side-door led up a short staircase and into a combination living room and dining area. The left side of the space had a short diagonal hallway that seemed to lead to the back of the property.

I headed that way as Bill and Leanne checked corners, guns leading the way. If Roust was there, we couldn't see him.

With the bedroom clear, I poked my head in, finding a hideaway that should have belonged to a teenager. There were two consoles of the Nintendo and Sony varieties hooked up to one of those gigantic televisions you'd be more likely to see in a bar than a bedroom. Movie posters best left in a freshman dorm's end of semester dumpster, all

Tarantino and *Boondock Saints*, lined the walls. I heard something crunching under my feet and realized I was standing on the shattered screen of what looked to be a PC monitor. I spotted a logo that looked like a Martian with glowing blue eyes on the front of the equally trashed CPU. Roust appeared to be forty going on eighteen based on the amount of gaming hardware in his possession.

I moved onto the kitchen, swapping places with Leanne and Henniman. The whole area was a mess, punctuated by a recycling can overflowing with spent soup containers and takeout menus.

I took another step and felt my feet almost slip out from under me, then looked down to see shattered glass, probably the bottle of whatever had been dropped when Bill pounded on the door. I reached down to see what it was and felt more glass crunch under my feet as my weight shifted. I back pedaled and something slipped under my heel, forcing me to turn and find a broken picture frame, the image it once held face down and damp in whatever liquid I was standing in.

A stench hit my nostrils as I raised the picture, enough to make me shudder. I shrugged it off for a second and flipped the image over. Roust was on the left, younger and thinner, maybe in his late teens or early twenties. The picture seemed like it had been taken before the one in Henniman's file. There was someone next to him, but I couldn't focus too long as the smell hit again, almost making me gag.

It was sour, acidic, pungent. Cleaning product? Bleach?

"He's not here," Henniman growled, stomping back into the kitchen. "There's a back window and a fence leading onto another property. Maybe he jumped it."

I stood up, my head suddenly feeling a little disconnected from my shoulders. I looked over at Bill, who seemed red-faced from anger but otherwise fine. Leanne was behind him, flush with embarrassment, or adrenaline, or both.

I'd always hated the smell of bleach, but I was struggling to think that one whiff would make me feel woozy. Or account for the sudden burning in my eyes. I looked over at Bill and Leanne again, noticed them dabbing at their faces too. I turned my watering eyes toward the stove, noticing the faintest hint of blue around the burners.

"Out!" I shouted. "Out! Now!"

Henniman and Leanne looked confused.

"The gas is on!" I screamed.

Their expressions changed. We all started moving for the door, just in time to see a glass bottle come flying up the stairs. In spite of my blurred vision, I was able to make out a small orange flame at the tip of a rag stuffed into a bottle of vodka.

As soon as the glass exploded, that one flame grew into several tongues.

All of them racing along the floor. All of them following the bleach trails we'd stepped in.

All of them hungry and headed our way.

CHAPTER
NINE

O N INSTINCT, I backpedaled away from the flames until my spine hit the stove range. I stumbled, elbows too close the vents. The little blue flames singed some arm hair, providing a preview of how I was very possibly about to die.

The spot where the Molotov had crashed was filled with bright fire, cutting off the front door completely. Henniman was moving toward it with his gun drawn anyway, but thankfully Leanne grabbed his arm.

"Gun's not gonna help us in a fire," she shouted, tugging him back toward me.

She started for the rear of the apartment. I followed her and Henniman came along.

The hiss of the stove filled my ears as we ran for the dining room, the flames lapping up the bleach and giving chase. I looked back to see the yellow tongues licking at the edge of the stove range, just in time to feel Leanne grab me by my shirt collar and pull me in the other direction.

The sound of the hiss disappeared, overtaken by a boom that ripped through the air and sent all three of us flying toward the back of the property. The flames and the gas had made first contact, and it was not peaceful. The stove range turned into a pipe bomb, spewing metal like shrapnel, jagged pieces going every which way.

Leanne and I had already been moving away from the blast and were lucky enough that the force knocked us across Roust's dining room table and onto the floor. Henniman had been a step behind and it cost him. I watched him lurch as the force of the explosion caught him square in the back, launching him into the air and onto the dining room table, which immediately collapsed under him.

The metal missiles flying from the blast mercifully whistled overhead, embedding themselves into walls, but Bill was still in a bad way. There was blood trickling down his forehead and his eyes looked glazed over. If he wasn't concussed, he was close.

I tried to stand up, but felt my chest turning to concrete. The smoke in the air was thickening fast as the fire found more oxygen to feed it. The blast had blown out some windows but also shot embers onto blinds and furniture. More kindling. More fire. Less space in the room that wouldn't kill us. I placed a hand on the ground to steady myself and felt more wetness. Maybe more bleach.

Did Roust know we were coming? And how much advance notice did he need to try to burn us alive like the kids whose deaths we were seeking answers for?

Another wave of heat chased away those questions. I saw the flames advancing again, slower this time. Stalking us.

"Bill! Bill!" I shouted, immediately regretting opening my mouth that far. I choked and coughed and sputtered as I shoved at his shoulder. Trying to roll him over, trying to move him away from the inferno.

Leanne was up, moving with a slight limp toward the hallway leading to the back.

"There's a window!" she shouted, her voice muffled by the undershirt she'd pulled over her nose and mouth. "We can get out!"

Bill was up to his hands and knees now, but still struggling to get on his feet. I ducked my head under one of his arms to help prop him up, and he looked at me genuinely confused. Maybe not even sure where we were, just that it was a bad place to be.

"Help me!" I shouted to Leanne. It took her a second to register the situation but she got under Bill's other arm and we got the lieutenant's stocky frame upright. We hobbled, limped and stumbled toward the back hallway, the fire only a breath behind.

My vision started to dim. Sweat was pouring out of my hair and into my eyes, the salt only adding to the sting from the bleach and the gas. I'd written about enough fatal fires to know smoke did the real killing. The flames just picked the bones.

Breathing was starting to become a borderline impossible task. My knees weakened and we fell forward through a partially open door and into Roust's bedroom. My hands found the remnants of his computer screen on the floor again, little pieces now sticking into the meat of my palms.

Leanne bounced up. I continued to crawl forward, looking behind me to see that the fire had converged on the hallway. It had already claimed the front rooms of the apartment. We were cornered.

Henniman was up a second later. Whether instinct had kicked in or the second fall had shocked him back to alertness I had no idea, but at least he was moving under his own power now, flailing for the window.

"Open it!" I shouted to Leanne.

She looked uncertain for a second, but we didn't have any other options. The rush of fresh air felt amazing as she shoved the window up. Then I turned around.

I'd heard the word backdraft hundreds of times. I didn't know what it meant until the sudden dose of oxygen functioned like adrenaline for the flames trying to eat me alive.

Leanne was out the window by the time I turned around. Henniman was stumbling in the same direction, but not quick enough. I put my hands into the big man's back and shoved him out, hoping the drop wasn't too far.

The lieutenant ducked his head as he slipped through the open space. I waited a second to give him time to clear, relieved to see he'd only fallen six feet and turned his body on the way down, taking the brunt of the landing with his shoulder instead of his skull.

All that relief disappeared when I started to feel the burning.

The fire had caught up to me, and its teeth were in the meat of my left shoulder. Shockwaves of pain radiated through my body and I started to fall. If I hit the floor inside the apartment, it would be my tomb.

Through luck or karma or magic my right arm hooked onto the windowsill, and I managed to drag myself through as the flames leapt out after me.

When I landed, the pain of my right shoulder hitting the cement briefly distracted me from the fact that my left shoulder was still on goddamn fire. I dropped and rolled and screamed and cursed but still felt my skin turning extra crispy as every pain receptor in my brain overloaded.

As I rolled around and howled, water hit me from somewhere. I looked up, thinking maybe it was raining and maybe it was time to start wondering if God existed, but somewhere at the edge of my blurred vision was Leanne, spraying me with a yard hose.

I flattened out on my back, looking left to find Henniman. He was down and groaning and bleeding, but most importantly, breathing. Then I looked up, watching the fire continue to climb and claim the rest of the building.

One yellow tongue kept flitting in and out of the window we'd fallen from. Almost like it was winking at me.

Almost like it knew how close it had come to claiming me too.

About an hour later, I could still feel the smoke in my nostrils, the heat radiating off my shoulder.

As I sat up on a gurney on the other side of the street, staring at the smoldering wreckage of what used to be Isiah Roust's apartment, I rubbed at my eyes and tried to understand what had just happened.

Someone, presumably Roust, had tried to kill us before we'd even asked a question, meaning there was an answer out there someone believed to be worth at least three people's lives.

After we'd escaped, Henniman and I limped to the front yard just in time to be met by a rush of Asbury Park police, firefighters and EMTs. Leanne had suffered the least damage, so she took on the task of bringing the first responders up to speed.

Someone guided Bill toward a gurney and an oxygen mask while another paramedic shined lights in his eyes, probably checking for a concussion. Another EMT checked out my left shoulder to determine if it was medium rare or well-done.

The paramedics said I might have suffered second-degree burns as they cut away singed pieces of my shirt. They applied salve to my left shoulder and wrapped it in bandages, while I took inventory of the rest of the damage. The opposite shoulder, the one I'd landed on as I fell out the window, felt awful, probably bruised, but the pain was dull, not blinding, so I assumed nothing was broken. A coughing fit made me guess I'd need treatment for smoke inhalation, as did the stream of multi-colored phlegm that left me in the process.

I just kept staring at the blackened outsides of the building, watching the fire's furious climb. I looked down, noticed my hand was shaking. Maybe it had been the whole time.

Without that window, I might have known what Shayna Bell and her sister and her cousins knew. A death so horrible it was too sickening to consider. A death like the one Isiah Roust had described to a courtroom years ago, when he put an innocent man in jail for the better part of a decade. Now, when we'd come to question him about it, there had been another roaring blaze.

Roust needed to answer for this. The best I could figure, he'd jumped out the back window and tossed the Molotov as he fled up the driveway. I doubted he kept his apartment permanently rigged as a fire trap. Maybe he'd seen Henniman at the arcade and freaked out. He'd clearly deviated from the routine Leanne said she'd noticed he'd been following every Saturday. The smashed computer and picture frame made it seem like he was trying to hide something. Maybe the fire was meant to clean up whatever he'd failed to get rid of before we banged on his door.

My hand wandered to my back pocket, mind flashing to the shattered picture frame I'd noticed just before the apartment went up in flames. The photo I'd picked up in the pool of accelerants that nearly claimed my life and had swallowed Roust's apartment whole.

I studied the black-and-white image of a younger Roust. He had his arm around a man I didn't recognize, but the version of Roust I was looking at also had little in common with the flabby arcade employee who might have tried to set me on fire. Past Roust looked confident, wearing a smile that bordered on a smirk framing a thin, well-groomed goatee that came to a point at his chin. His neck lacked the disastrous tattoo, probably because he hadn't seen the inside of a Rahway prison cell yet. But mostly he looked young and hopeful, not ravaged by a few bad decisions and a few too many trips around the sun.

They both appeared to be wearing semi-formal clothing, maybe school uniforms. I flipped it over again, noticing pen strokes in the lower-left corner I hadn't the first time.

A date. The month didn't matter. The year did. 1996.

The same year Isiah Roust testified another fire had been set to hide something.

CHAPTER
TEN

I TOOK THE NEXT day off, spending most of it lying in bed, counting my blessings that I wasn't resting inside a hospital or a morgue.

The skin on my left shoulder screamed to the touch and it still felt warm, like there was phantom flame hovering around it. Its compatriot wasn't doing any better, stiff from taking the brunt of the impact of the fall out the window, keeping the rest of my right arm hostage. Bandages wrapped each shoulder.

A short stay at University Hospital ended with a painkiller prescription, but I'd written enough stories about opioid addiction to choose short-term agony over a future that would hurt a lot worse.

Besides, I wanted my head clear in case anyone had any news on the guy who'd nearly dropped a building on me.

I was waiting for a call from Leanne to tell me Roust had used his debit card to buy lunch at a Turnpike rest stop and we'd be able to question him in state police custody. I was waiting for a text from Key or, god help me, even Lynch, just to see if any rumors about our involvement in the blast had followed us back to Newark. I was waiting for an e-mail reply from one of the former colleagues I'd sent a message to, inquiring about freelance opportunities, not that I had a story to write.

I didn't know that Abel Musa was innocent, or at least I didn't know enough to print an article saying that. I knew Roust was a liar in one case, but not necessarily the one that may have put the wrong man in prison. I knew a house had blown up, but I didn't really know why. The apartment that had burned down around me was only connected to the Twilight Four case by Roust's name on a lease agreement, a piece of paper that was probably ash now.

So, I let the day slide away.

Then I started the next one by driving to University Hospital, hoping to make my own luck.

I hadn't seen my primary care doctor in the two years since I'd lost my job at the *Signal-Intelligencer*, which is what happens when you're young and relatively sure you're not dying and lack health insurance. Dr. Vercher's receptionist was in no mood to rush an appointment for an erstwhile patient like me, but they became a little more agreeable when I sent them a picture of my marbled shoulder.

Not that I was looking for urgent medical attention. But the appointment with Dr. Vercher gave me a reason to be at the same hospital where Abel Musa was located.

Between Musa's outcry and Lynch's actions during my last visit, I didn't want to take any chances with the first-floor security desk. An appointment was a hall pass, and no one paid too much attention when I took the elevator two floors past the one Vercher's office was on.

I slowed my walk as I entered the hallway near Musa's room, giving the nurse's station a once-over, making sure neither woman sitting there looked up or recognized me from my prior visit. With no alarm tripped, I slipped inside.

Musa was in the bed, his body tilted away from the door and toward the window. He wasn't laying on his side as much as he seemed to have fallen over in that direction. Maybe he was sleeping, or just curled up and ignoring the world, but either way, he hadn't seen me yet.

The line from the IV drip on the right side of Musa's bed was snaking across his body, gaining and losing slack every few seconds. I followed it back to his wrist and noticed his arm tugging ever so slightly. Something like a muffled groan followed the next movement of the coil, and I stepped closer. Musa was reaching for something out of my field of vision.

I moved slowly around the bed, crouching down to see what his withered hand was trying to grasp. A book was on the floor near the window, spread open like it had fallen there, just beyond the chewed edges of Musa's fingernails. It was a weathered copy of *The Count of Monte Cristo*, with a faded cover and pages so well-read they felt like blistered skin about to peel off.

"Still won't call the nurses?" I asked as I grabbed the book off the floor and held it up to Musa.

His eyes were bulging, the strain on his face evidenced by the sweat bubbles popping on his forehead. Musa had fought in a war, but now it was taking everything he had to reach a few feet under his bed.

"Not 'til…" he started, but his remark was interrupted by a long, defeated breath. "Not 'til I really need…" His voice trailed off, but he made sure to lift his right arm just enough to show the emergency buzzer hiding there.

He smiled.

I smiled.

Then I noticed the window was open.

"You sure you want to ring that?" I asked, as I moved the book ever so slightly toward the edge, lucky that a little wind rustled the pages for dramatic effect.

"That's cruel," he said.

"It is, and I'm not," I replied, placing the book gently on the foot of his bed. "So, can we talk?"

"You're with Henniman," he growled.

"Not that simple."

"Henniman put me in prison. I didn't deserve to be," he said. "That simple."

"Henniman almost wound up in the morgue yesterday trying to fix that," I replied. I showed him my bandages. "So did I."

Musa's expression changed, eyes bugging just slightly, enough to give away that he was curious. I picked up the book, noticing the dozens of dog-eared pages. He'd run the copy into the ground.

"How many times have you read this thing?" I asked. "Put the buzzer down. Let me tell you a new story. If you don't like what I have to say, then tell me to fuck off. I'll leave, and you won't even have to bother the nurses this time."

Musa chewed the corner of his lip and eyed me up and down, doing the internal math to determine if I was trustworthy. I wouldn't trust me either if I'd been through what he had.

"Better part of a decade, I sat in a prison cell. Filing appeals. Sending letters to reporters, what family I got left, lawyers, anyone who could read, swearing I was innocent. No one cared," he said. "Now it matters?"

He had leaned forward just a little as the passion rose in his voice, and even that miniscule motion took its toll. Musa shrunk back into the bed, breathing laboring a little, eyes still locked onto me like a target.

"Honestly? I'd never heard of any of this until, like, a week ago," I said.

"That's not a defense. That means you gotta read more," he hissed. "And that's not an answer. Why do you care?"

"Because if someone lied to put you in prison, that's wrong," I replied. "It used to be my job to try to expose things like that."

"Your job? You a superhero?" he asked.

"I was a reporter."

His face turned, like he'd sniffed vinegar.

"Here? With the Lack of Intelligencer?" he asked.

I rolled my eyes. The juvenile insult had made almost daily

appearances in poorly-worded, profanity-laden e-mails sent to reporters at Newark's hometown paper. But knowing how heavily we'd relied on the cops' version as gospel for stories in the past, I doubted my predecessors on the cops' beat had scrutinized the case against Musa closely. Captured serial killers sell more papers than thorough legal analyses.

"Yeah, but I never wrote about you. That was before I was there," I said. "Listen, man, I'm not saying you should trust me. I'm just trying to tell you what I'm doing. You're right. I'm working with Bill, and Bill's part of the reason your life went to shit. But he's not the only reason. Isiah Roust said you confessed when you guys were cellmates. Now, Bill has reason to think Roust cooked up that story. And when we went to challenge him on that yesterday, his goddamn house fell on us."

I pulled at the neck of my shirt, displaying the seared meat on my shoulder.

"Bill got a Grade 3 concussion. I got this," I said. "Trying to help you."

"So, it's my fault?" he asked. "I didn't ask you to take up my cause."

I grabbed at a clump of my hair and tried to quiet the hornets marshaling to sting in my throat. Musa had every reason to be fed up past the point of talking. He'd been fucked over in ways I'd only seen in movies. But that didn't make me less frustrated.

"Are you trying to tell me you don't care anymore? That you're over this?" I asked. "What do you want from me?"

"My life got hijacked because someone lied. I will never be over that and you..." He trailed off for just a second, catching his breath, then slid himself forward so he might look as strong as his voice sounded in that instant.

"You don't get to question if I care, or what I want," he said. "What I wanted was someone to listen. Someone to look around and see the case didn't hold water. Someone to grab Cynthia and tell her that I didn't rape her baby sister. That I'd never hurt anyone like that. That I was taking the bullet because someone else decided I had to."

"Then tell me about that someone," I replied. "Roust lied about you. Now, he's missing. You knew him."

"Knew him?" Musa asked. "We shared a cell for a few months. Clicked just a little bit 'cause we were both from Newark. He didn't cause trouble. I think he liked being friendly 'cause I was big then and he thought I'd help him out in the yard. Can't say I remember it ever coming to that, but he talked a lot. Helped pass the time."

"So you two were friendly?" I asked.

"About as friendly as I ever bothered getting with anyone inside," Musa replied. "I was just waiting to leave. The next time I thought about Isiah Roust was when I found out he was testifying against me."

"That makes less than no sense. The man goes from polite cellmate to cooperating witness after you were nothing but nice to him?" I asked. "How would he have even known you were connected to the victims?"

"He asked," Musa said. "So, I told him."

"Wait, what?"

"You ever spend most of twelve months talking to just one person?" Musa asked. "Roust loves garlic bread. Became a Jets fan because his uncle was a Giants fan, and that uncle used to smack him around. And he hates Puerto Ricans. Never explained why. We talked about anything and everything. At some point, we got to talking about women. Exes. Cynthia came up, and once I mentioned who she was, what'd she been through, he got real interested."

"And that didn't set off any alarms?" I asked.

"People get curious. Just 'cause the rest of the world forgot about those kids, doesn't mean Newarkers did. Roust grew up here, he knew the stupid name your paper made up for it. Twilight Four," Musa responded. "Besides, can't say it wasn't good to talk about. I always felt raw about leaving Cynthia how I did. When I did. But I just couldn't be around that. Her whole life became that mission, searching for them. I understood it. But I just wasn't strong enough to stand by her through it. I didn't want my life to be about looking for something we both knew was never gonna get found. I hate saying this, but I never believed they went missing. I loved those kids, I did. But people don't just vanish like that."

"And you told Cynthia that?" I asked.

"That was the last straw that ended it," he replied.

I remembered what Henniman told me, about Roust's terror at the idea of doing time again when they first crossed paths. What if he'd been the same kind of scared in Rahway next to Musa? What if he'd heard Musa's sad story and it inspired to him craft a different tale, one that would give him a card to play to in case he was ever at risk of a return trip to a prison cell?

The court records had me thinking Roust knew how the fire was set. Musa had given him intimate details of his breakup with Cynthia. Details he could twist and color to look like what Henniman wanted to see years later. It also helped explain why Cynthia was so breathless in testifying against her ex.

I'd been too hard on Henniman. Roust's story was the best kind of lie, the kind that contained just enough truth to make it plausible.

"This mean anything to you?" I asked Musa, producing the picture I'd taken from Roust's apartment.

Musa leaned forward, cocked his head to the side.

"That Roust? He looks…healthier," Musa said. "I don't know the other one."

So much for making my own luck.

"Abel," I said, using his first name for the first time. "You know Roust set you up. I believe you. There's got to be something you can tell me about him that'll help you."

Musa's breathing picked up again. He pointed a shaky finger at himself, right at his chest.

"Help me? How exactly are you gonna help me? The doctors say I've got weeks, at most. And that's just what the optimistic one says. Could be tomorrow just as easily," Musa replied. "Besides, I don't know who would've hurt those kids. I never have."

Musa's trembling finger now turned toward the TV bolted to the far wall.

"This ain't on me to fix anyway. I'm as much a victim as the people in the park the other night. That TV gets the news. I saw Cynthia, refusing to speak my name, calling me a monster," he said. "What I want is for her to remember who I was, not who someone else said I am. But it doesn't matter now. Lie's been true so long nothing can change that. I'm gonna die that monster in her head. You're too late."

He was right. Pulling the sword out now wouldn't matter. Abel Musa had already been run through.

I looked up at the TV and thought about the park, about Cynthia's speech. How she knew her sisters and cousins up, down, left and right. Maybe Musa didn't know why someone would want them hurt.

But if anyone did, it was her.

"What if I got her here?" I asked.

"What now?"

"Cynthia. What if I got her to come up here? Got her to listen to you," I said. "You're right. I'm too late. No matter what I find out, the damage is done. But maybe at least you get a chance to tell her what really happened."

Musa pressed two fingers to his lips, like he was smoking an invisible cigarette, mulling his options. His left eye had the slightest sheen to it, a teardrop thinking about forming. There was fresh pain on his face.

He picked up *The Count of Monte Cristo* again, turned a page, watched it rip slightly. They were both reaching the end of their road.

"I guess I can't just sit here and read this all day," he croaked.

I nodded. I meant what I said. I hoped giving Musa a chance to speak to Cynthia gave him the slightest bit of shelter from the torrential downpour of shit he'd experienced.

But if that conversation even happened, it was going to be tense. It was going to be emotional. And I was going to be there, hoping that the ferocity of the moment prompted Cynthia to say something that helped me figure out who really stole her family from her.

Promising Musa a visit from his lost love was one thing. Delivering was another.

I'd met Cynthia Bell for all of three minutes at the end of the memorial in Weequahic Park, and even then, she'd barely said two words to me. Her relationship was with Henniman, who was still dealing with the after effects of a concussion and struggling to keep his eyes open in well-lit rooms.

I'd seen the way her face turned at the mere suggestion that someone other than Abel Musa had killed her family. She wasn't going to meet with a man she'd long seen as a killer, no matter who asked.

Getting her in that room would require a little subterfuge. I needed bait. I needed help from someone who didn't mind running up against the edges of decorum for the sake of doing the right thing.

I needed Key.

Throughout my entire career as a reporter and PI, Keyonna Jackson's nickname had been literal to me. She unlocked doors. She opened paths. Or to put it more bluntly, she took aggrieved and justifiably untrusting members of Newark's Black community aside and told them they could talk to me without wondering if it would bite them in the ass.

Over the years, relatives of crime victims had been blindsided by one too many television reporters who I shared a skin tone with and little else. They wanted misery porn. I just wanted to tell a story accurately, but even then, sometimes I'd let my desire for a good quote barrel past my compassion.

Key reined that in. Kept me honest. Kept the interview subjects comfortable and me telling the right tales. The kind that helped people, the kind I desperately wanted to tell again.

If she could get Cynthia Bell and Abel Musa in the same room having anything approaching a productive conversation, it would be her finest work.

But Key had someone else to help these days. Someone who was paying her. Someone who could effect change on a level I couldn't reach most days without a trampoline and a grappling hook.

I understood why Key was too busy to take my calls which was I was walking into the Mary Burch Theatre at Essex County Community College, passing under a banner advertising a debate between the mayor and the woman Key seemed to believe could fix all the broken things in Newark.

The auditorium was surprisingly full as I stepped through the doors twenty minutes before the candidates were to take the stage. Newark's voter base was historically apathetic, but maybe the chaos of the past year and the youthful energy of Mariana's campaign could change that.

Watkins had been in office for sixteen years since Newark didn't believe in term limits. He'd overseen his share of law enforcement scandals, but the city never seemed to hold him responsible for the things his police department did, at least not come election day.

That was probably a combination of chronic low voter turnout and racial politics. Watkins was a Black mayor in a city whose populace was fifty-five percent Black. By the grace of the machinery of Essex County's Democratic machine, or just dumb luck, he'd never been challenged by a rival Black politician. That usually gave him enough entrenched support to be virtually invulnerable.

Or it had, until Newark got the CNN treatment the year before and became the latest flashpoint in the never-ending national conversation about police violence. Until the last scandal put Watkins's police department under the watchful eye of the U.S. Department of Justice.

The ordeal had blown a hole in the barricade between Watkins and accountability, and he knew it. The mayor was synonymous with police misconduct now. A few stories in my old paper about the absurd amount of police union money pouring into his campaign weren't helping, and neither were the constant images of Watkins being flanked by his city security detail, the same cops turned political goons who had grabbed me at the hospital.

I took out my phone and pulled up the most recent *Signal-*

Intelligencer article on the campaign. If polls were accurate, Mariana held a fifty-four to forty-six advantage over Watkins among likely voters, with policing and criminal justice reform ranking as the most important issues among those polled. Sure, Watkins was within the margin of error, but he was still on the wrong side of the scoreboard.

Overseeing the police force that caught the Twilight Four killer was one of his last unassailable accomplishments. That positive turning into a scandal, with Watkins already trailing, could have ended the contest.

Unless something dramatically altered the course of the race. Something like a sex scandal involving his challenger.

I scanned the room, looking for each side's appointed spin doctor. The back of Lynch's head gave off a sheen, even from a distance. The light and his hairspray collided to create a lens flare bright enough to make me squint. He was seated in the front row on the left side of the auditorium. Key was ten seats to the right. There was a podium halfway between them.

While roaming the auditorium for a place to sit, I noticed another familiar face about five rows back from the podium. The man's head was down, if not outright bowed, mumbling.

I shuffled into the seat next to Tiago Pereira as he clutched a small crucifix near his neck and whispered words I didn't understand, but in a cadence that sounded familiar from Sundays in my childhood.

"Our Father?" I asked.

Tiago snapped to attention and shot me a look of slight annoyance. He prayed deep, entering a trancelike state that I'd only seen my grandparents in before. The kind of prayer where you don't just step into another room to talk to God but lock the door behind you.

"Mr. Avery," he said, adjusting his glasses and trying to shake the surprise from his face. "What are you doing here?"

"My civic duty. Need to be informed before I head to the voting booth in November," I replied. "What about you? Last we spoke, you were less than enthusiastic about your daughter's mayoral bid."

"Maybe when you have children, you will understand, Mr. Avery.

You don't have to love what they do, but you have to support it, within reason," he said.

That was two chances to call me Dick Tracy that he'd passed on. That was odd. Then again, it was odd for us to be discussing his daughter's political prospects instead of the way he managed to get a perfect sear on grilled octopus.

Still, Tiago seemed more nervous than he had the other day when he'd expressed concern about people hanging around the bakery. I looked over to Lynch again, who was lost in his phone, and remembered my last run-in with the mayor's master manipulator. I thought about the photos and messages of Mariana stashed in my office.

"Do you remember what we talked about the other day?" I asked him. "About people coming around? About how you were worried?"

He blinked and squeezed the cross on his neck again. I nodded my head in Lynch's direction.

"Any chance that guy was in the restaurant?" I asked.

Tiago adjusted his glasses and looked where I'd suggested.

"No...no, I don't think so," he replied. "Why are you asking?"

I didn't want to freak him out, but at the same time, I worried about the Pereira family being blindsided by the bomb Lynch was building. I'd shrugged off Tiago's concerns the last time I'd seen him because I hadn't known his family might have something to hide. At the same time, I had to wonder how much the father who had his rosary beads out in public knew about his daughter's sexual identity.

"That guy is the mayor's right hand," I said. "And as much as I hate admitting it, if there's something you're worried about him finding out, he's the type who will find it. If you were trying to tell me you needed help the other day—"

Tiago cut me off, gently placing a hand over mine.

"You're a good customer, Russell. I like you. I truly do," he said, smiling at me just long enough for me to focus on his expression as it turned grim. "But do not make the mistake of thinking you are more. If my family has a problem, we will handle it as a family. *Entiendes*?"

The crowd got quiet around us and I pulled my hand back from Tiago's, not sure the exact wire I'd tripped, but sure I'd need to figure that out soon.

Someone in a bow tie came out and welcomed the crowd to the night's debate. Tiago went statue still as Mariana entered from stage left, wearing an elegant ankle-length green dress and offering a tight smile and a big wave as the crowd met her with polite applause. She turned her head to the right before Watkins started his own walk-up. Mariana looked focused, coiled, locked in on the man holding the seat she planned on taking.

The mayor paid her no mind. Watkins was in a charcoal three-piece and pointing to people in the crowd like he recognized them, showing all his teeth for those unaware they were fangs. The guy looked like he was entering a party, while his challenger cracked her knuckles for a fight.

Bow Tie announced it was time for each candidate to make an opening statement and produced a silver dollar, but Watkins interrupted the coin flip.

"I think in this case age can wait for beauty," he said, flashing another shark grin.

Knowing what I knew about Watkins's history with young attractive women, the line made me cringe.

"Cute. But not surprising," Mariana said, moving toward her podium. "My name's Mariana Pereira. I've represented Newark's North Ward for the last two years, but I've lived in Newark my entire life. Cleanthony Watkins has been mayor nearly half that time, and I've been sick of him for exactly all of it. And what he just did there, that's exactly why. He smiles and defers to me, when he really wants you to focus on two things—that I'm inexperienced and, in his eyes, that I'm pretty. But before I've said one thing, referenced one issue, that's what he wants you to see. I actually want you to thank him for it, because this is what he does. Smiles while he pushes you off a ledge. For sixteen years, he has cozied up to police unions, developers, power brokers.

He's told you he's here to keep you safe while never really trying to fix a police force whose members have beaten and shot your fathers and brothers and sisters and cousins without cause. Even last year, when things got so bad that parts of downtown burned, was the mayor the one stepping in to say enough is enough? No, he was out in Morris County, sleeping in his Victorian. I was here, in the street, facing the same unjust treatment you all have. Getting brutalized at the hands of the officers who want this man re-elected."

A murmur rose through the room like a wave. She'd practiced that line, likely planned to conjure the viral image of her getting hurt during the Kevin Mathis protests for the crowd, the idea that she was on their side of a line.

"I want to tell you who I am, but I also want to tell you who Cleanthony Watkins isn't. He's not your protector. He's not the man who has guided this city toward a bright future. He's the one who would rather get re-elected than repair what's broken," she continued. "He's going to spend the night telling you I have no record to run on. I'm here to tell you neither does he. But I can, and I will, build a record you can be proud of. I will stand up for people, not systems. Because it's systems that get people like Kevin Mathis killed."

I looked over toward Key and noticed her clutching the hand of an older Black man. It took a second before I recognized Austin Mathis, Kevin's father. The client who'd hired me a year ago, setting me on a path that changed a lot of lives for the better, just not mine.

He was standing and applauding. I briefly remembered out last conversation, when he told me, in tears, that he didn't want his son's story to be indistinguishable from any of the hundred or so homicides that stained Newark each year. Looking around the room, I hoped it was clear to Austin that Kevin's tale was now Newark legend.

Bow Tie turned the floor over to the mayor, who looked like he wanted to spit venom. But in the time I'd spent covering Watkins, he'd never been much of a counter-puncher. Ducking and dodging was more his style, but that's hard when your opponent's holding a flamethrower.

I looked over toward Lynch, hoping to enjoy a brief glimpse of him mumbling curses. Instead, I found him looking in my direction, but not at me. He was nodding at someone. I followed his sight line and found a person I didn't recognize returning Lynch's look, craning his neck toward the stage. The man was fiddling with something in his pocket, but I wasn't sure what.

"Well, that was certainly loud. And I can respect loud," Watkins said as he took the podium. "Angry is loud. And why shouldn't Miss Pereira be angry after last year? Last year made me angry too. Mr. Mathis, your son deserved better. It still breaks my heart what happened to him. We need to learn from last year. But as Miss Pereira points out, I've been mayor for sixteen years. I know her generation is notorious for its short attention span, but I'm hoping you all can see the long view."

Watkins paused. The older members seemed of the crowd seemed to be nodding, a few chuckling. Watkins knew where he had firm ground to stand on, and he was going to root himself to that spot instead of fighting Mariana on her turf. That was smart, and it smacked of how Lynch dealt with me earlier in the week. You don't have to beat your opponent's argument. You just have to change it.

"Does our police department need to make some changes? Hell yes. But let's not forget that same police department guided this city to yearslong dips in violent crime. Let's not forget that five years ago, before Miss Pereira had ever set foot inside city hall, that same police department led us to the lowest homicide rate in Newark's history. If Miss Pereira wants to lay the department's failings of the last year at my feet, she's welcome to, but I hope she remembers to put its successes there too. The department was having hiring problems before I changed the requirements that forced officers to live in the city, remember? And I seem to remember a few companies like Panasonic and Amazon decided to open up sites here—not in New York, not down in Philly, *here*—on my watch. Miss Pereira wants this race to be about one thing, and it's an important thing, but it's not the only thing. She's angry, and anger is powerful. But it's also fragile. Easily redirected. I've spent sixteen years bringing you jobs, bringing you safety, bringing you something stable that you can touch, feel and count. Do our police need some fixing? No doubt. But do our police need someone from Washington, DC doing the fixing, or do we need to do it our own selves? I've been mayor a long time, but most days, I'm a repair man. And I don't know about y'all, but I get real nervous bringing my car to a new mechanic."

As Watkins and Pereira started trading punches on the city's unemployment rate, I clocked Lynch's friend again. He didn't look familiar, and his combination of untucked flannel shirt and ill-fitting jeans made me assume he didn't work in Lynch's communications shop. But he was fidgeting with something in his lap again. I was a few rows back, too far to make it out for sure, but it looked like the man was reading something to himself. Repeating it. Memorizing it?

Pereira kept sticking jabs. Watkins took one on the chin for the police department's notoriously low rate of sustained citizen complaints alleging misconduct. A correct citation of stats showing the department arrested Black men at a rate of five times their census representation tagged the mayor in the ear. As the hour long back-and-forth headed toward its conclusion, Pereira reminded the crowd that Watkins had twice launched exploratory committees for Senate runs, her message clear: he's only here because he can't go someplace else.

But the mayor wasn't going away easy. He played the hits. He'd been the city's first Black leader. And over the long arc of history, the crime rates and economic data painted a rosy portrait of the Cleanthony Watkins era compared to the city under his predecessors. Whether that was worth the price of a department that had been so aggressive many of its citizens lived in fear of lights and sirens would be up to the voters.

Bow Tie thanked both candidates for their time and opened the floor for questions. That's when I noticed the guy in the flannel look at Lynch one more time. They exchanged another set of signals. The man stood up and headed for the Q-and-A podium.

I followed, not entirely sure what I was doing but certain I wasn't about to like the guy's next move. A few members of the audience were standing and stretching, but none seemed in as much of a rush to get to the microphone as Flannel. We'd be the first two up there. Lynch clearly saw me. So did Key, which was good, because I needed to get her attention somehow.

Flannel beat me to the microphone, placing what must have been the item he was fidgeting with on the podium. A white envelope with a polaroid peeking out.

One I was pretty sure I'd seen before.

"Please state your name," Bow Tie said.

"Will Malookin. My question is for Councilwoman Pereira. You've spent a lot of time tonight talking about accountability for Mayor Watkins, but what about you? When will you be held accountable for your conduct?"

He held up the envelope for the room to see, thankfully too dumb to realize no one could make sense of a blank white object. I must have been Lynch's last hope to place his salacious story in a legitimate publication. Now he just wanted it out in the air. I didn't know where he'd found this bumbling idiot or what he'd paid him to do his bidding, but I understood his goal.

He didn't need to plant the story. He just needed someone asking the question. There were enough cameras present that Mariana would have to at least acknowledge the accusations or provide the dreaded no comment.

Or she would have. If I was just a little less impulsive. 'Cause all it took was one glance at Lynch's smug grin for me to rip the microphone from Flannel's hands.

"Hey, man, sorry, I know there's probably some rules for this but I think it's important that I ask you a question before you ask the councilwoman one," I said, continuing to backpedal toward the right side of the room. "You mind telling this crowd where you got that envelope?"

I looked past Flannel. Lynch wasn't smiling anymore.

"That's alright. I can tell them if you're feeling shy," I said, continuing to retreat, hoping to make my point before the campus security officers who were headed my way could do anything. "My name's Russell Avery. I used to write for the *Signal-Intelligencer*. And before this toady tries to smear the councilwoman, I figured you all might wanna know he's working for the mayor's office."

Lynch was up now. I really, truly hoped he made a run for me, but one of the security guards was already past him. I wasn't done talking, so I vaulted onto the stage and jogged past Watkins, giving the visibly aggravated mayor a polite nod as I ran past.

"Yeah, him, right there. Dameon Lynch, the one with the hair. That guy," I said, pointing down. "Why is the mayor sending people to take photos of his opponent? Why is he giving them out to random people? Is that creepy? I don't know, but I feel like some of you might wanna use your time to ask him."

The guard in the black shirt was coming up the stairs behind Mariana now, and his partner was waiting for me at the foot of the stage. I tossed the microphone in his direction, and he bobbled the reception, giving me enough time to exit stage right and head toward Key.

"Gonna need to talk to you," I said, hearing four sets of feet coming up behind me.

"That makes two of us," she replied. "I'll be waiting when they're done."

Then I got tackled.

It took about a half hour for me to convince the campus security guards that involving the actual police was a bad idea.

The two men who had dragged me away from the debate stage seemed nice enough, as far as rent-a-cops go. No one had their pants tucked into their socks. No one acted like they were patrolling Kabul instead of a local college campus. No one was particularly rude, and neither reached for their stun gun when they realized I wasn't fighting back.

But they still did that thing all humans do when granted one milligram of power over another.

They used it.

They told me they would probably have to report me to Newark's police, let them sort out if I'd crossed any lines covered by the penal code. One of them seemed a little happy about it, maybe hopeful he'd get a medal.

I reminded them that calling the police would result in reports being generated and formal statements being taken. Meaning they would probably have to explain how they'd let me get on stage, close enough to two elected officials to do serious damage if that was my aim in the first place.

Then I asked them if they thought it was weird that the mayor's security detail hadn't gotten involved. I asked them if that probably meant the mayor didn't want any official documentation of the incident either, considering what I'd been yelling about. Before I could ask them if they were worried about being on a city hall shit list, they asked me to leave immediately and muttered something about me being banned from campus for life.

Fine by me. Between exploding homes and pissed off mayors, I didn't think I'd have time for night classes anyway.

My phone buzzed once I got back to the parking lot.

"Just remember, I tried to help you break that story," read the message in the Signal app, from the same thread that had baited me into the meeting at Don Pepe nights earlier.

It was Lynch, smart enough to text me from a number that likely didn't track back to him.

"That's not a story. It's a lame-ass character assassination attempt," I replied. "But at least now you won't have to worry about it anymore."

Had I taken the photos entirely out of Lynch's arsenal? Probably not. But I must have been caught on at least one camera shouting that the mayor's team was up to dirty tricks involving photos. Lynch would at least have to wait a bit to try making the images public again if he wanted people to see them as a scandal instead of a political hit.

"I've tried to be friendly, Russell," he wrote. "You really do not want to be my enemy."

"Why? You got photos of me in lingerie too?" I asked.

Digital ellipses popped up and disappeared a few times.

"Wait," I wrote. "Do you?"

"Being a credentialed member of the press afforded you certain protections, Russell," he wrote. "You would do well to remember you lack those now."

Before I could process Lynch's vague and mildly unnerving threat, Key emerged from the theatre laughing and clapping as she headed my way.

"Thought you might try to pull off a spin move or something when the guards came," she said. "Never thought I'd see the day where Russell Avery became an activist. Taking the mic, shouting down city hall. I'm starting to think you might finally be seeing past your 'both sides' bullshit."

"I saw something bad happening and I reacted," I replied. "Call it whatever you want."

Key had ditched the blazer, revealing the shirt underneath to be a Lauryn Hill graphic tee with some lyrics from "Lost Ones" tangled up in the likeness of the singer's hair.

"Well, the councilwoman noticed. She appreciated it," Key said. "And she wants to meet you."

"No offense, Key, but I've already had more dealings with city hall in a week than I'm usually comfortable having in a year," I replied. "I came here to talk to you, not her."

"You did, but you listened to her in there, right? Like the whole hour? Independent investigations of police shootings? Citizen review boards? Actually working with the feds, not fighting them tooth and nail over every change like Watkins will," she said. "We're talking real reform, Russ. She's legit. After everything last year, you telling me you don't believe this city needs that?"

"It's your job to get her elected, not mine. I'm trying to clear a man's name, remember?" I asked. "Or are you too caught up playing *West Wing* that you forgot about Abel Musa?"

Key sucked her teeth and shook her head, rolling her eyes before stepping right up in my face.

"Always the either/or shit with you. We work well together, Russ. Always have. But it goes a lot easier when you stop pretending we don't want the same things," she said. "I want to help Abel. But that's your job. So, what do you need?"

I took a second to look around the parking lot.

"Mayor's people left already," she said. "That crowd was small enough that this won't be a problem, but I imagine they wanted to be gone in case any media came around looking to ask follow-up questions about your performance."

"Speaking of, you want to tell me what I was defending?" I asked. "Those photos Lynch had…"

"Lynch is a propagandist. But if you want to know more about those photos, you need to talk to the councilwoman herself," Key replied. "That's not my place."

"So, you already knew about them?"

Key paused, held a hand up, but her stern expression melted before she could formulate a lie.

"Yes, and no," Key said. "Like I said, you should talk to her."

"Don't care. I don't need her help anyway. I need yours," I replied. "I'm running into walls with this Musa thing."

She laughed.

"What?" I asked.

"You need me to vouch for you with some Black folks, don't you?" she asked. "This is giving me flashbacks, like you're still at the paper."

"Only two of them are Black, Key, if that makes any difference," I replied.

"It doesn't," she said. "Out with it."

"The cousins. Lavell and Kurtis Dawkins. They were in foster care back when this all went down, and Lavell had previously alleged abuse. The allegation never went anywhere, but that seemed like a thread worth pulling. Seems everyone's always just assumed Shayna was the target because of the informant's testimony against Musa. Thought maybe we'd been looking in the wrong direction," I said. "The foster mother is still in Newark. I went over there yesterday. Weird scene. Foster kids looked terrified of her. Littlest one had his arms covered. In August."

"Done. Get me the name," Key said. "I'll pull whatever records I can, see if we can urge a wellness check."

"That easy?" I asked.

"You think I took this job just for the paycheck?" she asked. "I've got reach now. I'm gonna use it. Especially if someone's hurting a baby. Is that all?"

"No. I know you said you knew Cynthia Bell back when, but how close are you now?" I asked.

"Close enough for me to know she won't help you," Key replied. "She believes with every part of her body that Abel Musa killed her family. She's been furious about the appeal. She won't talk to you."

"That's fine. I don't need her to talk to me," I replied. "I need her to talk to Abel Musa."

"Did you listen to a word I just said?" she asked.

"Yeah. But it doesn't change what needs to happen," I replied. "Musa won't talk to us, says it's too late to make a difference. Cynthia won't talk to us either. But there are fewer and fewer people living and breathing who knew the victims. They're two of the last. I went up to Musa's room again this morning. From what little he said, he made clear he's still hurt by Cynthia thinking he's a monster. He wants a chance to make that right. If they end up in the same room, it gets them talking about back then. There's gonna be screaming, crying, it'll be ugly. It's a shitty thing to do, but maybe they say something useful. Something that helps us find the real killer."

Key chewed on her thumbnail and narrowed her eyes at me.

"That's a longshot, and a fucked up one to attempt. There's no way I can get her in that room if I tell her why you want her there," Key said. "I'm gonna have to lie for you, then. That's a big ask, which means I've got a big ask. Meet with the councilwoman. She has a job for you."

"Key..." I started.

"I'm your only way to Cynthia Bell. This is non-negotiable," she said. "You want my help? Then you're getting into politics."

CHAPTER
ELEVEN

I HATED POLITICS, BUT not politicians.

Mariana Pereira seemed like a well-intentioned woman. She came up waiting tables at her family business and would likely remain rooted in the same reality as the people she hoped to govern. She talked about police like someone who lived in a world where sirens could mean salvation or serious trauma, depending on the day.

Pereira saw Newark as a community. Watkins saw it as a fiefdom. If the Brick City chose to make her its next leader, I wouldn't have a problem with it. But I didn't want to be part of the reason it happened either. It just wasn't in my DNA.

I'd spent years as an arbiter of fact from horseshit, and no matter how highly I thought of a politician, I didn't want to be in a position where I was required to live on their side of every and any argument. I didn't want an employee ID number and tax return that put me in their camp. I didn't want to be part of their team, on paper, at the inevitable moment where they fucked up in grandiose fashion under a spotlight.

I'd spent the entire morning reviewing my misgivings, hyping myself up to say all this to Key or the councilwoman herself, hoping they'd respect my principled stance and agree to help Abel Musa anyway because it was the right thing to do.

But I wasn't that naive. Leverage was currency. Key had it.

So, I put on a dress shirt, sprayed my hair into a manageable condition and took a long look in the bathroom mirror.

Had Dameon Lynch looked like this once, before the first time he shook hands with Cleanthony Watkins?

That thought was enough to make me claw at my hair, messing up the polite part before I rolled up the sleeves of my dress shirt. I kicked off the half-tied dress shoes and grabbed a pair of Converse instead.

Doing the job was one thing. Looking happy about it was another.

I stepped out my front door and started the nine-block walk toward the meeting that would mark my first foray into politics, hoping maybe some kind of divine intervention would prevent me from getting there.

Just as I got in view of Marisqueira Pereira, my phone rang.

"What the fuck are you doing?" a voice growled.

Well, it wasn't God. But Henniman would do in a pinch.

"Do you mean, like, at this exact second? Or with my life in general?" I asked.

"I already have a concussion. I don't need a migraine," Henniman replied. "You started shit with the mayor last night? Did you miss the part where we're supposed to be doing this discreetly?"

That word had traveled faster than expected.

"I don't know if I necessarily started shit with the mayor," I said.

"The Internet disagrees. You got on a microphone and accused Watkins's staff of something sideways," he said. "What would you call that?"

Starting shit with the mayor. Though Lynch had started shit with me on the mayor's behalf by trying to leak those photos. So technically, I was only continuing shit with the mayor.

"Listen, I hear you, but this had nothing to do with our thing.

I didn't mention Musa, the fire, Roust, any of it," I said. "This was a separate issue I had to take care of, and it may have helped us."

"Helped us! Helped us? How the fuck did it…?" His voice trailed off. I heard a low growl and the sound of something tumbling. It took about twenty seconds and a lot of static before Henniman got control of the phone back. "Goddamn head still isn't right," he said. "Doctor said I'd be getting these lightning bolt headaches."

"There's no shame in that, man. But you need to get back in one piece, and you hired me for a reason. So, let me do my job," I said.

"I told you. I made this mistake. I'm fixing it. You're just adequate cover for me in case the department starts asking questions," he replied. "Speaking of which, our new friend, the probation officer? She managed to keep my name out of the police reports down there, and the fire seems to have stayed out of the news."

With no one dead or hospitalized and the Asbury Park Press criminally understaffed, that made sense.

"So, we seem to be in the clear, for now," Bill continued. "As long as you stop being a pain in the mayor's ass or doing anything else that draws attention to us."

I looked up at the ebony wood framing the restaurant's entrance, where the name of the mayor's political rival was carved in red letters.

"Russell?" Bill asked. "You understand?"

"Yeah, of course. Absolutely," I replied, entirely too cheerful.

"Then why are you about to walk into a meeting with the Pereira family?"

"The fuck did you…?"

"You're standing outside a seafood restaurant at nine a.m.," he replied.

I pulled the phone from my ear, looking at the screen for a second in complete confusion as I tried to make sense of Bill's psychic powers. Then I swiped to the home screen and remembered why there was an image of two stick figures arm and arm there. The app Bill had put on my phone as a condition of employment.

"You paranoid motherfucker," I said. "You're really monitoring me? That wasn't a joke?"

"I'm not particularly funny," Bill replied.

He wasn't.

"What are you doing, Russell?" he asked.

"Musa talked to me yesterday, which I guess you know since you're cyber stalking me," I replied. "He wasn't that helpful, but he didn't demand the staff throw me out either. He wants to talk to Cynthia, and I'm thinking—"

"If you want to put him and Cynthia in the same room, then you're not thinking," Henniman replied. "That woman has had so few certainties in her life. Abel Musa's guilt is one of them. She's not going to help us."

I held the phone slightly away from my face, knowing he was gonna yell when I told him I had a workaround.

"Keyonna Jackson thinks she can change that," I said.

Henniman cleared his throat like he had to spit something up.

"*That* Keyonna Jackson? Thinks they should abolish the police, Keyonna Jackson?" he asked. "Megaphone calling for my colleagues to be indicted anytime we sneeze on a perp, Keyonna Jackson?"

"I mean, I usually just call her Key."

"We are not working with that woman. Or the mayor's enemies," he said.

"Then what's your play here?" I asked. "This happened when you were barely out of the academy. Before I was in junior high. We're chasing ghosts and the only people who knew what was happening in 1996 won't speak to us without something in return."

"We need to find Isiah Roust," he said.

"Who's we? You can barely get out of bed. My shoulder looks like an overcooked steak. And we have no idea where he is," I said. "Sure, the Asbury cops and firefighters are looking for him and maybe you get a heads-up when or if that BOLO pops. Maybe you don't. Maybe he's in Canada by now. You didn't meet Cynthia until fifteen years after the crime. Musa's barely ever said two words about the case other than to plead not guilty. Putting those two in a room, with all the history and hatred between them, you don't think we learn something we didn't know before?"

"Maybe," he said. "Or maybe we just give her more pain that she doesn't deserve."

"Bill, you saw her the other night at the park. Did that wound look closed to you?" I asked. "Only thing worse than her hurting, is her hurting over a lie. Someone made her suffer that way, someone made her carry all that. And we both know it's not the man she thinks it is. She deserves—"

"Do not tell me what she deserves," he replied. "I call her once a month. Just to check in. Just to make sure she knows someone else thinks about them. 'Cause otherwise, she carries all of that alone. What she deserves is a better life than the one she was handed."

"She deserves to know the truth," I replied. "And she deserves to hear it from you. Think about it, Bill. If we figure this thing out, she's going to learn it wasn't Abel anyway."

Bill went quiet. I waited, knowing him, knowing he'd have to get there on his own.

"What's Miss Megaphone's plan?" he asked.

"She hasn't given me one yet. You have any ideas?"

"One. And I hate it. Your paid protester friend is still going to need to approach her," he said. "But from when Roust came forward, through the trial, even after the DA petitioned for Musa's release, Cynthia's always wanted to hear it from him. A confession. That's how you get her there. Tell her he's ready to give it up."

"Thank you," I replied.

"Fuck you," he said. "We're gonna hurt this woman, and it can't be for nothing."

He hung up. It was well-timed. Because as I walked up to the side entrance of the Pereira family restaurant, I heard screaming.

Twelve hours earlier, I'd seen Mariana Pereira stand tall as an older man talked down to her, fire sparking in her eyes as she expertly counterpunched Mayor Watkins's every insult and condescension.

As I walked into Marisqueira Pereira, those eyes were filled with the same fury but the flames were doused by what looked like tears. Tiago stood at the center of the restaurant's dining room, face reddened as he launched into a shout that seemed to require the effort of his entire body.

"I told you! I told you this would happen if you ran. Disgrace at our door," he howled. "Because you can't control yourself."

I hadn't met this version of Tiago during our occasional polite banter about breakfast pastries. But I'd gotten a preview the night before, when he made clear I'd crossed a line by offering to get involved in his family's business. That was only minutes before I actually got involved in his family's business. Hours before I showed up at his family restaurant for the same reason.

I probably wasn't getting free Pasteis de Nata anytime soon.

"I can't control myself?" Mariana asked. "That's your takeaway from last night? Not that someone's trying to blackmail your fucking daughter?"

Mariana was seated at a two-top to her father's left, one of the many solid black tables that lined the always dimly-lit interior of the restaurant. Pictures of the eatery's humble beginnings showed a simpler open space design with tables under plain cloths that draped to the floor like curtains, the whole room arranged based on how many customers Tiago could pack in after the Sunday church rush. But as his restaurants grew in stature, someone must have pushed a more refined approach on him.

There was a solid black oak bar to the right of the entrance, and a dining space that sprawled out into two wide rooms, both with small tables in neat rows of three. None of them could have sat more than four patrons. The back of the restaurant even spilled into a small patio area, with hung lanterns and ivy winding up the brick face that divided his property from the apartment complex behind the restaurant. It all presented a sleek, romantic atmosphere.

If either Tiago or Mariana had seen me, they weren't acting like it. Key had told me to enter through an unlocked service door, probably wanting to minimize the chance of anyone seeing her mayoral candidate meeting with the guy who'd made a spectacle of a recent mayoral debate. The entranceway brought me through the kitchen and past the restrooms, the complete opposite side of the restaurant from the spot where the Pereiras were folding their dirty laundry.

"There would be nothing to blackmail if you weren't doing things you're not supposed to," Tiago said. "You promised me this was a phase. You swore to your mother. Something from college, that's all."

Mariana ran her hands down her face, fingertips dragging over the puffy skin forming under her eyes.

"A phase? You're talking about this like it's a hobby!" she shouted. "How is this...why is this how you are? You're my father! Why are you not on my side?"

"You know why," he said. "And you know your mother would agree with me."

Mariana was out of her chair now, venom clearly surging through her. But as she stood, we made eye contact, and that was enough to suppress the bile in her throat. Tiago followed her eyes, and his withering glare found a new target.

"We're closed, Mr. Avery," he said.

"I know, Tiago. It's nine a.m.," I replied. "I'm not here for the clams."

Mariana turned her back on her father, blinking away the tears and extending a hand toward me.

"It's okay," she said. "Russell is just a little early for our meeting."

She'd flipped the switch from aggrieved daughter to professional in about four seconds. I was as confident in her political aspirations as I was concerned for her mental health.

"Meeting? What meeting?" Tiago asked, before turning his furious gaze from his daughter to me. "I told you last night not to involve yourself in my family's business."

Mariana kept moving, shook my hand and closed her eyes for a brief second at the sound of her father's voice.

"This is campaign business, not family business," she said, every word coming out like it was a strain. "It stopped being family business the second you chose to act this way. I'll handle this on my own. Discretely."

"Discretion," Tiago said, a wheezing laugh following the word. "What would you know about discretion?"

"She probably knows enough to stop having this argument in front of me and anyone else who can walk in off the street," I said. "Seems a little more discrete than what you're doing."

Tiago's eyes bugged. He didn't look like someone who suffered backtalk often. Those were my favorite people to mouth off to.

"This is my business. If I say you leave, you leave," he replied, stepping closer to me.

Tiago was a tall man, maybe six foot three or four, and as he got near, I saw the ropey muscle on his forearms. I'd heard the stories about Tiago Pereira, the Ironbound Mayor, building up Marisqueria Pereira from a glorified lunch counter, battling away the occasional Italian or Pole irritated by his presence in a neighborhood they thought they might have claimed before the Portuguese influx chased most of them to Bayonne. He was used to fighting for his share, defending it from threats a little more malevolent than borderline unemployed ex-reporters.

"Well damn, I must have set my watch to CPT if you're all this heated this fast."

Key's voice cut through the room like a referee's whistle, stopping the play before Tiago and I could collide. I turned around to see her walking through the dining area, left arm holding up a bag that looked like it came from the other Pereira family property down the block.

"How are you, Mr. Pereira?" she asked, moving in for a half hug with her free arm, forming a natural barricade between me and the restauranteur. "I've got enough for four if you want to join us. I see you've already met Russell. He's an old friend. Here to make sure we don't have to deal with any more nonsense like last night. Right, Russ?"

I looked at Mariana, then Tiago, then Key. The daughter looked relieved. The father looked perplexed. I wondered if my expression belied the same confusion. I was used to watching Key start shit rather than defuse it, but I guess her time in city hall had helped vary up her skill set.

"He does not need to be involved in this," Tiago said. "Neither do you. This is a personal matter."

"Tiago, maybe you want it to be a personal matter, but the other team came pretty close to making it a public one last night. Hell, if it wasn't for Russell, it might have been in the paper this morning," Key said, patting her hand gently on Tiago's meaty wrist. "You're welcome to be part of this. Are you sure you don't want to join us? I got a bunch of custard cups…sorry, wait, that's not what you call them. Patsy's…"

Tiago looked like he wanted to continue the argument, but realized he was outnumbered.

"Pasteis de Nata," he replied, the fire in his voice extinguished. "And no, thank you. I have to get us ready to open."

Tiago slumped his shoulders before looking in his daughter's direction, his face flaring one last bit of defiant frustration.

"We will finish this later," he said, echoing the famous last words of every parent in recorded human history.

Tiago stalked off to the back, and I followed Key and Mariana to the table she'd been seated at when I came in, pulling over a third chair.

"Does CPT mean what I think it means?" I asked as I sat down.

"Yes, it does. And no, you can't say it," Key replied, laying out the pastries before looking over her shoulder. "Now what did y'all do to get Westboro Baptist riled up this early?"

"Keyonna," Mariana said, her face caught between blushing and scowling. "I told you to stop calling him that."

"And I told him to stop being a bigoted jackass," Key replied, her voice just low enough that it might not carry to the kitchen. "Guess we're at an impasse."

I looked over my shoulder to make sure Tiago had disappeared into the recesses of the restaurant before raising my hand tentatively like I had a question in class.

"So, does someone want to catch me up here?" I asked, looking at Mariana. "'Cause I think I got arrested helping you last night and your dad seems like he wants to kill me."

"I'm sorry about my father. He's very protective," she said.

"Yeah, he's told me about that before. But that didn't seem like someone being protective," I said. "That seemed like someone being an asshole."

"Mr. Avery, Key has been with me for a little bit, so I don't mind when she takes the occasional jab at my father," Mariana said, her smile fading. "We just met. You don't get to insult him."

"I insult everyone. Kind of just comes naturally to me," I said. "But I'm easily distracted, so why don't you tell me what I'm doing here."

She looked at the pastry Key had placed in front of her and picked at the edges of the crust.

"Listen, Councilwoman, you grew up in Newark and you hired one of the only people on earth who can shut me up," I said, pointing at Key. "I know you're not a fragile bird. So, can we just be straight with each other? I need Key's help with something. Key said you need my help with something first. It's obviously got to do with those pictures, so why don't you tell me what's so bad about them?"

Mariana looked like she was going to open her mouth, but Key held a hand up.

"You spill, then we spill," Key said. "I wasn't exactly taking notes, but your speech made it seem like you knew what was in that man's envelope. You'd seen those before. Yet you didn't say word one about them to me before last night."

"Key, I didn't…" I stopped myself, looked toward Mariana instead. "You're not out, right? I mean, I don't care, at all, but that's the whole score here, isn't it? That's what I just walked in on now, with your dad. How was I supposed to know if Key even knew about this?"

"You expect me to believe you were trying to be delicate, Russ?" Key asked. "Your softest touch usually hits like a cinderblock."

"I wasn't trying to be anything, Key. I don't know the councilwoman. I didn't know what I was being handed or why someone who hates me as much as Dameon Lynch was handing it to me," I said. "All I knew was it was toxic, so I put it in a drawer and stopped thinking about it until last night. When, as you noted, I did everything in my power to keep a lid on those pictures. The only damn I give about those photos is how me helping you deal with them gets you to help me with my other problem. But first, someone needs to tell me what the hell is going on."

I turned back to the councilwoman.

"Or, more specifically, you need to tell me what the hell is going on," I said.

Mariana looked around the empty room, checking for I don't know what. She clocked something, leaned back in her chair and forced a smile. A younger busboy appeared with black gauges in each of his ears and a tray in his hand. He placed two cups of coffee down, one for Mariana and another for Key. All he had for me was a scowl, but that seemed preferable to the café au phlegm that might have been headed my way otherwise.

When he left, she leaned forward, resting her elbows on the table. The shift in her body language from when Tiago was there to when he wasn't was like her slipping off a mask.

"Well, you've seen the pictures," she started before scanning the room again, voice growing smaller by the second, like she was about to confess to a capital crime.

"You're gay," I said. "I think the three of us and Pops at least know that much."

Anger flared in her eyes, and the same rage refracted in Key's. This might not have been the best arena for my flippant attitude about, well, everything.

"I'm bisexual, and if you don't realize why that might be a campaign issue, then maybe you're the wrong person for this job," she said.

"Then educate me," I replied.

"How much do you know about Portugal, Mr. Avery?" she asked.

"Absolutely nothing. Sure, I live in the Ironbound, but I eat a lot of Italian food too and I couldn't tell you shit about Florence."

She turned her palms up and looked at Key, exasperated.

"This is how he is," Key said. "He really does mean well, I promise. Even if he's bad at reading the moments when he needs to tone it down."

I was. Thankfully, Key had a habit of guiding me to those moments via death stare.

"Nearly eighty percent of the country is Catholic. It actually used to be the state religion," Mariana said. "The families that came here packed their rosary beads, and they handed them down throughout the neighborhood. My father would not be the only one using words like 'disgrace' to describe my sexuality."

"I thought this pope was supposed to be a progressive or something," I said.

"That doesn't erase decades of people being told my preferences are a sin," she said. "You saw my father. This isn't the first time we've had this conversation, and he chooses to live in a fantasy world. He Googled the word 'bi-curious' once and has decided that's all this has ever been. He can't accept it, and I'm his daughter. How do you think others will react? I'm not afraid of who I am, Russell. But my neighbors might be."

"Watkins is vulnerable right now, Russ, but he's not anywhere close to dead," Key chimed in. "The police department's sins are on him. All of last year is on him. That's hurting him. We got the protesters. We got the young voters. But if this gets out, she could start bleeding in her own backyard. And the church isn't the only group that might get shy about voting for an LGBT candidate."

Key looked like she was waiting for me to catch up to her. I took a bite out of the pastry in place of having anything useful to say.

"We pull some Black voters from Watkins on criminal justice, but his whole base is older. Black folks who have lived here for years. Who have been voting for him for years," Key said. "They go to church too."

"You really think this might be enough to cost you the election?" I asked.

"If it wasn't, do you think Watkins's people would be spreading it? He's already tried to leak them twice, that we know of," Mariana said. "Thank you, by the way, for refusing to go along with that."

"I'm not a reporter anymore," I replied. "That's why I'm sitting here, right?"

"Would you have run with this nonsense if you were?" she asked.

"Of course not," I spat back. "Some stories aren't worth telling. But that doesn't mean I want to be involved with this either. I know this shouldn't affect how people vote, but people are going to feel like you lied to them if you slip into office in the closet."

Mariana's shoulder twitched, just for a second, small enough that I'd have missed it if I wasn't staring at her. Her eyes met mine, and they looked tired. She raised her coffee cup and took a long sip, keeping me in her view the whole time.

"Russell, when you first broke into journalism, did you have to hear about how you'd be the first Irish reporter at the *Signal-Intelligencer*? The first straight man to run the police beat?" she asked. "Or did you just get the job you wanted because people thought you were good enough to do it."

I shook my head, looked at Key, and realized this was a good time for me to shut up.

"This race is about past and future. It's about Cleanthony Watkins letting this police department do whatever it wanted to deliver crime stats that upped his approval rating. This is about me being in that seat when the Department of Justice finishes up its investigation and moves to put this police department under a consent decree so the changes happen in reality. Not just on paper. Because if Watkins is there, he will fight it all tooth and nail," she said. "This is about getting financing for mental health diversion programs so truly damaged people arrested for misdemeanors don't end up in a system that breeds them to be felons. This is about making this city's budget about more than just public safety. Knowing who I go to bed with won't fix Newark. I want to be the city's mayor because it's what the city needs. But if we don't cut Lynch off at the knees, well…you know how this goes. The narratives. Is Newark ready for an LGBT mayor? That's a race for small minds. That's a race we can lose. There's too much at stake to risk this on people's tolerance."

I leaned back in my chair, thinking about all the time I'd spent chronicling the ills of Cleanthony Watkins's Newark. The murder rate that always seemed to yo-yo from terrible to tolerable. The names that kept appearing in stories I wrote about officer misconduct because the discipline review board only sometimes suspended cops and rarely fired them. The women who'd come to me trying to implicate Watkins in his own, much more severe, sex scandal before Lynch intercepted my story.

"So, what are you asking? You need me to figure out where Lynch is getting his intel?"

Mariana flashed a little smile. It looked forced.

Then she got up and walked away.

"That's a yes," Key said.

"'Cause she can't say it out loud," I replied. "Just like she can't say that you need me to shut them up."

Key nodded.

"Welcome to politics," she said.

With her sales pitch finished, Mariana Pereira asked us to leave the restaurant. Whether that was to placate her father or claim plausible deniability, I couldn't be sure.

Key had agreed to help me make a list of people who might want to see the councilwoman's political fortunes ruined and followed me back to my place, showing brief astonishment that I lived in Newark, much less the Ironbound.

That made me feel a little bit of pride, like I was really a part of the city without growing up there. Then again, it also made me wonder how Key and I had been sources, or friends, or something, for years and we'd never even considered setting foot in the other's home.

"This is it?" she asked as we entered the office where Henniman first told me about the Twilight Four case a few days earlier. "This looks like a storage closet."

I rolled my eyes, even though she wasn't wrong. Sit-down meetings weren't a common occurrence for my PI business, even when I had actual business. When I was helping the cops, they didn't really want to be seen coming and going from my place. When Key had hired me the year before, I'd done most of my work in the field.

I pointed to the knockoff Ikea chair facing my desk, the only other item in the room besides the two filing cabinets. Even the walls were bare, except for the one framed article that sat opposite the desk. The last good thing I did at the *Signal-Intelligencer*.

"I'm not sitting in that," Key said. "That thing looks like it's gonna collapse any second."

"It hasn't collapsed in a while," I said, promptly sliding into the chair that was really a stool with a U-shaped metal backing held in place by a washer and screw on each side.

"See?" I said, tugging at the backing, smiling right up until the second it gave way and I crashed onto my burned shoulder.

Key laughed hard enough that she needed to cover her mouth. I peeled myself off the floor and leaned on the stool portion that was still standing while she waltzed over to my desk chair and took a seat.

"You gonna tell the councilwoman this counts as hazard pay?" I asked.

"We're trading in favors, Russell. You're not getting paid," she said. Story of my life.

"You also haven't done anything yet," she continued.

"Then let's get started," I said, walking over to her side of my desk and pulling the envelope Lynch gave me out of a drawer. "Who's in this photo?"

"She's not the problem," Key replied.

I traced my finger over the woman caught in a lip-lock with Mariana Pereira. She couldn't have been older than twenty-five. Younger than me, but still stuck in the same generation that winced every time we looked at our bank accounts.

"Lynch said she was a staffer. You pay her enough that Lynch couldn't buy a story out of her?" I asked. "Also, by the way, the fuck is the councilwoman doing messing around with a staffer?"

"The girl's only two years younger than Mari. It was years ago anyway. She made a mistake," Key replied. "It started at the League of Municipalities in Atlantic City. From what I hear, that's two days of meetings that ends in a weekend-long city government version of spring break. Mariana said it evolved into a bit of a fling. Maybe a few months, but it never got complicated. They both knew what they were after. She left the team on good terms."

"And stayed on good terms?" I asked.

Her expression soured.

"Key, we're, like, twenty minutes into me working with you on this," I said. "Don't hold out on me."

"She died, Russ," Key responded. "About a year later. Sideswiped by a drunk driver in Wall while visiting her family. It was completely unrelated, obviously, but…"

"If a story gets out about Mariana sleeping with a staffer who turned up dead, the conspiracy nuts will run with it," I replied.

Key nodded. The amount of people dumb enough to use words like "sheeple" or affix a Q to their bumper in Newark was mercifully small, but it wasn't insignificant.

"So, you guys have no leads? No ideas?" I asked.

"Well, we know the how, but not the who," Key replied. "A few months ago, Mariana started getting alerts on all her devices. All her social media. Account logins from unrecognized devices. It started during a council meeting, so she wasn't checking her phone."

That had to have been done on purpose.

"She didn't notice until hours later," Key continued. "We went through every account. No messages were sent. Nothing was deleted, but whoever went looking probably had at least two hours to go through Mariana's private conversations uninterrupted, and she isn't exactly shy."

"Plenty of time to find things to fill other envelopes," I replied. "Also, back up. Was she getting password reset notices? Or just the login e-mails."

"The latter. Which means it was someone who knew, or could guess, her password," Key replied.

"So maybe it's personal, not professional," I replied. "An ex?"

"That's where she wants us to start," Key replied.

I leaned forward on the broken stool, rubbing two fingers on my temples. Pestering a politician's ex-lovers to determine their potential risk to her campaign was the exact PR-type task I'd always dreaded. I was going to hate this, but then again, Key was going to hate what I asked her to do.

"You're sure you can deliver on Cynthia Bell?" I asked.

"Once we take care of—"

"No, not once we take care of anything. I need her and Abel Musa in the same room tomorrow," I said.

"Russell…"

"Key. Time's a factor here. For both of us. Musa's dying. And you don't know how long Lynch is going to wait to try to do something with these photos again," I said. "You didn't sound all that sure you could deliver Cynthia for me, so I asked Bill for advice."

"Bill Henniman?" she asked. "I'm not working with that piece of shit."

At least there was one thing they'd agree on.

"Just like I told you I wouldn't work for a politician?" I asked. "C'mon Key. I'm holding my nose. You owe me the same. He thinks he knows how you can convince her to walk into that hospital room."

I told her what he'd said about Cynthia's lifelong desire to hear a confession.

"I am not gonna lie to that woman," Key said.

"You're only lying to set her up to hear a more important truth," I replied, hating myself for the way it sounded. "If we ever find out who really did this, she's going to learn it wasn't Musa anyway, right?

Key leaned back in my desk chair, eyed me for a second like she wanted to argue, but for once, I had the high ground in one of our disagreements. She nodded, and I left it at that, taking the silence as a yes.

After Key left, I spent the next few hours going through the list of Mariana Pereira's lost loves she'd put together for me. Background checks, lawsuits, arrest records, social media. Whatever I could find to determine what they had to gain, or lose, from throwing knives into the councilwoman's back.

. The first name on it was Marisa Latyn, Mariana's longest and apparently most serious relationship since she'd been elected. They'd been together about a year, cutting things off not long before Mariana announced her mayoral bid. Key said they kept their relationship out of the public eye, and I had to wonder if Mariana ended it due to fear of her sexuality becoming a campaign issue.

LexisNexis—the public records dragnet that saves journalists, investigators and attorneys hours of leg work each year—told me Ms. Latyn had never been arrested or sued, at least not in New Jersey. Her mailing address came back to downtown Jersey City, and it hadn't changed in three years. She was local, but she had to be making good money to afford a place in a gentrification hotbed like that.

Latyn's Facebook and Instagram pages weren't public, and if she had a Twitter account, I couldn't easily find it. I pulled up the Essex County Registrar's website next, and after a few errant clicks on some poorly worded tabs, I found the campaign finance page. I ran the last name Latyn, and found two $500 donations to the Pereira campaign that appeared to be from the councilwoman's ex. Nothing came up under Watkins's donors.

It was possible she made the donations as cover, but it was also possible I'd get hit by lightning while doing a handstand, just not likely.

I moved to the next name: Leslie Canino, an on-again, off-again dance partner Key said had been mostly off for the past two years. There had been the occasional late-night Facebook message, but the councilwoman had no interest in rekindling things.

Spurned love would have made sense as a motive. But Leslie's Facebook page was public, as was her album of profile pictures. The last three showed the future Mrs. Canino smiling as a man dropped to one knee in front of her, blushing in a wedding dress and then pressing her hand to what looked like a baby bump. All the pictures had been posted in the past two years, which made me wonder if her now-husband was a then-boyfriend when Leslie and the councilwoman had their dalliance. Seemed like Leslie would be risking a lot to expose her relationship with Mariana.

It went on like that for another hour. Me scrolling down Key's list. A public record or Internet search disqualifying a name. Frustrated and needing a bit of a break, I did what came naturally to anyone in their early thirties when they had a difficult work task to tackle: I started dicking around on Facebook.

Just not my own.

Mariana had three pages. One a sanitized "official" profile of Councilwoman Pereira posing in front of city hall with a confident smile. Another seemed to be the Facebook hub for her mayoral campaign. Neither of those interested me. They were probably run by interns.

The third one, with her last name intentionally misspelled, showed a slightly younger Mariana, arms draped around two friends in what looked to be a bar, a much looser smile spread across her face. Like she wasn't entirely sure the flash was coming.

This was probably her personal page, but the terms of my potential new employment didn't come with a Facebook friendship. At least not yet.

Key could probably fix that, but I wanted to poke around without her over my shoulder. An ex who wanted to cause headaches for Mariana might have kept tabs on her through social media, and he or she would know the real accounts. I tried my luck on Twitter, though the only account that obviously belonged to Mariana had a blue check mark and the language on it screamed public relations team.

MariPosa872 on Instagram had some potential. The profile picture was the same image from the councilwoman's personal Facebook page. I recognized the Spanish word for butterfly, but maybe the handle was more a play on the councilwoman's name. Either way, it was vague enough that it wouldn't have come up on a cursory search of "Mariana Pereira." But a few competent reporters I knew followed the account, and so did Key. Not that they needed to. The page was public. The councilwoman was going to need to learn better Internet discipline if she wanted to be mayor.

I scrolled down and found pictures uploaded years ago, from the early stages of Mariana's entry into political life. There were college graduation pictures, workout pictures, some images that might have been taken after more than two drinks had been consumed.

The mouse wheel wandered through years of photos, until I slowed down around late 2017. The League of Municipalities' annual conference was in November, when Key said Mariana's fling with her staffer started. Sure enough, I found a picture of the woman from Lynch's envelope and the councilwoman clinking glasses in workout clothes, smiling over a caption that read "Brunch After Barre With The Best."

The picture didn't tell me anything about their relationship, but one look at Denise's finely toned body in yoga pants made it obvious why the councilwoman wasn't thinking too clearly about the politics of their affair. I briefly stopped to think about the last time I'd been on a date, then went back to work before I had a chance to come up with an answer I didn't like.

The photo had about one hundred likes. I opened up a Word document and started scribbling down any names of interest, leaving off accounts that had a large number of mutual friends with Mariana. I whittled that down to about twenty, and then started checking them against the likes on other images where the councilwoman was either posing with another attractive woman or showing off her own form. After a sampling of about thirty-five pictures over a few years, one account kept popping up over and over that didn't have any mutuals with Mariana. The same account that seemed to have stopped liking pictures after Mariana announced she was running for mayor.

I clicked on the profile for Agony Doll. The woman behind the page had posted picture after picture of herself in corsets, modified and mutilated wedding dresses, and black cross earrings. She didn't smile, so much as gasped or smirked in each image. She was incredibly attractive, but also kind of terrifying. I assumed that was the point. Other photos showed her wearing black headphones, tinkering with knobs while purple light and shadow filled the frame.

I ran "Agony Doll" through a search engine and came across a music blog that identified her as a dark wave, synthpop DJ whose real name was Celia Cain. Before my imagination got out ahead of the facts, I went back to LexisNexis and ran that name. I got two hits for an arrest and a petition for a restraining order in Passaic County Superior Court.

William Paterson University was in Passaic County. Mariana, according to her campaign page, had graduated from Willie P. I couldn't see the files without driving to Paterson, but I thought back to a few hours earlier. Tiago shouting in the restaurant about his daughter's sexuality being a college phase.

Agony Doll's Instagram was back on my screen. I looked at the last image posted. It was the bill for her next performance, later that night, at a venue called QXT.

People are always surprised when I remind them Newark has a goth club.

Especially one so close to city hall.

CHAPTER
TWELVE

THERE WAS A long line outside QXT, filled with enough people sporting black boots, garters, dreadlocks, latex and leather to make the cast of *The Matrix* blush.

I didn't have the wardrobe to hover around that crowd for too long without drawing attention, and attention is bad when you're trying to have a private conversation with the woman whose presence is the reason for the line.

Downtown Newark tends to clear out at night unless there's a Devils game drawing thousands to the Prudential Center. But with The Rock's lights dimmed, the entire neighborhood was a shadow: darkened buildings, shuttered storefronts and yawning, vacant parking lots. The only activity around the neighborhood was the old sandstone building with the ominous black doors that swung out to the sidewalk.

If you weren't in line for QXT, you had almost no reason to be around. Every leather Daddy hat, chainmail corset attachment and mohawk turned my way as I trudged up Mulberry. It wasn't their attention I wanted though. It was the guy with the bullseye tattoo on his forehead at the door.

The heavyset Black man with the shaved head and the frosted white contact lenses fit the part of QXT's gothic guardian. He was short and chubby, but eighty percent of what hid under his trench coat was muscle, not fat. His hair was close cropped and dyed green, and a ring sat hooked under his nostrils, peering down at the snakebite piercing near his chin.

The gargoyle might have dissuaded anyone else trying to cut the line and get access to the venue's top talent, but thankfully, I knew his first name. And he owed me a favor.

"Obie," I shouted as I stepped to him, drawing looks from the line.

An arm blocked my path. It belonged to the other security guard who was checking IDs. If Obie heard me, he wasn't acknowledging me, keeping his gaze on the line.

"Obie," I said again. "Your friend here seems a little confused."

I looked up at the head controlling the arm blocking my progress. Obie's partner was a white man with longer black hair that curled at the neck and a goatee that seemed shaved into a point at his chin. He was in the prototypical black security shirt and pants, not trying to fit the mood of the building. Probably just an extra hand for a busy night.

"There's a line," the other guy said. "You should get in it."

"I'm impatient. Also, I'm not here for…whatever that is," I replied. "Obie, I really don't have time for this."

Obie uncrossed his arms and turned his artificially deadened pupils my way. Then his hands shot up and under my armpits as I turned around, lifting me straight off the ground.

I felt my legs kicking helplessly as Obie flung me over his shoulder and carried me like a rolled-up carpet. A few members of the line started laughing, and the other guard seemed satisfied with the departure of my mouthy ass, unaware that I'd gotten exactly what I wanted.

When we were out of view and around the left side of QXT, Obie put me down gently, then immediately shoved me into a wall. The burned part of my shoulder took the brunt of it, sending pain radiating into my neck.

"If you want to keep having an in with the doorman," he said, his voice now an octave or two up from the cement mixer put-on he demonstrated out front, "then maybe stop bragging about it at the fucking door."

"I'm sorry, but you won't have to worry about that after tonight," I said. "I'm cashing in."

I didn't know Obie because I'd gotten really into The Cure in college or previously dated a woman from the leather and lace crowd. I'd never even been inside QXT.

But the cops had. Multiple times.

In the summer of 2015, relatively early in my *Signal-Intelligencer* career, there had been a spate of sexual assaults in a six- to eight-block radius around the nightclub. With almost no other businesses open in the area at that time of night, the NPD got it in their heads that someone was targeting women leaving QXT. They were right, but lacking for suspects, it didn't take long for them to zone in on the club's Black bouncer who was always sober and always aware of who was leaving the place in the worst condition each night.

It didn't help that the bouncer looked like he could punch through granite and went by Obsidian, which likely sounded like a gang nickname to a cop. The moniker actually referred to the black stone that formed from cooling lava.

With public pressure mounting on the police and city hall, someone got it in their heads to leak the identity of a "serious person of interest" in the case to me, hoping maybe a story about how police were closing in would stifle concerns. Except when I went to QXT to confront Obsidian, he got his manager to show me security footage they'd provided to the police. Security footage that, once the detectives got around to reviewing it, would show he was at his post the exact time two of the assaults took place.

I killed the story and decided to stop trusting leaks from Dameon

Lynch.

Obsidian, relieved to not be wrongfully linked to a serial rape investigation, told me to reach out if I ever needed anything. I laughed it off, wondering what possible favor I'd ever need from the head of security at a goth nightclub. Right up until the second I did.

"I need a minute with your headliner," I said, rubbing at my still throbbing shoulder.

"Agony Doll?" he asked. "You're writing about the scene now?"

I didn't know exactly what scene he was referring to, but it seemed Obie thought I still worked for the *Signal-Intelligencer*. Guess he hadn't picked up the paper in a while. For once, I was thankful for declining readership. Now, I knew what string to pull.

"Not exactly. I don't really want to get into it right now, but she's being accused of some things and I haven't been able to get a hold of her through her website or on the phone and, well, if she doesn't say something, then…" I let the sentence trail off, not wanting to make the lie too elaborate.

"You can't just wait to talk to her after the show?" Obie asked.

"Middle of the night after a set doesn't sound like the best time for an interview," I replied.

"Maybe I can help you get in contact with her another day. I'm sure the managers have a cell number or something if they booked her," he said.

"Obie, man, you know better than anyone how this stuff could go if I don't have her response in the first story."

His white capped eyes wandered down the alley, toward what looked like a service door. He was on the hook.

"It's just that… she's got fans. Some of them are creepy. She's not gonna like being approached at random," he said.

I wanted to comment on the idea of me being creepy as compared to the Transylvanian delegation out front, but then realized I was the one out of place here.

"I'll be delicate, I promise," I said. "You're doing a good thing for her here, Obie."

He scratched at his nose and narrowed his eyes, before nodding slowly. He walked over to the service door and pounded on it twice, waited a beat and then smacked it twice more. It opened.

"I better be," he replied. "This makes us even. And if you do anything to distress her, I'm going to treat you like anyone else who isn't supposed to be back there. Understand?"

I nodded.

"Down the hall, make a right, second door. It's the closest thing we have to a green room," he said.

I followed his instructions, moving through mostly darkened passageways toward the pulsing beats and droning synthesizers that had to be emanating from the main room. Occasional beams of purple and white mood lighting were all I had to make sure I didn't trip over anything.

The second door on the left was cracked slightly, a streak of fluorescent light peeking out into the hall. I nudged the door a bit with my foot and waited for any kind of response. When nothing came, I tried my luck a little further and stepped into the room.

The green room, as Obie called it, was really just a place the venue seemed to be stacking spare parts. There was an old couch, a cooler full of what looked like the best of a Rite Aid's beer selection, and a wide mirror where I found the woman I assumed to be Agony Doll.

She was focused on her eyeliner and didn't seem to notice me. She wore a pink corset, red thigh-high boots, and the kind of makeup that seemed to absorb the light of the room and spit it back out. Her platinum-colored hair framed her face and fell toward her shoulders, stopping about halfway down her neck. I could only see the side of her face, but her lipstick appeared to be green.

I waited there a second, hoping she'd notice me on her own, not wanting to do anything approaching sneaking up behind a woman wearing what most people would barely consider clothing.

"Ms. Cain?" I asked.

She didn't react. The song in the front of the room had picked up, a blare of synth and haunting guitar likely to swallow anything quieter than a shout.

"Ms. Cain!" I tried again, turning up the volume.

Agony Doll's shoulders twitched. The makeup pencil she was running across her face stopped moving.

"I can hear you. I'm just ignoring you," she said. "No one is supposed to be back here."

"No offense, but this doesn't really look like a 'follow the rules' kind of place," I replied.

She put down the pencil and turned my way, revealing a face that looked younger than the date of birth I'd spotted in court records. Maybe that was where she took the "Doll" half of her stage name from. Celia Cain looked like she was twenty-five going on fifteen, in spite of her sex fantasy attire. Maybe that was the point.

"So, you snuck into my dressing room, now you're being judgy, and I don't even know who you are or what you want," she said. "I've done enough shows to know this is the part where I call for security and the creepy guy gets dumped onto the sidewalk."

"Security let me in here, Celia," I said.

"Bullshit," she replied.

"It's true. I'm a reporter. I've written about this place before and I know some people. But that's not important," I said. "I'm sorry if I upset you, sneaking in like this. Not the best look, I agree. I just had a question for something I'm working on, and you happened to be here tonight, and I didn't want to wait."

Concern crept onto her face. The optics were not lost on me, especially after what Obie told me about her having obsessive fans. I was a lot bigger than her. We were alone. Whatever song the warm-up act was playing was barreling toward its high point. There was probably a part of her brain wondering if anyone would hear her scream.

I stepped further into the room but then moved to the right, giving her a clear path to the door.

"If you don't like what I have to say, nothing's stopping you from leaving or telling me to fuck off," I said. "I'm not one of those guys."

"That's, like, the motto of those guys," she replied.

She wasn't wrong. But I wasn't convincing her, and it didn't matter. She wasn't going to like me very much in a matter of seconds anyway.

"I just wanted to ask you about your relationship with Mariana Pereira," I said.

"Didn't we already do this?" she asked, annoyance spreading across her face as she abandoned her makeup and headed towards the door.

More than a little confused by her question, I broke my promise on instinct and started to step in her way, reaching out a hand toward her arm to slow her.

Agony Doll lived up to her namesake, driving the point of her knee into the meat of my right thigh, nearly crumpling me. She slipped by as my leg gave out, turning left, toward the stage. I hopped up and tried to follow, but she moved quicker in heels than I could after she'd bashed my quadriceps.

I followed the echo of her boots and the rising voice of a singer who sounded like a cross between Ian Curtis and a ghost into the main room. Agony's distinctive platinum hair still shined in the light bath coming from the overhead rig, and it was all I had to track her into the tangle of bodies dancing and mashing together near the QXT stage. Whoever was up there was in all black, sporting a leather jacket and sunglasses inside, one hand bouncing on what looked like an electric keyboard.

Each note seemed to pulse through the crowd, adding to its energy, making it harder to push through as they all surged toward the stage. I couldn't see Agony Doll, but I kept moving against the procession, assuming she was looking for security. If she got to Obie before me, he was going to do a lot worse than he had when I got to the club.

About halfway to the door, I heard a woman's voice cry out, loud enough that it overtook the song. I looked left and saw the shape of a man reaching for Agony Doll.

She recoiled from his touch, and he stumbled into my path, forcing me to stop short as she opened up the distance between us.

The guy called out to her and she spun around, a mix of anger and panic on her face. Maybe Obie was serious about her having obsessive fans. Maybe she had reason to be worried when I showed up in her dressing room.

She tried to reward the man's interest with a backhand just as I pushed past him. One of her knuckles caught me in the left eye, and I was starting to see why Mariana got a restraining order. She could handle herself better than someone dressed like a *Blade Runner*-themed stripper should have been able too.

Half-blind on my left and partially hobbled on my right, I stumbled toward the door. Agony made it through first. I heard shouting, but I couldn't tell if it was about me or the other guy or both. When I made it to the door, the sight of Obie's tree trunk arm swinging my way clarified that.

The bad leg made it easier for me to fall forward, and I executed a far less athletic than it looked dodge of Obie's baseball bat of a limb, forward rolling to the sidewalk. I got to my feet and backed up toward the street, finding Agony to my right hollering to the other guard and pointing at me. Obie made sure I had no room to escape his next move.

"What did I tell you?" he asked.

"All I did was ask a question!" I shouted back.

"I already told your boss no!" Agony screamed. "Why won't you scumbags just leave her alone?"

My boss?

Obie got his hands on my shirt and threw me up against a car.

"You fucked up, man," he said.

"There's a mistake!" I shouted back. "My boss is harassing her? Does that make any sense to you? The newspaper is harassing a DJ?"

Obie paused for a second. I looked over at Agony Doll, who still looked pissed, but not entirely sure at who.

"Newspaper?" she asked.

"Lady, if someone's been asking you questions about this, they've got nothing to do with me," I said. "I didn't even get to tell you why I'm here."

"You mentioned Mari," she started.

I held a finger up to my lips.

"And if I wanted her name being shouted in public, I wouldn't have asked you about her in private," I replied, starting to move toward her before Obie's forearm cut me off.

His limb moved like a piston, sending all of me back into the car again. The burned shoulder connected with the roof, causing me to grimace and clutch at the torched skin. I fell to my hands and knees, not sure where to clutch in pain, until her boots filled my field of vision. For a brief second, I was worried she was gonna kick me or stomp on me and live up to her outfit, until I realized she was the only thing keeping Obie from doing that.

"Hang on," she said, stepping toward him, putting the same hand that had slapped me on his arm. "Let him go."

He looked back and forth between us, then toward the other guard, who just shrugged. This was probably more bullshit than they got paid to deal with.

A minute later, Obie walked us back over to the side alley where he'd first let me sneak into the back of the club, a move he likely regretted.

"Who are you?" she asked.

"My name's Russell Avery. I used to work for the *Signal-Intelligencer*," I said, briefly looking at Obie, watching fresh fury appear in his dead pupils as he realized I'd lied to him. "And I'm trying to figure out if someone is harassing the councilwoman and why. You two used to date, right?"

She stayed quiet.

"I saw the restraining order, Celia, that's why I'm here," I said. "Someone's trying to out Mariana."

Agony rolled her eyes, then motioned toward Obie with two fingers in front of her lips. He produced a cigarette on command.

"Maybe that's a sign she should just be honest about who she is," Celia said.

"That's not up to me. Or you," I said. "But someone apparently thinks it's up to them. There are pictures floating around, and given your history, I had to ask."

"Our history. You sound like her. Like it was something cold, or professional," she said, taking a drag, letting out a sad little laugh. "You know that restraining order fucked me up for a bit. We were together for a year. That was an L-word serious relationship, not some experiment like she told her family. I wanted to meet them, that's what messed it all up. She said it wasn't time. I wouldn't let it go. So, she went to court. Made me out to be some kind of stalker, just so she wouldn't have to face that asshole father of hers."

"Doesn't exactly sound like you're over it," I said.

"I can be over it and still pissed when people keep asking me about it," she said. "It hurt. It sucked. But that doesn't mean I'd out her. That's nobody's choice but hers. That's what I told the other guy."

"And that other guy was…?"

"I don't know. Someone else who didn't fit in here. Even less than you," she said, waving her cigarette toward the club. "Wore a suit. A lot of hairspray. Looked like he was disgusted to even be here. He wanted to know about Mari's past, and he was willing to pay. I told him to go fuck himself."

Dameon Lynch's office was four blocks away. I wasn't surprised, but I was annoyed about being back to square one. After Celia, I was out of ex-girlfriends.

"I've got a pretty good idea who that is. He's who I'm trying to stop," I replied. "I thought you were the one feeding him information."

I looked toward Obie, who appeared to be fantasizing about removing my head from my shoulders, slowly.

"Banned for life," he growled.

"That's fine. *The Addams Family* is on Netflix," I shot back.

I turned to leave, my back tensing up with each step. I was going to feel every inch of Obie in the morning, and that was the least of my problems. If Key found out I'd come up empty, she might stop Cynthia Bell from going to Abel Musa, stonewalling the investigation I actually cared about.

"Wait," Celia said.

I turned back, watched her drop the cigarette and grind it out slow.

"This might be a longshot, but there was someone else from back then who wasn't too thrilled with Mariana seeing me. With her seeing a woman," she said. "Though it'd be fucked up if he was the one doing what you think someone's doing."

"He?" I asked.

"One night we were messing around at her family's place. Her parents were out of town," she said. "Her younger brother walked in on us and freaked out."

"She has a brother?"

"Had," Celia shot back. "I wasn't the only one who got thrown away."

Mariana Pereira had a brother.

One she neglected to tell me about.

One who might have shared Tiago's weirdness about her sexual orientation.

One who had been cut out of the family in a manner ugly enough that Mariana's ex didn't hesitate to suggest he was behind the circulating pictures and texts that were costing the councilwoman sleep.

Now her problems were keeping me up. I really needed to crash after my visit to QXT, between the burns and the way Obie had rag dolled me. But the why of it kept bouncing around my head, tiptoeing around my brain, making the floors creak.

Mariana had an estranged brother who might have a less than progressive view on her choice in romantic partners. How was he not at the top of the list Key gave me to look into?

I dropped my laptop onto my bed, laid on my side and absent

mindedly searched for information about the younger Pereira, pretending the effort might tire me out again.

The name Angel Pereira was a little too common, turning up way too many results. Without a date of birth or anything more specific, he'd be invisible to me in court record searches or criminal databases or any of the other quick scans I could do. But when I started joining the name with Tiago's and Formosa and Marisqueira Pereira, I stumbled upon some archived pages of the *Luso-Americano*, Newark's Portuguese language newspaper.

I couldn't read a word, but the magic of Google meant a readable, if Frankenstein-ed, English translation was just one right click away. An article which focused on the opening of Marisqueira Pereira in 1989 spoke of Tiago's ascent from waiting tables at various restaurants in the neighborhood to owning one of his own. Even back then, Tiago looked strong and determined, never smiling but also far from angry, just focused. The article referenced how the rising restauranteur's family represented the changing dynamics of the Ironbound, how it had grown from a landing spot for Portuguese immigrants to the hub of Newark's Latin and South American communities. His wife, Clara, was a beaming Brazilian woman who appeared wrist deep in dough in one of the featured images. Apparently, she'd tweaked his recipe for Pasteis de Nata, the pastries I'd been devouring for years.

Unfortunately, Clara's improvements to the family's famous dessert would mark one of the last times she appeared in the *Luso-Americano*'s pages. Two clicks took me two years into the future, where I found her obituary. Breast cancer had cut her life short at the age of forty-seven. Tiago's insult to his daughter, about how her mother would have judged her life choices, seemed doubly cutting now. He'd invoked a ghost.

My eyes wandered back to the photos of the younger versions of Mariana and Angel, which showed brother and sister locked in one of those way too tight childhood hugs, smiles only interrupted by lost baby teeth.

The kids grew up through the pictures attached to each piece.

There was string bean Angel, with chestnut eyes and black hair flipped up, probably around age twelve in a soccer jersey. A slightly younger Mariana standing up on a chair to help her dad clear a table in an obviously staged, but nonetheless adorable, snapshot. Teenage Angel, skinny but not sickly, dressed up in the white collared shirt and black pants I'd seen the Marisqueira Pereira busboys sporting the other day. Black hair on the longer side then, curling a bit at the neck. A fully grown Angel probably in his early twenties, still smiling but in a way that seemed just a bit forced, as Tiago mugged for the grand opening of Formosa, the bakery and second business that locked in the Pereira as neighborhood institutions in the mid-1990s.

Something clicked. My eyes bounced between Angel's face and the year in the caption. The brown eyes, the smirk. The way he leaned on the wall with the kind of confidence that said, "I'm holding it up, not the other way around." I'd seen that before.

I jumped out of bed and half ran, half stumbled into my office, opening the desk drawer, swatting aside the envelope of blackmail Lynch wanted to use against Mariana, looking for a different picture, hoping I was remembering it wrong.

The image still smelled a little of bleach, the sting forcing me to recoil just a bit. A warning of danger just like the first time.

Roust and the other person in the picture I'd found weren't wearing dress clothes. They were wearing work uniforms. For a restaurant.

I had seen Angel Pereira's face before. Inside the photo in Isiah Roust's apartment. Right before it caught fire around me.

CHAPTER
THIRTEEN

THE PICTURE DIDN'T mean anything.

At least that's what I told myself over and over again as I lay in bed, waging a futile battle with my brain's off switch for several hours, eyes finally slamming shut just as the sun came up.

Isiah Roust and Angel Pereira were in a picture together. So what? They'd both grown up in Newark. They worked at the same restaurant. Maybe they went to high school together and Angel got his buddy a job.

There was no reason to think Angel had anything to do with the Twilight Four, other than the fact that I'd only learned his name while I was looking into the case. That I'd only found his picture in the home of one of the only leads I had on the case. That it was soaked in the same liquid that set the fire that served as Roust's only response to any of my questions.

Nope. Angel only mattered to me as part of the job I'd taken in exchange for Key's help. At least that's what I told myself when my sleep-starved brain reactivated at 9 a.m. When my fingers wandered back to Nexis and started looking for Angel Pereiras who would be in their forties. Angel Pereiras with past addresses in Newark. Specifically, ones who used to live in the apartment above Formosa.

Two coffees and one questionable diner omelet later, I was awake enough to drive to the Clifton address that I was pretty sure belonged to the Angel Pereira I needed to talk to. Maybe he was just trying to profit off his estranged sister's dirty laundry. Or maybe that picture wasn't a coincidence and he knew where Isiah Roust was. Maybe neither.

But I wouldn't know unless I talked to him, and I had four hours to kill until Key brought Cynthia Bell to University Hospital. Until I could bait a still grieving woman into a room with a non-existent promise of justice so I could pump her for information.

Maybe I deserved those burns on my shoulder.

Angel's apartment appeared to be above a strip club disguised as a corner store. Delilah's, which sat on an otherwise forgettable corner three blocks up from the Passaic River, had a roll down gate over its entrance and its unlit neon sign announced a lunch special. It didn't say what that entailed, and I didn't want to meet anyone who would know. I'd always hated strip clubs and anything strip club adjacent, but this setup looked so sad I actually felt a little pity for whoever was going to have to open up the place later in the day.

I got out of my car and patted each of my pockets. The left one contained the envelope Dameon Lynch had given me. The right one had the bleach-scented polaroid from Isiah Roust's apartment. Hopefully, I'd only need one of them.

The thought of Mariana Pereira's brother having any connection to the Twilight Four case, however tangential, should have excited me. It was another hook for the story I eventually hoped to write. The story that was supposed to act as a defibrillator for my journalism career, even though the vague pitch e-mails I'd sent to a few old reporter friends had yet to earn any responses.

But as I entered the apartment complex, stepping on seafoam

green carpet that smelled like it had soaked up every mistake ever made in the building, I couldn't shake the idea of what would happen if Dameon Lynch found the same picture. He'd been desperate enough for a hit piece on Mariana that he'd turned to me, and once that failed, he'd hired a random idiot to bring up the pictures in a public forum.

The Twilight Four case was a serious weakness for his boss, and Lynch knew it. He'd treat that picture of Roust and Mariana's estranged brother like the Zapruder film if he found it. The facts wouldn't matter at that point. Even if Roust and Angel hadn't spoken since that picture was taken, Lynch would find a way to glue the issues together. Especially if he found out what happened down in Asbury.

Jogging up the stairs to the third floor, I froze at the door leading into the hallway. I needed to get my head right. I didn't know shit about Angel's connection to the Twilight Four case, if any, and that didn't matter right now.

What I knew was that he'd had a falling out with his family. That Mariana's ex seemed to think it had something to do with his sister's sexual preferences. And I knew there were pictures of Mariana and another woman floating around that could have only been accessed by someone who knew one or two of her passwords. Someone close to her.

This was about Mariana. If Isiah Roust happened to be chilling on Angel's couch, so be it. Maybe I'd call the police then. Maybe I'd set Angel's apartment on fire and see if Roust could think as fast on his feet as we had.

But I wouldn't get any answers unless I talked to him. And that meant getting the door knock right.

There are a lot of unglamorous parts of journalism that any honest reporter will tell you they hate. Stakeouts. Contacting a crime victim's loved ones. Transcribing recorded interviews would have its own wing in a museum in Journalism Hell.

But the blind door knock was among the most frustrating because you could fail so quickly. In my experience, the door got slammed within fifteen seconds unless you did something that made the person on the other side incapable of exiting the conversation.

Each time I pounded on what I presumed to be Angel Pereira's apartment door, my hand instantly traveled back to my left pocket, ready to draw what was holstered there. It took four bangs before I heard the knob start to turn.

The face that appeared behind it lacked the confidence and knowing smile I'd seen in the picture next to Roust. The Angel Pereira who answered the door had his neck hunched toward his shoulders, eyes wet and narrow, face the textbook definition of exhausted. The long hair was still there, but it was thinning, silver lines not exactly well hidden in the strands that fanned out to the sides of his head and fell toward his ears. There were little red splotches on his face, burst capillaries, the kind that form when you wretch up the events of the night before. He was wearing a polo shirt with "Delilah's" embroidered over the left side of his chest, meaning he was either an employee or a regular of the C-list strip joint downstairs, neither a fitting fate for a member of the Ironbound's first family.

Angel looked up at me with a face undecided between surprise and outrage.

"The fuck are you banging for?" he asked.

Words were not going to keep him from shutting the door. So, I held up two of the photos of his sister in positions that no brother outside of Joaquin Phoenix's weird ass in *Gladiator* would ever want to see.

He wiped his hands down his face, tungsten rings on each middle finger pressing toward his corneas. Angel shook his head, blinked a bunch and took a long look at me, maybe trying to focus in on my face over the images of his sister no brother should want to view.. A reasonable choice.

"You recognize these?" I asked.

Angel's eyes narrowed. He checked over his shoulder then turned back to me. I tried to lean in and see what caught his attention but his palm found my chest fast and shoved me back. I stumbled, more out of surprise than anything else. He stepped into the hallway, revealing stained cargo shorts below the Delilah's polo and a pair of bare feet with nails so mangled they belonged in a scared straight program for podiatrists.

"You sure you want to have this conversation out here?" I asked, holding the photos up in his face again.

"Who the fuck are you and why the fuck do you have those?"

I flashed an old business card from the *Signal-Intelligencer*, handed it to Angel and then tried to stitch as much truth into the lie as possible.

"I'm a reporter in Newark. Some people don't think your sister should be mayor. Same people think photos like this are why," I said. "Same people said you might agree and might have more to say."

"My sister is gonna be an amazing mayor and those pictures don't mean shit," he replied. "Can you fuck off now? Or do I have to, like, officially say no comment or something?"

"Technically the first sentence was a comment."

"You woke me up with naked pictures of my sister," he replied. "Getting cute isn't gonna help your cause."

I wasn't sure if he was being genuinely defiant about the pictures or just covering his own ass. Either way, I had his attention now and I had to keep it.

"Listen, man, your sister is on her way to running the biggest city in the state. It's my job to vet people like that. I know what these pictures are and I know what kind of scandal they might entail," I said. "What I don't understand is why I keep hearing you're the reason they're floating around. Or why you're living above a strip club you look like you got thrown out of last night when your family runs two of the most successful restaurants in Newark."

Angel's eyes wandered up to the ceiling and the muscles around his jaw tensed up.

"Those aren't the same story," he said.

"I can write both."

"My family's drama counts as news now?"

I took a step closer to him.

"Your sister wins that race, and your family is news. Period. Anything and everything in your history becomes fair game," I replied, making sure to strain the last sentence. Just in case that other picture in my pocket meant anything.

Angel's face didn't change, but his reply didn't come as quick as the earlier ones had. He looked like he was thinking before talking for a brief second, a habit I might do well to pick up one day.

"What makes you think I put those pictures out there?" he asked. "What makes you think I'd betray my sister like that?"

"'Cause you haven't denied it," I said, then decided to pile on before he could push back on that. "And because the guy who gave them to me said you might have more to offer. For the right price."

I almost winced, throwing out a lie that huge, but it was a worthwhile gambit. Dameon Lynch had used bribes to kill my stories before. It stood to reason he'd do the same to gin up controversy against a political opponent.

"He tell you how much?" Angel asked, an embarrassed, almost resigned look blooming across his face as he did.

I wanted to judge him for selling out his sister like that. But a small part of me wondered how many missed rent checks I was above his rung on the ladder.

I stayed quiet and simply shook my head no.

"Well, ask him. Then come back here with double that if you want the rest of the pictures," Angel replied.

"Double?" I asked.

"The price went up because I love my sister, and I'm pretty sure you're an asshole," he said. "But I'll make you a deal. You want to know why I'm living out here? Then I'll talk to you about my scumbag father all day. Free of charge."

sat in the lobby of University Hospital the next afternoon waiting to see four different people, wondering which one was going to be the angriest with me when the day was over.

Up in his hospital room, Abel Musa was waiting too, probably counting down the final few minutes before a face-to-face he'd hoped for every day since his arrest.

Musa wanted a reunion, a reckoning, maybe both. I doubted he'd get either.

I'd done what he asked and convinced Cynthia Bell to speak with a man she believed murdered her younger sisters.

But Musa didn't know how I'd pulled that off. When he learned she was there for a confession instead of a conversation, there was a good chance he would try to have me thrown out of the hospital like he did the first time.

That might be the only thing Cynthia and Musa would agree on once they figured out I'd arranged the meeting under false pretenses. Henniman had inspired the lie, and Key had passed it on in exchange for my help with her Dameon Lynch problem, but ultimately, I was the one who had moved the pieces around the board. When Cynthia understandably started screaming, they would point her in my direction.

Maybe Key would join in. She'd helped arrange this powder keg thinking my trip to QXT would end with me fixing her client's problems. Instead, my visit to the goth club had only exacerbated them. I fingered the photo of Angel Pereira in my pocket, thinking about how my last conversation with him was probably going to make my next conversation with Key deeply unpleasant.

I was relieved when Henniman walked through the building's automatic doors first. At least the lieutenant's baseline annoyance with me was something I was used to managing.

Bill was sporting a bandage over the right side of his forehead that partially covered his eyelid, drawing attention to the splotches of purple bruising on that side of his face, battle scars from our visit to

Asbury Park.

He looked steady on his feet, but the lights of the waiting room were still forcing him to squint. I reached for my shoulder, which was raw from Obie smashing the burned flesh there against a wall and a car the night before.

"You look better," I said.

"I look like shit," he replied.

I waited for Henniman to sit down, but he motioned toward the elevator.

"Uh, shouldn't we wait for the guest of honor?" I asked.

"Russell, I haven't seen Abel Musa since I watched a jury convict him of a crime he thinks I framed him for," he said. "We want him and Cynthia focused on each other, right? Then he's probably got some things to hash out with me first."

I checked my phone. Key had sent a text that she was on the way, but I had no idea from where.

"They'll be here soon," I said.

"Then we should hurry," he replied.

Henniman marched to the elevator, leaving me little else to do but follow.

Bill remained quiet until we got to Musa's room. He wasn't the kind of guy who engaged in small talk, but even his breathing seemed to slow as we got closer to the door. He stopped right at the entrance, closing his eyes, lightly bowing his head and mouthing something. His right fist clenched and unclenched several times. I couldn't tell if he was mumbling a prayer or a mantra, but the message seemed to be the same. Gimme strength. Or sympathy.

As we turned the corner, I noticed the hospital bed in Musa's room was empty. He was standing on the right side of the room, both hands wrapped around his IV pole for support, a practiced smile clinging to his face, quivering like the muscles there were straining to keep it in place.

He'd gotten hold of a black suit jacket and pants that hung loosely from his withered frame, the sleeves slack at his wrists like a priest's cloak. The pants were draped over his ankles, nearly obscuring the loafers on his feet. Musa's entire form was shaking, from either nerves or the strength it was taking to remain upright. It only made the whole getup look sadder, the suit moving like there was wind blowing through it. His hospital gown peeked out from under the breast of the blazer. Whichever one of the nurses brought him the suit had failed to find a matching dress shirt.

Musa looked like he'd gotten a last-minute invite to the prom, only to be stood up anyway. His pained smile gave out as he locked eyes with Henniman.

"What the hell is this?" Musa asked, his voice a throaty growl.

"Cynthia's coming. She's coming, I promise," I said. "Any minute. But Bill wanted to talk to you first."

"Who says I want to talk to him? I barely wanted to talk to you," he replied. "I want to talk to her. That's what you promised. That was the deal. This is…"

The excitement was too much for what little his body had left to give. Musa lurched forward, hands slipping from the IV pole. He was going to collapse. But as he crashed toward the ground, Henniman cut across the room with more speed than I thought the beat-down cop possessed, dropping to one knee and getting his body under Musa's falling frame.

Musa hooked an arm across Henniman's shoulders, using the lieutenant to prop himself back up, slowly regaining control of his failing body. It took a minute, and his breathing was labored, but Henniman eventually helped Musa return to the proud stance he'd wanted to present when Cynthia Bell arrived.

"Need to keep this sharp for when she gets here," Henniman said, trying to flatten any creases in the blazer as Musa stood upright.

"Last time I was in a suit around you, things didn't end so well for me," Musa spat back. "Don't touch me."

Henniman backpedaled, looking at me for a lifeline. I had

entirely too much practice apologizing, but this was a whole different stratosphere of fuck up from anything I'd experienced.

"I'm sorry," Bill said.

"You're sorry?" Musa said. "Sorry for...for what exactly? For ruining my life? Putting me in a hole with killers? Making me out to be a monster?"

"I'm sorry for—"

Musa held up a hand.

"Don't. Don't come here thinking we're gonna talk after all this time. I'm gonna talk. You're gonna listen," he said. "I'm dying. I'm dying and I'm happy about it. Do you have any idea what that's like?"

Bill shook his head no.

"Every day I wake up, I'm not Abel. Not to anyone outside my own head. I'm the Twilight Four killer," he said. "I'm some...shadow that massacred children. Children. I'm a bogeyman. That will never end. I have to die and hope I go somewhere where they know the truth."

Tears came from Musa's eyes, and they looked like the furious kind, the ones that felt so hot they might evaporate once they found skin.

"But that's what you did to me. Left me somewhere that dying is all I got for hope. That's on you," he said. "My clock is running out. All I got left is to try to explain this to Cynthia, to hope maybe I die innocent in her mind. That's why I got up this morning. Not for whatever you're here for. You're sorry now? You want forgiveness? Well, fuck you. This isn't about you."

Henniman just stood there, hands folded, head dipping almost imperceptibly in agreement. A year earlier, the man had stood next to me at a memorial for a kid killed as a result of his police department's desperation to protect itself, and he'd been almost unable to comprehend the role he played in that nightmare.

That version of Bill seemed to have gone missing, at least for the moment.

"I don't want your forgiveness, Abel. I don't think I'm ever going to be able to earn that," Henniman said. "All I know is I took this job to protect people like Cynthia. That's what I was trying to do when we first crossed paths. And I failed. You, and her. That's what I'm trying to make right. That's why I wanted to talk to you before she gets here. That's what today is about."

Musa looked over Henniman's shoulder at me.

"We had this conversation," he hissed. "You want to find the real killer, fine. But don't put it on me to help. It's too damn late for me and it ain't on me to fix."

"It's not too late for her though," Bill replied. "Cynthia deserves the answer, right? You told Russell you didn't want her thinking of you as a monster. Solving this thing, for real, is the only way to change that. Do you know how we got her to come today?"

Musa's eyes wandered toward me, widened and fearful.

"She thinks you're going to confess," I said. "I had to lie just to get her through the door, just so you could tell her your side."

Slowly, Musa unclasped one of his hands from the pole. His fingers shook and fluttered, almost tapping out a rhythm as he placed them across his chest. I watched something break in his expression, his righteous fury at Henniman melting away as he looked toward me. I thought he'd lash out or curse, but whatever was wound up in his chest stayed there. Barricaded in by the return of the smile he'd worn when we first showed up.

I turned around to find Cynthia Bell standing in the doorway. She was wearing a yellow Sunday dress that fit her broad form well, the bright color accentuating the shine from the earrings and choker she'd chosen. She looked elegant, except for her lips, which appeared to be curling into a scream.

"What did you just say?" she asked, staring right at me.

For every ounce of longing in Musa's eyes, there was an equal amount of hatred in Cynthia's. I'd wanted a confrontation in the hopes it would shake something loose from the last two living links to a decades-old crime. I'd engineered this. But it was still awful to see.

Cynthia turned to Key, briefly made eye contact with Musa, then looked away in disgust as Henniman came across the room to her now, clasping her hand.

"Detective," she said. "Bill. What's happening here? What's he saying?"

"Cynthia…" Musa said, his voice croaking when it tried to form a second word.

"Don't," she replied, keeping eyes trained only on the lieutenant. "They told me he was confessing. I don't want to hear his voice unless it's for that."

I took a step toward her, but Henniman held a hand up. He guided her to a lounge chair near Musa's bed, but she refused to sit down.

This was the moment Bill had been dreading. It was one thing for Henniman to carry the weight of his mistake. It was another to burden her with it.

"Cynthia," Henniman said. "I made you a promise when we first met, didn't I? Do you remember?"

She nodded, eyes registering something between realization and horror.

"I told you I'd follow this wherever it led. That no matter what, you'd know everything we found, when we found it," he said. "No matter how painful."

"Don't say it," she said, voice barely above a whisper but quaking with rage. "Don't take it from me."

Henniman took her hand in both of his, squeezing hard, drawing her focus.

"Cynthia. I was wrong," Bill said. "Someone lied. Roust lied. Abel didn't do this."

"No. No!" she screamed again, causing Key to rush over as Cynthia lurched toward Musa. "He…who else? Who else could have…?"

Cynthia recoiled, panicking, screaming "no" over and over again. Each howl got weaker, more resigned to the fact that her reality just got ripped out of her hands.

Musa dragged the IV pole as he moved toward her, nearly falling.

Cynthia kept sliding away from Henniman and his words and the truth she didn't want to hear, falling into a chair as she retreated.

Nurses ran in. They offered help, but the pain that Cynthia Bell and Abel Musa were experiencing was far beyond medicine.

CHAPTER
FOURTEEN

NO ONE MANAGED to speak for a solid five minutes. People tried. They just didn't succeed.

Twice, Abel Musa held up his hand, like he was waiting to be called on at school, hoping Cynthia might give him the chance to plead the case he'd been making for a decade. For as fierce as he'd been toward Henniman, the old man acted as frail as he looked around his ex.

Cynthia was too busy crying to acknowledge him. She was slightly hunched over, clutching something I hadn't noticed her carrying when she'd arrived. It was a bound book. A sticker bearing Weequahic High School's outdated logo—a brown-skinned Native American woman in a headdress—was visible on the cover.

Key patted Cynthia on the shoulder. Henniman tried to do the same but she slapped him away, briefly looking up to display eyes that were bulging and red and furious.

It took time, but slowly, her breathing returned to normal. Cynthia pressed her hands together in front of her face. To an outsider, it might have looked like a prayer pose, but I wondered if she was just keeping her lips from opening until it was safe for the rest of us to hear what was behind them.

"Tell me," she said, finally looking at Henniman. "Tell me all of it."

The lieutenant was red faced and flustered. Embarrassed. Maybe hurt. A stream of "ummms" and "wells" started to spill out of him.

"Well, Mrs. Bell, Bill came to me because—" I started.

"Not you," she said, eyes not moving off Bill. "Him. It was his job. His responsibility. He owes me that."

Her arm flew out to the side, one long nail aimed at Musa.

"Tell me why it's not him," she said. "Then tell me who it is."

"I can do one of those things," Bill replied. "The other is why you're here."

Henniman exhaled, then spilled everything into Cynthia Bell's lap. Isiah Roust's deceit. The prosecutor's office's decision to seek compassionate release before Musa could file an appeal that might make the lies public. The NPD's refusal to consider Musa might be the wrong man despite the credibility of the witness who put him away being ruined because the mayor couldn't afford the publicity hit. The department blocking Henniman from looking back on the case. The assumption that the edict not to dig deeper came from city hall. Henniman going to me. Us going to Roust. Our last lead literally going up in smoke.

When Bill finished, Cynthia made eye contact with Musa for what had to be the first time in a decade. Her gaze did not soften.

"It's still him," she said.

Musa looked like someone had slid a knife between his ribs. Bill and Key exchanged confused glances, possibly as perplexed by Cynthia's reaction as they were by the fact that they finally agreed on something.

"Maybe that other man did lie. Maybe you didn't actually confess. But it's still you," Cynthia said. "There's no one else it could be. This doesn't change anything."

"Cynthia," Bill started. "Without the confession, there's almost no evidence."

"There's no evidence it's anyone else," she spat back, jumping out of her seat. "This isn't... No. This just isn't happening."

She stepped to Musa. I was starting to regret this whole "make them talk and see what happens" plan.

"I know what you are. I know what you did to her," she said. "Even if they can't understand, you know what I know."

"Cyn, I'd never have hurt them," he said. "You know that. You know me."

He reached out to touch her, but she slapped him so hard and so fast that her hand was back at her side before Musa's face had time to register the hit.

"I knew you then. Not now. Don't call me Cyn. Don't touch me," she said. "Don't act like who you were, or who I thought you were. The man I knew? The one who loved me? He wouldn't orchestrate all this. He would admit what he did. He would give me peace."

Musa rubbed at the spot where she had struck him, dried out fingers turning his lips inside out.

"Peace? I know you're hurting, but don't talk to me about peace," he said. "The hell I've been through..."

"You don't know hell," she replied. "Hell is losing your family."

"I lost my family too. You, those kids, were my family," Musa shouted back. "You were at the trial, Cynthia. I didn't have no one. No one's visiting now! I'm alone because someone lied and too many people fell for it! You were desperate for an answer, I get it. But Roust is a liar. There's proof! There's more proof that I'm innocent than there ever was that I was guilty!"

Cynthia puckered her lips and exhaled through her nose, the flare loud like an animal's snarl.

"You want to talk about proof?" she asked. "We can talk about proof. You think I really spent all these years believing what I believe about Shayna's murder because some man I never heard of said so? You think it's that simple?"

"Why else would someone want them dead, then?" I asked. "If you know something, now's the time to tell us."

Cynthia glared at me, chewing the corner of her lip, neck flaring like she was choking on something.

"A few months after they vanished, I started to come unglued. The police weren't doing nothing. I was in Shayna's and Adriana's bedrooms one day, fixing things up, dusting, trying to make everything perfect for when they came home. Back when I thought it was just a matter of when," she said. "And I don't know what it was, if I just caught sight of a picture of Shayna or a rogue thought, but I just snapped. Started knocking things over, howling, crying like a banshee. No one else was home. No one came to stop me. And as I thrashed and started pulling things apart, I ripped one of her drawers out of her dresser and threw it at a wall. And something came flying out."

Something flickered in Musa's eyes. Cynthia held up the book she'd been carrying.

"Her diary. Hidden. You taught the kids that trick once, didn't you, Abel? How to make a false bottom, their own little hiding places? They were always so amazed by how handy my man was. So, of course, that's where she stuck her diary. I used to tease her all the time that she was too old to keep one, that she was of the age where she might be writing down things that it might be a problem for people to know. I was talking about my parents, but that was when I didn't know they'd die not knowing what happened to their daughter," Cynthia said. "About two months before they disappeared, she started writing entries about a man. Not a boy, and certainly not one she'd told any of us about. She kept referencing a love we wouldn't understand, one she needed to keep hidden. I didn't know what to make of it, until I got to one of the last entries. She was scared. She was panicking. Things had gotten out of her control and she needed help."

Cynthia's tongue flicked out of her lips before the next sentence, like she was spitting it up.

"Shayna was pregnant when she went missing," she said.

Henniman's hand shot toward Cynthia's shoulder. He didn't grab her, but he came close.

"How could you not tell me that?" Bill asked. "All this time, you don't think that was something that might have changed things?"

"What does it change, Bill?" she asked. "It's obvious he was…it was his. Why else would she hide it? Why else would he leave so soon after? It didn't matter once you got the confession. And if I told the police back then, if I told a reporter, what do you think would have happened? How long do you think a missing pregnant Black teen stays in the news? Where's people's sympathy go then? Then it's she ran away to get an abortion. Then it's she ran off with the baby daddy. You know that's how people would have reacted. Don't tell me otherwise."

Bill looked apoplectic. I wanted to be right there with him, livid about this giant puzzle piece that had been hidden from the board. But Cynthia was right. I'd worked in newsrooms long enough to know what missing white woman syndrome was. Cynthia had probably kept her family's story on the front page by hiding the most likely reason their loved ones wound up dead.

"How could you do this, Abel?" she asked.

"I didn't," he said. "And I couldn't."

Cynthia seemed to be gearing up to shout at him again, but his response slipped under her guard and stunned her for a second.

"Cynthia, my swimmers they, umm, they were never the strongest," he said. "I don't want to be disrespectful, but we weren't exactly careful, if you remember. And nothing happened, right? About two years after we ended things, I met someone else. We talked about kids. But I thought about us, went to a doctor and, well…I can't believe this is what it came to, but aside from the fact that I'd never, ever, ever have touched Shayna in that way, I couldn't have done what you think I done anyway. They said I couldn't get anyone pregnant, ever. They said I was infertile, had been for some time."

Cynthia raised her hand again, mouth hanging opening, but whatever words wanted to exit turned back and sat down.

"They probably have it in my medical files here, Cynthia. If you want to see it and be sure," he said.

She turned around and walked out of the room. Key followed her. Musa looked like he wanted to do the same, but the IV tethering him prevented that, which was probably for the best. I couldn't even imagine what she was going through, to have her entire reality challenged in such sudden fashion.

I looked across the room at Bill. He was staring at nothing, visibly exhausted. Maybe replaying how he would have handled the investigation differently if he'd known about the pregnancy. Maybe wondering if he could have done more to coax the information out of Cynthia when it mattered.

It could still matter now, though. The fresh pain she was suffering didn't have to be useless.

Isiah Roust had been in his early twenties the night Shayna Bell lost her family. He easily could have been the man referred to in her diary. He almost certainly knew what happened that night. And the burns on my shoulder were proof he had no problem setting fires to hide secrets.

CHAPTER
FIFTEEN

L ATER THAT NIGHT, when the crying and screaming were done, when no one could see me, I let myself be just slightly satisfied by the day's events.

The emotional car wreck that had played out in Abel Musa's hospital room had been a net negative for every party involved. Except me.

Now, I had a top. An opening scene. A reason to write, even if I wasn't entirely sure what I was writing yet.

It had been hard to focus between the exploding apartments and goth club bouncer beatings and hospital room dramatics, but I still had a story to work on.

Most reporters don't have a set process for how they put a piece together. Sure, we'll babble a response that sounds convincing if you ask, because the only thing we fear more than a blank page is not knowing something. But generally, we stumble around an idea or premise or case, poking and prodding at the edges until something reaches back and grabs us.

Might just be hubris, but we tend to think the thing that hooks us on a story will do the same to a reader.

I couldn't get Cynthia Bell's face out of my head. The gamut of reactions she had run through, from shock to righteous fury to indignance to rage. She was what the cops and some crime writers call a "true victim." A pure innocent. Someone who no reader or malcontent or errant Twitter account could slime in any way. Someone who legitimately deserved peoples' sympathy. Her world had been taken from her twice over—once because of someone's monstrous actions and a second time because of the toxic combination of a lie and an overeager detective. She had to be the center of the story.

The story that didn't have an editor. Or a home to publish. Or really any life expectancy beyond my imagination and a laptop screen for the time being.

But I couldn't fix that until I had something on the page. So, I started typing:

By Russell Avery
Signal-Intelligencer Staff

I stopped, stared and backspaced. It was just reflex. I hadn't written an article since I was at the paper.

By Russell Avery

I stopped again, let the cursor blink. Wrote and deleted Cynthia Bell's name about a dozen times. Waited twenty minutes for the excitement of inspiration to sit down and clink a glass with the reality of writing something. Then I started again.

Cynthia Bell walked into University Hospital in Newark hoping to unearth one secret, but she ended up revealing another.

The last surviving relative of the victims of the city's infamous "Twilight Four" murders, she had been told the man convicted in the gruesome slayings was finally willing to confess.

The meeting was supposed to mark the end of decades of tumult for Bell, a 57-year-old Newark native. Her younger sisters, Adriana and Shayna, and cousins, Kurtis and Lavell Dawkins, disappeared from Newark's South Ward in 1996. What started as a little-known missing persons case evolved into a homicide investigation that clawed at the poor relationship between the city's police and its citizens as Bell continually blasted the department's sluggish response to the teens' disappearance. As the case continued to garner media attention from outside New Jersey, tabloids began referring to the vanished teens as the "Twilight Four."

After more than 15 years, Bell finally saw a breakthrough in the case in 2012 when Newark Police arrested her ex-boyfriend, Abel Musa, in connection with the murders. An informant came forward and said Musa had confessed to trapping the teens in an abandoned Newark rowhouse and setting it ablaze. Musa, the informant alleged, had a sexual relationship with 16-year-old Shayna and had been trying to silence her. The other children were caught in the crossfire.

Musa has always denied wrongdoing, and prosecutors faced an uphill battle at trial with no forensic evidence to corroborate the informant's testimony. But Musa lacked an alibi for the night the teens disappeared, had a prior criminal record and faced a jury of Newarkers who would later admit in media interviews they were relieved to play a role in closing one of the city's oldest wounds. Bell also testified at trial that her sister, Shayna, had always seemed infatuated with Musa and that she often regretted leaving the two alone together.

Musa was convicted after two days of deliberation. Cynthia Bell, it seemed, could finally rest.

He appealed his conviction once and lost. But a hearing for a second appeal was vacated earlier this year, when Musa was granted compassionate release from a state prison facility after he was diagnosed with pancreatic cancer. The news, coupled with rumors that Newark's police were taking a second look at the Twilight Four case, left Bell furious.

So, when the lead investigator, Newark Police Lt. Bill Henniman, arranged a meeting between Bell and Musa based on the promise that the accused killer would finally confess, she marched into the hospital room ready to get answers to questions she'd been asking for thirty years.

By the time the meeting ended, Bell was in tears. Musa had professed his innocence. The lieutenant said he no longer believed Musa was guilty. And Bell admitted to hiding a key fact from investigators for decades, information that cast serious doubt on Musa's involvement.

In thirty minutes, Bell had been dragged back nearly thirty years. Just like the moment she'd learned of her sisters' disappearance, she was desperate for answers again.

It was one of those breathless, sprint writing sessions where the words just spill out of you. The prose was purplish at points, and it skirted the facts at others. I'd need quotes. I'd need better attribution.

But I knew the bones of a good story when I saw one.

I couldn't show it to anyone, not yet. But the piece was no longer an idea. It existed outside my head now.

A yawn rumbled from my stomach. Before I drifted off, I opened up my e-mail and searched the names of the colleagues I'd reached out to when Henniman had first hired me, the ones I'd sent cursory messages to about freelance work. None had written back, but I knew more now than I did when I'd first reached out. Looking over the names of the people I'd contacted, one seemed like he might be receptive to a follow-up.

Neal Goldberg. A former *Signal-Intelligencer* reporter, now an editor at a criminal justice non-profit in New York City. He'd always had an eye for a good narrative when we worked together, even on a public health beat that didn't really lend itself to yarns. I sent him another message, kind of a loose story pitch. I referenced the Twilight Four, the possibility of a wrongful conviction, the fact that I had an in with the victims' family and that there would be good photos. A combo that would claim the attention of any decent editor.

I crawled into bed after that, hoping I'd wake up with confirmation that my first attempt at writing in two years hadn't been a waste of time.

I woke up to a bunch of missed calls, none of them from anyone interested in what I'd written the night before.

It was 8 a.m., too early to have pants on, much less talk to anyone. Henniman and the blocked number that had rang me six times already apparently disagreed.

Key's name flashed on the screen before I could even wonder who the mystery caller was.

"Pick up the next one," she said, then immediately hung up.

The word "Unknown" appeared on my phone five seconds later.

"Do you not understand the definition of the word discreet?" Mariana Pereira asked as soon as I answered.

"Mariana," I started.

"It's Councilwoman," she said. "At least when you're working for me, which might not be much longer."

I rubbed at my eyes and slapped at the sides of my face, briefly hoping this was the end of a lucid dream. But the sting was enough to let me know I was in the joyous real world, where I got talked down to by a politician that I was technically an employee of. The laptop was within reach, so I pulled it closer and decided to let the maybe future mayor stew for a bit.

"Russell. Russell!" she shouted. "I'm talking to you! Why the hell were you harassing my brother?"

The Pereiras made less sense by the second. Angel was supposed to be estranged from the family. He'd offered to give me dirt on his father for nothing, while demanding an undisclosed sum for compromising pictures of his sister. Now, I had to assume he'd called and let her know I'd knocked on his door.

"You told me to investigate where the pictures were coming from," I said. "That's where the investigation led."

I neglected to mention there was another picture connected to her brother she might need to worry about, even though I had no proof to back that assumption. The coffee maker called to me. This was not the kind of conversation I could be civil for under the best of circumstances. Without caffeine? We were two exchanges from me throwing the phone out the window.

"My brother is not a part of this," she replied.

"You mean your estranged brother you didn't tell me about? The one who hates your dad and got excommunicated from the family and lives above a strip club while you take meetings in the dining room of a Zagat-rated restaurant?" I asked. "That brother? You're sure he couldn't use a bribe or three?"

The coffee maker hissed to life, but it was going to take a few minutes for the empty pot to fill with life-giving liquid. Mariana's attitude was wearing thin. I wanted to tell her that Angel had all but confessed, but I had a feeling that would only make her angrier.

"You talked to him one time. You don't know him" she said. "We're still close in spite of—"

"In spite of what? What happened?" I asked. "Councilwoman, you asked me to figure out who would leak those photos to your opponent. People who do those things usually have motives. Money and anger seem like good ones. Why isn't your brother in any of the pictures in the restaurant? How come I've never heard his name before?"

"That's none of your concern," she said.

Mariana sounded like her father now. If the Pereiras wanted to make it anywhere in politics, they were going to need to develop a thicker skin for questions about their past.

"I talked to your ex. Celia," I said. "Mentioned your brother was more than a little judgmental about the kinds of things that are in those pictures."

"Christ, you have no idea what you are talking about," she spat back. "Angel is not a bigot and that was a lifetime ago. He got over it. This is not him. He would not betray me like this."

"I'm no expert on your family, Councilwoman, but based on how your father was acting the other day, it seems like your family's got some flexible rules on loyalty," I replied.

I felt the phone buzz and pulled it away from my ear. Henniman was calling again. I sent it to voicemail. Something started pounding on my front door almost immediately.

"Avery," Bill growled from the other side. "Open up. We have shit to do."

"Russell," Mariana said. "I am telling you my brother's not the problem. We are fine. It's someone else."

My clients did not respect my personal space. Or sleeping habits. Or the fact that it was too early to have pants on. I needed to decide between Mariana's bullshit and Henniman's.

"Well, then give me a hint," I said to her. "Or better yet, let's discuss my fee. Because I don't know if you forgot, but our arrangement was based on a quid pro quo, and I got my favor last night. So, if you're not paying me to look into this, you're sure as hell not telling me how to look into this. Why don't you call me back when you're serious about finding out whose messing with you? Because I have better shit to do."

And with that, I hung up, likely ending a political career that had mostly involved getting smacked around in a club filled with people who looked like they paid money to get smacked around.

Henniman called two more times and smashed his fist against the door two more than that while I poured a cup of coffee and located my only clean pair of jeans.

"The hell took you so long?" Bill growled as I opened the door.

"I don't really function before nine," I replied, raising the coffee cup toward him.

Henniman walked past me into the kitchen, briefly looking around and sniffing the air. The trash needed to go, and he wasn't shy about reminding me. He grabbed the coffee pot and started to open cabinet doors.

"Mugs are second from the left," I said. "Wanna tell me why you're trying to take my door off the hinges and stealing my coffee this early?"

"We need to find Roust," he replied.

"That's been true since he dropped a building on us," I said. "The wake-up call doesn't change that."

"No, it doesn't," he said. "But the call I got from Internal Affairs last night does."

Henniman poured himself a cup and moved onto the refrigerator. He took a look around before turning to me wearing his default annoyed expression.

"No creamer?" he asked.

I looked past him. The fridge contained a half loaf of whole grain bread, two takeout containers that belonged in the already pungent trash, and the survivors of a six pack of Presidente. The lack of creamer was the least of my worries.

"How do you live like this?" he asked.

"I take it black," I replied. "Now what did IA want?"

"To notify me that I'm now the subject of a formal complaint. Insubordination, interfering with an investigation. They even tacked on something about inappropriate disclosure of departmental materials," he replied. "They knew we were in Musa's hospital room yesterday. They knew your activist friend and Cynthia were there."

I thought about my first visit to Musa's room. The one that ended with Dameon Lynch and two plain clothes officers bracing me. They'd been there that day because the mayor was visiting Musa, but given how politically toxic the case could be, it didn't stretch credulity that they'd keep eyes on Newark's most famous cancer patient.

"That sucks. But what does that change for us? You already knew you weren't supposed to be looking into the Twilight Four case," I said.

Bill took a long sip from the mug and frowned. I wasn't sure if he was mad about what he'd just put in his mouth or what was about to come out of it.

"I want to do right by Abel, Russ. But I'm not about to lose everything doing it. My career was already on life support after last year, but at least I was going to keep my pension," he said. "This is going to end up before a disciplinary board if we don't find out something they can't keep quiet soon. They're going to come for my badge. And we're going to need my badge to find Roust."

"Do we? 'Cause the Asbury Park cops, the state police and that probation officer who saved our asses down the Shore are all looking for him, and they've all got badges," I replied.

"That's why I'm here so early. We've got some driving to do," Henniman said. "They're not looking in the right place."

"And what's the right place?" I asked.

"Prison," he said.

The texts flooded in almost as soon as Henniman started driving.

"You still interested in that story?" one read.

"You got the money to cover it?" read the next.

I didn't recognize the number, but I'd only given my business card to one person who'd put a price tag on my last few shreds of journalistic integrity in the last twenty-four hours.

"Angel?" I wrote back.

"You know who this is," the text replied. "It's a yes or no question."

I looked over to Henniman, who hadn't said much about where we were going or what we were doing since we'd left my apartment. I assumed we were headed into New York, based on his decision to cut through Elizabeth toward the Goethals Bridge, but other than that and the word "prison" he hadn't offered me any other hints.

Bill almost seemed pleased that I wasn't asking questions, and for once, I was thankful for the clogged pipe flow of information between us. I hadn't told him about Angel's presence in the picture in Roust's home yet. Partly because I wasn't sure he needed to know. Partly because I worried if he did, he might be desperate enough to use the info to curry favor on Broad Street. Bill's politics were anything but aligned with Mariana's, and he might not be above ferrying dirt to someone like Lynch in exchange for the mayor's office exerting its influence to rescue his cratering police career.

"It was a yes or no question yesterday," I typed to Angel. "Now I'm trying to figure out why you're selling me blackmail on your sister one day, then sending her after me the next."

"Gotta cover my ass in case she goes looking for the source. Which she apparently hired you to do," he wrote back. "So maybe I'm trying to figure out if you're a real reporter or just running errands for her."

My body let out an involuntary shudder at the last few words. Those were the sentences that made up my nightmares about public relations. Fuck being an errand boy.

"It's complicated, man," I wrote. "Complicated like you telling me you love your sister when you're willing to try to wreck her campaign for a few dollars."

"More than a few dollars."

"Not the point. Not sure I can do business with someone whose motives don't make sense to me," I wrote back, words coming out almost as fast as I thought of them.

There are a lot of different methods to source-building. Usually, I preferred the earnest, empathetic approach. Camouflaging myself as a friend, a guy you feel compelled to talk to when I don't need something, so you pick up the phone on instinct when I do. But when you're firing off texts to a guy you barely know in a car headed for a prison, you do what you can. In this case, I was sticking with a classic: he needed me more than I needed him, so I had no problem making him chase. Making him prove himself. Making him give up info before he'd even agreed to it.

"I don't hate my sister. But I hate how unfair shit is," he wrote. "If she winds up mayor, she winds up mayor. I hope she does. But how come she doesn't have to own her mistakes? How come I'm the only one Tiago punished?"

"These would be good things to explain in an interview," I wrote back. "With a reporter."

The ellipsis that meant he was typing popped up. Then it stopped.

That pattern played out for a few minutes before the text window went still. He was stewing. I could have pressed him harder, but he'd already reached out. He wanted the story out. I needed to let him make the decision on his own.

As we crossed the Brooklyn Bridge into Manhattan, I turned to Henniman and asked exactly where we were going.

We were driving toward the Metropolitan Correctional Center, a faded brown tower that somehow operated within a mile of the United Nations despite prison reform groups constantly describing conditions inside that would violate the Geneva Convention. The federal lock-up largely housed people who were supposedly presumed innocent while awaiting trial or prisoners transferred down from larger institutions for court appearances. Before they'd even been convicted, many of them had seen water bugs crawl over them in showers or rat droppings appear in their barely edible meals. Guards often reacted with batons or chemical spray or worse when they complained about either.

More than one suicide had taken place in a wing of the facility where cameras weren't working properly.

For people in MCC, a boring day was worth celebrating. One where you got called into a room where you were the only one in a jumpsuit was a nightmare. Henniman's plan involved the latter.

The man we'd driven over ninety minutes in traffic to see was Jaquan Crowley. He'd been sitting next to Roust in the car Henniman stopped as part of a federal gun running sting all those years ago, the day Roust became an informant and Abel Musa's life started turning to ruin.

"Crowley's been doing federal time, real time, for eight years, while Roust has been out in the open," Henniman said as we pulled into a garage. "The two had priors together before I ever crossed either of their paths. He'll have an idea where Roust would lie low."

Henniman nodded toward a man in a suit in the guard shack in his fifties with a thick moustache and black hair I'd only hope to have later in life. Bill gave a big smile and reached out the window to shake the hand of the guy he called Jimmy before looking back to me, like he needed to show off that he had friends here.

"And if Crowley's such an obvious expert on Isiah Roust, why haven't the other three police agencies hunting for him driven up here for a visit?" I asked.

"Roust wasn't mentioned in the federal indictment with Crowley and the rest of that gun operation since he flipped almost immediately," Henniman replied. "I put them both in cuffs the same day, only reason I thought of it."

"What did Crowley go down for?" I asked.

"He got caught in a car with an ass load of unregistered weapons, and he crossed state lines," Henniman replied. "Federal weapons trafficking. Ten-year minimum. Means he has less than two years to go."

"You think he'll flip to shave less than two when he's already done eight, risk getting a snitch jacket inside?" I asked. "That's not usually how this works."

"Roust killed kids," Bill said. "Changes the bullshit code of honor inside."

"We don't know that Roust killed anyone," I replied. "We think that."

"Well, we're going to tell Crowley we know that," Henniman said. "This will work. He's in there. We're out here. He doesn't know shit."

I checked the phone one more time as we went through security. Angel had made a decision.

"You get the interview once you buy the pictures. I'll tell you whatever you wanna know, give you whatever you need to knock down the Ironbound Kennedy family bullshit my father likes to pretend is our truth," he wrote. "But the pictures need to be part of it. $5K. Today."

I went to type something back, but before I could even figure out if I had enough in the bank to display money to Angel that I'd never actually give him, a guard told me to give up my phone if I wanted to enter the prison. Henniman got to keep his, but I apparently wasn't allowed the same courtesy.

Once inside, I tried to focus on Crowley again. To remember he had helped smuggle guns into Newark, guns that killed kids, probably kids I'd written about in the past. But my attempts to conjure him as a hardened criminal failed once I actually saw him.

The man looked skinny, tired and stiff. He was moving more like he was being dragged, shuffle steps with his hands cuffed out in front. The corrections officer who placed him on the other side of the table from us wore a blank expression, transporting Crowley with all the care of a bag of groceries. He plunked the man down into the chair and snapped his handcuffs in place to a table anchor, ensuring Crowley's arms wouldn't be much use until the CO decided to change that. Then he gave Henniman the slightest of nods and moved to the corner of the room, where he stood at parade rest. The whole thing had an assembly line vibe to it.

One of Crowley's eyes was a little purple. It could have been a stye or a bruise, but given our setting I tended to think it was the latter. He lolled his head to one side, eyes drifting up and to the right. I followed his stare and noticed he was checking for a camera, seemingly more concerned about where he was then who he was there to meet.

"Help you?" he asked.

"You don't recognize me?" Henniman replied, voice tinged with annoyance.

"Nope," Crowley said.

"I arrested you. Eight years ago. I'm the reason you're in here."

"Cool," Crowley said.

"You got driven all the way down here from Ray Brook at the ass crack of dawn, put in a box with the person who put you away and you don't care why?" Henniman asked.

"Oh, I care. But you acting like I'm supposed to be impressed? That's different," he said. "And they brought me down last night. Ray Brook's five hours up. No one was bringing me down here at five a.m. in traffic and shit."

"That's not the poi—"

"It's the point for me. Days melt together in here, but I know when summer is," Crowley said. "Least a nice drive might have made me wanna act like I'm gonna help you."

Henniman looked flustered. I was usually a fan of anyone who could fluster him.

"Hey, uh, Jaquan, right? My name's Russell, my partner here's a little pissy this morning. We hit traffic, you know. Why don't we start over? You want anything, like a coffee?" I asked, turning toward the CO. "Can we get him some coffee?"

The CO looked at me like I'd just asked him to shit out the Hope Diamond.

"What are you supposed to be?" Crowley asked.

"I'm Russell…"

"No, I got that. That's who. I asked what," he said. "You ain't a cop. And if you're a lawyer, you ain't mine."

Now I was flustered. Announcing myself as press or a PI was always a coin flip. It was just as likely he'd shut down and end the meeting as it was he'd talk more. But the lawyer comment had touched a nerve in my head. If he knew he was talking to cops, why didn't he have one?

"You remember Isiah Roust?" Henniman asked. "Skinny piece of shit you got arrested with. You ran with him a bit in Jersey before that."

"Sure. Izzy. He ain't been up to visit. And they don't let us use Facebook in here, so it's been hard to keep in touch," Crowley said.

"Izzy? That was his nickname?" I asked.

"Nah, not Izzy. Like, Is. He. Two words," Crowley said back. "Is he gonna puke? Is he gonna cry? Is he gonna run? Izzy was fun to have around, but he was kind of a bitch."

Crowley swiveled in his seat, positioning himself to look at Henniman. The movement was sudden enough that the CO took a half step forward.

"So, what'd ol' Izzy do? And how much did y'all fuck up that you actually need help finding a punk like him?" Crowley asked.

"He tried to kill us," Henniman said.

Crowley started laughing under his breath.

"I once saw Izzy get punched in the mouth in a bar and apologize for it," Crowley said. "He ain't never tried to kill no one."

Henniman pointed to the bruising around his face.

"This is him," Henniman said.

Crowley scratched at his chin. If nothing else, he was at least interested. Maybe Bill had been playing with him when we got there. Setting the hook. Getting him curious enough to talk too much. Just like he'd done with me the first time he brought up the Twilight Four.

"You seriously sitting here and telling me Izzy messed you up?" he asked. "This I gotta hear. At least tell me he hit you when you wasn't looking."

Now it was my turn to let out a little laugh, even though I felt it in my burned shoulder.

"You could say that," Henniman said.

"What'd he jump you with, a bat?" Crowley asked.

"He dropped a house on us," I replied. "Blew up his own goddamn apartment when we came knocking."

Crowley leaned forward, eyes bouncing from me to Henniman and back again.

"Bullshit," he said. "Izzy would never take a shot at a cop. Hell, what would he even do worth taking that shot anyway?"

"Killing four kids qualify?" Henniman asked.

Crowley turned back to me now.

"If you convince him to get me that coffee, you're gonna need to pour something in it for me to believe that nonsense," he said. "Izzy couldn't kill no one. Definitely not a kid, much less several. When the fuck...why?"

Henniman reached into his suit jacket's breast pocket and started laying down Polaroids, one by one like a poker flop. They were the pictures from the case file. Shayna. Adriana. Kurtis. Lavell.

"Bullshit," Crowley said. "I grew up in Newark. Don't come at me with that. Izzy did not…the Twilight Four? You coming in here telling me Izzy did the Twilight Four? He the one who really shot JFK too?"

"What I'm telling you, Jaquan, is that you've been in here for eight years and Isiah Roust hasn't because he spun us a bullshit story about this case," Henniman said. "I'm telling you we need to find him, and I'm betting you might know some places to look. I'm telling you that you do that, maybe you and him switch places."

If there was a deal on the table, there would have been an assistant U.S. Attorney out of the Newark office in the room. Henniman was lying.

Crowley started chewing on his pinky nail, sucking his teeth, thinking.

"So, you're telling me I can be on my way home sooner, and all I gotta do is point you to where Izzy might go to hide out?" Crowley asked.

Henniman nodded. His face went blank. His breathing slowed, like he was hunting something and closing in.

"That ain't the worst deal I ever been offered. Wanna hear about the worst one?" Crowley asked. "'Cause I do remember you, Detective. Course I do. You tried to run the same game you must have run on Izzy. Telling me I'd get put in some lock-up in North Dakota. That my family wasn't gonna be able to see me without getting on a plane, like my people have money for that. That you'd make sure I got the max if I didn't help you. That you'd make sure word got out to wherever I went that I was a snitch, even if I wasn't."

Henniman's face flushed red. I couldn't tell if he was blushing because he hadn't remembered how he'd treated Crowley, or that he hadn't expected Crowley to remember it himself.

"Eight years I sat up there, did my time, shut the fuck up. I got less than two to go. I'm gonna be home before my fortieth birthday. I can wait that out, especially if it means leaving you as fucked as you left me," Crowley said. "What's that thing they used to say in church? Unto others, right? Should've thoughta that, Billy. 'Cause you could tell me

Izzy shot up a school. You could tell me Izzy was running the KKK. And I'd still tell you to go fuck yourself."

I was waiting for the explosion. Few people had talked as much shit to Henniman as I had, so I knew his limit and I usually knew when I was approaching it. When he hit that red line, there wasn't much time between you thinking you had the last word and him having the next two hundred.

Except he wasn't talking. Or moving. I was only sure he was breathing because he looked up at the CO, nodded and stood.

"You sure?" the guard asked.

"Absolutely," Henniman replied.

The guard moved toward Crowley, calmly reaching for his wrists and producing a key. Henniman took his suit jacket off, folded it in half and draped it neatly over his chair.

"Uh…Bill?" I asked. "What are we sure about?"

"Same question," Crowley said as the guard fiddled with the anchor point on the table. "The fuck is this?"

"You said before this wasn't the worst deal you'd ever been offered, right?" Henniman asked.

He rolled up his sleeves, stopping at the forearm on each.

"Bill. What the fuck are you doing?" I asked.

"This doesn't concern you."

"I'm standing so close to you I can smell the coffee on your breath," I replied. "It fucking concerns me."

Henniman turned to me. Eyes dead. Fists balled up. Despite being in his fifties, his arms still had definition. The guard stopped messing with Crowley's shackle, adopted the same glare and let his hand wander to the chemical spray at his side. His arms were thicker than Henniman's.

I felt the room get smaller. Crowley looked at me for help.

But all I did was take a step back from Henniman.

It sucks learning you're not a hero.

Henniman turned back to the CO, who finished unlocking Crowley from the table. His handcuffs were still on, but he wasn't anchored to the metal furniture anymore.

"I had a feeling it was going to go this way. Like you said, you did eight years, you can do two more," Henniman said. "But what about twenty?"

"What the fuck are you talking about?" Crowley asked.

The guard set his feet apart, one foot back and to the right of the other. Henniman stood up tall and jutted his chin out, just in time for the CO to throw an overhand right that came across Bill's cheek hard enough that the lieutenant's legs went spaghetti for a second.

I backed up against the wall. Crowley did the same, hitting the door loud enough that someone probably heard it.

"Yo, what the fuck!" Crowley shouted. "The fuck is going on in here?

Henniman looked at the guard and nodded again. The CO tagged him with a left hook, painting the lieutenant's mouth with blood. The shot turned Henniman's face toward me, crimson framing an unnerving smile.

Henniman turned back to Crowley. The guard moved to the side as the lieutenant closed the distance between them. He reared his right arm back. Crowley reacted, swinging his cuffed hands in the air. I don't know if he was trying to block or attack, but his clasped hands caught Henniman's face.

They came back bloody.

"Twenty years is what they give you for assaulting a federal corrections officer," Henniman said, his voice coming out in a hiss, slipping between the spit and blood in his mouth. "Maybe they give you the same for hitting a cop while in custody."

"This is bullshit! There's a fucking camera right there," Crowley said, pointing over my head.

"Doesn't work," the guard said. "Repair requisitions aren't fast around here."

"He saw it!" Crowley said, turning to me. "You're not gonna let them do me like that, right?"

I wasn't, but I wasn't going to point that fact out in a locked room with two cops and zero recording devices.

"He can't help you. I can," Henniman said. "Someone heard you yelling. Someone definitely heard you bang against that door. And when that someone gets here, they're going to see blood coming out of me and blood on you. They're gonna hear a story. One is you got loose and attacked us. That puts you in here for twenty more. The other is Russell over there got into a fight with me, he tends to be emotional, so it'll add up, and you just got caught in the middle of it. Tell me what I want to know, and it's the second story."

Crowley was fuming. He had every right to be furious, but no time to be. He was fucked. Henniman had checkmated him before he even knew he was in a game. I'd have been impressed if I wasn't livid.

"You're fucking insane," Crowley said. "I ain't seen Roust in years. You know that. How the hell am I supposed to know where he is?"

"Clock's ticking," Henniman said.

"Alright, Jesus, fuck. Jesus. Okay. Okay. Ummm…okay…"

Crowley's voice was shrinking. He was quaking. He knew how close he was to being in prison until he qualified for AARP.

"It's only your life, Jaquan," Henniman said. "Don't rush."

"Newark! When, before you, like 2010. We did a few smash and grabs outside the city. Maplewood. South Orange. But someone saw enough of us that there was a sketch on the news and…"

Henniman looked at the guard.

"Maybe you should radio for help?"

"NO!" Crowley shouted. "There was a woman. Lived near Branch Brook. He said he grew up with her! Or used to work for her. Both maybe. Either way they was close. That's where he went when shit hit the fan last time! Laurie or Lacy or Lauren. Italian last name."

"Lorena?" I asked. "Lorena D'Agostino?"

"Yeah. Yeah!" Crowley shouted. "That's it. Lorena! If he's hiding anywhere, it's there."

I'd been where we needed to go a few days earlier. The foster home where Kurtis and Lavell Dawkins lived before they vanished. The home Lavell claimed he'd been beaten inside of. The one where the young boy looked scared enough like he'd experienced the same.

"You know who he's talking about?" Henniman asked.

I nodded.

"Now, you gonna tell them I didn't do anything to your face, right? Right? We good, right?" Crowley asked, basically pleading.

Henniman wiped some of the blood away, stared at Crowley for a second, then let out a shark's smile.

"Yeah, we're good," he said, before turning to me. "We're good, right?"

We were not good.

CHAPTER
SIXTEEN

I LET HENNIMAN FEEL clever for a good chunk of the drive back to Newark.

Bill spent most of the ride rambling about how he had a friend or two in the New York chapter of the Council of Prison Locals, the union that represents federal corrections officers. How that contact was able to arrange Crowley's visit to the private, unmonitored room in MCC where Bill had just terrified both of us. How an assistant U.S. Attorney in Newark had lubed up the process to get Crowley transferred south for a chat.

I stayed quiet the whole time, except for a question here or there to spur Bill along. My phone was in my lap, under the guise of its GPS guiding us to Lorena D'Agostino's address in Newark. The recorder was running in the background, making sure to capture any name or detail Henniman let slip, anything that might prove useful when I decided to make him answer for this later.

While he rambled, I checked for new messages from Angel. There was just one.

"You want the interview?" he'd asked. "It's gotta be today."

Sources never want to connect when it's convenient. But I couldn't meet now, not if we were this close to Roust. Maybe tracking down the erstwhile snitch would answer my questions about why he and Angel were in a photo together, rendering Angel a problem I'd only care about if I chose to keep working for his sister.

By the time Henniman was done talking, we were already through the Lincoln Tunnel and into Jersey City, a short drive from our best shot at finding the guy who tried to burn us alive. We needed to focus. We needed a game plan. There would be a time and place to deal with the fact that Henniman had explicitly threatened to frame someone for assault while we were trying to hunt down another man who might have framed someone for murder. I needed to be patient.

Then I thought about how Jaquan Crowley looked to me for help, how I'd shrunk away from the moment.

"You know, maybe it's a good thing they're thinking about taking away your badge," I said as we got onto the Turnpike south.

"It got us what we needed," he replied. "I didn't like what you did with Cynthia the other day either. But it got us what we needed."

"So, what? You were just getting even?" I asked.

"No, I was getting us Roust," he said.

"By torturing that guy?"

"Torturing...for fuck's sake," he said. "You know, I try not to generalize about the whole millennial thing. But your generation really turned out to be a bunch of pussies."

I turned away for a second, looking out the window and watching the exits countdown. We were almost back to Newark.

"I'm a pussy because I got an issue with you threatening to steal a man's freedom?" I asked.

"You act like that was my first move," he replied. "You were there. I tried to see if he'd take a deal. I tried to see if he'd just be a decent human and help us."

"If there was a deal on the table, how come there weren't any lawyers in the room?" I asked.

Bill didn't answer me, suddenly very focused on a lane change.

"Right. And that guard was in on it, so you clearly planned that in advance," I said. "What was next, huh? If he didn't crack, were you gonna start beating on him right in front of me?"

"I wasn't going to hit him," Bill said, the reply fast enough that I felt like it might be true.

"So then what? You let him stew on that charge? Let the CO report it as the assault you staged until he gives us Roust? If he doesn't, or he just doesn't know anything, what happens then?" I asked.

"Didn't come to that," he said.

"It could have! Are you even sure you could have walked all that back if it didn't go how you wanted it to? Or does Jaquan just get twenty years added to his sentence while you go on with your life like nothing happened?" I asked. "Do you ever think about the consequences when you do shit like that?"

"I think about consequences all the time, Russ," he said. "You were in that hospital room the other day. Cynthia. Musa. All that pain. All because I fell for a lie. What just happened in that jail was ugly. But it was an ugly thing done to an ugly person, Russ. That was a gun runner. Doubt he's thought much about the consequences of the things he's done. Chancing that piece of shit's freedom to get Cynthia answers? To try to do one decent thing by Abel Musa after what I caused him? I'm okay with that. And I notice you're not offering a Plan B here."

"Excuse me?" I asked as the car came to a stop on Highland Avenue.

The last home that Kurtis and Lavell Dawkins had ever lived in was on our right, the two-story with the large-lacquered wood frame and wide porch that belonged to Lorena D'Agostino.

"How else were we going to end up here, Russell?" he asked. "You didn't like my play. Fine. What was yours?"

Now it was my turn to stay quiet.

"What happened last time you came here?" he asked, waiting

about a minute after I ignored his last question.

"I tried to talk to Lorena," I said. "Approached her as a reporter. She was not interested."

"Aren't you supposed to be some kind of a storyteller?" he asked. "Was she mad? Afraid? Nervous? Panicked? Was anyone else around?"

"She was agitated. Not scared. She seemed more concerned with the kids than me," I replied.

"So, she's still fostering?" he asked.

"At least three kids," I said. "Two of them were coming home on a bike. Little one maybe twelve, other one probably fifteen or sixteen. They were arguing over something, the teen knocked the younger one on his ass. The young one looked scared. He was wearing long sleeves. Made me think of—"

"Lavell Dawkins. The abuse complaint from back then," Bill said. "That's why you came here in the first place."

Henniman chewed his lip and scratched at his nose. He'd dismissed the abuse allegation as a motive in the Twilight Four killings when we first talked about the case. It seemed like he'd done the same when Roust came forward in 2012. Even now, after Cynthia's revelation that Shayna had been pregnant, it was hard to think the D'Agostinos and their foster care checks were actually the heart of the matter.

"Wait, where was the third kid?" Henniman asked. "The last time you were here."

"Maybe kid was the wrong word. Might have been nineteen, maybe twenty," I said. "Pretty built. Seemed to be the enforcer in the house. But even then, he shrank from Lorena."

Henniman let out a groan and started running his hand over the ridges on his bald head.

"Kurtis Dawkins had a marijuana arrest back then too," he said.

"Don't try to make this a drug thing again just because you don't want to admit you were wrong about the abuse maybe having something to do with the fire," I replied.

"I was wrong about the abuse. We're here, aren't we?" he growled.

"But it might still be a drug thing. Think about it. There's a pattern here. Bad things always happen in threes."

"I don't speak in riddles."

"Try not speaking. Just for a second and you might learn something," he said. "Dealers use minors to transport product all the time. The younger they are, the tighter the rules on using them as informants, the lighter the sentences. You said you saw three, right? It would make sense. Youngest carries the product. Middle child is the runner. Big one is the enforcer."

He held up three fingers in front of my face and counted them down one by one.

"Little. Big. Biggest," he said. "Lavell. Kurtis. Roust."

"Roust?"

"The hell else would he have been doing here?" Henniman asked. "He never came up in the initial investigation, so he probably wasn't the D'Agostinos' foster kid. But Jaquan said he worked for her. Roust had priors for drugs too."

There were more than a few assumptions in there, but I had to admit Roust fit into the story Henniman told better than he did the one in Shayna Bell's diary. He clearly knew how the fire was set. Lavell's abuse complaint had been a threat to the D'Agostinos. Between Kurtis's and Roust's criminal records and connections to the family, it was somewhat likely they were subsidizing their foster income costs with a weed business.

Whether Roust was covering up an unwanted pregnancy or taking care of a problem out of loyalty to who I now assumed were his former employers, he had two more motives than Abel Musa ever did.

I looked over the house, trying to determine how to get past the latest locked door between us and Roust, hoping this one didn't self-immolate after we passed through. The big kid, the one I think called himself Ray last time, was slouching in a folding chair on the porch again. He'd swapped his wifebeater for a blank blue t-shirt, and he'd added a fitted Yankee hat to his look. I didn't see the bike in the yard this time, so maybe the two younger kids were out on a run again.

Something flared under the porch. My eyes tracked the latticework of cross-stitched wood there, but I couldn't find the source. I looked up to see if Ray reacted to it, but the big man wasn't moving, and I briefly wondered if I was just seeing things.

A minute passed. The flash came again, same spot, but it stayed long enough that I was able to trace it to the lower left corner of the space under the porch. I saw the light move left to right. Like someone was tracking something.

I thought back to my last visit. To the scared little kid and what fell out of his backpack.

The light wasn't tracking something. It was helping someone read.

"I got an idea," I said to Bill. "But you need to keep the kid on the porch and whoever else is inside busy."

"Don't we need to get inside?" he asked.

"We need a reason. I think I know how to get us one," I replied. "Just go up there and be an asshole for a bit. Do the cop thing. Keep them occupied."

Two minutes later, Henniman was loudly announcing to the D'Agostinos' oldest foster son and/or bodyguard that he was there to conduct a wellness check, that he was going to need to search him and go inside. On a normal day, I'd consider that two civil liberties violations too many, but it was just a feint and I needed to get to the kid hiding under the porch.

Once Henniman had the man turned around, I got out of the car and jogged across the street to the cover of a parked van. An exchange of profanities confirmed to me that Bill had Ray's undivided attention, so I crept toward the darkened underside of the porch, following the flashlight to the little boy's hiding spot. The beam was concentrated on an issue of Spider-Man, but not the one I'd grown up on.

"Sometimes, man, I really do start to think Miles is a little bit cooler than Peter," I whispered.

The kid spun around and began scooting his butt backwards in the grass to get away from me. I was lucky he hadn't screamed.

"Hey, relax, relax. You remember me from the other day?" I whispered. "I was trying to help you then. I know what's going on here."

I didn't, but I knew enough. The kid's eyes stayed wide with fear, just like they had been when he'd run out the door from Lorena the other day, fleeing a beating he'd surely received after I left. He was wearing long sleeves again. It was still eighty-five degrees out.

"I know what she does to you," I said. "So does the man on the porch right now. He's a police officer. We're going to help you, but we need a little help from you first."

The kid went to move back again, but he bumped up against the house itself. Surprise spread across his freckled and dimpled face. Both of our eyes traveled to the comic book he'd dropped. Miles Morales— the younger Spidey who looked more like the kid than me—was leaping across a panel, web line shooting out of one hand, electricity coiled around the other.

"Listen, I know you don't know me. I know you're scared. She probably told you not to talk to anyone else. But that's because she knows how much trouble she'd get in if anyone found out she's hurting you," I said. "We can make it stop. As long as you talk to us."

The kid shook his head no, head moving back and forth so fast I thought it might fall off, the curls in his hair trembling like a hedge in the wind. I looked at the comic book again.

"You know, you might be stronger when you're scared, just like Miles," I said, reaching my hand through a space in the wood slats, tapping on the lightning around the character's fist. "The Venom Blast. Miles only figured out he could do that when he was so afraid, he didn't know else how to protect himself. When he was so scared, his body just knew it had to do something different."

Something changed in the kid's demeanor. I hadn't been abused as a kid, but I'd sure as hell been a bullied nerd, and I knew the relief that came when you found someone else who spoke the same language.

"Nah, man, Miles can just do that. He's just different like that," the kid said.

"Nuh-uh. You need to read the earlier issues," I replied. "The electricity. Turning invisible. All the stuff Peter can't do? It's self-defense. It's because Miles knows how to use being afraid to his advantage."

The kid scooted forward now, picking up the comic. He kept a nervous eye on me while he traced his finger over the panel.

"I've told people what she does before," he said. "Teachers. But they say they need proof. And they can't get it. And then it just gets worse."

Kid had been talking to the wrong people. My mind flashed to Key, her city hall secure pass and direct line to the new mayor. That should have been more than enough to get something useful done.

"I know you don't know me, but you're going to have to trust me, I'm going to send someone who can fix this. When she gets here, just tell her you're the boy Russ mentioned, okay?" I asked. "I can do that, but I just need you to tell me something first."

The kid looked at Spider-Man again, lowered his head, let loose a long exhale, and said, "Okay."

"Was there a man in your house today?" I asked.

The boy looked over my shoulder and to the left and right, just to make sure there were no witnesses, then nodded.

"A man who's not normally here?" I asked.

The boy shook his head no.

"Is his name Isiah?"

A nod, yes.

"Is he still there?" I asked.

"No," the boy croaked.

Something in my face must have shown that wasn't what I wanted to hear, because he flinched immediately. I wondered how long it had been since he answered a question without the risk of being met with a fist.

"It's okay. It's okay," I said. "Do you know where he went?"

"Baltimore," he said.

"Wait, what?"

"Miss Lore made me call him a cab to the train station before she sent us out," he said. "She told me if I got it wrong, she'd…"

The bottom fell out of his voice, and the whisper became a blubber as tears started to leak.

"I'm sorry. I'm so, so sorry," I whispered back, pressing my hand against the wood. "We're gonna get you out of this soon. I promise. How long ago did he leave?"

The kid blinked a few times.

"Maybe a half hour? Why?"

Because if Lorena D'Agostino had sent Isiah Roust to Newark Penn station, that meant our last lead on the Twilight Four case was about to disappear.

Roughly thirty thousand people walk through Newark Penn Station's doors every day. Henniman and I only needed to find one of them, but we needed to do it fast.

Nothing I'd read or heard about Isiah Roust led me to believe he was particularly smart, but he'd done enough to make tracking him difficult. He must not have touched his bank accounts or used a credit card, any of the obvious things that would have allowed any of the police agencies hunting for him to pick up his trail after the explosion in Asbury Park. Meaning he either had a cash reserve, or someone was feeding him enough money to get by undetected.

We'd only caught up to Roust based on his connections in New Jersey. I didn't know anyone in Baltimore. I didn't know what to do if he got there.

Newark Penn didn't give off the same iconic aura as its New York counterpart—it wasn't nestled under Madison Square Garden, after all—but its large sandstone façade and long, yawning window panes still signaled Penn was a grandiose, important building in a city that lacked them.

We moved through the front doors and into the vestibule that sat under Penn's ancient train information board. They hadn't digitized, so the track names and destinations and delay warnings all had to be swapped out mechanically. With every loud click and whirr, dozens of the hundreds of people lining the wooden pews on either side of the vestibule looked up to see if it was their turn to get out of the Brick City.

I checked the board. If Lorena D'Agostino's youngest, most terrified foster child was right and Isiah Roust really was running to Baltimore, then he'd be on a DC-bound Amtrak. The board told me that train would be departing Platform 2 in less than ten minutes. I scanned the crowd in the vestibule, not seeing anyone with Roust's signature stupid ace of spades neck tattoo.

Henniman started marching deeper into the station, toward the platform entrances. As we got close to the stairs leading to Track 2, something dropped in my stomach. I started thinking about what happened the last time I walked through a doorway that was supposed to lead us to Isiah Roust.

"Should we call any of your friends?" I asked.

"You want to involve the department?" he asked. "I'm on thin ice with them as it is."

"I know. But after last time—" I started.

"Last time he had a house rigged to blow. Here, he's just a shit heel, and there are two of us," Bill responded. "Besides, once anyone else with a badge gets involved, we won't get to talk to him."

Henniman stared at me for a second. As pissed as I was about what he'd done in the jail, I still had to be impressed by his ability to read me. Even though I hadn't told him I was working on a story about the Twilight Four, he probably suspected I was. We both knew I wouldn't get a chance to talk to Roust after he was in police custody.

I nodded, and we kept moving up the stairs.

The platform was its usual mob scene, with hundreds of people shuffling from foot to foot, waiting for trains while the occasional behind schedule commuter sprinted through crowds hoping not to miss the 3:15 to wherever.

Bill and I moved cautiously. We had no idea where Roust would be standing and if he saw us first, he'd run, and I didn't love the idea of a foot chase near train tracks. We started checking benches, looking down staircases and peeking into the enclosed waiting areas. They were normally meant for the winter, but we gave Roust the benefit of the doubt that he might be smart enough to try to remain hidden until his train arrived.

Halfway down the platform, we'd come up empty. I checked my phone. His train was scheduled to depart in five minutes.

"Not seeing him," I said.

"Then keep looking," Bill replied.

Henniman nudged his head left, indicating he'd split to that side of the platform while I stayed to the right. I kept advancing, starting to focus on people's neck lines, hoping the t-shirt weather would make it impossible for Roust to hide his atrocious ink.

Two minutes ticked by. No ink. I half jogged down the rest of the platform and started weaving through small crowds, like I was the obnoxious guy running late for his train, using the excuse to invade personal spaces and get some close looks. Nothing.

The intercom system barked to life, announcing that a Washington Union Station bound train would be arriving in two minutes. I looked across the platform to find Henniman frantically searching for Roust but failing.

Maybe the poor kid was wrong. Maybe his piece of shit foster mother had hit him so many times he was afraid to say no to any adult, even a stranger.

Something bumped into my leg. I looked down to find another unattended child, screaming and crying as she rebounded off my shin and to the dirty platform floor.

"Gracie! Gracie!" shrieked the woman running toward me as I scooped her child off the floor. The mother snatched her daughter away without even making eye contact, shouting at her not to run off like that.

The intercom buzzed again. One minute until Roust's train arrived. Wouldn't be much longer than that before it departed. My eyes traveled to one of the pillars at the center of the platform. There was a call box bolted to it. In the first bit of good luck I'd had in weeks, the cover seemed to have been left open by a nearby NJ Transit employee.

I had no idea if the line went directly to the public announce system. I had no idea if you could get arrested for misuse of a train station's intercom system. But I didn't have any better way of trying to stop the guy who'd nearly burned me to death from escaping the platform.

I grabbed the phone, put on my best official-sounding voice and said: "Attention all NJ Transit Riders. If you are looking for your lost son Izzy, he is at the first-floor ticket booth. Again, if you are looking for your lost son Izzy..."

I scanned the platform for someone to look up. Nothing. Somehow, the NJ Transit employee still hadn't turned around. I glanced at his phone, noticed he seemed to be involved in an extremely personal and graphic text exchange, and decided to press my luck.

"That's Izzy. I-S-H-E, like Jaquan spells it," I shouted, invoking the name of Roust's former partner in crime. "Lorena really wants to know where you are Izzy. She's worried."

The Baltimore bound train was pulling in. Some passengers started moving toward the doors, fighting for first position to get a choice seat. But as they clawed forward, I noticed a neck craning up, looking for the speaker box, face twisted in confusion.

As the man looked around, his terrible ace of spades tattoo became more visible.

It might as well have been a bullseye.

I had no idea how many feet and inches were between Roust and I, but I probably broke the land speed record to cover it, getting low and wrap tackling him around the waist.

Roust rolled away from me as we hit the ground, spilling dangerously close to the tracks before his body came to rest at the yellow line near the edge.

"This time we should talk before you blow up the building," I said, hopping to my feet as he continued backpedaling.

Roust's eyes widened. He was wearing a white t-shirt and jeans that hung too loose, like they weren't his. The shirt had at least one stain on it, and his curly hair was a complete mess, standing up at odd angles.

After spending five days looking for him, I wasn't giving him any breathing room. I closed in and reached for his left shoulder, but he swung the duffel bag up. Whatever was inside was heavy enough to stagger me for a second. One second too long, because Roust was running the other way by the time I'd regained my balance.

He'd dropped the bag and taken off in a full sprint, throwing a forearm into the chest of someone coming up the stairs to the platform. I went after him, dipping my shoulder and bowling over the unlucky older gentleman in the process.

Henniman's bald head popped into my peripheral vision. He'd probably followed the commotion to us, but the heavyset lieutenant wasn't built for a foot chase. His labored breathing got more and more faint behind me as I raced down the steps, leaping to the floor with about five to go.

I looked left and right, seeing if Roust had headed back to the main entrance or deeper into the station. A bush of wild dark hair was moving fast on my right, so I went after it, following it into an auxiliary hallway.

I knew the layout of the station fairly well. There was a side exit to a bus terminal ahead of him, another crowd he could get lost in. I picked up the pace, driving my elbows through my hips, getting up on my toes as I ran.

Roust was looking over his shoulder every few seconds, face red and out of breath. I remembered the overflowed ashtray in his apartment, and as the gap closed between us, felt a little prouder than usual that I'd cut the cigs out almost two years earlier.

He swung right. I was maybe ten feet behind. The space turned out to be a blessing, as Roust didn't realize he was running straight onto an escalator toward the underground platforms. He tried to pump the brakes but wound up executing a cartoonish banana peel slip kind of fall.

Roust rolled over and tried to find his feet, but I got my hands under his shoulders and drove him against the wall before pinning him there with my forearm.

"We need to talk," I growled, trying to arrest my breathing.

"Let me go. Let me go!" he shouted, squirming against the wall, trying to wrest himself free. "I'm sorry, I'm sorry, okay! But I…"

I didn't realize the pleading was a distraction until his foot crashed down on mine. The jolt of pain forced me back just enough that he had room to run again. He headed back the way we came but wound up on the floor as soon as he rounded the corner back to the hallway.

The forearm that nearly took his head clean off belonged to an extremely out of breath Bill Henniman.

Roust's head clattered off the tile floor hard. Bill was too tired to stop Roust from running again. But that wouldn't be a problem anymore. The informant turned flight risk looked equally out of gas and possibly in need of a neurologist.

With his hands on his knees, Henniman motioned across the hall to an alcove with two heavy green doors. There was a sign over it that read "No Public Access."

"In there," Henniman said. "We need privacy."

Being a cop in Newark for twenty years, I imagined this wasn't the first suspect Bill had tried to stop from fleeing the city via train or bus at Penn Station, so it was no surprise to me he knew the building's layout. But after what happened at the jail that morning, I briefly worried about Bill knowing exactly where to secure alone time with someone on the wrong side of the Twilight Four case.

Then my shoulder started acting up again, the burned skin from my first run-in with Roust now aching from the physical strain of the second. I started to give as little of a shit about his well-being as he had about mine.

I dragged Roust to the heavy doors while Henniman shoved them open. They led into a sparse hallway with white brick walls, a few doors on either side and crates at the end. I assumed it was a storage or maintenance area. Once we were alone, Bill grabbed Roust off the floor and put him against a wall again. I flinched, worried Bill might hit him but not entirely sure I wanted to stop him.

"I said I was sorry!" Roust screamed.

"Sorry for what exactly?" Bill asked. "Trying to kill us? Ruining a man's life? You recognize me, right, Roust? That's why you disappeared on us the first time, back in Asbury?"

"You, yeah," he replied, voice more stammering than speaking as he turned to me. "Who's that?"

"Oh right. We haven't been properly introduced," I said. "My name's Russell. You tried to kill me. I'm pretty sure I fucking hate you."

"I didn't want to do that. And I said I was sorry," he said. "I mentioned that, right?"

I took a step toward Roust, but Henniman shoved me back with his free hand.

"If you didn't want to do it, then why did it happen, Roust?" Bill asked. "You do understand what's going on here, right? You're looking over the same ledge as the first time we met, only this time the fall is a lot further. He's one attempted murder charge. I'm the other. With your history, that's life. Your last memory as a free man is this hallway, right here, right now."

"What? No. No! I didn't set that fire," Roust shrieked.

"Your apartment was covered in accelerants when we got there, and it blew up five seconds after you left," Henniman replied. "You sold me one bullshit story years ago. That's not happening again."

Roust swallowed hard. His Adam's apple looked like it wanted to burst through his neck. Sweat was staining his shirt and his beady eyes seemed like they were going to retreat out the back of his skull.

"We know Musa's innocent," I said. "We know you cooked the

confession all those years ago. And after what happened the last time we knocked on your door, I think we've got a pretty good idea of how you put together all those details on the fire in the first place."

Roust started to writhe against the wall, trying to slip Henniman's grasp, but the lieutenant's forearm had him flush. He might as well have been bolted into position. His eyes darted between Bill and me, looking for sympathy that didn't exist. There was something manic in his pupils. This was the moment he'd spent his whole life running from, and it didn't appear he'd ever made plans on what to do if he fled into a dead end.

"You're not listening. I didn't set the fire. Either fire. Any fire," he said. "I'd never even met Shayna before that night."

"So, you were there?" Henniman asked.

"You just said you fucking knew I was there!" Roust shouted back. Confirmation never hurt though.

"You're out of moves, man," I said, stepping closer to Roust, slipping my phone from my pocket so I could record what I hoped came next. "The harder you try to untangle yourself from this, the tighter the rope gets. You lied about Musa to save your own ass once. Look where it got you. Now you say someone else burned your house down, almost killed us, just to keep you from telling us why. Why the hell should we believe you? Do you even remember how to tell the truth?"

Roust stopped fighting. His arms went slack. It looked as if Henniman was holding him up now instead of trapping him. I let my reporter brain take over. Roust's best move was to shut up, but he didn't seem to know it. I couldn't give him any time to breathe and realize that.

"We get it. You're loyal to Lorena. She looked out for you as a kid. She helped you again now. She's got some sway over you," I said. "We know she beat on those kids, on Lavell. Maybe you were scared and felt like you had to go along with it. But we came straight here from her house. You can't protect her anymore."

Roust cocked his head to the side.

"You think…Lorena?" he asked. "She was just giving me a place to hide. This doesn't have anything to do with Lorena."

He trailed off, mouth snapping shut before anything real could come out.

"I can't talk about it," he said. "I didn't want to hurt them, or you, or Abel, or anyone. That's not…I mean, I'm a fucking thief, sure. I've sold drugs. But I don't hurt people."

"You don't hurt people?" Bill asked, his face reddening. "What do you call what you did to Abel Musa?"

"Desperation," he said. "I liked Abel. Really. I did. But you didn't give me any other choice."

"Me?" Bill asked.

"You told me you were gonna put me in jail for the rest of my natural life. I couldn't handle that shit," he said, pointing to the disastrously bad tattoo on his neck. "I know everyone looks at this shit when they see me, but they never ask how I got it. That was my last trip inside, before I went to Rahway, before I went to Musa. Some big Aryan motherfucker decided he liked the way I looked, like pulling my hair when he…" Roust's voice trailed off. He didn't need to finish the sentence.

"He had someone put this on me, as a reminder. I couldn't live like that again. As someone else's property. As their fucking toy," he said, his voice a mix of a cry and a shriek now. "That's why I got so close to Musa in Rahway. Figured he was big enough to keep me safe. And he was. But then he told me who he was. How he was connected to those kids. And every night I got to thinking…I hoped it never came to that. That I'd never be staring down a long stretch again. Because knowing what I know, about what really happened…he just fit too well. I fucking hated doing it. But once you put those handcuffs on, it was him or me."

I searched Roust's face, trying to find something alien in it, trying to convince myself I'd be braver in the same situation. Bill did not share my empathy, shoving Roust against the wall again, hard enough that his ex-informant rebounded off the brick and fell face first into the cop's chest.

"Don't expect me to feel any fucking pity for you," Bill said.

"I don't want pity. I just want you to understand. I...I heard them scream. Do you have any idea what that's like? To hear people, hear... fucking kids, man," Roust said, his body quivering from head to toe. "They...the girl. It was the girl. The littlest one. She was screaming. She was begging. And I didn't stop it. I couldn't. It wasn't up to me then. And afterwards, well...they paid me to keep quiet. And I needed that money."

"Stop with the I can't and the I'm sorry. Like you didn't have choices," Bill said. "You chose to run guns. You chose to do dumb shit that put you in an interrogation room with me. You chose to ruin Abel Musa's life. You chose to run from us and you chose to leave us to die. No one had a gun to your..."

Now it was Henniman's turn to go quiet, still. His right hand started moving down toward his waist.

"Bill..." I said.

"Shut the fuck up, Russell," he replied.

Roust tensed up, pressing his back further against the wall, maybe hoping he could slip through it and escape.

"Do not do whatever you're thinking," I said. "He's not worth that."

"He's not? 'Cause there are four graves, a dying man and a grieving woman who probably fucking disagree with you," he said, face half-turned to me. "Every goddamn step of the way, this snake has lied and dealt and danced to keep from owning his shit, and each move has left wreckage. Everywhere. He's done. Today. He's telling us the fucking truth *today*."

Bill's right hand was at his holster now.

"What it takes to get us there is entirely up to him," he said.

Roust seemed to be studying me, waiting to see if I'd leap forward to his rescue as Bill's fingers started to walk around the grip to his sidearm. I wasn't sure what I was going to do. The last time I'd fought a Newark cop with a gun in his hand, Henniman had been the only reason I survived.

"Hey, Detective," Roust said, voice now down to a whisper. "How would you know anyway?"

"What?"

"If I was telling the truth," Roust said, a sad smile creeping across his otherwise desperate expression. I couldn't tell if he was trying to distract Henniman or get himself killed, probably whichever one he thought might keep him out of a jail cell.

"'Cause you were pretty sure the first time and, well…"

Bill's hand came up from his holster and flew forward, ending Roust's comment. I was too slow to react, but thankfully the gun stayed home. Henniman's fist, however, turned Roust's face into an explosion of blood and spit, impacting his front teeth with all the force of a line drive.

"You motherfucking worthless piece of shit, cunt bastard," Bill screamed, an unholy exorcism of profanities spewing forth as he rained haymakers on Roust. I grabbed him by the waist and pulled backwards. I might as well have tugged a lion's mane.

Henniman's elbow swung high at my chin, but his arc was just wide enough that I managed to avoid the blow. I caught sight of Roust's bloodied face as I lowered my center of gravity, wrapping Henniman's gut in a bearhug and driving him into the wall. The battered ex-informant fell out of the way more than he dodged, but he cleared a path for me to drive Bill's spine directly into the wall.

The force of the impact made Henniman cough and shot me backwards.

"Bill, wait," I said, but he closed the space between us with a wild right that I just barely managed to avoid.

"Bill!" I shouted again, as a weaker follow-up jab caught me in the chest.

I stumbled back. Bill shouted and charged, pinning me against the wall.

"Bill!" I screamed.

"Enough of you. Enough of your fucking questions," he said. "You haven't been living with this."

He got his hands up under the neck line of my shirt, hands close enough that they could choke if they wanted to.

"I am going to fix this. I do not care how. And not you, him, or anyone else, is going to get in my way anymore. Do you understand?" he asked.

"Bill!" I shouted, but he slammed me against the wall before I could get the words out.

"Do you understand?" he asked again, voice so loud it echoed down the hallway, making it seem like he'd asked the question six different times.

The sound was only drowned out by the loud thud of a door slamming.

Bill turned around to see what I'd been trying to scream to him. Droplets of Roust's blood led from the wall to the door and back out into Penn Station.

I brought my forearms down in a sledgehammer maneuver, breaking Bill's grasp for a second. As he stumbled, I shoved him toward the wall, the back of his head striking the brick. The aftereffects of our first clash with Roust seemed to kick in, the last concussion he suffered getting queued up for a re-run, stunning him long enough that I had a second to run after Roust.

As soon as I got out the door, I heard him begging again. His desperate, helium whine filling the otherwise empty hallway. I looked up just in time to see the reason his pleas stopped.

Roust was stumbling back toward me, hands clutching at his stomach as he fell to the side, eyes bulging with panic as they stared at a kitchen knife drenched in his own blood. The person holding the blade was clad in all black, a hoodie and jeans covering anything that could identify him, a balaclava wrapped around his face.

All I could see were chestnut eyes that looked as scared as Roust's did, and the hands holding the knife. There were two tungsten rings on the fingers wrapped around the handle of the blade, ones that looked eerily similar to those worn by a man whose apartment I'd visited because of a picture I found in Roust's apartment.

The man with the knife stepped toward me.

"I didn't want this," he said. "You could never understand how much I didn't want this."

Before the man could punctuate that sentence with the weapon in his hand, someone came up the escalator from the nearby underground Light Rail platform. They did the smart thing and screamed as loud as I probably should have.

The man in the balaclava ran back toward the lobby, tucking the blade inside his sweatshirt as he fled. I ran over to Roust, looking in the direction his killer was running, sure I'd lose him in the crowd as fast as any witness would.

Roust was breathing in panicked heaves, clawing at me as I leaned in, spilling blood he couldn't afford to lose. I pulled out my phone and started to dial 911 as he reached up and grabbed my wrist with his blood slick hand.

"Tell Abel," he hissed. "Tell him I'm so goddamn sorry. I never should have—"

"If you're sorry, prove it," I replied. "Tell the truth. One time."

Roust's eyes started rolling into the back of his head. I grabbed his shirt, not caring how much blood got on me, and slapped the dying informant twice.

"Angel?" I asked, shaking him. "Was it Angel?"

He nodded, finally confessing before his eyes rolled into the back of his head.

Isiah Roust was gone, taking the only truth that could help Abel Musa with him.

CHAPTER
SEVENTEEN

ENNIMAN AND I were standing over Isiah Roust's body when the first wave of Newark cops arrived. They noticed Bill's badge and whisked us off in separate directions.

The detectives gave each other a "this fucking guy" look after learning my name. Knowing Henniman was likely somewhere else in the building answering the same questions, I didn't bother lying. I told them we were trying to talk to Roust when he ran from us. I described all the completely discardable features I could about the man holding the knife. The mask and the sweatshirt that were probably in a trash can somewhere nearby.

And no, I told them I couldn't think of anybody who would want Isiah Roust dead.

I couldn't give the detectives the name that Roust had given me. His lies had already stolen one man's life. I couldn't risk it happening again, especially considering the name. Not unless I was sure.

But if Roust was telling the truth, that raised even bigger questions.

Had Mariana known? Had Tiago? Was that why they hired me?

Realizing I was somehow less helpful than the already vague witnesses they had, the detectives cut me loose but told me not to go far.

I stumbled outside the train station, hoping the fresh air would help. But I just kept looking at my hands and the specks of dried blood there, watching my fingers tremble just a bit and inhaling deep when somebody nearby lit a cigarette.

Roust had built his entire survival on fiction. How the hell could I take anything he said seriously? What if he was just pulling his trick again, escaping so far away in death that it wouldn't matter by the time the lie fell apart?

Then again, there was still the decades-old photo in Roust's apartment. The one I'd been telling myself didn't mean anything out of context. Roust's dying words and the fact that the man who killed him was wearing the same exact jewelry Angel Pereira had been the one time I met him seemed like pretty important context.

There were blanks Roust needed to fill in. And he might have been on his way to an interrogation room instead of a morgue if Henniman and I hadn't been complete fucking morons.

This was our fault. How could it not be? Henniman and I had done everything but stick the knife in Roust's gut.

He'd only had time to set the fire at his apartment because we missed him at the arcade in Asbury. He only had room to flee through the train station and into the path of a blade because we'd been selfish and chosen to interrogate him head-on instead of calling any of the police agencies that wanted to put him in handcuffs.

Even my attempt to record what should have been the last useful thing Isiah Roust said had gone wrong. Henniman must have slammed up against my phone when we fought in the hallway, because the file I'd started either hadn't saved or got itself deleted during the struggle.

In trying to get justice for four deaths, we'd caused one more. And we had absolutely nothing to show for it.

What the hell was I supposed to do with Roust's dying words? How would I even corroborate them?

Cynthia Bell's pain was for nothing. The brief hope we'd given Abel Musa was little more than dangling keys just out of the reach of a man in chains. He couldn't be helped now, and once he learned what had happened, he'd suffer just a bit more before he died.

I turned to my right and noticed the smoke smell wafting over from the left hand of an NJ Transit employee. The distinctive filter told me it was a Parliament. I'd hated Parliaments back when I smoked. I reminded myself that I'd saved thousands of dollars in the years since I'd quit, that every single one of those dollars was going to be critical since my brief foray into politics hadn't produced any revenue and my lone avenue of PI work had just ended in a homicide.

My index and middle finger extended themselves on reflex. The smoking fingers. I saw Roust's blood on them, and started moving toward the smell.

"Haven't you made enough mistakes for one day, Mr. Avery?" asked the last voice I wanted to hear at that moment.

I turned around to see Dameon Lynch walking toward me. Over his shoulder, a group of people in suits appeared to be berating Bill Henniman near a row of Newark PD cruisers, probably a mix of bosses from Broad Street.

"I remember your ever-present cigarettes after press conferences. I was genuinely proud when I heard you quit," he said, each word dripping with condescension. "You wouldn't want to backslide now, would you?"

"If you're here, Lynch, then you know I've got bigger problems than cigarettes," I replied.

"Oh, of course," he said. "I'd imagine you've got a lot of concerns about your future after today."

"My future?"

"Well, from what some witnesses have told the police, you were chasing the poor man who was murdered shortly before he was killed,"

Lynch replied. "I imagine there are going to be some questions if it gets out that a member of Councilwoman Pereira's campaign team is connected to a murder. Much less the killing of a man so central to one of the city's most infamous crimes."

It had been a while since Lynch spoke to me in that way, warping reality with every breath, twisting words so confidently that I almost agreed with his version of something I'd lived.

"Before you tell me you aren't working for the councilwoman, I'll note you didn't deny it right away," he said.

I was too busy trying to figure out how he knew to even pretend he was wrong. It wouldn't have made any sense for Key or Mariana to dime me out to their political nemesis, and I didn't think Tiago had a direct line to the mayor's office. Bill couldn't cough up that information without hurting his own standing with the people who ran Newark.

Only one other person knew I was working for Mariana. The same man Lynch was already paying for information. Angel had apparently fucked me over even before he killed Roust.

"Do you have a point, Lynch?" I asked.

"You know, while the circumstances are unfortunate, I do prefer you this way. Docile. Not in a rush to insult me," he said. "My point, Mr. Avery, is that your presence here today could go unnoticed, or it could not."

"The fuck do I care if people knew I was here?"

"Perhaps you don't. But your future editors might. If you are to have any," he said. "I did some checking up on you after you decided to become a problem in my life again. It sounds like you're trying to get back to being a working journalist. Considering the state of your PI business, that's understandable. But I wonder how your job prospects would fare if any of your former colleagues were to learn that you're running errands for a mayoral candidate, that you've actually been trying to suppress a scandal on her behalf. That your efforts today— whether they be for your public relations job or your little freelance gambit—led to a man's death."

"That's a lot of ifs and maybes for blackmail, Lynch," I said.

"Observations aren't blackmail, Mr. Avery. And I did warn you about the loss of the protections you enjoyed as a reporter," he replied. "You crashed and burned out of the business two years ago. Doesn't everything I just described sound like a lot of baggage for someone looking for a second chance?"

It did. Which was why I let Lynch enjoy himself. I didn't have anything to counterpunch with, and he had a lot of ways to make my already disastrous day worse.

"What do you want?" I asked.

"The same thing I wanted when we first reconnected. I want to help you get back in the game. I want to help you tell a story," he said. "Now, you've obviously had a day. So, I'm going to let you be. But we're going to have this conversation again. Soon. And I'm going to offer you a story again. And if you've any interest in self-preservation, I'd suggest you take it."

Lynch met me with a high-beam smile, fidgeted with the Bluetooth in his ear, and walked away.

But before I could think too long about Lynch's blackmail attempt, I saw Henniman headed in my direction. His mouth was drawn tight and his head was pitched forward as he stepped away from the crowd of suits that had been berating him.

"You should leave," Henniman said as he got close.

"Are…are we not going to talk about what just happened?" I asked. "Roust, when he was dying, he confirmed—"

"Russell. This might be the last conversation we ever have, so for once, listen," he said.

"Bill, you don't understand. Roust told me who it—"

"It doesn't matter anymore," Henniman said. "You see that crowd I was just getting reamed out by?"

I nodded.

"Those are deputy chiefs. Watkins's people have their ears or vice-versa," he said. "They're putting this on me. What happened here, they're saying it's the direct result of me defying a direct order to leave the Twilight Four case alone."

His breathing picked up slightly, big draws in and out through his wide nose.

"This is going to a disciplinary board. They will take my badge. My pension. They want to march me out, Russell. In handcuffs, if they get particularly angry. This is not how it's supposed to end for me. I didn't give twenty-five years for…"

Bill looked away from me, up into the bright summer sky, squinting as he took one elongated breath.

"I am not going to be a cautionary tale. I have, I had…a history in this department. A legacy. If they put me down this way…if they make me a pariah…I can't deal with that," he said. "I have to drop this. Or else I lose everything."

I thought back to the inside of Henniman's home. The pictures of police functions that far outweighed mementos of wives or kids. That was all he had to go home to, and he couldn't have that corrupted.

"It's over, Russell," he said. "It has to be."

"What about Musa?" I asked. "What about Cynthia? Don't they deserve answers?"

"Cynthia had an answer she could live with until we took that away from her," he said. "And Musa…there's nothing left we can do for him. Look at what happened today. Look at what happened in Asbury. Hell, even this morning. Every step of this, we've hurt people. And for what? We have nothing we can prove. Nowhere else to look. Without Roust, it's done."

"I'm not giving up on this," I said.

"That's up to you," he said. "But I can't be a part of it. I don't have a choice."

"What are you saying?" I asked.

"I'm saying go home, Russell," he replied. "You're fired."

My trip home was interrupted by a desperately needed piece of good news landing at the exact wrong moment.

I'd been walking down Ferry, head buried in my phone to avoid human contact after a day of almost universally terrible interactions with the rest of my species, when an e-mail I'd normally have prayed for appeared.

It was a response to one of the freelance pitches I'd sent out. Neal Goldberg, the reporter-turned-editor friend of mine, said he might have an appetite for a wrongful conviction story like the one I'd pitched about the Twilight Four. But I'd need to get beyond the holes in the case and Musa's claims of innocence. Neal wanted to know what I had on the police missteps that put Musa behind bars in the first place, any information I could provide on alternate suspects. Basically, he wanted to know if I could answer the first question any reader would have: if Musa was innocent, then who was guilty?

He asked if there was a problem with the informant. The man whose blood I needed to wash off my forearms.

I deleted the e-mail and picked up the pace as I turned onto my block. I definitely needed a shower. Maybe a beer, and an intervention after that.

The closer I got to my apartment, the more I thought about breaking something once I got inside. If I'd been a better reporter, or PI, or whatever the fuck I thought I was supposed to be, I wouldn't have wound up in this situation.

I'd have tracked Roust down before he got to the train station instead of chasing him into the path of his killer. Or I'd have found someone else who could point me toward the secret lover detailed in Shayna Bell's journals, the father of the unnamed fifth victim of the Twilight Four killings.

The baby that was never born because her mother died before they could meet.

That concept turned my stomach to lead as I reached the door of my apartment. Whoever killed those kids was even more of a monster than I'd realized. They had to have known she was pregnant when they lit the match.

Not whoever. I had a name. If nothing else, I had that.

Angel Pereira. The estranged brother of Newark's potential next mayor. The man who'd stuck a knife in Isiah Roust's gut and might have done the same to me if he had a clean chance at it.

He had to be the man in Shayna's journals. Why else would he have killed Roust? He would have been in his late teens or early twenties around the time the Twilight Four vanished, old enough to be the man Shayna described in the pages that haunted her older sister.

It made sense. But did it matter?

The only person who could put Angel Pereira at the scene of one of Newark's most horrific crimes had just bled out in front of me. Without Roust, there was no story to write. And without Henniman, there was no one in law enforcement who would even consider listening to me. Not with my reputation.

The only person who I knew could confirm Angel Pereira's involvement in the Twilight Four killings was Angel Pereira. I liked to think of myself as a gifted interviewer, but talking someone into confessing to a quadruple-homicide was probably beyond my skill set.

Especially someone who had to know I was looking for them now. Someone who had locked eyes with me while they put an end to my last lead.

I pulled out my phone, scrolled to the text message conversation I'd been having earlier in the day. Angel had suggested meeting up. Maybe he hadn't connected the dots. Maybe he didn't know the person looking into his sister's dirty laundry was also the man chasing his past sins.

Or maybe he did, and the interview setup was just a pretext to do the same thing to me that he'd done to Roust.

I thought about texting him. About chancing it. But I wasn't sure I had that in me. At least not right that second.

But without it, I had no story to write.

Even though I had one to tell.

No matter what could or couldn't be published, what would stand up in court, Abel Musa still deserved to know what I'd learned.

Laughter was not the sound I expected to hear coming from Abel Musa's room the next day.

I'd gone to University Hospital to tell him about Isiah Roust, to tell him I'd fucked up his best, maybe last, chance at clearing his name. To at least let him know that someone was straight with him before it all ended.

I was walking through University Hospital, bracing myself to be yelled at, told to leave, told I should have just left him in peace, when I heard the laughs.

His, and a woman's.

I turned the corner to find Abel Musa sitting in a chair on the left side of his bed, IV pole wheeled forward so the line didn't strain too much. His gaunt face was lit up with a cheek-to-cheek grin as his shaking hands tapped excitedly at a book in his lap.

Cynthia Bell stood next to him, hand over her mouth, trying to stifle a smile as she pointed at the same spot.

I hovered at the edge of the doorway, extremely confused but also slightly concerned about interrupting what might have been a rare blip of joy on Abel Musa's radar.

"You were not ready," Cynthia said, the laugh escaping over her palm as her voice cracked.

"Look at that boy. He was a goddamn thoroughbred, and I was already halfway to the glue factory," Musa responded. "Guess I was trying to impress you."

"By getting bowled over by my little cousin?" she asked.

"It worked, didn't it?"

"I think they call that pity," she clapped back.

Musa looked up at her with wanting eyes. Cynthia bit her lip, holding back the littlest bit of affection he'd been chasing for decades.

She stood up straight when she spotted me and pulled away from Musa, whose wet puppy eyes had turned feral when they realized why she was withdrawing.

"Mr...Avery, right?" she asked, face still slightly flush from my sudden appearance.

"Yes, ma'am," I replied. "Sorry, I guess. I wasn't expecting him to have company."

"Well, I do," Musa said, his voice a little weaker than it had been during my other visits. "And this room cramps with more than two people in it."

Cynthia placed a hand on his shoulder, and Musa's entire face changed. I wondered how long it had been since he'd had physical contact with someone who wasn't wearing scrubs.

"I'm sorry. And it's been a hell of a two days," I said, scratching the side of my head. "But the last time I was here, Miss Bell, you two were not so..."

"A lot's changed since the last time you were here, hasn't it?" Cynthia asked, removing her hand from Musa and regaining a more formal posture.

"You could say that," I replied. "But I'm not really sure I understand."

"I'll tell you later. Hell, I'll sing you a song about it," Musa hissed. "But later. Come back later."

He started to shake again. His body just didn't have the energy to fight even the smallest battle. Cynthia patted him on the shoulder and walked over to the doorway, prompting another smile from Musa before she hooked my arm and led me out of the room.

"I wanted to hit you the last time we were here," she said. "Lying to get me up here. Spouting what you did about my family. That was wrong. But honestly, I was angrier with Bill. All these years, and he couldn't just tell me to my face that he thought Abel didn't do it? I couldn't understand why he hid that from me."

"Ma'am, all due respect, your sister's death has been a legend around Newark for half past forever and you hadn't told a soul she was pregnant until two days ago," I replied. "People keep secrets for a reason."

"Do you want an explanation, or do you want to interrupt me?" she asked.

"The first thing," I said.

"Thought so," she replied. "I left here demanding to talk to Bill's boss at the police department. I wanted to file a complaint. But they wouldn't meet with me. Wouldn't take my calls. Told me there was nothing to worry about and nothing had changed and to go home. They'd never been like that with me before. So, I went to city hall, thinking after the mayor's speech at the memorial the other night that he'd listen, tell me what could be done about this. I waited three hours for some secretary to tell me his schedule was full but someone on his staff would call me soon. Then I saw the news yesterday."

"Roust," I said.

"Not twenty-four hours after you tell me this man set Abel up and he might have a different story about what happened to my family, he dies? That's suspicious," she said. "And the police and city hall people who swear up and down to call whenever I need anything won't even look me in the eye? That sound right to you? I'd spent so long focusing on Abel and Shayna and that disgusting thought. Now, you're all telling me that wasn't possible, that he couldn't have gotten her pregnant. So, I started thinking, devil's advocate. If not Abel, who?"

Her gaze lingered on me longer than I felt comfortable with, almost like she knew I had an answer. I was exhausted, and maybe projecting. There was no way she could know what Isiah Roust had whispered to me as his soul fled his body. But she deserved to. She deserved for someone to validate or disprove that claim, no matter the consequences.

"I don't understand," I said. "You think he's innocent now? 'Cause we tried to tell you that last time and—"

"You talk a lot better than you listen. I'm a woman of God, but I'm no fool either. I don't forgive all that easily. And he still disappeared on me not long after we lost them. But I wanted answers, so I came to talk to him, and, well…almost no one else is left who remembers them like I do," she said. "We were looking through Shayna's yearbook, and we came across a picture of Kurtis in his football uniform, and I just remembered this time Abel promised to help him with a drill for practice and Kurtis, well…he just put Abel right on his butt. And that was the first time I thought of that, or had someone to share that with, in so, so long."

I nodded. Not because I entirely understood what she was going through, but because I was happy to see her and Musa no longer divided by someone else's lie. Whatever their dynamic became, for however long it functioned, at least in this moment they would be governed by the truth of their shared pain and past.

"Does he know?" I asked. "About Roust?"

Cynthia shook her head imperceptibly.

"Well, that brings us to the other reason for my compassion," she replied. "When I came up here, the nurses stopped me. They thought I was family, 'cause I guess I'm one of the only people they've seen up here more than once. He doesn't get many visitors, from what they said. But he's getting worse. It could be days, they said, not weeks."

I looked over at Musa and Cynthia turned with me. He'd dropped his "Russell, get the fuck out" glare and tried to plaster his grin back on before she noticed. It almost looked like he was waiting for her to pet him. He was so sickeningly gleeful it briefly allowed me to forget that I was there to ruin his hopes to clear his name.

As Cynthia swung back to his side, I remembered what he'd said the last time we'd been alone together. How it was too late to change the way his story would be told. How those were my goals, not his. How he'd just prayed and wished and begged that one day, Cynthia wouldn't consider him a monster.

Maybe he'd gotten what he wanted. Who was I to take that away from him?

Maybe I didn't need to drag him back to the reality where his last, best hope at innocence had died bleeding in my arms.

Except it hadn't. I still had a name.

Cynthia Bell had seen through decades of bullshit to give Abel Musa one overdue smile.

Abel Musa had survived cancer long enough to earn that little bit of joy.

If they could persevere through that kind of pain, what was my excuse?

CHAPTER
EIGHTEEN

YOU NEVER WANT to do an interview hungry. Especially when it
might be your last one.

I flopped into the seat that had become my unofficial table at
Hobby's, the best deli in Newark and probably the entire solar system,
falling into the ripped cushioning and pushing the menu away as soon
as the waitress put it down. Bowl of matzoh ball soup and a Number 5,
which was corn beef and pastrami on rye covered in enough slaw and
Russian dressing to drown in. It really should have been a meal for two,
but I was incapable of wasting food at Hobby's, even if my stomach was
so full I might need medical attention.

Considering my plans for the day, I was probably going to end up
at a hospital one way or the other.

I pulled out my phone and scanned over the texts from Angel
Pereira. He hadn't contacted me in over a day. The last message was
him asking me to meet, sent just a few hours before he plunged a knife
into Isiah Roust. Was he really planning to sell blackmail photos to

me and kill who I now presumed to be his accomplice in a quadruple-murder in the same day? Or was I supposed to meet the same end?

The soup came first, and I shoveled a spoonful of the matzoh ball at the center into my mouth, wanting to enjoy some before my guest arrived. I needed to have at least two conversations before I tried to have one with Angel. And this one was probably going to involve yelling.

As the salted broth warmed my insides, the taste so good I didn't care it was making me sweat a bit, my mind cleared for a blissful sixty seconds. I stopped thinking about teens burned to death, lives stolen by a sideways prosecution and a selfish informant's lie, witnesses silenced and whether or not I was about to become one of them. My sandwich arrived and I got exactly one glorious bite down before reality interrupted me.

"Your obsession with this bland-ass food is not one of your better qualities, Russ," said Keyonna Jackson as she sat down, her knee banging the underside of the table, causing a not insignificant amount of my soup to splash out.

That move had become a running joke between us, one I was kinda done laughing over.

"Key, you know this place is the closest thing I have to a church, right?" I asked. "The day, no, the week, I'm having, you really feel the need to insult me in my house of worship?"

"You worship cold cuts?" she asked.

I held up the sandwich, pointing to the beautiful cut of corned beef I would have already inhaled if she hadn't started with me.

"One, this shit is as close to cold cuts as Popeye's is to Cajun food," I replied. "Two, these sandwiches have done a lot more for me than Jesus."

"I had six missed calls from you," she said. "I assume those weren't so we could fight about lunch meat."

I took an oversized, defiant bite, making sure to chew long and slow and disgusting, just so Key had to make a face like she was embarrassed to know me.

"You hear about what happened at Newark Penn?" I asked.

"Hear about it? Yeah, from just about everyone except you, who I should have heard it from first. I'm getting a little tired of that pattern, Russ," she said. "First, you don't tell me the informant who testified against Musa is sideways. The informant turned up by this mayor's police department, by the way. Now you're standing there when he dies and I gotta hear that shit from some cop I don't even like on Mariana's security detail?"

"I was being delicate with incomplete information. That's a trait you're going to be thankful for in a minute," I replied. "That's why we're here."

I slid my phone across the table, the screen open to the texts with Angel. I figured that'd catch her up and buy me time to finish my sandwich.

Key picked up the device and started absent mindedly scrolling with her thumb. It took about twenty seconds for her to start scowling.

"This what you called me here for, an 'I told you so' about the photos?" she asked. "Is that really the most important thing right now?"

"I wish it was," I replied, dropping the rest of the sandwich on the plate before scanning the room for anyone whose good hearing might have been problematic. Hobby's was close enough to Broad Street, the Essex County Prosecutor's Office and the federal courthouse that I didn't want to chance it.

Then I whispered the few facts I knew about Angel Pereira, each of them more troubling than the last. The picture in Roust's apartment. The jewelry I'd seen on Angel one day, then on the hands of the man who'd taken a life in front of me the next.

"Who else have you told?" she asked.

"No one," I replied. "Can't exactly run around telling people the next mayor's brother might be—"

Key slapped a hand on the table, loud enough to draw the entire room's attention and shut my mouth without her having to physically close it. I hadn't said it out loud yet, and she clearly didn't want me to, to give it the power of being spoken into reality.

"I don't know that it's him, Key," I said. "I can't know that. Not yet."

"So then why are you telling me all this?" she asked

"Because I don't know who else to tell it to. Henniman fired me, and the way he's been the past twenty-four hours, I can't say I really trust him with this anyway. I went to Musa's hospital bed, but Cynthia was there, and for once, he looked happy. I wasn't taking that away from him for something I'm not sure of," I said. "But considering where this could go, I just wanted to make sure someone else knew what I knew before I do what I've gotta do next."

Key looked down at the phone again, retracing the text conversation until she found my meaning.

"You're gonna meet with him?" she asked.

"I'm gonna try. What else am I supposed to do?" I asked. "I can't ignore it. But I can't raise the dead either. He killed Roust. Which means he either killed those kids, or he knows who did, but either way, he might be the last chance we have to make sure Abel dies an innocent man. The only way we're going to know for sure is if I confront him. But if I'm really going to try to talk him into a confession, I need to go in there knowing everything I can about him."

"Meaning you need me to get Mariana to talk to you again," Key said. "She ain't thrilled with you after your last conversation."

"I'm assuming you can fix that," I replied. "Tell her what I showed you about the pictures. It's him. We at least have proof of that."

Key nodded. Then she exhaled. For a moment we just stared at each other, letting the heaviness of it all fill the air between us. Hobby's had basically functioned as a field office for me when I was a reporter. I'd talked about dozens of depressing stories and controversies between bites of the deli's perfectly crusted rye. But talking about this toxic, political mess in my happy place felt wrong. So did the question I had to ask Key next.

"Do you remember last year? We were sitting right here, a few days after I found out who shot Kevin Mathis. You asked me what I would have done if you weren't involved," I said. "If I was the only one who knew, if I would have been the one to make it public. To turn on my friend and do the right thing."

"'Course I do. And you said you didn't know," Key said. "So what, you wanna ask me the same thing now, hoping I'll actually give you a straight answer? What do I do if you're right?"

"If I'm right, that could be the end of your candidate," I said.

"If you're right, then you're right. But you're the reporter. You're the one who'd have to tell the story, not me," she replied. "Besides, shouldn't you be asking yourself the same question. What if you're right? If it was Angel in the train station, if it's been Angel this whole time, keeping this a secret for more than twenty years…what do you think he's gonna try to do if he gets you alone?"

I picked up the last bite of the best sandwich I'd ever had.

"Well, if it goes that way," I said. "At least I had a great last meal."

No matter what Key did to smooth things over with Mariana, she held little sway over the man who owned the building where I needed to meet her.

Tiago was standing outside Marisqueira Pereira as I approached, his hands wrapped so tight around the broom he was sweeping back and forth that I thought it might splinter in his hands. He hadn't seemed to notice me as I crossed Ferry in his direction, though given the look of intense concentration on his face, I wasn't sure if he would have noticed much of anything. He was sweeping like he wanted the bristles on his broom to push away not just the dirt and other sidewalk detritus, but the concrete itself.

For a second, I thought I'd be able to slip past him without issue. But the broomstick tapped my chest as I approached the restaurant's heavy wooden doors.

"You need to stop this," Tiago said. "I asked you twice. Once politely, once less so, to stay out of my family's affairs. I heard her on the phone the other morning. I know you contacted her embarrassment of a brother. That's why you are here now, correct? I have worked my entire life to keep her clear of his whirlpool, and yet here you are, trying to drag her back in for your own benefit."

Tiago's descent in my eyes from kindly pastry merchant to probable bigot and definite asshole had been swift.

"Do you have any idea what he's been doing?" I asked, surprising myself with the weight of the question, the heft he couldn't recognize.

Tiago met my eyes, something between exhaustion and disgust swimming in them.

"You seem to think he is behind the smut being peddled involving my daughter," he said.

"Smut?" I asked. "Dude, do you even know what decade it is?"

Tiago pulled on the necklace he was wearing, the simple silver crucifix hanging from it.

"My beliefs do not change with the calendar. Angel has many, many failings, but even he would not sink to the level you are accusing him. Nor would he have reason to. He is far more forgiving of his sister's behavior than he should be," Tiago said. "I have asked you to back away as a friend. Again, as a father. I am asking once more, as a man, that you leave this alone. God willing, my daughter is about to become the most powerful woman in this city. Angel is poison. Everything he touches crumbles. I have spent much of my life keeping him away from her, so she could reach her full potential. She does not need this right now."

I wanted to unload on him. To tell him his son was far more dangerous than whatever little monster he imagined he had raised, but I couldn't risk tripping that wire.

"Why do you think he's poison?" I asked. "What the hell did he do?"

"All I am trying to impress upon you is that what you are doing will only lead to more harm for my daughter than good," he said. "If you persist on this path, I will do what is necessary to protect her."

"Did you really wait out here all day to threaten me, Tiago?" I asked. "Because that's really sweet. Usually people just call me or send poorly written e-mails, but you went with the in-person touch."

"Understand that whatever happens next, you had choices," he replied. "We are not all given that luxury."

Tiago stomped away, so I stepped inside. The restaurant's sleek, romantic vibe was being disrupted by the construction of a lengthy buffet line and the noise of a half-dozen employees moving around with ladders and stepstools. Some of them chattered excitedly in the language it would have done me well to learn as an Ironbound resident. Two men were climbing the ladders, each holding one end of a blue banner that bore Mariana's name. Her campaign slogan, "Leaders Are Homegrown," was embroidered across it in white. I wasn't partial to it, but that might have been colored by my last few run-ins with her father.

Not seeing Mariana immediately, I stepped behind the unoccupied bar and reached for the soda gun to pour myself a water. It was hot as hell out, and I didn't think grand theft aqua was enough to make Tiago hate me more than he already did. As I crouched down to fish a clean glass from a rack, I noticed the long, smooth black snout of a Remington and traced the nose back to the body of the 12-gauge that was sitting on two hooks behind the ice bin.

The shotgun made me give a second thought to how casually I'd dismissed Tiago's polite threat outside.

"Working for me doesn't mean we comp your drinks, Russell."

Mariana Pereira was standing across the bar from me when I stood up.

"What's all this?" I asked, gesturing toward the banners and buffet setup.

"We're having a fundraiser tonight. Watkins has a lot of independent expenditures backing him. Using Dad's place to cut down on overhead is really all I can do to counter that," she replied. "So, as you might imagine, I don't have a lot of time."

"I understand. Key caught you up? She told you what I found?" I asked.

She met me with a short, wobbly, nod, her lips pressed together like they were sealing something off.

"Well, then it's your call. You asked me to find the source of the photos. I found them," I said. "Now what?"

"Find out how much he wants," she replied. "Then we pay him. Then this can end."

Mariana turned and walked away from me, waving her hand to call over a man who I assumed was one of Tiago's busboys. Like ordering me to pay off her brother the blackmailer was just a simple task to be completed so she could get back to her day.

"That's it?" I asked, stepping out from behind the bar.

She spun on her heel and looked at me like she was annoyed I was still there. For the briefest second, I saw the father flash in the daughter's eyes.

"What else do you need to know?" she asked.

"Do you really want me to answer that question out here?"

The busboy she'd been directing was still standing on a nearby ladder, maybe wondering if he was safer up there.

Mariana bit her lip slightly, darted her eyes toward the kitchen and motioned for me to follow. We traveled through and out a back door, stepping into a space littered with cigarette butts that I imagined functioned as the staff's break area.

"I don't mean to sound like my father, but there does come a point where this genuinely stops being your concern," she said. "I have appreciated your help in this. I should have listened when you tried to warn me about Angel the first time. But what does it matter to you how I handle this now?"

I might have lied to Key about my reasons for wanting to talk to Mariana before going after Angel. Yes, I did want to know more about his excommunication from the Pereira family before confronting him. But Mariana's sudden shutdown the first time I'd suggested her brother was behind the photos had unnerved me. She was a smart woman, and I had to be sure she wasn't walling me off to try to block me from a far worse truth. The one I was going to try to convince her brother to confess to.

"Because I don't understand this. At all," I said. "You're just going to let your brother profit off having the same ass backwards opinions about your sexuality as your father?"

"Angel and my father agree on almost nothing, least of all who I let in my bed," she replied.

"I talked to your ex, remember? She told me how Angel reacted when he saw you two together."

"I talk to my brother at least once a week, Russell, trust me, I understand his opinions on my lifestyle a little better than you," she said.

"I thought he was persona non grata around here."

"He is," she replied. "My father doesn't know we talk. And it needs to stay that way."

The Pereiras had way too many secrets for a family whose name was on the verge of being stenciled on the door to the mayor's office.

"I'm a few train stops past confused, Councilwoman," I said.

Mariana patted at her jeans, fishing a vape pen from a pocket that seemed too tight to hold anything. She took a long pull and let out a plume that looked like a mushroom cloud.

"I'm guessing Angel didn't tell you why he's no longer welcome here?"

I shook my head no.

"Celia put you on the right track. My interest in women played a part, but it wasn't because Angel had a problem with it," she replied. "My father is barely hiding his disgust for my choices now, but when he first found out, he was vicious. Threatening to cut me out if I ever brought a woman home again. He told me I would ruin all that we'd built. That people would stop coming to the restaurant if they knew. That we'd lose friends. That we'd lose everything because of who I am."

It occurred to me that in all my interactions with the Pereiras the past few days, I hadn't seen a warm embrace between Tiago and Mariana. He'd talked her up to me, but in an almost clinical way. Admiring her professional success, how she reflected on him. But he'd offered no plaudits of his daughter as a person.

The only time I'd seen them speak, they were screaming. Angel was onto something when he called out their Ironbound Kennedys charade.

"I played along. For years," she said. "I even introduced them to two boyfriends. One was real. One was someone I met at an internship who was doing me a favor. But one of Dad's friends saw me out at a club in Elizabeth one night. Dancing too close to another woman. Close enough that he had to make a comment. My father exploded. Right here. In the restaurant one day while we were opening. He…"

The sentence stopped in her throat. Mariana took another long drag, refusing to let the tears come. As far as I was concerned, Tiago didn't deserve them.

"He told me I'd be on the streets. I was barely out of college at that point. I was still working in the restaurant. I was terrified," she said. "And Angel saw that. And he couldn't stand it."

She walked over to the kitchen door that looked out of place with the rest of the older building.

"Angel beat my father so badly that he didn't come in for two weeks," she said. "Both of my father's eyes were swollen shut. He could barely see the first few days. I had to take care of him. When he finally got on his feet again, he stopped asking about who I dated. And he never said Angel's name again."

Mariana took another drag from the vape. I wouldn't have begrudged her if she pulled out a real cigarette.

"I doubt he planned it that way, but Angel jumped on a grenade for me," she said. "He had to know things would never be the same after that, but maybe he didn't know how scared my father would be in the days after. That he'd depend on me like he did. Tiago even apologized, not for what he said to me, but how he said it. Angel left home so I didn't have too. So, I could benefit from my father's name, from our standing here. I'm not even a councilwoman if he doesn't do what he did, much less running for mayor."

"That's commendable," I replied. "But it doesn't excuse what he's doing now."

"Angel didn't have any prospects outside of the restaurants, Russell. He didn't go to college. He didn't do anything except work here until my father kicked him out," she said. "He gave up what little he had, protecting me. I've been helping him out, for years. Slipping him whatever I could every month, just so he has a place to sleep. But three months ago, he started asking for more than I could get my hands on without asking my father for help."

Three months. It had been about three months since Isiah Roust's lies in a Monmouth County criminal trial had first surfaced, imperiling Abel Musa's conviction. Three months since Roust's probation officer said he started taking meetings with someone every Saturday in Asbury Park, like the one we'd interrupted the day we got caught in the fire.

If Angel managed to siphon any extra cash from his sister, I doubted it was destined for his own pockets.

"My mother left us bonds when she died. They should have appreciated to well over twenty thousand dollars by now. I was supposed to save them to pay for a wedding, that's what she asked," Mariana said. "But if Angel is this desperate for money, he clearly needs them more than I ever will. I'll cash them out. This way, at least he gets something good from one of my parents."

She took one more drag.

"He still thinks you're a reporter, right?" she asked. "That's what Key said."

I nodded, thankful her question didn't require a further response.

"Keep it that way," she said. "He can't know that I know this was him. Things won't be the same between us if he does. And he's all the family I really have left."

With that, Mariana Pereira disappeared back into the restaurant, back to her fundraiser, back to all the things that hopefully distracted her from the toxic ties binding her family.

I pulled out my phone and texted Angel a dollar figure and a time.

It didn't take long for him to respond with a Newark address, one that didn't make a lot of sense when I searched the location.

"There?" I asked. "Are you sure?"

"Save your questions for the interview," he wrote back. "It's all part of the same story anyway."

CHAPTER
NINETEEN

THE MEETING PLACE Angel Pereira chose had been dead to Newark for about as long as he had.

Standing five stories tall, the buildings that were once intended to be the Segura-Dahl homes now haunted a tract of land just outside Weequahic Park, peering over anyone enjoying the golf course and lake nearby, reminding them of the urban blight waiting just beyond the eighteenth hole.

The buildings were skeletons now. Dirty brick face and boarded up windows were all that remained of an affordable housing project no one ever got to use as intended. Most of the people who had found shelter inside had done so after the project got murdered in a city council budget session knife fight. Now, the only tenants were homeless folks who had slipped inside the property's lifeless husks.

Constructed in the late 1990s as part of a previous mayor's attempt to revitalize the city's South Ward, the 300-unit complex only ever got close to a third of the way full before that same mayor got himself indicted in a scandal connected to the grants used to break ground in the first place.

Cleanthony Watkins, then the South Ward's councilman, won the open contest to fill the mayor's seat not long after. But by that point, many of the complex's vacant units had been taken over by squatters, addicts and other characters who drove the Segura-Dahl homes' few paying tenants to look for safer ground. The project turned into a pariah for the city housing department. No one wanted to buy the land, and while demolition doesn't cost as much as construction, it still costs. Watkins chose to let the buildings hang around in a state of suspended animation. Withering, but never truly dead.

That was Watkins's mayoral tenure: an exercise in managing to not trip over the lowest possible bar. The three mayors before him had been indicted or resigned in disgrace.

Things wouldn't get better under Cleanthony Watkins, but they probably wouldn't get worse. They would just…be.

In my past life as the kind of reporter cops didn't spit on, I'd been out to the Segura-Dahl homes a few times on ride-alongs. Stomping through overgrown weeds and stray cat shit behind narcotics detectives after the crumbling complex had devolved into an open-air drug market. I knew the property half decent, enough to know the spots the dealers used as lookouts over what was intended to be the main courtyard. The place where Angel Pereira had told me to meet him at 8 p.m.

I peered out of the small rectangle cut into the rotting wooden boards covering a second-floor corner unit that had its back to the park, giving myself a view of the two main approaches to the courtyard. I checked my phone—7:45 p.m.

In that past life, I'd have arrived early for an interview, so I had time to go over the order of the questions I planned to ask, get myself in the right frame of mind for the personality I planned to sit on the other side of a notepad from.

In my current life, arriving early was a tactical decision. In case

Angel Pereira was planning to kill me. The longer I sat there, the easier it was to convince myself that was the case.

He had to have recognized me at Newark Penn. I'd given him a close enough look when I confronted him at his apartment, after all. Had he seen me in Asbury Park too? Roust's probation officer made clear he'd been meeting with someone, and after my conversation with Mariana about her financial contributions to her estranged brother, I started to wonder if those meetings were actually money drops. Roust appeared to be the only living witness to the Twilight Four killings, the only person who could make Angel Pereira answer for his gruesome crime.

But I'd seen the look in Angel's eyes as he put Roust down in the train station. He seemed on the verge of tears. Maybe he'd been content paying the man to keep quiet until I kept pushing, until I backed Roust into a corner where Angel had been waiting with a knife.

Now I'd put myself in a similar one.

I had no idea how I was going to convince Angel to confess. Considering I was sitting in an abandoned apartment complex at least a half mile from anything a jury might consider a credible witness, I figured he had a pretty good idea how he was going to make sure no one else asked any questions about the Twilight Four.

The phone let me know it was 7:58 p.m. Two minutes until I maybe didn't have to care all that much about what time it was. Fuck. Was it really that soon? And had I really not said goodbye to anyone but Key? Had I not told anyone what I was doing, or why?

My parents hadn't been all that communicative or understanding after I got fired from the paper. Dina, the ex-girlfriend turned crime reporter who'd helped me unravel the police scandal that had massacred my PI business, was living her D.C. life now, getting her name plastered on "30 journalists under 30 to watch" lists. The few other people I considered friends were all reporters, and I usually wasn't the best company when we met in bars and they talked about their careers and I got drunk and bitched about my lack of one.

I checked the clock again—7:59 p.m. There was one call I had to make. He wasn't a friend, but he was the person I'd been spending most of my time with lately.

It took five rings for Bill Henniman's gravel voice to bark a command to leave a message.

"I know you don't want to talk to me, but I'm about to do something incredibly stupid, so I just wanted to give you one last chance to say I told you so. You might be done with this. You want to protect your legacy on the job. I understand that, even if I don't agree with it," I said. "But I can't let this go. I'm about to meet with the man Roust pointed me toward, so if this goes as badly as I think it could…"

The phone beeped. Angel Pereira was calling me. I switched over immediately, not even sure if the message saved.

"You're not here," he said.

I peeked out through the cutout in the wood, seeing no one in the courtyard.

"Neither are you," I replied.

"So which apartment are you hiding in?" he asked. "Gotta admit, I'm a little surprised you know this place well too."

"Is that why you picked it?" I asked. "Familiarity?"

"We'll get to that," he said. "I thought this was a face-to-face interview. What's the matter, you don't trust me?"

"We met one time for maybe five minutes, didn't think we really had the time to establish a deep soul bond," I said, hoping he didn't hear the slight stammer in my voice.

"Don't do that," he said, his voice losing what little playfulness it had.

"Do what?"

"Lie to me," he said. "You said you wanted the truth about my family. If you want me to be honest with you, you need to be honest with me."

He was giving me a choice with two problematic options. Play dumb and risk him walking away, or admit we had met one other time, when I'd seen him kill someone.

Something creaked behind me, and I turned to see dust belch up from the kitchen area of the abandoned apartment I'd been hiding in. Something or someone was moving, but it couldn't have been Angel. I hadn't heard his voice beyond the phone.

The screen flashed as I held up the device to try and illuminate the room. Key was calling. I couldn't lose Angel though, so I just pressed ignore.

"Russell," he said. "I looked you up. Read some of your stories. Read about what happened last year. You're not exactly TMZ. I don't think you really care about my sister's dirty laundry."

"If you looked me up, then you know I've been out of work for a minute now," I replied. "You're right. I don't care about those pictures. But I care about the paycheck they can deliver."

"You're really going to keep this up?" he asked.

Something creaked again. My hand shot to the dirty floor, fishing for something to defend myself with. A sting across the tip of my right pointer finger told me I'd found the remnants of a broken bottle. Now things were looking up, since whatever diseases were on the jagged remains of the Mad Dog 20/20 I'd grabbed would kill me before Angel did.

"I'll make this easier for you," he said. "I don't need the money anymore because the person I needed to give it to doesn't need it anymore. And you know exactly why that is."

He was admitting to a murder that happened five feet in front of my face. He was admitting he wasn't here for the promised payoff that I hadn't brought. Which meant he'd only wanted us in the same place for one reason.

I rounded the corner into the kitchen with my right arm reared back, broken glass ready to stab. The source of the creaking was a human shape that I could barely make out in the shadows, save for a flash of white behind grime that appeared to be teeth. Teeth that revealed themselves when the homeless guy I'd walked in on opened his mouth into a surprised scream, matching the one that leapt from my lips.

"Fine. Maybe you'll be more talkative face-to-face," Angel said. "You need to hear this. Someone does."

He hung up. I looked down at the phone, seeing the call disconnected, and another two missed calls from Key. Probably a different fiasco I didn't have time for at the moment.

I didn't know what the fuck Angel was talking about anymore. But I knew the screaming had given away my position. If Angel was coming for me, I needed escape routes.

The door nearly came off its rusted hinges as I ripped it open and raced down the metal steps, gunning it for the courtyard. Open space was my friend, even with little else to guide me but moonlight, at least I'd have a chance to see Angel coming and a chance to move in the opposite direction.

Or I would have. If he hadn't been waiting for me. A knee slammed into my lower abdomen as I hit the bottom of the staircase, doubling me over just long enough for a pair of hands to grab the back of my jacket and toss me face down into the dirt.

I rolled over to thrust with the broken bottle, but I must have lost it in the fall. Angel Pereira stomped on the inside of my elbow, rendering the arm useless anyway and forcing me back long enough that he was able to drop his knee on my chest, pinning me down.

I could barely make his face out due to the darkness and the fact that his messy hair was framing it like a hood. But the shine of the knife he was holding was familiar enough. I'd seen it end one life before. I assumed it was about to claim mine to keep Roust's company.

My eyes closed involuntarily. The way they would when a doctor aims a needle at your arm. One quick prick and it would be over.

I don't know what I thought I'd feel as I was about to die, but I didn't think it would be relief. For the briefest of seconds, I didn't have to worry about why anyone in Newark did anything. I didn't have to worry about who had done what or when. I didn't have to worry about my next paycheck.

I could relax.

A few seconds passed. I didn't die. And my curiosity overtook my momentary peace.

"You didn't kill me," I said.

"Not yet."

"Why?"

"Because someone needs to know the truth," he replied. "Someone needs to know why my life went to hell. Someone needs to understand what happened here."

"Here?" I asked.

Angel hung his head low, muttered something I couldn't hear, then pressed two fingers to his lips and kissed them before rubbing them into the ground.

"This is where my life changed," he said. "This is where they died."

I didn't know who I was looking at.

From the moment I'd first heard about the Twilight Four killings, I'd imagined the man holding the match to be a monster. A snarling demon, happily presiding over a fire that reduced four teenagers to ash.

The version of Angel Pereira I thought I'd understood, at least up until about twenty minutes ago, was a blackmailer and a fuck-up and a desperate killer who had stolen Abel Musa's last chance at redemption.

But the person in front of me just looked tired.

Angel was sitting in the dirt of the courtyard, head slouched down, hands resting over his knees. A revolver hung limp from his left hand, its barrel making the occasional lazy pass in my direction. The knife he'd killed Isiah Roust with, the one I thought would end me as well, had disappeared into a backpack that hung from his right shoulder.

My wrists were bound with a pair of zip ties he'd produced from the same backpack, hands stretched over my head and attached to the half-collapsed remains of a jungle gym someone built before the courtyard looked like the exact opposite of a place children should be.

A few minutes had passed since Angel pounced on me at the bottom of the stairs. Since he'd informed me that I was standing in the space where someone had last laid eyes on the Twilight Four. Since he'd politely declined to kill me. Unlike the other five people whose lives he'd stolen.

Not five. Six. The baby Shayna never got to meet made six.

Angel hadn't spoken. He'd simply sat back down, exhaled a bunch and cycled through all the bored neck cranes and static stretches people do when they're waiting for a bus.

"Angel?" I asked.

He looked up like he was surprised to find me there.

"Why am I not dead?"

"That's your first question?"

"It seemed like an important one."

"I'm not really sure how to do this," he said.

"Do what?"

"You're not going to understand, are you?" he asked. "I thought, with everything you'd written about, maybe you'd understand."

I didn't know what I was supposed to have understood or misunderstood. But considering he had two lethal weapons and I had zero free hands, I was going to need to get empathetic in a hurry.

The man in front of me was a killer. But he was also clearly a mess. I tried to focus on the latter, the man Mariana had painted for me: the excommunicated son and brother, the unloved member of the Ironbound's royal family. That was the man I needed to keep talking if I wanted to keep breathing.

"You said you wanted this to be an interview, right? About your family, the truth about your family?" I asked.

Angel nodded, neck bobbing like it was on a string.

"Interviews are about relationships, rapport. And, well, fuck, man, we do not have a good one," I said. "You killed someone in front of me. You tried to kill me down the Shore. You're holding me prisoner now."

"I wasn't trying to kill you in Asbury," he said. "I just wanted you to back off. I didn't want things to get out of control."

"Burning a building down was your way of keeping things under control?" I asked.

He stood up fast enough that the pearl handle of his revolver caught the moonlight, a bright reminder that I needed to watch my mouth.

"This is what I meant about not understanding. You can't. You won't. How could you?" he asked. "There's so much I need to say, and I have no one left to say it out loud too. There was only one person I could talk to about this, but you made me…"

He trailed off. I guessed he was talking about Roust.

"This all went too far. It started out too far. But now, all this, again?" he asked, looking down at the revolver, his face recoiling in disgust. "How am I standing here, in this spot, like this, again?"

"I don't—"

"And to involve my sister? I mean, I don't even believe in him, but fucking Christ! How did it get to that?" he asked. "But I needed the money. To keep Roust together. To get him out of here before you got him talking about—"

"What happened here?" I asked.

The interruption stunned him like a quick jab. I had the reins of the conversation for a split second, and I needed to hold them. Angel was unfocused, coming apart at the seams, talking to God and Buddha as much as he was talking to me.

"Whatever you've done these past few days. Whatever you've been hiding. It all stems from what happened here," I said. "You said you couldn't talk to anyone but Roust about it. That's not true. You can talk to me. It's why you didn't kill me, right? Because you wanted someone to know. Then tell me."

"I want to. I need to. I can't carry this on my own. I've never been able to," he said. "I talked to Izzy all the time, at least once a week. Even when he was locked up. We'd write letters. Vague ones. We switched to e-mail when he got out. It was just easier to write it down than to say it out loud. He was supposed to delete them, but Izzy was never the most responsible person."

I thought of the picture frame soaked in bleach before the apartment exploded.

"So that fire wasn't just about scaring me," I said. "You were worried about what was on his computer."

"I knew I should have never written any of it down, but I couldn't swallow it all myself," he said. "I couldn't keep their screams to myself."

"You don't have to, Angel," I said. "I'm right here."

He raised the gun again, but this time the barrel wandered in his direction instead of mine. Killing me was one way of dodging the consequences of what happened, but given the mental cliff he was standing on, I wondered if he'd considered other options.

Angel holstered the weapon and clapped his hands together, fingers brushing the edge of his nose. He was mumbling something again, looking up to the sky. I briefly thought of Tiago during the debate. Maybe religion still bridged from father to son, even if nothing else connected them anymore. Then he shook his hands and rocked his head from side to side for a second, like this was a warmup for a performance. Like whatever he was about to say had been practiced in a mirror.

"You didn't grow up here, right?" he asked.

I shook my head no.

"They still didn't trust us, back then. The rest of the city. The Blacks. We were still the mystery in the Ironbound, even years after the big migration from Lisbon, they looked at us like invaders," he said. "But as much of a piece of shit as he is, my father was always right about a few things. He always said food could overcome any divide. Even race."

That sounded like the Tiago I knew before the past week. The nice guy with the bomb breakfast pastries. Not the stealth bigot whose kids despised him.

"We started getting customers from outside the neighborhood, beyond the off the boat Portuguese who looked at my father like some master of the universe. It was right around the same time I graduated from busboy to waiter. That was the first time Shayna and her family came in," he said. "She was in a flower dress. Hair tied back in braids. She seemed like the type who smiled at everyone, but for whatever reason, the one she shot me seemed special that day."

I shifted my weight, trying to find a way to slouch and keep my shoulders from burning as the zip ties trapped them in an upward stretch.

"I don't know if you've ever waited tables before, but when you do it well, it's a performance," he said. "I had jokes about all the entrees. I talked the little one, Adriana, into trying octopus. I just wanted to make sure Shayna kept flashing that grin. Left my name and number on her napkin when she wasn't looking."

Based on what I'd read in the neighborhood newspaper, Angel would have been around twenty-two at the time. Shayna was sixteen. I choked on every and any comment I wanted to make. Reminding Angel his meet cute was actually the first act in a statutory rape wasn't going to help anyone if he shot me.

"Two months. We snuck around, me and her. My parents' place, mostly. Dad was always at the restaurant and Mari was away at college," he said. "She wanted me to be her first. I just wanted to be with her."

Angel's expression changed from wistful to confused, maybe angry.

"I saw her journal, Angel," I said. "I know she was pregnant. You in your twenties, her being sixteen, I assume that was not the plan."

His lip started to quiver. I choked on the bile again, knowing sympathy was my best and only move.

"She loved you. And you, bubbling up like you are here, you cared for her too," I said. "You've done some horrible shit the past few days, Angel. There's no way around that. But...why back then? Why her? How could you do that to someone you loved?"

"I couldn't! I didn't! That wasn't...that wasn't why I asked her to come here that day," he said. "I just had to convince her that it wasn't time. That we could go to the clinic together. That it'd be alright. That God would understand we just weren't ready to be parents yet, but we would be one day. So, I told her I had a surprise, that we needed to talk. She said she did too, but I didn't understand what she was planning."

He held his hands out.

"This was all vacant rowhouses before they tried to make it a project," he said. "Places that got foreclosed on about a year or so before I met Shayna. Trapped in bank limbo. Just enough attention that the junkies hadn't closed in yet. But a few of the units still had furniture. Sure, they were a little grimy, but we had no place to ourselves. So, we made our own. She joked it'd be practice for when we moved in together one day. Our own private world. So, of course, it's where she wanted to meet."

Angel wiped at his cheek with the back of his hand, taking a second to gather himself. My eyes darted around the graveyard of buildings, thinking about Angel's proclamation that the Twilight Four had died here and the timing of it, tapping my feet on the concrete beneath me. If Angel was telling the truth, if they'd been burned in the basement of abandoned buildings marked for condemnation anyway, the site of a future housing project, then that explained why there had never been a crime scene, why the four were always ruled missing, but never dead.

Maybe the bodies were destroyed in the fire. Maybe the remains had deteriorated enough that the crews didn't notice or didn't look closely for bone fragments when they cleared the site years later.

Either way, Newark had literally paved over one of its worst crimes.

"Roust and I had become fast friends at the restaurant," Angel said, gathering himself enough to stumble on, his voice still trembling and weak. "He'd been bussing tables about as long as me. He was the only person who knew about Shayna, so he came that day for moral support. But she thought this was something else. She brought her sister. The cousins. She said she didn't want to hide anymore. That she was ready to tell her family, and she wanted to introduce me to the people that mattered most first," Angel said.

"I was scared. I freaked out. I started screaming at her, that it wasn't supposed to be like that," he continued. "When I told her why I'd really asked her to meet, she just cried. More like howled. She was so hurt that I asked her to get rid of…"

Angel turned away from me and dropped his head into his left hand. Maybe he'd gotten so used to his private pain that he couldn't look at someone else when he shared it.

"Her cousin came at me. The big one. Kurtis. And that's when it got out of hand," Angel said. "That's when he started hurting them."

"Roust?" I asked.

"No, not Roust," he said, whole body shaking as he hissed the words out. "We had to do whatever it took to protect the family. That's what he said."

I'd heard that line before. Just a few hours ago outside Marisqueira Pereira.

"Your father did this?" I asked.

Angel nodded as he leveled the gun at me.

"Twenty-five years," he said. "That's how long it's been since I could say that to anyone but Roust. It's been so long that sometimes I forget. Sometimes, I dream it was me walking her down those stairs. Me soaking the rags in oil. Burning my…"

He stopped himself. The gun changed its mind again.

"Burning my own baby to death."

"Holy fuck," I replied, as if any words would be sufficient.

I stayed quiet for a minute. Giving him time to unknot his shoulders as he felt the weight release. Giving myself precious seconds to process what he'd just said.

"Angel, I…I'm sorry, but why not turn him in?" I asked. "After all this time?"

"Could you send your own father to prison? My mother had been dead for years. He was all we had. All Mari had," he said. "I've thought about it. Hundreds of times. Whenever I see a cop. I think maybe today's the day I'm brave. Today's the day I tell the truth. But it would destroy Mari. And as the years went on, I started to think, what difference would it make? By the time Roust put that man in prison for it, Mari was already starting to make her way in politics. She had a future. One I couldn't risk destroying with our past. I didn't want to hurt anyone else with our mistakes. But then you started going after Roust. Made me do what I did the other day. Left me completely alone. That's when it changed."

Before I could ask any more questions, someone screamed my name.

It was near impossible to see through the darkened courtyard, but the frame moving our way was too wide to be anyone else's.

"Russell!" the voice screamed again, the unmistakable cement mixer owned and operated by Bill Henniman.

Angel's eyes widened. He spun around with the gun, searching the dark for the source of the sound. I didn't know why or how Bill was here, but his timing was terrible. The man we'd been chasing was finally done running, his shoulders releasing a weight that even Atlas could have sympathized with. But the sound of Bill's voice had changed something in Angel and brought back the feral animal I thought I'd been dealing with in the days prior.

"Is that your cop friend?" he asked. "The one from the Shore?"

"Russell?" Bill asked again, as if Angel needed more proof.

"Angel, Angel, wait," I said.

He shook his head, the gun wandering again, ready to kill any of us or none of us based on its owner's ever-changing whims.

"You brought him here," he said. "You weren't trying to understand. This was a trap."

Angel smashed the gun into my face. He didn't break my nose, but it felt like he wanted to.

"It's just as well," he said, voice sounding like it was getting further away as he spoke. "I knew how this night had to end either way. I just wanted someone to know. Someone else to carry the weight."

By the time my vision cleared from the pistol whipping, Angel was gone and Henniman was struggling with the elastic tying me to the old playground equipment. It took a few seconds, but his pocketknife eventually set me free.

"How did you…?" I asked, wiping blood from the cut that had opened on my nose.

"My paranoia paid off," he said. "You called me. You never call me. So, I checked that app I put on your phone when we started this, and you were in this shit hole a little longer than I was comfortable with. So who exactly did I just save you from? And what are you doing out here?"

Any other time, I would have needed a minute to process the fact that Bill's overbearing bullshit might have actually saved my life. But I'd have to catch him up a little later, because everything Angel said was already pooling in my head, an overfilled glass splashing everywhere.

The decades he'd spent knowing what it sounded like to hear his first love die screaming, knowing his father was the reason he'd heard that pain.

The fact that he said he knew how this night would end.

The fact that he'd killed one of the only two men who could understand the truth of his nightmares.

The fact that we were only three miles from the place he could find the other.

"Where's he going?" Henniman asked.

"Home," I replied.

CHAPTER
TWENTY

MARIANA'S FUNDRAISER MUST have been well attended. I could tell by the number of people running out of Marisqueira Pereira screaming.

Bill pulled his truck to a stop in front of a fire hydrant across from the restaurant and hopped out into the street, service weapon in the low-ready position.

"Bill," I said, following as he started advancing on the building. "Might not be the time for the direct approach."

"Avery, this really isn't your area," he replied.

"I know. But there's a kitchen entrance where they take their supplies. Has a straight shot into the dining room," I said. "Just figured you'd want an option that wasn't the front door. I already had Angel talking, maybe I can get him going again until you come in."

Henniman nodded and muttered a thanks. He would have been marching toward his entry point if I hadn't said his name again.

"We don't have time for a chat here," Bill said.

His eyes simmered behind the deadpan expression. The last time we'd been that close, he'd punched me in the face. It hadn't been the first time he'd threatened me. It probably wouldn't be the last. But that was tough to square with what just happened.

"You saved my life. Twice. Probably tonight and definitely last year," I said. "I know you don't like me, Bill. And I can't say I'm your biggest fan either. But I should be dead. You've risked a lot to make sure that I'm not. And I've never said thank you."

The old cop rolled his eyes, keeping up his lifetime streak of being annoyed by just about every breath I'd ever taken.

"You've never needed to. And you're right. I've never really liked you, Avery. But I understand you," he replied. "I get up. I try to make this city a little less terrible, protect the people who need it. And I don't really care what people think about how I do it. We're on the same side. Even if you're really goddamn obnoxious about it."

Bill pointed toward the restaurant.

"Now let's end this," he said.

I nodded. Bill raised his gun again and started moving down the side of the restaurant. As I headed for the front door, my eyes wandered down Ferry, where Newark Penn loomed in the distance. My mind wandered back to the last time I'd been this close to answers and how Angel's knife had robbed me of any proof. I brought up the recording app, hoping for Abel Musa's sake that I came away with something useful this time, then moved for the front door.

The flow of people fleeing had stopped. That was good. Less people for Angel to hurt.

Except for me. And the two members of the Pereira family I assumed he was looking for.

I stepped inside and found myself interrupting a surreal dinner scene.

The restaurant was all done up for Mariana's mayoral fundraiser, with the dining room divided by a lengthy buffet line, still steaming trays placed over blue flames belching from vents. Balloons and streamers hung from the ceiling, a mix of reds and whites.

But the floor told the story of an event interrupted. Discarded plates, mussel and clam shells cracking underfoot, some already partially shattered by the stampede of people fleeing before I got there.

On the left side of the dining room a lonely table was occupied by Key, Mariana, Tiago, Angel and Angel's favorite knife.

He was at the far end, Mariana to his right, closer to the blade than anyone should have been comfortable with. Tiago and Key had their backs to me.

"This family owes you a great debt," Angel said, standing up and aiming the gun at his father's head. "Dad would have never invited me back here on his own."

"Angel, you need to stop," Tiago said, before his reply was cut off by the crack of metal against bone as the revolver slammed into the side of his forehead.

"I haven't been home in how long? I think, maybe for once, just once, I'll do the talking," Angel said.

The gun jerked toward me. I raised my hands, slow.

"You don't need that, Angel," I replied.

"I'm starting to think you want to die," he shouted, moving toward me with the gun extended.

"Angel!" Mariana screamed. "Stop this! Whatever this is! You can talk to me! You've always talked to me about everything!"

Angel kept the gun trained on me, letting his head loll to the right just a bit. A wounded smile crept across his face. I searched his eyes, finding nothing but burst vessels and the sheen of tears that had been flowing since he started telling me his story at the place his life apart.

"Everything?" he asked. "I don't know about everything."

"Is this about him? The pictures? You know I didn't believe him, right?" she said, lying to preserve their connection, just like she'd asked me to hours earlier. "I know you wouldn't do something like that. I know you're better than that."

Angel turned to her, and I backed away a few steps, hoping if he moved toward me, I'd be able to draw him into Henniman's path. I couldn't see where Bill was, but if he came in the way I suggested, he'd wind up near the bar.

"You hear that, *papai*? At least someone thinks your son is worth something," Angel said to Tiago, who was still dabbing at the cut on his head with a large cloth napkin. "You know, maybe if you hadn't been so selfish back in the day, maybe if you saw a life outside of this fucking neighborhood, things could have been different."

Angel put the gun under his father's chin, raising it slowly until their eyes met.

"Now look where we are," he hissed.

Mariana started to move around the table, screaming no over and over again. Angel raised the knife, but only high enough that the sight of it stopped his sister cold.

"Please, Mari," he said. "This isn't about you."

"It was always about her," Tiago replied, teeth clenched, spit punctuating every word. "Look at you. Is it any wonder why I always tried to protect her? She's made mistakes, yes, but you. No self-control. No discipline. You were always mad I kept you in the restaurant. Did you ever wonder why? It was the place I thought you'd do the least damage."

Angel started looking at the gun longer than I was okay with.

"How's the story end?" I asked, backing up toward the bar.

"This doesn't concern you anymore," Angel yelled, pressing the barrel to his father's temple.

"Yeah, your family keeps telling me things like that. But we know it's not true," I replied. "Think about what you told me before. If you shoot him, how does your story end? How does it get told?"

Angel shook his head, pulled the gun away from Tiago. I exhaled in relief for the second between that and the one where he started marching toward his next target. Me.

This time, I was happy to have the gun's attention. I kept backpedaling, drawing him in. He kept following.

But my eyes betrayed me, wandering to the right to see where the lieutenant was. Angel followed them, to find Bill creeping up to the side of the bar.

Two shots flew just over Henniman's head as he dove for cover. The sound made Mariana scream, and that was enough to distract Angel for a half second. I grabbed for the revolver and got hold of the weapon just long enough to get slashed by the knife coming up in Angel's other hand.

The blade caught the outside of my right arm, and the flash of pain sent me stumbling backwards toward the bar, allowing Angel to easily regain control of the gun.

Key used the distraction to drag the still-shrieking Mariana out the front door. It slammed shut just as Angel grabbed me by the shirt and pulled me to my feet, holding me up as a shield as Henniman rose, gun trained on the younger Pereira. Tiago was stumbling toward us but stopped when he saw we were now in a hostage situation.

"You're the detective, right?" Angel barked toward Henniman.

Bill nodded, his body barely moving, eyes searching for a place to put a bullet.

"How bad did you want Roust to tell you what happened that night?" Angel asked.

"I'll take the story from you all the same," Bill replied. "There's a woman who deserves to know why her family died."

"Oh, I agree. And I guess we can be as honest as we've ever been now, with Mari out of the room," Angel said, pressing the knife closer to my throat, extending the gun again toward Tiago. "Why don't you tell them, Dad?"

"Angel..."

"Do you think he's the only officer coming?" Angel asked. "Do you think I came here for any other reason? I've lived a fiction for half my life. I've done terrible things to keep that story safe, for this family, and for what? I killed my only fucking friend the other day, Dad, to protect a legacy that's never once protected me. That tends to shift your priorities. This needs to end. And this is how it ends. The only question is how much more blood winds up on your hands."

"Think about your sister, Angel," Tiago replied. "I know you hate me. But for all your flaws, you were always a good brother. We've done so much to protect her. Why risk it all now?"

"We? What do you mean, we? I had to try to scare them off Roust. I had to kill my friend. I was ready to kill him," he said, pressing the gun against my temple to punctuate the sentence before turning it toward his father. "Why should I keep getting blood on my hands?"

Angel waved the gun toward the front door.

"Lock it. Pour us a drink," he said to his father. "And tell the story well. We might be the only people left who ever get to hear it."

Tiago did as his son asked, bolting the front entrance to the restaurant before moving toward the bar. Angel turned toward Henniman.

"You, gun down," he said as he pulled on my neck to walk backwards with him. "Kick it over."

Henniman dropped the weapon, looking livid about it. I decided to count that as the third time he'd kept me breathing.

"What do you prefer?" Tiago asked.

"Jameson's," Angel replied.

Tiago shook his head in disgust.

"Sorry, I lost the taste for the *ginja* when you told me to leave home," Angel said.

The father took out two glasses and fished around for the bottle while the son walked me toward the bar. He snatched up his glass of whiskey then pulled me back until we were almost flush against the door.

"Tell them," Angel said.

"All these years wasted," Tiago muttered.

"All these years I suffered. Cleaning it up. Helping you hide it. All so Mari could make something of herself. All for the family name!" Angel shouted back. "Isiah was my friend. And when they came looking for him, when he freaked out, I had to…well, you know what I had to do. Tell them why. Tell them or God puts another life on your ledger."

He pressed the barrel against my head to punctuate the sentence, clearly overestimating how much Tiago valued my life. The father took a long, slow sip from his glass, wincing as he swallowed.

"I would have paid for the abortion," Tiago said. "I offered to when he came to me, when he told me he'd made a mistake. It was not…what happened was not my intention. Was never my intention. You have to understand. At that time? With her being underage? Do you think people would have accepted it? Her family? Their neighbors?"

"We never gave them a chance to," Angel hissed back.

"No one else lived up here then. Little Portugal? It used to be literal, Angel. Don't be delusional," Tiago said. "At best, at best, you would have had a child you couldn't support. I would have had to pull Mari out of school. And when the parents found out. They might have involved the police. Shayna was sixteen, Angel. They could have charged you with something. There was too much to lose. We all had too much to lose."

"So, you killed four children instead?" I asked.

"That was never my intention. How many times do I have to say that?" Tiago asked. "But he was weak. Foolish enough to think he was in love. I knew, I felt…no, I just sensed he would fail to convince her. So, I followed him that day. The day he promised me he would handle this. And when I saw them start arguing, I marched over. I had about six thousand dollars to spare. I hoped that would be enough for her. But when I came up shouting, the big one rushed me…"

"And you had this," Angel said, briefly pulling the revolver from my head. "I kept it all these years. In case I ever found the courage to come back here. To send you where you sent them."

"It was self-defense. But he was a child, and I knew how that would end in a courtroom," Tiago said. "I would go to prison. The restaurants would have collapsed. My children would have had nothing. Everything I built in the neighborhood, gone in an instant. I knew I had to decide. Us or them. So, I marched them inside, and I swear to you, I prayed. I went to the back of my truck and I asked God what to do…"

"But God doesn't exist. And you saw the cooking oil and the bleach," Angel said. "He told me I had to decide, right then and there, if I wanted my father to spend the rest of his life in prison."

Angel loosened his grip on me, the gun wandering between my head and where Tiago was standing.

"He told me Mari would never forgive me," Angel said. "He told me I'd lose my whole family. He told me if God wanted them to survive, they'd find a way out. And I fucking believed him. So, I let it happen. Because I trusted you. Because sons are supposed to believe in their fathers."

I felt the knife move away from my neck. Angel stepped around me and started marching toward Tiago. I looked down by my feet. Henniman's gun wasn't far away.

"You told me I had to let Shayna die for my family, then you took my family away, threw me aside all those years later anyway," Angel said. "Shayna died screaming my name. All these years, I've had to live with that. Knowing you killed the first girl I loved, the baby I never got to meet. All these years, I've had to keep doing shit to keep it quiet for you. Because if it ever got out, it would destroy Mari. I've been living in hell, alone, all to protect this family from what you did. That ends today. Today you join me there."

Angel shoved me to the ground, lowering the gun for the briefest of seconds as he stomped toward his father. He was halfway there when Tiago popped up with the shotgun. The one I'd seen under the bar the last time I was behind it.

The blast ripped through the room, cutting Angel Pereira in half, turning off his tortured mind once and for all.

It was probably the only decent thing his father had ever done for him.

Tiago leveled the weapon at me, not wasting a second.

"I warned you to stay away from my family," he said, racking the next round into place.

Henniman bowled into Tiago's side before he could put me down. I dove for Bill's handgun, not entirely sure how to use it. I raised the weapon, hands sweating and shaking, barely able to aim as Tiago and Bill struggled for control of the shotgun.

Bill's eyes were bulging, his face fire red.

He'd finally gotten what he wanted, even in all the carnage. The monster he'd been hunting for years, the man he'd promised Cynthia Bell he'd find, was inches from his face.

Tiago jerked the shotgun backward, pulling it from Bill's grip, but the old cop delivered a kick to Tiago's stomach, doubling him over. Bill followed it with an overhand right to the back of Tiago's head, nearly crumpling him.

"Everyone is going to know what you did, you piece of shit," Bill shouted, throwing another punch to the back of Tiago's head. The older man fell to a knee.

Bill reached for the gun, but I saw Tiago throw something up toward his eyes. Maybe he'd reached into the ice bucket. Whatever it was, the spray was enough to force Bill back and give Tiago time to raise the shotgun again.

Three more blasts filled the room, the loudest I'd ever heard, probably because they were the first I'd ever fired. Tiago turned toward me, bewildered and aggravated. I'd missed, only managing to open wounds in a number of liquor bottles around him.

Splashes of rum and whiskey and broken glass dotted Tiago's face as he aimed at me, a mix of blood and liquor dribbling down his chin.

I raised Bill's weapon. Shots rang out again, and I found myself being driven to the floor.

I hadn't seen Bill come racing out from around the bar. Tiago probably hadn't counted on the lieutenant's body eating the buckshot meant for my face.

We rolled to the ground. Bill bleeding. Me screaming. We'd landed inches from Angel's body. I looked up to see Tiago take cover behind the bar. He was reloading.

Blood bubbled up between Bill's lips as I handed his gun back to him.

Tiago would be up any second. I watched Bill's fingers scramble over the weapon. I looked at Angel's corpse and noticed what had fallen out of his pocket as he died. A Zippo lighter. Maybe the one he'd used to light the Molotov cocktail in Asbury Park, the one that burned the skin on my shoulder into a marbled mess.

Tiago rose again, shotgun primed, body outlined in dripping liquor bottles.

I flicked the lighter and threw it.

The shotgun blast sprayed high into the ceiling as fire erupted around Tiago Pereira. He shrieked as hungry tongues lapped up the liquor trails around him, chewing at his clothes, scorching the bar top.

Tiago howled, shotgun still in his hands as the flames screamed up his body. He looked like the monster we'd learned he was.

One more time, Tiago raised the weapon.

One more time, Bill Henniman saved my life.

Tiago's body shook and spasmed as the last bullets in Bill's service weapon tore through his chest, sending his flaming form to the ground.

I struggled to my feet, trying to get Bill's shoulder over mine, surging toward the front door as the flames started to spread. He was dead weight. I had no idea how much longer he'd be conscious, much less breathing.

We crashed through the front door and collapsed onto the sidewalk as sirens filled the street. Bill's face turned white. Whatever he had left, he'd used to fire the rounds that kept me breathing.

I looked at Marisqueira Pereira as I fell, watching the fire grow and grow, bursting through the restaurant's front windows, the legacy Tiago Pereira had set one blaze to preserve now consumed by another.

CHAPTER
TWENTY-ONE

'D STARTED OUT chasing the Twilight Four case by walking into University Hospital, hoping I could try to repair the damage done to one man's life.

Now I was sitting in the same building, wondering how many lives had been ruined by that same pursuit, and for what purpose.

My hand traveled to the meat of my left arm, fingers tracing the raised and red skin where they'd stitched the wound from Angel's knife. The gash had been deep, bleeding more than I realized in the moment, dyeing my shirt half in crimson. But I was lucky compared to the other attendees of what was probably Marisqueira Pereira's last supper.

Paramedics and police descended on the restaurant less than a minute after Henniman and I crashed onto the sidewalk outside the building. Bill's upper torso was ruined. The color had drained from his face. He was coughing more than breathing, the quiet seething that always seemed to fuel him finally leaving his eyes.

I knew it was the last time I'd see him alive, but that didn't make it hurt any less when the nurse attending to me in the emergency room hallway told me the man I'd come in with hadn't made it.

The lieutenant had stuck to his words. For all his stubbornness, for all his faults, for all the sins he'd committed in the name of protecting the city of Newark, he'd still put everything on the line to save one of its residents one last time.

I liked to think he passed on with the image of Tiago Pereira burning and collapsing to the ground in his mind, warm in the knowledge that he'd solved his last case. That if he was going to die, he'd died vanquishing the shadow that haunted the final stages of his career.

Not his career. His life. There had never been any difference.

The sounds of a TV newscast coming from the nurse's station caught my attention, so I rose slowly, waiting to see if anyone official cared if I moved from my hallway gurney before advancing.

The chyron underlining the broadcast shouted "Ironbound Bloodshed" as an entirely too handsome news anchor named Rick Holmes rattled off the details I already knew. Tiago and Angel Pereira were dead. A Newark police officer had shared their fate. Councilwoman Mariana Pereira had been at the scene but escaped uninjured.

Dameon Lynch popped up on the screen briefly, reading a statement from the mayor, who apparently couldn't be moved to deliver remarks about an attack on his political nemesis in the middle of the night. Lynch was doing his best impersonation of genuine concern, and I would have been furious if the sight of him didn't lead me to one calming thought in the chaos.

If nothing else, his blackmail gambit was fucked now. There was no way he could use the pictures after this, risk pushing a sex scandal in the wake of this kind of attack, not with the sympathy Mariana was about to rightly earn.

Reaching for my phone gingerly, careful not to disturb the stitches, I pulled up my old newspaper's website looking for more information. The *Signal-Intelligencer*'s story had slightly more detail. My replacement on the crime beat, a young kid with the last name of Dazio, who I vaguely remembered being a way too competent intern a lifetime ago, had confirmed with police sources that witnesses described Angel as the aggressor. It was true, but it still felt wrong, considering the match that led to the fire inside the restaurant had been lit so long ago by his father.

But there was no mention of the Twilight Four on the TV or in the article. I blinked to keep my strained eyes focused, letting loose a long yawn that was more of a howl. Exhaustion hit me in waves.

They hadn't made the connection. Maybe they couldn't. Everyone who had heard Angel and Tiago's terrible story was dead. Except me. Sure, witnesses would probably come forward to the cops and the press in the coming days that knew Angel was estranged from the family, that he had a long running feud with his father. But they wouldn't know why. Not really.

Not unless I told the story.

I thought back to the housing complex, when Angel had held me at gunpoint and recounted his father's hellish crimes. He said he knew how the night would end. He said he couldn't carry the weight anymore.

He'd had no intention of walking out of his father's restaurant alive. He'd had every intention of passing the story and the burden to someone else.

I pulled up the recorder app on my phone. This time, the file had saved. "NewRecording1" was about ten minutes long, and while I didn't dare press the play button in the crowded hospital hallway, it almost certainly had captured Angel and Tiago's last words. Their confessions. The things Abel Musa had waited years to hear.

Abel.

I needed to talk to him. To tell him it was finally over. That he was clear of the crime he'd always proclaimed innocence from, even if the people who needed to answer for it were gone.

But as I walked toward the lobby, I saw Keyonna Jackson step off an elevator, her eyes as puffy and exhausted as mine. But there was something else there too. They were damp.

"Russell," she said, almost like she was surprised to see me up and walking around. "You alright?"

"No, but I'm doing better than everyone else who was in that room," I said. "We need to talk. Angel. Tiago, they…"

She pressed a finger to her lips, eyes scanning the hallway for I didn't know what, before tugging on my bad arm and pulling me away from the people milling near the elevator.

"Key?" I asked. "What are you doing?"

"Not here," she said.

I followed her around a corner, toward another hallway that led toward the hospital chapel. No one was praying at 4 a.m., so we had the space to ourselves. I obeyed her request for silence until a millisecond after the doors closed.

"Key," I said, holding up my phone, pointing to the still-open recording app. "We got it. We can clear Abel with what's on here. We can finally…"

These were the moments Keyonna Jackson lived for. Exposing police fuck-ups. Saving people from what she considered an unfair and unbalanced criminal justice system. But the more excited I got, the sicker she looked.

"Key," I said. "This is what you'd been hoping I'd find since this all started. Why are we not up in Abel's room right now? He needs to hear this."

She pursed her lips, looked at me and started shaking her head violently.

"He couldn't hold on," she said.

"What?"

"Cynthia called me right before the fundraiser started. It's what I was trying to reach you about before it all went to hell tonight," she said.

I thought back to the missed calls from when I was looking for Angel in the courtyard.

"Abel died about three hours ago," she said.

I nearly fell over, hand stabbing out and grabbing a pew at the last second. Isiah Roust. Angel Pereira. Bill Henniman. All dead. All killed in pursuit of justice for a man who hadn't lived long enough to receive it.

My eyes wandered between Key and the crucifix on the wall. I'd never really believed in God, but I'd have taken any advice in that moment.

"We need to talk about what happens next," Key said, her voice taking an edge that told me somehow, some way, my night was about to get even worse.

Abel Musa's headstone stood alone, unadorned on a plot that seemed just a bit further away from the rest in a row on the far west side of Woodland Cemetery. There was no epitaph written, no bouquets left from past visitors. Just a name and two dates. The grass at the base of his grave stood tall, unbothered by visitors' feet.

I crouched down to place a hardback copy of *The Count of Monte Cristo* against the side of his headstone. A newer, tightly-bound edition to replace the tattered one I'd seen him clinging to in the hospital.

"At least you finally escaped," I said.

It was pointless optimism, but I felt the need to say something. The man hadn't been mourned or eulogized. Just carted out of the hospital like meat. I imagined he would have been cremated and tossed into a potter's field as part of Newark's annual grim honor to its unclaimed dead, if not for the interference of the woman who had asked to meet me at Abel's final resting place.

A week had passed since Key sat in a pew inside the University Hospital chapel and asked me to betray everything I thought we both believed in.

In all the time we'd known each other, Key had lived to expose the Newark Police Department's every sin and right the innumerable wrongs they'd visited upon people who looked like her. At almost any other point in the six years we'd spent as uneasy allies, the story sitting on my phone's recorder would have been one she wanted screamed, printed tweeted and livestreamed on loop for days.

But now she was worried about bigger pictures and broader implications. Phrases I'd never heard her use before she had a city hall access badge.

I wasn't naive enough to think I'd lost my friend to a political power fantasy, not entirely. But the Key who taught me how to function in Newark as a cub reporter, who invited me to my first protest in the Brick City, who led a de facto uprising the year earlier, was not a woman who compromised. And maybe she wouldn't have been that type now, if Abel Musa was still alive.

But his trip to the other side, followed closely by the departures of Angel Pereira and his animal of a father, had cracked her typically absolutist stance. A year ago, I'd sat across from her as someone showed me a cell phone video of a police shooting and asked her to consider the weight of truth against consequence, to hold off on releasing it. She'd more or less told me to go fuck myself and done what she thought was right.

Now the roles were reversed, and she was asking me to ignore those same instincts.

We'd avoided the conversation for a week. I might have waited longer, if not for the e-mail I'd received the day before from Neal Goldberg, my former colleague turned editor, curious if I'd gotten anywhere on the cold case story I'd pitched. While no one knew the national headline writhing underneath the chaotic scene at Marisqueira Pereira, the combination of blood and palace intrigue that stemmed from the enjoining of murder and politics had reinvigorated interest in news about Newark.

CNN wasn't here yet, but they might be soon. Like any good editor, Neal sensed an inside track with me.

I had the story. At least a version of it. No one could corroborate Angel or Tiago's telling, but I had the recording and there were police records to prove I was the last person in the room the night they died. My conversations with Cynthia Bell could connect more than a few dots. It wouldn't be clean, but if I wrote it well enough, the true story of the Twilight Four was too compelling to stay untold.

It would publish. It would spread. It would resurrect my career.

Unless the woman who had shuffled up behind me at Abel Musa's grave could stop me from telling it.

"You know, they almost wouldn't take my money," Key said as I turned to find her in a black t-shirt and jeans.

Her New Balance sneakers crushed blades of grass as she moved. It was the first time I'd seen her completely free of the city hall getup in a long time. She looked good. She looked like herself.

"Once I said the name, the owners made up every bullshit excuse they could think of. No plots. Something about it being a Catholic cemetery, like this place isn't stacked three-deep with corner boys who only yelled out Jesus's name with their last breath," she said. "But between the new job and some of the leftover community donations from the marches last year, there was enough there to make them look past what they thought he'd done."

"There was an easier solution to that problem, Key," I said.

"Easy for you," she replied. "But that just tells me you're not done thinking this thing through. That's why we're here, isn't it?"

"We're here because I want to answer a question that's been hanging over this city for twenty-five years, and you don't," I said. "Don't try to color it any other way than what it is."

"It's not that simple," she said. "If Abel were still here to rescue, it might be. If that monster Tiago or his son were still here to own it, it might be. But that's not how it worked out. You've got to ask yourself what happens next now. Because I know you see it, even if you don't want to. You know where this goes if you write your story."

I looked down at Abel Musa's headstone in place of a response, half hoping his strained rustle of a voice would come on the wind and tell one of us we were right.

"When this all started, you were trying to help your cop friend hold the right man accountable. And maybe there was some politics in it for me, but mostly, I wanted to see the wrong man's name cleared," she said. "There's no one to set free now, Russell. No one else to put on trial. You tell that story now, and the only person who pays a price is Mariana."

"No one's going to blame her for what happened," I said.

"You really believe that? In a race this close?" she asked. "Russell, you print that story now, and she loses. People will look at her differently. They'll look at her and think of murdered teens and a wrongful conviction. They'll wonder if she knew, even though she had nothing to do with it. It could be enough to keep Cleanthony Watkins in city hall. And maybe that doesn't mean something to you, but it means plenty to people in the houses near this cemetery. To the people in the South Ward. It means the police department gets reformed in name only. It means the same people who ruined Abel Musa's life, the same lieutenants and captains who got promoted behind that investigation, stay in power. It means a whole lot more trouble for people who look like me than it does for people who look like you."

Key stepped in front of me, cutting off my view of Abel's grave, forcing me to focus on justice for the living rather than the dead.

"You'll destroy her. Politically, and maybe personally too," she said. "Think about everything that happened this week. How many people died because of mistakes people made decades ago? Does someone else need to get swallowed up in that wave? For what?"

"For the truth, Key. Did you just forget about that?" I asked. "Look where we're standing! Abel Musa lived his whole life wearing a scarlet letter he didn't deserve. Where's the justice in that? He just goes down as a monster and that's that? We throw the truth out the window? And for what? Because it's good for a politician we think might be right for the city? That's who we are now, Key?"

"Abel's dead, Russell," she said. "If he wasn't, don't you think for one second we'd even be having this conversation. But he is. If there's a God, he knows the real story and Abel walked right through the gates. If there isn't, and there's just nothing after, well…at least he's not hurting anymore. But Mariana is here. This city is here. And as much pain as the lies caused getting us here, the truth is gonna ruin a lot more people going forward."

I looked over her shoulder at Abel's headstone. Wishing he was here to cast the tiebreaking vote. It was his story, after all.

"I'm just trying to make you understand you lived your whole life one way, telling stories to help people. I understand that. I respect that," she said. "But you need to think hard about this. About what this story means, and who it could mean things for. I guess what I'm trying to ask Russell, is who are you really helping?"

A series of footfalls caught our attention. Both Key and I turned to find Cynthia Bell making her way across the grass, a funeral wreath in her arms.

The woman who had spent her entire life convinced Abel Musa had stolen her family was about to become the first one to decorate his grave site.

Because she knew part of the truth now, but not the whole of it.

Because she knew he wasn't the monster, but she didn't know who was.

"She deserves better," I whispered to Key.

"So does Newark," Key whispered back.

CHAPTER
TWENTY-TWO

WROTE THE STORY that night.

I had to.

There were too many voices bouncing around in my head, too many ghosts demanding escape. Too many tales untold.

I had to get it out, just so I could sleep.

The words fell from me like fruit grown strong enough to break from the branch. Natural. Smooth. Obeying gravity more than anything else.

I printed the pages out, poured a glass of bourbon, grabbed a red pen and walked to my front stoop. The summer humidity was still merciless. Sweat started pouring out of me within seconds, desperate to flee my body as fast as the words.

This was the editing process an old colleague had taught me, a veteran *Signal-Intelligencer* reporter who could write more important stories in five weeks than I had in the five years I spent at the paper. Write in one place. Clean it up in another. The story doesn't live on your screen anyway, he'd said. It's going out into the world and so should you.

I'd seen him outside the building so many times, ever-present cigarette in one hand, pen in the other, surgically striking the piece he'd just given birth to. I was about to do the same, but I wasn't all that worried about the quality of the copy. Not yet anyway.

Key's question had burrowed deep into my head.

Who are you trying to help?

I circled every name in the story, big red ovals like little spotlights for my eyes.

Bill Henniman.

Angel Pereira.

Tiago Pereira.

Cynthia Bell.

Shayna and Adriana Bell.

Kurtis and Lavell Dawkins..

Mariana Pereira.

Abel Musa.

The murdered. The dead. The survivors wronged by both and left with their respective tabs. The story might correct some legacies. It might destroy others. It might swing an election.

But who was I trying to help?

Who would gain the most from me pouring twenty-five years of Newark whispers and sins and tragedies onto a page?

My eyes wandered to the top of the story.

By Russell Avery.

I took a big gulp from the bourbon glass, draining most of the three fingers I'd poured in the time it took to pull the lighter out of my pocket.

The page went up fast, yellowing, curling, blackening and gone. One last fire closing the loop on the first, all the ashes cleansing Newark of a twenty-five-year history that might only serve to make it a place ripe for more monsters and monstrous acts.

I watched the flames swallow my byline, knowing what it meant.

Knowing I'd mortgaged the truth.

Knowing I might be setting fire to my last, best chance to get back to the life I wanted.

But some stories aren't worth telling.

ACKNOWLEDGMENTS

While the idea of a wrongful conviction drives this work of fiction, it's an all too real nightmare for many Americans who sat in prison while you read it.

There is no reliable data on the number of people wrongfully convicted in the American criminal justice system, but the Innocence Project has documented more than 365 exonerations based on DNA evidence alone. The vast majority of those defendants had been convicted of sexual assault or murder, meaning they had been sentenced to life in prison, or execution, for crimes they did not commit.

This novel was inspired by two real-life tragedies that I covered as a reporter, one in Newark, the other in Los Angeles. I think it's important to share both of those stories, as they highlight the pain that wrongful convictions visit not just upon the erroneously accused, but crime victims as well.

The Twilight Four are a nod to the Clinton Avenue Five: Alvin Turner, Melvin Pittman, Randy Johnson, Ernest Taylor and Michael McDowell. None older than 17, the boys vanished from Newark in 1978. Their bodies were never found and the entire truth of their disappearances, and in all likelihood deaths, remains unknown.

Based on little evidence beyond a confession offered up by another person implicated in the crime, Newark's police and the Essex County Prosecutor's Office chose to bring murder charges against a man named Lee Evans. A jury acquitted him of all charges, but as Evans has said time and again, his name is permanently slandered now, irrevocably linked to the crime. The victims' families remain robbed of answers or anything resembling closure. Somehow, their story isn't known much beyond New Jersey. If nothing else, I hope this book changes that.

The character of Abel Musa is an homage to Bobby Joe Maxwell, a man I've devoted thousands of words to in the *Los Angeles Times* but never once had the chance to speak with. Maxwell was once better known in my newspaper as the "Skid Row Stabber," after he was convicted of terrorizing homeless victims with a knife. Again, his conviction was based largely on the word of a jailhouse informant who was later found to be manufacturing confessions.

Maxwell spent decades in prison, fell ill and slipped into a coma. His conviction was eventually overturned on appeal, but the Los Angeles County district attorney's office decided to try him a second time. It took months of fighting by Maxwell's lawyers and me making noise in the paper before the D.A.'s office thought better of prosecuting a man who would never have known he was on trial. Bobby died in 2019, unaware he was a free man.

This book doesn't exist without conversations with the wrongfully convicted, their loved ones and the people who fight on their behalf. Thank you to Laurie Levenson, Rosie Harmon, Fred Alschuler, Dupree Glass, Juan Rayford, Annee Della Donna, retired LAPD Lt. Dan Mulrenin and so many others who have shared their stories and their frustrations with me over the last few years. I hope this book did some justice to those conversations.

They warned me the second book would be extremely difficult. They didn't warn me about writing it during a pandemic. But none of us do this alone, and a few writer friends were pivotal in pushing me to finish this thing. Julia Dahl, Alex Segura and Todd Ritter, I cannot thank you enough. If you've enjoyed this novel, you will love their work too.

Jason Katz and Krystal Spencer, I rarely see either of you anymore and you owe me nothing. Yet, you both made the time to give me honest beta reads and this novel is so much better because of it.

Finding motivation to write was hard during the pandemic, but finding the right soundtrack wasn't. If one good thing came out of the pandemic, it was the formation of the Album Consumers. One record a day for nearly 18 months might seem crazy, but I think it gave us all something we needed in a time of mind-bending isolation. Eternal thanks to the rest of the Council of Nine: Patrick Polimeni, Scott Latyn, Greg Miller, Chris Kubak, Ray Adams, Dave Damiano, Daniel Miller and Michael Canino.

Speaking of music, this book does not exist without the band Dogleg. I listened to Melee basically every other writing session. Get to L.A. soon so we can punch dance our rage out. (Preferably not at a venue run by the scumbags at Live Nation.)

This book also doesn't exist without Jenny Tsay, because I wouldn't exist without her. Russell won't take another case until after we're married, I promise. Love you more than the most.

ABOUT THE AUTHOR

James Queally is an award-winning crime reporter for the *Los Angeles Times*. Throughout his career, Queally has covered hundreds of homicides as well as national use-of-force controversies. His short stories have appeared in *Thuglit, Crime Syndicate Magazine, Shotgun Honey* and more. He is the author of two novels: *Line of Sight* and *All These Ashes*. Follow him at @JamesQueallyLAT.